THE LOST CHRONICLES
VOLUME TWO

DRAGONS OF THE HIGHLORD SKIES

Margaret Weis and Tracy Hickman

The Lost Chronicles, Volume Two
DRAGONS OF THE HIGHLORD SKIES

©2007 Wizards of the Coast, Inc.

Published by Wizards of the Coast, Inc. DRAGONLANCE, WIZARDS OF THE COAST, and their respective logos are trademarks of Wizards of the Coast, Inc., in the U.S.A. and other countries.

Printed in the U.S.A.

Cover art by Matt Stawicki
First Printing: July 2007
Library of Congress Catalog Card Number: 2006937509

9 8 7 6 5 4 3 2 1

ISBN: 978-0-7869-4333-3
620-95979720-001-EN

U.S., CANADA,
ASIA, PACIFIC, & LATIN AMERICA
Wizards of the Coast, Inc.
P.O. Box 707
Renton, WA 98057-0707
+1-800-324-6496

EUROPEAN HEADQUARTERS
Hasbro UK Ltd
Caswell Way
Newport, Gwent NP9 0YH
GREAT BRITAIN
Save this address for your records.

Visit our web site at www.wizards.com

By Margaret Weis and Tracy Hickman

CHRONICLES
Dragons of Autumn Twilight

Dragons of Winter Night

Dragons of Spring Dawning

LEGENDS
Time of the Twins

War of the Twins

Test of the Twins

The Second Generation

Dragons of Summer Flame

THE WAR OF SOULS
Dragons of a Fallen Sun

Dragons of a Lost Star

Dragons of a Vanished Moon

THE LOST CHRONICLES
Dragons of the Dwarven Depths

Dragons of the Highlord Skies

Dragons of the Hourglass Mage
July 2008

To "Sir Chris" and the men and women of
the United States military and their families who have
sacrificed so much. You are the real-life heroes!

INTRODUCTION

The Story Thus Far

Many years after the War of the Lance, one of the Aesthetics, a woman named Lillith Hallmark, devised the idea of inviting the children of Palanthas into the Great Library to hear accounts of Krynn's history. Lillith was at the time one of the most powerful and influential of the Aesthetics, second only to Bertrem, and though many of the other Aesthetics were alarmed at the prospect of sticky fingers and runny noses and shrill voices disturbing their studies, Lillith had her way.

Lillith Hallmark never married—some say she bore in her heart a secret sorrow—but she was fond of children and she was an excellent historian. Even many of the parents who brought the children stayed to listen.

Since it could be that you, our readers, have not read the stories of our heroes in a long time—or perhaps you have never read anything about them before picking up this book—we decided it might be wise for us to listen in on Lillith's story this day. She is going to be telling the children the story of two women of importance in the life of one

---

of the heroes—Tanis Half-elven. The women, Laurana and Kitiara, are featured in the book you are holding.

Before launching into her tale, she is giving a summation of what has gone before. Let us listen in.

"Seven friends swore an oath to meet in Solace after a five year absence, during which they went on a search ostensibly for some sign of the true gods, but in reality, they sought themselves. These seven were Tanis Half-elven, the twin brothers Raistlin and Caramon Majere, the dwarf Flint Fireforge, the irrepressible kender Tasslehoff Burrfoot, the knight Sturm Brightblade, and Kitiara uth Matar, half-sister to the twins.

"Sturm and Kit traveled north to Solamnia, both of them seeking information about vanished families. The others went their separate ways. All of them returned to the inn at the appointed time except Kitiara, who sent a message saying she could not come. Tanis, who was in love with Kit, was saddened and deeply disappointed.

"The arrival at the inn of a mysterious woman bearing a blue crystal staff plunged the remaining six friends into an adventure known as *Dragons of Autumn Twilight*. Their journey took our heroes from Solace to the haunted city of Xak Tsaroth, where the true gods manifested themselves and gave them the Disks of Mishakal. The disks were said to bear the knowledge of the true gods, but none could read them. They set out to find someone to translate them.

"Returning to Solace, Tanis met an old friend, an elf named Gilthanas. Tanis and Gilthanas had been raised together, and they had once been close, though time and circumstance had since severed those ties. All of them were taken prisoner by the army of a vainglorious hobgoblin Fewmaster named Toede. Locked up in prison wagons, the slaves were being transported to the city of Pax Tharkas when they were freed by a small band of elves (contrary to the story the Fewmaster would later tell!).

"Tanis recognized one of the elves as Porthios, brother to Gilthanas. Hearing that the companions claimed to have found evidence of the true gods and that they brought healing back into the world, Porthios took Tanis and his friends back to Qualinost. Here Tanis met again a young woman to whom he had once been engaged, daughter of the Speaker of the Suns, Laurana. She loved Tanis, but he no longer loved her. His love for Kitiara still burned inside him and he broke off their engagement because of his divided heart—though her brothers and father had not approved anyway, for Tanis had human blood in his veins.

"The elves persuaded Tanis and his friends to go to the city of Pax Tharkas, ruled by Dragon Highlord Verminaard. Tanis and his friends planned to start a slave revolt, hoping to keep the dragonarmies, which threatened the elves, from launching an attack on the elf kingdom, allowing the elves to escape safely into exile.

"The friends, accompanied by Gilthanas as guide, set out for Pax Tharkas. Hurt by Tanis's rejection, Laurana ran away from home to be with him. He tried to send her back, but she willfully refused. On their way to Pax Tharkas, they were joined by a man named Eben Shatterstone, who claimed to be running from the dragonarmies, but who was, in reality, a spy for the Dragon Highlord Verminaard.

"The heroes sneaked into Pax Tharkas and mingled with the slaves. Here they met a man named Elistan. He was dying of a wasting disease when Goldmoon, a new follower of the goddess of healing, Mishakal, prayed to the goddess on his behalf. Elistan was cured, and asked to know more about these gods. Goldmoon gave him the Disks of Mishakal and found that he was able to read them. He became a cleric of Paladine and worked to bring knowledge of the true gods to the rest of the people enslaved in Pax Tharkas.

"Tanis and his friends led the slaves in revolt and killed Verminaard. Eight hundred men, women and children fled south and managed to evade pursuit. They holed up in caves, hoping to be able to spend the winter there.

"Meanwhile, an aurak draconian masquerading as Verminaard marshaled a force of red dragons and set off in pursuit of the former slaves, who were forced to flee the valley and seek refuge with the dwarves in their lost kingdom of Thorbardin. These adventures are related in the book *Dragons of the Dwarven Depths*.

"During this time, Laurana continued traveling with the group. Danger, sorrow, and fear forced her to grow up. The once-spoiled and willful girl grew into a serious, thoughtful young woman. She used the skills she had learned in her father's court to assist Elistan in his work, and Tanis found himself charmed by this beautiful young woman, so different from the girl he'd known. He began to fall in love with her and became torn. Which woman did he truly love? As for Laurana, her love for him never wavered.

"After much hardship and peril, the heroes found and restored the Hammer of Kharas to the dwarves. In return, the dwarves permitted the refugees to remain in Thorbardin until they could find safe passage to new homes. Tanis and his group set out to the seaport city of Tarsis, there to buy passage on the white-winged ships for the refugees, who sought a new homeland. Their trek and adventures along the way are described in *Dragons of Winter Night*.

"As for Kitiara uth Matar, she followed a different path from that of her friends. Whereas they walked the path of light, she walked a path that led to darkness. She joined the dragonarmies of Queen Takhisis, and it was not long before Kitiara's skill and ambition caused her to rise to become Dragon Highlord of the Blue Dragonarmy, known to most of Ansalon as the Blue Lady.

"The individual adventures of Kitiara and Laurana and what happens to them at this point in time have never been told—until now. In the book *Dragons of the Highlord Skies*, the two women in the life of Tanis Half-elven each go on separate journeys whose perils will lead both of them to face their greatest challenges. I myself play a small part in this tale.

"It all begins . . ."

BOOK I

PROLOGUE

Over three hundred years had passed since he had last heard the sound of a human voice. Or rather, since he last heard a human speak. He had heard screams since then; screams from those who had come to Dargaard Keep to confront him, screams that ended in gurgling gasps as they choked on their own blood.

Lord Soth had no patience with such fools. He had no patience with those who came seeking his storied treasure. He had no patience with those who come on gallant quests to rid the world of his evil, for he knew the truth (who better than one who had once ridden on his own knightly quests?). He knew the knights were self-serving, self-seeking, interested only in glory, in hearing their names spouted by the bards. He saw through the shining armor to the spots of darkness that stained black the white purity of their souls. Their courage leaked through those spots when he confronted them, oozed out of them, and they clattered to their knees, trembling in their shining armor, and begged for mercy.

Lord Soth had none to give.

Who had shown him mercy? Who had heard his cries? Who heard them now? The gods had returned, but he was too proud to beg Paladine's forgiveness. Lord Soth did not believe forgiveness would be granted, and deep within, the death knight did not think it should be granted.

He sat upon his throne inside the great hall of his ruined keep listening, night after endless night, to the spirits of the accursed elf women who were doomed to sing as he was doomed to hear the ballad of his crimes. They sang of a gallant and handsome knight whose wayward passions led him to seduce an elf maiden and get her with child. They sang of the betrayed wife conveniently removed, so the elf maid could be welcomed to Dargaard Keep. They sang of the new wife's horror when she learned the truth and of her prayers to the gods, pleading with them that there was yet some good in Soth and begging them to grant him a chance for salvation.

They sang of the gods' answer: Lord Loren Soth would be given the power to persuade the Kingpriest to abandon his notion of proclaiming himself a god, thus averting the wrath of the gods. Soth could prevent the disaster of the Cataclysm, save the lives of thousands of innocents, leave his child a name of which he would be proud. They sang of Soth's journey to Istar, determined to save mankind, though he himself would be lost. They sang of their part, these accursed elf women, who halted him on the road, telling him lies about his lover. They sang of secret trysts with other men and a child that was not his.

They sang of Soth's rage as he rode back to his castle, and of how he ordered his wife into his presence and there denounced her as a whore, her child a bastard. They sang of shuddering earth as the fiery mountain cast down by the gods crashed into Istar, causing the huge chandelier, resplendent with a hundred flaming candles, to fall from the ceiling and crash down upon his wife and child. They sang about how he could have saved them, but he was consumed with hate and the thirst for revenge and he watched his wife's hair catch fire and heard his little child's frantic screams as soft flesh blistered and bubbled. They sang, every night, about how he turned upon his heel and walked away.

Last they sang—and he would always and forever hear his wife's curse upon him—that he would live forever, a knight pledged to death and darkness, forced to dwell upon his crimes as time passed him by, his minutes endless as hours, his hours endless as years, his years hollow and empty and cold as only the unredeemed dead are cold.

In all those years it had been so long since he had heard a voice speak to him that when one did, he thought for a moment it was a part of his black musings and he paid it no heed.

"Lord Soth, I have thrice called out to you," the voice said, imperious in tone, angry at being ignored. "Why do you not answer?"

The death knight, clad in armor that was blackened by fire and stained with blood, peered out through the eyeslits of his helm. He saw a woman magnificent and beautiful, dark and cruel as the Abyss over which she ruled.

"Takhisis," he said, not rising.

"*Queen* Takhisis," she returned, displeased.

"You are not *my* Queen," he said.

Takhisis glowered down at him and her aspect changed. She transformed from a human female into an enormous dragon with five writhing, hissing, and spitting heads. She towered over him, a creature of terror, and each head shrieked at him in rage.

"The gods of light made you what you are, but I can unmake you!" Takhisis hissed. The dragon heads with their dripping fangs darted at him, menacing him. "I will cast you into the Abyss and break you, smite you and torment you for all eternity."

The goddess's fury had once shattered a world, yet Lord Soth did not quail beneath it. He did not fall to his knees or shake or shiver. He remained seated on his throne and gazed up at her with eyes of flame that burned calm and steady, unafraid and unimpressed.

"What would be the difference between that tortured existence and the one I now endure?" he asked her quietly.

The five heads ceased their attacks and hovered over him, five brains confounded. After a moment, the dragon disappeared and the woman returned, a smile upon her lips, her tone seductive, purring, persuasive.

"I did not come here to quarrel, my lord. Though you have hurt me, wounded me deeply, I am prepared to forgive you."

"How have I hurt you, Takhisis?" he asked, and though there was nothing left of his face it seemed to her he smiled sardonically.

"You serve the cause of darkness—" she began.

Lord Soth made a gesture of negation, as much as to say he served no cause, not even his own.

"—yet you hold yourself aloof from the glorious battle we are waging," Takhisis said. "The Emperor Ariakas would be proud to have you under his command—"

The flame of Lord Soth's eyes flickered, but Takhisis was so caught up in the passion of her cause that she did not see this.

"Yet here you sit," she continued bitterly, "locked up in this blackened keep, bemoaning your fate while others fight your battles."

"From what I have witnessed, Madame," Soth said dryly, "your emperor is winning his battles. Much of Ansalon is under his control now. You have no need of me or my forces, so take yourself away and leave me alone."

Takhisis regarded the death knight from beneath long lashes. The locks of her dark hair lifted and fell in the chill wind that gusted through the cracked and broken walls. The black tendrils reminded him of the writhing heads of the dragons.

"True, we are winning," Takhisis stated, "and I have no doubt but that we will ultimately prevail. However, I say this to you and only to you, my lord, the gods of light have not been crushed as swiftly and as easily as I anticipated. Certain . . . um . . . complications have arisen. Emperor Ariakas and my Dragon Highlords would be grateful for your help."

Certain complications, she had said. Lord Soth knew all about these "complications." One of her vaunted Dragon Highlords was dead. The other Highlords each wanted the Crown of Power for himself, and while they drank wine from the loving cup in public, they spit it on the floor in private. The elves of Qualinesti had escaped the dragon armies sent to annihilate them. The dwarves of Thorbardin had defeated those same armies and driven out the darkness from beneath the mountain. The Solamnic knights had been defeated, but were not yet destroyed. They wanted only a champion to lead them and at any moment one might rise up from among their ranks.

The metallic dragons, who had thus far remained out of the war, were starting to grow uneasy, to think perhaps they had made a mistake. If Paladine's powerful dragons of gold and of silver entered the war on the side of Light, the red and blue dragons and the green and black and white would be in serious trouble. Takhisis needed to conquer Ansalon immediately, before the metallic dragons entered the fray; before the armies of Light, now divided, came to their senses and formed alliances; before the Knights of Solamnia found a hero.

"I will make a bargain with you, Takhisis," said Lord Soth.

The Queen's dark eyes flared in anger. She was not accustomed to making bargains. She was accustomed to giving commands and to being obeyed. She had to swallow her anger, however. Her most effective weapon was terror, and its cutting edge was blunted and useless against the death knight who had lost everything and thus feared nothing.

"What is your bargain?"

"I cannot serve someone I do not respect," said Lord Soth. "Therefore I will pledge my loyalty and my army to the Highlord who has the courage to spend the night alone in Dargaard Keep. Or rather, let us say, the Highlord who *survives* a night alone in Dargaard Keep. This Highlord must do so freely, not under duress from you or anyone else," Lord Soth added, knowing how the goddess's mind worked.

Takhisis glared at the death knight in silence. If she had not needed him, he would have been crushed in the coils of her fury, torn apart by the claws of her rage, and devoured in the maw of her hatred.

But she needed him, and he did not need her.

"I will bear your message to my Highlords," said Takhisis at last.

"The lord must come alone," Soth repeated, "and not under duress."

Takhisis did not deign to respond. She turned her back on him and swept into the darkness over which she ruled, leaving him to listen again and yet again to the bitter song of his tragic life.

I

Grag reports to the Emperor.
The Blue Lady receives a shock.

ate autumn and the leaves, their colors once bold and defiant, were dead, their brittle brown corpses scattered by the winds to lie upon the ground, waiting to be mercifully buried beneath the coming winter snows.

Winter was almost upon Ansalon, and with it would come the end of the campaign season. Takhisis's forces under the leadership of Emperor Ariakas occupied much of Ansalon—from Nordmaar in the west to Kalaman in the east, Goodlund in the north to Abanasinia in the south. He had plans for conquering the rest of Ansalon, and Queen Takhisis was impatient for him to act on those plans. She wanted him to push on with the war, but she was told this was not possible. Armies cannot march on snow-choked roads. Supply wagons tumble down ice-rimed cliffs or get bogged down on rain-wet trails. Better to wait until spring. Winter was a time to hunker down and rest and heal the wounds of autumn's battles. Her armies would emerge in the spring, strong and rejuvenated.

Ariakas assured her, however, that just because her soldiers were not marching, the war was still being waged. Dark and secret schemes and plots were in the works. Once Takhisis heard this, she felt better.

The dragonarmy's soldiers, pleased with their recent victories, occupied the conquered towns and cities, lived in the comfort and warmth of captured castles, and enjoyed the spoils of war. They commandeered the grain from the barns, took any woman they fancied, and ruthlessly killed those who tried to protect property and family. The soldiers of Takhisis would live well this coming winter, while those under the claws of the dragon faced starvation and terror.

But not all was going well for the emperor.

He had been planning to spend the winter in his headquarters in Sanction when he had received disturbing reports that his campaign in the west was not going as intended. The goal had been to wipe out the elves of Qualinesti and then to seize and occupy the dwarven kingdom of Thorbardin by year's end. First there came word that Verminaard, Dragon Highlord of the Red Army, who had conducted such a brilliant campaign in the land of Abanasinia, had met an untimely death at the hands of his own slaves. Then came the news that the Qualinesti elves had managed to escape and flee into exile. Then the emperor was informed that Thorbardin was lost.

This was the first real setback the dragonarmies had suffered, and Ariakas was forced to travel across the continent to his headquarters in Neraka to find out what had gone wrong. He ordered the commander currently in charge of the fortress of Pax Tharkas to come to Neraka to make his report. Unfortunately, there was some confusion over who was in charge now that Verminaard was dead.

A hobgoblin—one Fewmaster Toede—claimed the late Verminaard had made him second in command. Toede was packing his bags for the trip when word reached the hob that Ariakas was in a towering rage over the loss of Thorbardin and that someone was going to be made to pay. At this, the Fewmaster suddenly remembered he had urgent business elsewhere. He ordered the draconian commander of Pax Tharkas to report to the Emperor, then Toede promptly decamped.

Ariakas moved into his quarters in the military headquarters in Neraka, capital city of the Dark Queen's empire, and awaited the arrival of the commander with impatience. Ariakas had valued Verminaard and the emperor was angered at the loss of such a skilled military commander. Ariakas wanted answers and he expected this Commander Grag to provide them.

Grag had never been to Neraka before, but he did not plan to take in the sights. Other draconians had warned him that their kind were not welcome in the city, though "their kind" were giving up their lives to help the Dark Queen win her war. Grag did see what he'd wanted to see and that was the Dark Queen's Temple.

When Istar had been destroyed by the gods, Takhisis had taken the foundation stone of the Kingpriest's temple and carried it to a high plain in the Khalkist mountains. She placed the stone in a wooded glade and slowly the temple began to grow around it. She was secretly using the temple as a gate through which to travel to the world when her gate was inadvertently slammed shut by a young man named Berem, and his sister, Jasla.

Coming upon the foundation stone, Berem was entranced by the jewels adorning it and he wanted to pry one loose. His sister, Jasla, sensed the evil in the gems and sought to prevent him. Berem grew angry. He dug out the stone, and when Jasla tried to stop him, he shoved her from him. She fell, striking her head on the stone, and died. The green gem fused to Berem's chest and he was fused to that point in time. He could not die. He did not age. Horrified at his crime, he fled.

When Takhisis next went to leave the Abyss through the gate, she found the good spirit of Jasla had entered the foundation stone, there to await the return of her repentant brother. Takhisis was barred. Only her avatar could now walk Krynn, thus greatly reducing her power to affect world events. But she foresaw a greater danger to herself. If Berem returned and joined with his sister, the gate would slam shut and she would be forever barred from the world. The only way to reopen the gate and ensure it stayed open was to find Berem and slay him. Thus began the search for the Green Gemstone Man.

The temple continued to grow around the foundation stone that was buried far beneath it. The temple was now an immense structure, dominating the land all around it, visible from miles away. Its walls twisted and distorted, it looked much like a claw thrust up out of the earth, trying to snag heaven. Grag considered it impressive and he paid his reverence to it, albeit from a distance.

Commander Grag did not have to enter the city proper to make his way to the Blue Army's barracks where Ariakas had established his headquarters, and that was fortunate for the draconian. The city's narrow streets were clogged with people, most of them human, with no love for the likes of Grag. He would have been in a fight before he walked a block. He kept to the byways and even then ran into a slaver leading a clanking row of chained slaves to market, who said something to his companion in a loud voice about slimy "lizard-men," adding that they should crawl back into the swamp out of which they'd emerged. Grag would have liked to have broken the man's neck, but he was already late and he kept walking.

Ariakas had formal chambers inside his Queen's temple, but he did not like to conduct business there. Although he was a devout worshiper and highly favored by his goddess, Ariakas had little use for his Queen's priests. He suspected they spied upon him when he was in the Temple, and he was right. The High Priest of Takhisis, known as the Nightlord, thought that he should be the Emperor of Ansalon, and that Ariakas, a mere military commander, should answer to him. He was particularly outraged that Ariakas had direct access to Her Dark Majesty instead of going through him as an intermediary on his behalf. The Nightlord spent much of his time working to undermine Ariakas and end his reign.

Ariakas had therefore ordered Grag to meet him in the Blue Quarter, where the Blue Wing of the dragonarmy resided when they were in the city. Currently, the Blue Wing was in the west, preparing for the invasion of Solamnia in the spring. Their commander, a Dragon Highlord known as the Blue Lady, had also been ordered to Neraka to meet with Commander Grag.

With the Blue Wing in Solamnia, their quarters had been commandeered by Ariakas, who had brought with him his staff and his bodyguards. An aide found Grag wandering about lost and escorted him to the short, squat, and unprepossessing building in which Ariakas lived and worked.

Two of the largest ogres Grag had ever seen stood guard outside the door. The ogres were clad in plate and chain mail armor and were heavily armed. The draconian detested ogres as being thick-skulled and brutish, and the feeling was mutual, for ogres considered draconians arrogant upstarts and interlopers. Grag tensed, expecting trouble, but the two ogres were members of Ariakas's own personal bodyguard and they went about their business in a professional manner.

"Weapons," growled one, and held out a huge, hairy hand.

No one entered the presence of the emperor armed. Grag knew that, yet he had worn a sword from practically the moment he'd been able to shake the eggshell out of his eyes, and he felt naked and vulnerable without it.

The ogre's yellow eyes narrowed at Grag's hesitation. Grag unbuckled his sword belt and handed it to the ogre, also turning over a long-bladed knife. He was not completely defenseless. He had his magic after all.

One ogre kept an eye on Grag while the other went in to report to Ariakas that the bozak he was expecting had arrived. Grag paced nervously outside the door. From inside came a human male's booming laughter and a human female's voice, not quite as deep as the man's, but deeper than that of most women, rich and husky.

The ogre returned and jerked a sausage-like thumb, indicating Grag was to enter. He had a feeling this interview was not going to go well when he saw the gleam in the ogre's squinty yellow eyes and saw the ogre's comrade show all his rotting teeth in a wide grin.

Bracing himself, folding his wings as tightly as possible, his bronze-colored scales twitching, his clawed hands flexing nervously, Grag entered the presence of the most powerful and most dangerous man in all of Ansalon.

Ariakas was a large and imposing human male, with long black hair and, though clean-shaven, the dark stubble of a black beard. He was somewhere near the age of forty, which made him middle-aged among humans, but he was in superb condition. Stories about his legendary physical prowess circulated among the ranks of his men, the most famous being that he had once hurled a spear clean through a man's body.

Ariakas was wearing a fur-lined cloak, tossed casually over one broad shoulder, revealing a hand-tooled, heavy leather vest beneath. The vest was intended to protect against a knife in the back, for even in Neraka there were those who be glad to see Ariakas relieved of both his command and his life. A sword hung from a belt around his waist. Bags of spell components and a scroll case were also suspended from his sword belt, something remarkable, for most wizards were prohibited by their gods from wearing armor or carrying steel weapons.

Ariakas had no care for the laws of the gods of magic. He received his spells directly from the Dark Queen herself, and in this he and Grag shared something in common. It had not occurred to Grag until this moment that Ariakas actually made use of his spellcasting abilities, but the fact that he carried magical paraphernalia alongside his weapons proved he was as comfortable with magic as with steel.

Ariakas had his back to Grag. The man merely glanced at the draconian over his shoulder, then turned back to his conversation with the woman. Grag shifted his attention to her, for she was as famous among the soldiers of the dragonarmies as was Ariakas—if not more so.

Her name was Kitiara uth Matar. She was in her early thirties, with black curly hair worn short for ease and convenience. She had dark eyes and an odd habit of quirking her lips when she smiled, making her smile slightly crooked. Grag knew nothing about her background. He was a reptile, related to dragons, who had crawled out of an eggshell himself, and he had no idea who his parents were, nor did he care about the parentage of others. All he had heard about Kitiara was that she had been born a warrior and Grag believed it. She wore her sword with jaunty ease and she was not the least bit intimidated by the size and strength and physical presence of Ariakas.

Grag wondered if there was truth to the rumor that the two were lovers.

At length, their conversation ended and Ariakas deigned to give Grag an audience. The emperor turned around and looked straight into the draconian's eyes. Grag flinched. It was like looking into the Abyss, or rather, it was like entering the Abyss, for Grag felt himself drawn in, skinned, dissected, pulled apart, and tossed aside—all in an instant.

Grag was so shaken he forgot to salute. He did so belatedly when he saw Ariakas's heavy black brows contract in frowning displeasure. Kitiara, standing behind Ariakas, folded her arms across her chest and smiled her crooked smile at the draconian's discomfiture, as though she knew and understood what Grag was feeling. She had evidently just arrived, for she still wore her blue dragon armor, and it was dusty from her journey.

Ariakas was not one to mince words or waste time in pleasantries. "I have heard many different versions of how Lord Verminaard died," he stated in cold and measured tones, "and how Thorbardin came to be lost. I ordered you here, Commander, to tell me the truth."

"Yes, my lord," said Grag.

"Swear by Takhisis," said Ariakas.

"I swear by my allegiance to her Dark Majesty that my words are true," said Grag. "May she wither my sword hand if they are not."

Ariakas appeared to find this satisfactory, for he indicated with a gesture that Grag was to proceed. Ariakas did not sit down, nor did he invite the draconian to be seated. Kitiara could not sit down either, since her commander was still upright, but she made herself at ease by leaning back against a table.

Grag related the tale of how Verminaard had died at the hands of assassins; how the aurak, Dray-yan, had conceived the idea of masquerading as Verminaard in order to keep up the pretence that the Dragon Highlord was still alive; how Grag and Dray-yan had plotted the downfall of Thorbardin; how they would have been successful, but their plans were thwarted by magic, treachery, and the gods of Light.

Grag could see Ariakas growing more and more enraged as he went on with his report. When Grag reluctantly reached the part where Dray-yan toppled into the pit, Kitiara burst out laughing. Ariakas, infuriated, drew his sword from its sheath and began to advance on the draconian.

Grag ceased talking abruptly and backed up a step. His clawed fingers twitched; he was readying a magic spell. He might die, but by Takhisis he would not die alone.

Still chuckling, Kitiara casually reached out her hand and laid it restrainingly on Ariakas's massive forearm.

"At least do not slay Commander Grag until he has finished his report, my lord," Kitiara said. "I, for one, am curious to hear the rest of the story."

"I'm glad you find it so damn amusing," Ariakas snarled, seething. He slammed his sword back into its sheath, though he kept his hand on the hilt and eyed Grag grimly. "I do not see anything funny about it. Thorbardin remains in the control of the Hylar dwarves, who are now stronger than ever, since they have recovered that magical hammer, and they have opened their long-sealed gates to the world. The iron, steel and wealth of the dwarven kingdom which should be flowing into *our* coffers is flowing into the hands of our enemies! All because Verminaard managed to get himself assassinated and then some fool aurak with delusions of grandeur takes a dive into a bottomless pit!"

"The loss of Thorbardin is a blow," said Kitiara calmly, "but certainly not a fatal one. True, the wealth of the dwarven kingdom would have come in handy, but you can get along without it. What is more to be feared is the dwarven army entering the war and I do not see that happening. The humans hate the elves, who distrust the humans, and no one likes the dwarves, who despise the other two. They're far more likely to turn on each other than they are to fight us."

Ariakas grunted. He was not accustomed to losing and he was still not pleased, but Grag, glancing at Kitiara, saw from her slight wink that the crisis was past. The bozak relaxed and let go of the magical spell he'd had ready to use to defend himself. Unlike some of the emperor's human toadies, who would have said meekly, "Thank you for the attention, my lord," as Ariakas chopped off their heads, the draconian would have not gone to his death without a fight, and Grag was a formidable foe. He might not have been able to kill the powerful Ariakas, but the bozak, with his massive scaled body, clawed feet and hands, and large wings, could at least do some damage to the human. The Blue Lady had seen the danger, and this had been the reason for her intervention.

Grag was a descendant of dragons, and like dragons, had little use for any human, but he gave the Blue Lady a slight nod of gratitude. She flashed her crooked smile at him and her dark eyes glittered and he realized, suddenly, that she was enjoying this.

"Regale us with the details of Verminaard's death," said Kitiara. "He was set upon by assassins masquerading as slaves. Are these assassins still on the loose, Commander?"

"Yes, my lady," said Grag stiffly. "We tracked them to Thorbardin. According to my spies, they are still there."

"I will offer a bounty for their capture as I did with the Green Gemstone man," said Ariakas. "Our forces all across Ansalon will be on the lookout for them."

"I would think twice about that, my lord," said Kitiara, with that strange quirk of her lips. "You do not want to advertise that slaves were responsible for slaying a Dragon Highlord."

"We will find some other excuse then," Ariakas stated in cold fury. "What do we know of these men?"

Grag's tongue flicked out from between his fangs and slid back in. In truth, he didn't know much. He glanced at the Blue Lady and saw that she was losing interest in the conversation. She lifted her hand to her mouth to conceal a yawn.

Grag scanned his mind for all that his late partner, the aurak Dray-yan, had told him about the assassins.

"Verminaard had placed a spy in their midst. He reported that they were from a town in Abanasinia, my lord. A place by the name of Solace—"

Kitiara's boredom vanished. "Solace, you say?"

Ariakas glanced at her. "Isn't Solace where you were born?"

"Yes," Kitiara replied, "I grew up there."

"Perhaps you know these wretches," Ariakas remarked.

"I doubt it," Kit answered with a shrug. "I have not been back to my home in years."

"What were their names?" Ariakas asked.

"I only know a couple—" Grag began.

"You must have seen them during the battle," Ariakas said curtly. "Describe them, Commander."

"I saw them," Grag muttered dourly. He had seen them close up, in fact. They had captured him at one point and only by the Dark Queen's mercy and his own wits had he been able to escape. "They are a rag-tag lot. Their leader is a mongrel half-elf called Tanis. Another is a gray-beard dwarf, and yet another is a sniveling kender. The rest are human: a red-robe wizard, a foul Solamnic knight named Sturm, and a muscle-bound warrior named Caramon."

Kitiara made a slight sound, a sort of strangled gasp.

"Do you recognize these criminals?" Ariakas demanded, turning to her.

Kitiara composed her features in an instant. She smiled her crooked smile and said, "I am afraid not, my lord."

"You better not," said Ariakas grimly. "If I find out that you had something to do with Verminaard's death—"

"I assure you, my lord, I know nothing about it," Kitiara said with a shrug.

Ariakas regarded her intently, trying to dissect her. Assassination was one means of rising to higher rank in the Dark Queen's army, viewed as a way to provide the strongest possible leadership. But Ariakas had valued Verminaard and Kitiara did not want to be accused of having arranged the man's death, especially when the loss of the kingdom of Thorbardin had been the disastrous result.

"Solace has a population of several thousand, my lord," Kitiara said, growing annoyed. "I did not know every man in town."

Ariakas stared at her and she met his gaze unflinchingly. At last, he let her off the hook.

"No, but I'll bet you slept with half of them," he said, and turned his attention back to Grag.

Kitiara smiled dutifully at his lordship's jest, but her smile vanished when he was no longer watching her. She leaned back against the table, her arms folded, her gaze abstracted.

"Where are these assassins now, Commander?" Ariakas asked.

"The last I heard of them, they were hiding in Thorbardin, my lord." Grag hesitated, then said, with a curl of his lip, "I believe the hobgoblin who styles himself Fewmaster Toede can provide you with more information about them."

Kitiara stirred slightly. "If your Lordship would like, I could travel to Pax Tharkas, talk to this Fewmaster."

"The Fewmaster is not in Pax Tharkas, my lady," said Grag. "That fortress is in shambles and is no longer defensible. The Red Wing has relocated to the city of Haven."

"I will go to Haven, then," Kitiara said.

"Perhaps later," Ariakas told her. "Solamnia takes priority."

Kitiara shrugged again and subsided back into her reverie.

"As for these assassins," Ariakas continued, "they will most likely remain skulking in the caves of Thorbardin through the coming winter. We will hire some dark dwarf—"

"I wouldn't be too sure of that," Kitiara interrupted.

"What do you mean?" Ariakas turned to glare at her. "I thought you didn't know these men!"

"I don't, but I know their type," she said, "and so do you, my lord. They are most likely rovers, itinerant sellswords. Such men never remain in one place long. Rest assured, they will soon be on the move. A little snow will not stop them."

Ariakas gave her a strange look, one she did not see, for she was staring down at the toes of her dust-covered boots. He regarded her in silence a moment longer, then turned back to Grag.

"Find out from your agents all you can about these men. If they do leave the dwarven halls, report to me at once," Ariakas scowled, "and put the word out that I want them captured alive. The death of a Dragon Highlord will not go unpunished. I plan to make an example of them."

Grag promised he would find out all he could. He and Ariakas spent some time talking about the war in the west and who should take over command of the Red Wing. Grag was impressed by the fact that Ariakas knew all about the Red Wing's status, the disposition of its forces, the need for supplies, and so forth.

They discussed Pax Tharkas. Ariakas said he had considered retaking it, but given that the fortress was in ruins, he had decided that it would not be worth the effort. His armies would simply go around it.

All this time, Kitiara remained silent and preoccupied. Grag thought she wasn't listening until he mentioned—with another curl of his lip—Fewmaster Toede's ambition to become the successor to Verminaard. At that, Kitiara smiled.

Grag did not like to see her smile. He feared she was going to advocate promoting Toede, and Grag did not want to take orders from the bloated, arrogant, self-serving hob. Although, on second thought, having Toede for a commander might be better than some arrogant human numbskull. Toede could be manipulated, flattered, and cajoled into doing what Grag wanted, whereas a human commander would go his own way. Grag would have to think about this.

The discussion ended soon after. Grag was dismissed. He saluted and walked out the door, which Ariakas shut behind him. Grag found to his amazement that he was trembling and he had to stop a moment to regain his composure.

Once he was himself again, Grag confronted the ogres, who appeared surprised to see him return all in one piece. They handed over his sword and knife in silence, regarding him with more respect.

"Is there a tavern close by?" Grag asked. He held the sword belt in his hand. He wasn't at all sure he could buckle it without fumbling and he wouldn't give the ogres the satisfaction of seeing his weakness.

"I could use a shot of dwarf spirits."

The ogre guards grinned.

"Try the Hairy Troll," one said, pointing in the tavern's general direction.

"Thanks," said Grag and walked off, still carrying his sword belt.

There was no doubt in his mind. The Blue Lady knew the assassins, and Ariakas knew she knew—or at least suspected it.

Grag would not have been in her boots for all the dwarf spirits in Thorbardin.

2

Kitiara's strategy.
Ariakas's scheme. The witch.

ou know, I've half a mind to promote that Grag to Dragon Highlord," said Ariakas, gazing speculatively after the departing draconian.

"A draco?" Kitiara was amused. "The lizard-boys are excellent fighters, to be sure, my lord. They were bred for battle after all, but they lack the brains and discipline needed for command."

"I'm not so sure," said Ariakas. "Commander Grag has a good head on his scaly shoulders."

"He's smarter than Verminaard, at least," Kitiara muttered.

"I remind you that I highly valued Verminaard," stated Ariakas heatedly. "His campaign in the west was brilliantly conducted. Any man—no matter how powerful—can fall victim to fate."

Kitiara shrugged and stifled another yawn. She hadn't slept much the night before, her sleep broken by disturbing dreams of a fire-ravaged keep and an undead knight clad in blackened armor adorned with a rose. Kitiara had no idea what the dream meant or why she had dreamt it, but she had woken suddenly, filled with an unnamed fear, unable to return to sleep.

Ariakas didn't look as if he'd slept well himself. His eyes had dark circles beneath them and he blinked them constantly. Kit wondered uneasily if her dream had been a dream or if Takhisis was trying to tell her something. Kit was about to ask Ariakas when he startled her by saying, "Or *was* it fate, Kitiara?"

"Was what fate, my lord?" Kitiara asked, confused. She'd completely forgotten the subject of their conversation.

Ariakas exploded. "By Takhisis, I begin to think you were the one to have Verminaard killed! Quite a coincidence, these assassins coming from your hometown, and one of them a wizard. You had a brother who was a wizard, as I recall."

"I am flattered that your lordship remembers so much about me," said Kitiara coolly. "As for my brother the mage, Raistlin is only my half-brother and he was always weak and sickly. I doubt if he is even still alive, much less given to going about assassinating Dragon Highlords."

Ariakas glowered at her.

"Are you accusing me of Verminaard's murder, my lord?" Kit flared.

"What if I am?" demanded Ariakas.

He crowded close to her, using his massive body to physically intimidate her. Kitiara was shaken and for a moment she almost gave way to panic. She had been telling him the truth, but she wasn't telling him all the truth. She should never have made that crack about Verminaard. At that moment she was reminded of her father's teachings. Gregor uth Matar had once been a Solamnic knight. Dismissed from the knighthood for disgraceful behavior, he'd made a living by selling his sword to the highest bidder. Gregor had been a handsome, bold womanizer, always in debt, frequently in trouble, and Kitiara had adored him. One of his dictums—always attack, never defend.

Instead of falling back, as Ariakas anticipated, Kitiara moved in closer, so that they were practically toe-to-toe.

"You should know me well enough, my lord, to know that if I wanted to assassinate Verminaard, I would have done it myself. I would not have paid to have it done for me."

Ariakas seized hold of her jaw. His fingers clenched. A single move and he could have broken her neck. He stared down at her, waiting for her to whimper and weaken.

Kit did not so much as blink and suddenly Ariakas felt a tickling sensation, as of sharp steel, in the area of his groin. He looked down and was startled to see Kitiara's hand holding a knife, prepared to thrust it through the leather skirt into a very sensitive part of his anatomy.

Ariakas gave a great guffaw of laughter and shoved Kitiara away from him.

"Damn those guards of mine for slackers," he said, half-amused, half-infuriated. "I'll have their heads for this! They have orders to search everyone—even my most trusted commanders! Or perhaps I should say *especially* my most trusted commanders."

"Do not blame the ogres, my lord," said Kitiara. "They were not meant to find this."

She took the thin-bladed knife and slipped it into a hidden sheath that had been cleverly worked into the ornate design of her dragon armor breastplate.

Ariakas chuckled. "Would you really have stabbed me?"

"Would you have broken my neck?" Kitiara returned in arch tones.

Both knew the answer was "yes". They expected nothing less of each other.

"Now perhaps we can turn our attention to matters in Solamnia." Ariakas walked over to the desk where he had spread out a map. He bent over it.

Kitiara breathed an inward sigh. She'd survived yet another confrontation with her powerful master. Her boldness and daring had pleased him. The day would come, though, when they wouldn't.

"Did you have a strange dream last night, my lord?" Kitiara asked.

"Don't try to change the subject," Ariakas said curtly.

"I did," Kitiara continued. "I dreamt Queen Takhisis was trying to persuade me to travel to Dargaard Keep to confront the death knight who is supposed to reside there."

"Soth," Ariakas said. "Lord Soth. What did you tell Her Dark Majesty?"

He tried to sound casual, but Kitiara knew then that he'd had the same dream.

"I told her I didn't believe in ghosts," Kitiara returned dryly.

Ariakas grunted. "Soth is no ghost. He lives—if you can say such a thing about a man who has been dead for over three hundred years. Our Queen wants to recruit him to our cause."

"Would you do that, my lord?" Kitiara asked.

Ariakas shook his head. "Soth would be a valuable ally, but I could not trust him. He is far too powerful. Why should a death knight call any mortal 'master'? No, let Soth brood over his wrongs in his ruined castle. I want no part of him."

Kitiara had to admit his reasoning was sound. Queen Takhisis was often impatient with human frailties and weakness, and she could be impractical on occasion. Kit put the dream aside

"I read your latest proposal for Solamnia," Ariakas was saying. He picked up a thick sheaf of parchment. "You propose that the Blue Wing seize the High Clerist's Tower, occupy it, and from there march on Palanthas. A daring plan, Kitiara."

He took his seat behind the desk. "I am against it. It stretches our forces too thin, but I will listen to what you have to say."

Kitiara perched her hip on the edge of the table and leaned over to explain her idea.

"My spies tell me the High Clerist's Tower is manned by only a few troops, my lord." She put her finger on the map. "The Red Wing is here. You could order the Red Wing north. We could strike the High Clerist's Tower with troops and dragons from the Red Wing and the Blue Wing. We could easily wipe out the small force holding it, seize the High Clerist's Tower, and occupy it before the Solamnic knights knew what hit them. From there, we march on Palanthas, conquer the city and take over her seaports."

"Taking Palanthas will not be easy," said Ariakas. "We cannot lay siege to the city, not without blockading her seaports."

"Bah! The Palanthians are soft and pampered dandies. They don't want to fight. They might break a nail. Once the Palanthians see dragons flying in the skies, they will be so terrified they will piss their pants and surrender."

"What if they don't?" Ariakas pointed to the map. "We do not yet control the Plains of Solamnia, nor Elkholm, nor Heartland. You leave your flanks exposed, surrounded by the enemy. What about supply lines? You may take the fortress, but once you are inside, your troops would starve!"

"When Palanthas is ours, we resupply from there. In the meantime, we have red dragons ferry in what we need."

Ariakas snorted. "The reds will not be used as pack mules! They will have nothing to do with such an arrangement."

"If her Dark Majesty were to order them—"

Ariakas shook his head.

Kitiara sat back. Her lips pursed, her brown eyes glinted. "Then, my lord, we will carry our supplies with us and make do with that." Her fist clenched in her enthusiasm and passion. "I guarantee you that once people see your banner raised over the High Clerist's Tower, Palanthas will fall into our hands like rotten fruit!"

"It is too risky," Ariakas muttered.

"Yes, it is risky," Kitiara agreed eagerly, "but there is a greater risk in allowing the knights time to organize and send in reinforcements. Right now, the Knighthood is in turmoil. They have no Grand Master, for no man is strong enough to claim it, and they have two High Justices because two men claim the position and neither will acknowledge the rights of the other. They are running around like sailors on a burning deck quarreling over whose job it is to put out the fire and all the while, their ship is sinking."

"That may be true," said Ariakas, "but the Knighthood is still a powerful force in Solamnia and so long as the knights are around, the Solamnic people will never give up. The knights must be utterly destroyed, the knighthood vanquished. I want them crushed, shattered, and so demoralized they can never recover."

"That will happen if we rout the knights at the High Clerist's Tower," Kitiara argued. "If Palanthas falls due to the feeble folly of the knights, the people will turn from them in fury and disgust. The people already distrust them. The loss of the High Clerist's Tower and the invasion of Palanthas would be the final blow. The knighthood would crumble to dust."

Seeing Ariakas thinking this over, Kitiara pressed home her point.

"My lord," she said, "we use the blue dragons to strike like a thunder bolt falling from the heavens. We hit the knights quickly and we hit them hard before they ever see us coming. Give the command and my dragons can be ready to attack within the week!"

She paused to let this sink in, then said quietly, "It is said that the

High Clerist's Tower has never fallen while men of faith defend it. The men guarding the Tower have lost their faith and we must not give them the opportunity to find it. We must strike before the knights raise up a champion who will bring the feuding factions together."

Ariakas mulled this over. Her arguments were persuasive. He liked the idea of a swift, brutal attack on the under-manned tower. The knights would be demoralized. Palanthas would undoubtedly surrender, and he needed her wealth and her fleet of white-winged ships. The trade in slaves alone would send steel coins flooding into his coffers.

Ariakas was about to agree and then he looked into Kitiara's eyes. He saw what he wanted to see in the eyes of one of his commanders: the lust for battle. But he saw something else there, too—something that gave him pause. He saw smug certainty. He saw ambition.

She would be lauded and celebrated: Kitiara, the Blue Lady, the conqueror of Solamnia.

He could see her hand reaching for the Crown of Power. She had already, perhaps, removed one of her rivals . . .

Ariakas did not fear Kit. He feared nothing and no one. If he had thought her daring plan was his only chance for victory, he would have ordered her to proceed and he would have dealt with her when she challenged him. But the more he considered her plan, the more he saw the potential for disaster.

Ariakas mistrusted Kit's reliance on dragons. Before the Dark Queen's return, Ariakas had never brought dragons into battle, and while he admitted they had their uses for destruction and intimidation, he did not think it wise to rely on them to take the lead in a fight, as Kitiara was proposing. Dragons were arrogant beasts. Powerful and intelligent, they considered themselves as far above humans as humans considered themselves above fleas. Ariakas could not, for example, give a dragon a direct order. The dragons were obedient only to Queen Takhisis, and even the goddess had to be diplomatic in her approach.

Kitiara's reckless and unorthodox plan went against all Ariakas's notions of the proper way to conduct a war, and it wouldn't hurt her to get smacked down for once— remind her who was in charge.

"No," he said decisively. "We will strengthen our hold on the south and the east and then we will *march* on the High Clerist's

Tower." He emphasized the word. "As to the Solamnic knights, I have my own plan for their destruction."

Kitiara was disappointed. "My lord, if I could just explain the details, I'm sure you would come to see—"

Ariakas slammed the flat of his hand down on the desk. "Do not push your luck, Blue Lady," he said grimly.

Kitiara knew when to quit. She knew him and understood him. She knew he distrusted dragons. She knew he distrusted her and that his distrust was part of his decision, though he would never admit it. It would be dangerous to continue to press him.

Kitiara also knew, with a certainty bordering on the uncanny, that he had just made a serious mistake. Men would pay for that mistake with their lives.

Kitiara thought all this and then she let it go with a shake of her black curls and a shrug. Hers was a practical nature that looked always ahead, never behind. She did not waste time in regret.

"As you will, my lord. What is your lordship's plan?"

"This is the reason I summoned you." Ariakas rose from the desk and walked to the door. Leaning out, he shouted, "Send for Iolanthe!"

"Who is Iolanthe?" Kit asked.

"The idea is hers," said Ariakas. "She is my new witch."

From the glistening of lust in his eye, Kitiara guessed immediately that this new witch was also his new lover.

She leaned her hip on the desk again, resigned to hearing whatever lame-brained scheme Ariakas's latest paramour had whispered to him during the throes of their love-making. And she was a witch, a user of magic. That made this even worse.

Kitiara was more comfortable around magic-users than most warriors. Her mother, Rosamun, had been born with magic in her blood, given to strange visions and trances that had eventually driven her insane. The same magic flowed strongly in the veins of her younger half-brother, Raistlin. It had been Kitiara who, seeing this talent in him, understood that he could someday earn his bread with his art—provided it didn't kill him first.

Like most warriors, Kitiara did not like nor trust magic-users. They did not fight fair. Give her a foe who came lunging at her with a sword, not one who pranced about chanting sing-song words and tossing bat dung.

31

The witch arrived, ushered in by one of the ogre guards who couldn't quit ogling her. Iolanthe had responded to the summons with such alacrity that Kitiara suspected the witch had been ensconced in a nearby chamber. From the glance she and Ariakas exchanged, Kitiara guessed the woman had been invited to eavesdrop on the conversation.

Iolanthe was what Kitiara would have expected in one of Ariakas's lovers. She was human, young (late twenties, perhaps), and Kitiara supposed men might consider her beautiful, if you happened to like a nubile, sensuous, voluptuous sort of beauty.

There had been a time when Ariakas had liked Kitiara's lean and muscular sort of beauty, but that time was long gone. Kit was quite content to let it remain in the past. She'd slept with Ariakas for one reason and that was to gain an advantage over the hundreds of other aspiring and ambitious commanders clamoring for Ariakas's favor.

Kit greeted Iolanthe with a cool nod and a quirk of her lips, which let the witch understand immediately that Kit knew why and how Iolanthe came to be here.

Iolanthe returned the woman's crooked smile with a charming smile of her own. Iolanthe had heard a great deal about Kitiara uth Matar from Ariakas and the witch had been intensely curious to meet her. Iolanthe was not jealous of Kitiara. Jealousy of an individual means that one suffers from feelings of inferiority and inadequacy, and Iolanthe was supremely confident of her powers—both physical and magical. She did not see the need to be jealous of anyone.

Kitiara did have one thing Iolanthe wanted. Kit was a Dragon Highlord. She commanded men and dragons; she had wealth and status. She was an equal in the eyes of Ariakas, while Iolanthe was only his witch and his mistress—one in a long line of mistresses. The ogres standing guard outside treated Kitiara with marked respect. They leered at Iolanthe.

The witch wanted what Kitiara had—power—and she meant to get it, though Iolanthe had not yet decided how. She was from Khur, a land of fierce nomadic warriors who fought blood feuds dating back centuries. Iolanthe might make a friend of Kitiara. She might become her most deadly foe. Much depended on Kitiara.

"Explain your idea to the Blue Lady," said Ariakas, as Iolanthe entered.

Iolanthe made a graceful bow of acquiescence. Her eyes were violet, and she lined them with black kohl to enhance their unusual color. Those eyes met Kitiara's, their gaze one of cool appraisal.

Kitiara had little use for most men she met and no use at all for women, who, in her mind, tended to be soft creatures given to babies and hysterics. Kit could see why Ariakas had brought this woman to his bed. Iolanthe was one of the most striking, exotic females Kitiara had ever seen.

"You are of Solamnic descent, I believe, Kitiara—" Iolanthe began.

"I am properly addressed as Highlord," Kitiara stated.

Iolanthe's black lashes flickered. "I beg your pardon, Highlord. Forgive me."

Kitiara gave an abrupt nod. "Proceed. My time is short."

Iolanthe cast a covert glance at Ariakas. As she expected, he was enjoying this. He generally found it expedient to keep his subordinates at each other's throats, encouraging the survival of the fittest. Iolanthe had the idea that perhaps she could use them both, play one off the other in her own rise to power. A dangerous game, but Iolanthe was born with the blood of warrior-kings in her veins, and she had *not* come to Neraka merely to feel Ariakas's calloused hands groping her.

"Your father was a knight," Iolanthe added, refraining from adding that Kitiara's father had been a disgraced knight, "and therefore you are familiar with the politics of the Solamnic knighthood—"

"I know that I get a blinding headache whenever politics are discussed," said Kitiara disdainfully.

"I heard you were a woman of action." Iolanthe favored Kit with a pretty smile. "Do you know a knight named Derek Crownguard?"

"I know *of* him. I've never met him. He is a Lord of the Rose from a wealthy family, who is vying with Gunthar uth Wistan for the leadership of the knighthood."

Politics might give Kitiara a headache, but she took care to keep herself informed as to what was happening in the nation she was about to conquer. "Crownguard is ambitious. A glory-seeker. He is a strict follower of the Oath and the Measure. He will not take a crap but that he first consults the Measure to make sure he's doing it right."

"Crudely put, but accurate," said Iolanthe.

"This Crownguard is the key to the destruction of the knight-hood," said Ariakas.

"You want me to have him killed?" Kitiara asked.

She was speaking to Ariakas, but it was Iolanthe who responded with a shake of her head. She wore her long black hair shoulder-length with straight-cut bangs adorned by a slender gold band. Her thick hair swung when she moved her head, giving forth a hint of fragrant perfume. Her robes were made of black silk trimmed in gold, sewn together in layers so that the diaphanous, filmy fabric clung to her here and floated away from her there, providing a fleeting and tanta-lizing glimpse of brown flesh beneath. She wore golden bracelets on her arms and golden rings on her hands and around her ankles. Her feet were bare.

Kitiara, by contrast, was clad in dragon armor with tall boots, and she smelled of sweat and of leather.

"Assassination would make Derek Crownguard a hero," said Iolanthe. "The knights need a hero right now and only a fool would provide them with one."

"Just tell her the plan, Iolanthe," said Ariakas, who was growing impatient, "or rather I will do it myself. You have heard of dragon orbs?" he asked Kitiara.

"The magical artifact that holds the elf king Lorac in thrall?"

"Another orb like it has been discovered in Icereach. The Dragon Highlord of the White Wing, Feal-Thas, apparently just came across it while cleaning out his closet," Ariakas said dryly.

"You want me to go take it from him," said Kit.

Ariakas tapped his fingertips together. "No. Derek Crownguard should be the one to recover this orb."

Kitiara raised her eyebrows. Whatever she had expected, it wasn't this. "Why is that, my lord?"

"Because the orb will seize Crownguard, as it has seized the elf king, and bring him under our control. He will go back to Solamnia— the poison in the Solamnic well. Under our direction, he will lead the knights straight to ruin. This plan has the additional advantage of removing Derek from Solamnia during a critical time. You are familiar with Solamnics. What do you think?"

What Kitiara thought was that a bold attack now on the High Clerist's Tower could win the war, but Ariakas didn't want to hear that, and Kitiara suddenly understood why. He hated his foes, the Solamnic knights, but as much as he hated them, so too did he believe in them. He believed their mythology. He believed the legend of the knight Huma and how he had driven the Dark Queen and her dragons back into the Abyss. He believed in the myth of the knights' prowess and strength and he believed in their former glory. He had concocted this elaborate plan because, deep inside, he believed he could not defeat them militarily.

Kitiara was under no such illusions. She was not a believer. She'd seen the knights in the person of her profligate father and she knew their shining silver armor was rusty and dented and that it creaked when they walked.

This was all so clear to her, yet there was nothing she could do. What was equally clear was that if this scheme of Ariakas's failed, if the dragonarmies lost the battle for Solamnia, she—as commander of the Blue Wing—would be blamed. Never mind that she had given Ariakas the winning strategy and he had turned it down. He would conveniently forget that when the time came.

He and his witch were both waiting for her to tell them how brilliant they were.

She would do her duty. She was a soldier, after all, and he was her commander.

"It's an interesting notion," Kitiara said. "All Solamnics are deeply suspicious and distrustful of anything magic, but"—she smiled at Iolanthe—"I have no doubt some lovely woman could help Sir Derek overcome his misgivings. Now, if that will be all, my lord, I should be returning to my command."

Kitiara was thinking there might be some way around Ariakas's refusal to attack the High Clerist's Tower. He would be angry that she had disobeyed him, at first, but his rage would be mitigated by her victory. Better that than endure his fury after a defeat . . .

"Excellent," said Ariakas smoothly. "I'm glad you like the plan, Kitiara, because I've decided to send you to ensnare Crownguard."

His words came as a shock to both women. Iolanthe stared at him in amazement nearly as great as Kit's.

"My lord," Iolanthe protested, bristling, "you and I agreed that I should be the one—"

"My lord," Kitiara spoke at the same time, her dark brows

coming together in irritation, "I am commander of the Blue Wing. My place is with my troops—"

Ariakas was gratified. These two powerful women had been growing a bit too sure of themselves.

"I have changed my mind," he said, his sharp tone cutting them both off. "Iolanthe, the Highlord is right. The knights are distrustful of magic and those who wield it—a fact I had not taken into consideration when I agreed you could go. Kitiara is a warrior and far better suited to this task. As for you, Highlord, your forces are dug in for the winter. You can afford to spend some time away from them."

Kit turned away, determined to hide her disappointment. She walked over to stare out the window at the compound, where a group of prisoners, chained together at the ankle, was being lined up at the foot of a scaffold. Today was the day for hanging traitors. She watched dispassionately as the executioner placed the noose around the neck of a young man, who was groveling on his knees, protesting his innocence, begging for his life. The guards yanked him to his feet, put a bag over his head.

"Leave us, Iolanthe," said Ariakas, after a pause. "I need to speak to the Highlord."

Iolanthe cast Kitiara a baleful look, then took her leave, her silken garments flowing around her. She slammed shut the door behind her.

Kitiara had her feelings once more under control. "The lady was not pleased. I fear you will sleep in a cold bed this night, my lord."

"No woman ever says 'no' to me, Kitiara," Ariakas replied imperturbably. "You know that, and stop fingering that hidden blade of yours. I am convinced you are the one to handle this business with Crownguard. Once you have completed that assignment, which should not take you long, provided you handle it right—"

"I already have some ideas on that score, my lord," said Kitiara.

"Good. After that, I want you to fly to Haven and report back to me on this chaotic situation in the Red Wing."

Kitiara was about to argue against this, for she truly had no care about the Red Wing, when a sudden thought flashed through her mind. Haven was near Solace. A trip back to her old stomping grounds might prove most interesting.

"I am yours to command, my lord," she said.

"After that, you will travel to Icereach. I do not trust this elf wizard. I find the fact that he has suddenly 'remembered' he has a dragon orb in his possession disturbing."

Ariakas walked over to stand beside her. They both watched as the scaffold's trap door opened and the young man dropped to his death. Unfortunately for him, the fall did not break his neck, and he writhed and twisted at the end of the noose for some time.

"Ah, a kicker," remarked Ariakas, amused.

Kitiara watched until the body went still and hung twisting in the wind. Ariakas had more to say. She waited for him to say it.

"This is the main reason I am going along with Iolanthe's plan for this knight to steal the dragon orb. I do not want it in the possession of Feal-Thas."

"I could take it from him," said Kitiara.

Ariakas cast her a cool glance. "I don't want it in your possession either."

Kitiara half-smiled. She watched in silence as the soldiers cut down the body and prepared the noose for the next man in line.

"That being said, I don't want Feal-Thas to think I don't trust him," Ariakas continued. "He has his uses; I know of no one else I could convince to live in that frozen wasteland. You must be subtle in your dealings with him."

"Of course, my lord."

"As for the dragon orb, once I have no further use for this Crownguard, he will be disposed of and I will take the orb for myself. Don't you see the genius of this plan?"

Kitiara saw the genius of her own plan to attack the High Clerist's Tower. She sighed inwardly.

"Yes, my lord," she replied dutifully. Outside in the compound, the guards were dragging the next man up the stairs. She turned away from the window. "Your lordship must give me written orders for Feal-Thas. He won't believe me."

"Of course. You will have them by morning. Stop by before you leave."

"Do you know where I am to find Crownguard, my lord? I seem to recall destroying his castle some time ago. . ."

"According to my agents, he is on Sancrist Isle, residing at Castle Wistan. He leaves there to go back to Palanthas, however."

Kitiara stared at Ariakas, incredulous. "That is enemy territory, my lord!"

"A dangerous mission, Kit," Ariakas said imperturbably. "The reason I chose you."

Kitiara had the feeling there were other reasons as well. Up until a few moments ago, he had planned on sending Iolanthe to Solamnia. Ariakas was not one to act on impulse. He had a good reason for making the switch. Kitiara wondered uneasily what it was. Had she given herself away? Did he guess she had been planning to disobey him and attack the Tower? She thought back to her words, her actions, and decided she had not. No, he must simply be annoyed at her for pressing him on the issue of the High Clerist's Tower.

Their business concluded, Kitiara took her leave. The two parted, apparently on the best of terms.

"One thing I like about you, Kitiara," Ariakas said to her as she was walking to the door. "You take defeat like a man. No sulking or pouting just because you don't get your way. Keep me apprised of your progress."

Kitiara was so absorbed in her thoughts when she left that she did not see the door to another room open a crack, nor did she see the bright violet eyes, touched with kohl and shadowed by long dark lashes, watching her.

Kit retrieved her sword and her boot knife from the ogres. Unlike Grag, her hands did not shake as she buckled on her sword belt, but she felt a similar sense of relief. Few left Ariakas's presence alive without feeling relieved.

"Need the location of the nearest bar?" asked the ogre handing over her sword.

"Thanks, I already know it," said Kitiara.

3

The Inn of the Broken Shield. Silver Magic.

Iolanthe waited until she saw Kitiara walking down the street, then returned to Ariakas.

He was seated at his desk, writing the promised dispatch. Iolanthe went over to him, put her hands on his broad shoulders and rubbed his neck.

"I could send for your scribe to do that, my lord—"

"The fewer people who know of this, the better," said Ariakas. He wrote rapidly in large block letters, so that there would be no mistaking his words.

Iolanthe, looking over his shoulder, saw that he was writing about the dragon orb.

"Why the change in plans, my lord?" Iolanthe asked. "Why send the Highlord to Solamnia and not me? We had this all arranged . . ."

"As I told Kitiara, she is better suited to the mission. She already has a plan in mind."

"I have a feeling there is another reason, my lord." Iolanthe slid her arms beneath his leather armor, ran her hands over his bare chest. He continued writing.

"The Highlord was concocting some scheme to countermand my orders and attack the High Clerist's Tower."

Iolanthe bent closer, so that her hair fell around him, and he could smell her perfume.

"What else?" she said softly.

"She gave in too quickly, especially when I mentioned sending her to Haven. She is keeping something from me," said Ariakas. His voice had gone hard and grating.

"We all have secrets, my lord," said Iolanthe, kissing his ear.

"I want to know hers."

"This can be done," said Iolanthe.

"She must not suspect."

"That will be more difficult." Iolanthe thought a moment. "There is a way, but I must have access to her quarters. What barracks is she in?"

"Kitiara in the barracks?" Ariakas chuckled at the thought. "Sleep on a cot when there's a comfortable inn in town? I'll find out for you."

He took hold of Iolanthe's wrists, his grip hard, bruising, and with a sudden jerk, he dragged her off her feet and threw her down on the desk in front of him. He bent over her, pinning her arms.

"You do good work for me, Iolanthe."

She gazed limpidly at him, smiling, her lips parted. He pressed himself against her, his hands fumbling beneath her skirt.

"It is my pleasure, my lord," sighed Iolanthe.

Once she had finished her business with Ariakas, Iolanthe rearranged her robes and wrapped a shapeless black cloak around her shoulders, pulling the hood over her head. Runes stitched with golden thread on the cloak proclaimed her a magic-user and were meant to serve as a warning to any who might try to molest her. The streets of Neraka were narrow, vile, filthy, and dangerous. The Dark Queen's soldiers ran the city, feeling free to take anything or anyone they wanted, and because Ariakas promoted rivalry between the various commanders, the troops were constantly getting into fights. Their commanders might or might not decide to break it up.

In addition, the devoted followers of Hiddukel, the God of

40

Thieves, were always on hand to welcome visitors and pilgrims to the Dark Queen's temple, piously relieving them of any burdens, such as their purses. Criminals of all sorts could find safe haven in Neraka, at least until bounty hunters tracked them down.

Still, despite its lawless nature, Neraka was prosperous and thriving. The war was going well and her people were on the winning side. Spoils of victory poured into the city. The pawn shops were filled with gold and jewels, silverware and crystal, paintings and furniture looted from the conquered lands of Silvanesti, Qualinesti, Abanasinia, and eastern Solamnia. Human and elf slaves filled the slave markets and such was their quality that buyers came from as far away as Flotsam on the other side of the continent.

One entire street in Neraka was given over to shops trafficking in stolen magical artifacts, books and scrolls and potions. Many of these were fake, so one had to know what one was doing when shopping. A potion sold with the guarantee of a good night's sleep might mean one would never wake up. Holy artifacts were more difficult to come by. A person in the market for those had to go to the Dark Queen's Temple, and entrance into the walled Inner City was limited to those who had business there and could prove it. Since the Temple was a forbidding place and the dark priests, Takhisis's servants, were not disposed to welcome visitors, the traffic in holy artifacts was not a brisk one.

Iolanthe made her home in Wizard's Row, a street of shops and dwellings located outside the Temple walls. A relative newcomer to Neraka, Iolanthe had taken a small apartment above a mageware shop. Housing was difficult to find in Neraka, and she paid an extravagant amount for three small rooms. Still, she did not complain. She considered she was lucky to have a home at all. The city was so crowded that many were forced to sleep in the streets or cram together six to a room in squalid tenements.

The daughter of a well-to-do family in Khur, the fifteen-year-old Iolanthe had disgraced the family by refusing to marry the forty-year-old man they had chosen for her. When they sought to force her into the marriage, she stole the money and jewels that were to have been her dowry and ran away to the capital city of Khuri-Khan. Needing some way to make a living, she paid an itinerant wizard to teach her magic.

Eventually, her betrothed tracked her down and tried to force her to marry him by raping her. Iolanthe killed the man, but unfortunately she neglected to kill his servant, who ran back to tell the family, who vowed revenge. Iolanthe was now embroiled in a blood feud. Her life in Khur was worth nothing.

Her wizard teacher sought permission for her to find safe haven in the Tower of Wayreth, and she was accepted as a pupil by the famous wizardess, Ladonna. Iolanthe proved herself an apt student.

Iolanthe took the dread Test in the Tower of High Sorcery at the age of twenty-six, emerging shaken but unscarred to be confirmed as a Black Robe. Finding life studying magic in the Tower to be unprofitable and boring, Iolanthe searched about for a place where she could plant the seed of her ambition. The filth and squalor of Neraka provided fertile ground.

Wizards were not welcomed with loving arms by the clerics of the Dark Queen, and thus, upon first arriving in Neraka, Iolanthe found herself on the verge of starving. She made money dancing the exotic dances of her people in one of the taverns, and there she was fortunate enough to attract the attention of Lord Ariakas. He took her to his bed that same night, and when he found out she was a mage, he employed her as his own personal witch. Iolanthe's seed was planted and where once she would have been pleased with only a small tree, she now envisioned a veritable forest.

As she left the Blue Quarter behind her, walking toward Wizard Row, a hobgoblin soldier, whose intake of rot-gut liquor had apparently impaired his vision, grabbed hold of her, breathed his foul breath on her, and tried to kiss her. Iolanthe spoke a word of magic and she had the satisfaction of seeing all his hair stand straight up, his eyeballs bulge, and his big body vibrate from the jolt. The hobgoblin's companions hooted with laughter as he collapsed, twitching, into the mud.

Iolanthe reached her door without further incident. Removing the wizard lock, she entered her small quarters and went immediately to the library. She searched through her books until she found the one she needed: *Spells of Scrying and Far Sight with Particular Emphasis on the Proper Use of Spell Components*. Sitting down at her desk, she began to flip through the pages, searching for a spell. Those she found were far too difficult for her to cast or required rare components that she would not be able to acquire in time. She was starting to grow discouraged, but then, at last, she found one that would suit. There was some risk involved, but Iolanthe decided the ability to gain ascendancy over Kitiara uth Matar would be worth a little danger to herself.

Iolanthe descended the dark and narrow staircase that led from her apartment to the mageware shop below. She found the wizened old man who was the owner perched upon his stool behind his counter, drinking tarbean tea and watching the people passing in the street outside his window.

The old man's name was Snaggle and he was a half-breed, though he was so dried-up and wrinkled that it was impossible to tell what the two halves were. He claimed he was *not* a wizard, though he was so knowledgeable in the arcane arts that Iolanthe privately doubted this. He was known for the quality of his merchandise. No need to be concerned about purchasing lamb's blood that had been sitting on the shelf for three months, or crow feathers masquerading as raven quills. Snaggle had a knack for acquiring rare and precious artifacts, and the emperor himself made frequent visits to the mageware shop to see what new items might have come in.

Snaggle was Iolanthe's friend and also her landlord, since she rented her apartment from him. He greeted her with a toothless grin and an offer of tarbean tea, something he did only for favored clients.

"Thank you, my friend," Iolanthe said with a smile. She truly liked the old man and the feeling was mutual. She accepted the tea, sipping it daintily.

"I am looking for a knife," she said.

The mageware shop was very neat and tidy, unusual in the business. Most such shops tended to resemble magpie nests. All Snaggle's wares were stored in labeled bins and boxes stacked neatly one atop the other on shelves that went floor to ceiling. Nothing was on display or out in plain sight. The boxes were kept behind the long counter that ran the length of the shop. No customer was allowed behind the counter. The old man enforced this rule with a strange-looking staff said to possess lethal powers.

A customer would tell Snaggle what he or she needed. Snaggle would leave his stool and his tea and fetch the appropriate box, each labeled by a code known only to Snaggle.

"What sort of knife?" the old man asked Iolanthe. "Knife for protection, knife for dicing and chopping components, knife for conducting ritual sacrifices—"

"A knife for scrying," she said, and she explained the use.

Snaggle thought a moment, his brow furrowed, then, leaving his stool, he took hold of a ladder that ran on wheels along the floor, rolled it over to the correct shelf, and climbed nimbly about half-way up. He pulled out a box, brought it down to the counter, and opened the lid.

An array of knives were neatly arranged inside. Some of the knives were silver, some gold, some steel. Some were large, some small. Some had jeweled handles; some were plain. All had runes inscribed on the blades.

"This one is very nice," said Snaggle. He plucked out a gold knife adorned with diamonds and emeralds on the hilt.

"But very much out of my price range," said Iolanthe, "and it is too big and clumsy and made of gold. I have an affinity for silver."

"True," the old man said. "I had forgotten." He saw her gaze go to one slender blade near the back and he was quick to respond. "Ah, you have the eye, Iolanthe. This one is like yourself—delicate in appearance, but quite powerful."

He drew out the knife and placed it in Iolanthe's hand. The hilt was silver and simply made, banded with mother-of-pearl in a crisscross design. The blade was sharp. The runes etched on it were intricate as spider web. She hefted the knife. It was lightweight and fitted her hand.

"Easily concealed," said Snaggle.

"How much?" Iolanthe asked.

He named a price and she accepted. The two never haggled. She knew that he would offer her his lowest price at the outset, and he knew that she was an astute buyer who would not pay a copper more than what an object was worth.

"You will need cedar to burn," he said, as she tucked the knife up her tight-fitting sleeve.

"I will?" Iolanthe glanced up at him, surprised. "The instructions to the spell didn't say so."

"Trust me," said Snaggle. "Cedar works best. Half a moment while I put this away."

He shut the lid on the box of knives, climbed up the ladder, replaced the box, then propelled himself on the ladder across the floor to another shelf. He opened a box, drew out some sticks of wood as long as his index finger, and hopped back down.

"And add a pinch of sea salt," he added, as he tied the sticks together with a bit of string into a neat bundle.

"Thank you, my friend." Iolanthe was about to take her leave when a baaz draconian wearing the emblem of Lord Ariakas entered the shop.

"Can I help you, sir?" Snaggle asked.

"I seek the witch, Iolanthe. I am told she lives in the apartment above the store," said the baaz. "I come in the name of Lord Ariakas."

Snaggle glanced at Iolanthe, letting her know he would either acknowledge her or deny that he'd ever heard of her, depending on the sign she gave him.

Iolanthe spared him the trouble. "I am Iolanthe."

The baaz bowed. "I have the information you seek, Mistress. Broken Shield Inn. Room number sixteen."

"Thank you," said Iolanthe.

The baaz saluted, fist to heart, and turned on his scaly heel and left.

"Another cup of tea?" Snaggle asked.

"No, thank you, my friend. I have an errand I must run before darkness falls."

Iolanthe took her leave. Though confident of her ability to protect herself by day, she knew better than to walk the streets of Neraka alone after dark, and she had to pay a visit to the Broken Shield.

The Inn of the Broken Shield, as it was properly known, was located in the White Quarters district and was one of the oldest and largest buildings in Neraka. It looked very much like it had been built by a child playing with blocks stacked up one atop another. The inn had started as a one-room shack offering drink and food to those early dark pilgrims come to worship at the Temple. As its popularity grew, the shack added on a room and called itself a tavern. The tavern added on several blocks of rooms and named itself an inn. The inn sent out an entire wing of rooms and was now proud to call itself tavern, inn, and boarding house.

The Broken Shield was a favorite with the mercenaries, pilgrims, and clerics in Neraka, mainly due to the fact that it was "human only". Other races, most notably draconians, goblins and hobgoblins, were not allowed. The patrons themselves policed this policy and saw to it that "dracos" and "hobs and gobs" did their drinking at the Hairy Troll.

The inn was crowded tonight, filled with hungry soldiers just coming off guard duty. Iolanthe had exchanged her silken robes for the plain black robes of a dark pilgrim. Her face heavily veiled, she waited outside until she saw a group of dark pilgrims file into the inn. She joined up with them and they all entered the inn together.

She immediately spotted Kitiara. The Dragon Highlord sat alone, eating her meal with rapid efficiency and drinking a mug of ale. The pilgrims separated, seating themselves at various tables in groups of twos or threes. Iolanthe slid into a chair at a table close to the others, but kept herself apart. No one took any special notice of her.

She watched Kitiara shove back her empty plate and sit back in her chair, her mug in her hands. Kit was somber, lost in thought. One sellsword, a comely young man, with long blonde hair and sporting a jagged scar down one cheek, came over to her table. She did not seem to notice him. He started to pull out a chair.

Kitiara put her booted foot in the seat. "Not tonight, Trampas," she said. She shook her head. "You would not find me good company."

"Come now, Kit," the young man said persuasively, "let me buy you a mug of ale, at least."

She did not move her foot and there was no other chair.

Trampas shrugged and went on his way. Kitiara drank the ale in a long swallow. The barkeep brought her another and set it down before her, taking the empty mug away. Kit drank that one too, continuing to brood. Iolanthe tried to guess her thoughts. Kit did not look irate or angry, therefore she was not worrying about her rebuff from Ariakas. She looked introspective. Her eyes stared at the ale mug, but she was not seeing it. Occasionally she would smile to herself.

She looked like someone reminiscing, thinking over past times, remembering happy moments.

"How very interesting," Iolanthe murmured to herself. She thought back to the conversation she had overheard between Kit and Ariakas. They had discussed past times—Kit's days in Solace. They had talked about her brother the mage, but judging by the warmth of her smile and the flash of her dark eyes, Kitiara was not thinking about sickly baby brothers.

"My lord was right. You do have secrets," Iolanthe said softly. "Dangerous ones."

Kitiara took a long pull from the mug and, settling back more comfortably in her chair, she put both her feet in the chair opposite, letting everyone in the tavern know that she wanted to be alone this night.

"Good," said Iolanthe. The presence of a lover would have been a serious inconvenience.

Iolanthe left her table and walked up to a bar crowded with soldiers demanding ale or dwarf spirits, wine or mead or a combination of several. The bartenders, red-faced and sweating, bustled here and there, trying to keep up. The soldiers were loud and raucous, shouting insults at the bartenders and groping the barmaids, who were accustomed to the rough crowd and gave as good as they got. Iolanthe pushed her way forward. Seeing a dark pilgrim, the soldiers hastily drew back, making respectful, if grumbling, way for her. A man would have to be very drunk indeed to dare insult a priestess of Her Dark Majesty.

"Yes, Revered One?" said a harried bartender, who clutched three foaming mugs in each hand.

"I want my room key, please," said Iolanthe. "Number sixteen."

The bartender thrust the mugs into the hands of various patrons, then turned around to where the room keys hung on various hooks, each with a number attached. The soldiers cursed him for his slowness. He cursed back and shook his fist at them. Finding "16", he snagged the key and tossed it across the bar. Iolanthe caught the key deftly as it came sliding past her. Key in hand, she climbed the stairs that led to the upper chambers.

She paused in a dark hallway to look over the balcony down into the bar area. Kitiara still sat there, still staring into a half-filled mug of ale. Iolanthe continued down the hall, glancing at the room numbers on the doors. Finding the room she sought, she inserted the key into the door and walked inside.

The horned blue helm of a Dragon Highlord lay in one corner where Kit had tossed it, along with various other pieces of a dragon rider's habiliment. The armor was specially designed and had been blessed by the Dark Queen. It protected the rider not only from the buffeting winds of travel by dragonback but also from the weapons of an enemy. Other than her armor and a bed, the room was empty. Kitiara traveled light, it seemed.

Iolanthe paid no attention to any of the objects in the room. She stared about the room itself, committing it to memory. Certain that she could visualize it at need, she shut the door and locked it. She took the key back to the barkeep, and seeing he was busy, she left it lying on the bar and departed.

A glance over her shoulder showed her Kitiara, still sitting by herself, draining yet another mug of ale. Apparently she planned to drown herself in her memories.

Iolanthe sat in her small sitting room, studying the spell by the light of the fire. Beside her, a candle with the hours marked in increments on the wax burned steadily, the hours melting away one by one. When six hours had passed, Iolanthe deemed the time was right. She shut her spellbook, picked up another book and took that to her laboratory. She was dressed in her robes of magic, thick black robes with no decoration, to blend in with the night.

Iolanthe placed the second book on the table. This book had nothing to do with magic, being titled *A History of Ansalon from the Age of Dreams to the Age of Might with Annotations by the Author, a Learned Aesthetic of the Esteemed Library of Palanthas*. A more boring book one could not hope to find, likely to gather dust on any shelf. No one would ever pick up such a book, which was just what the maker intended, for it wasn't a book at all. It was a box. Iolanthe touched the letter "A" in Aesthetic and the cover that was the lid of the box popped gently open.

A glass jar sealed with a stopper covered with wax and trimmed with golden filigree nestled inside a hole cut in the "pages". Alongside the jar in another small pocket was a paintbrush, the tip made with hair from a lion's mane.

Iolanthe lifted the jar carefully. Placing it on the table, she broke the wax seal and pried out the cork lid. The substance inside the jar was thick and viscous, like quicksilver, and it shimmered in the light. This was Iolanthe's most valued possession, a gift from Ladonna, head of the Order of the Black Robes, upon the successful completion of Iolanthe's test. The substance quivered as Iolanthe carried the jar and paintbrush over to a portion of the room concealed by a thick curtain.

Iolanthe drew aside the curtain, letting it fall behind her. There was nothing at all in this part of the room. It was empty of furniture. No pictures hung on a wall made of bare plaster covered with white-wash. Iolanthe placed the jar on the floor. She dipped the paintbrush in the silver substance and, beginning at floor level, she painted a straight line up the wall, a line as long as she was tall. She painted another line perpendicular to the first, then added a third line down to the floor. This done, she carefully replaced the stopper in the jar. She poured melted candle wax over the cork and set it aside to let it dry. She checked to make certain the little silver knife was secure in her sleeve then returned to the curtained alcove.

Iolanthe stood before the lines painted on the wall and spoke the requisite words of the magic. The silver paint on the wall flared brilliantly, dazzling her eyes. For a moment all she could see was blinding white light. She summoned up an image in her mind of the bedroom in the Broken Shield Inn and forced herself to stare into the bright light.

The wall on which the silver lines were painted dissolved. The hallway in the inn stretched before her. Iolanthe did not immediately enter the hall, but looked about carefully, not wanting to be interrupted. She did not enter until she was certain no one was about, then she walked through the wall and the silver lines as another might walk through a door and, traversing the corridors of magic, she stood in room 16.

Iolanthe glanced behind her. The faintest gleam of silver, like the slimy trail made by a snail, shone on the wall, marking her return path. Embers burned in the fireplace, and by their light she could make out the bed and the woman sleeping in it.

The room reeked of ale.

Iolanthe drew the silver knife from her sleeve. She padded on slippered feet across the floor and came to stand beside the bed. Kitiara lay on her back, sprawled out, with one arm flung over her head. She still wore her boots and her clothes; either she had been too tired or too drunk to change. Her breathing was even, her slumber deep. Her sword hung in its sheath from one of the bedposts.

Knife in hand, Iolanthe bent over the slumbering woman. She did not think Kit was shamming sleep, but there was always the possibility. Iolanthe held the knife poised over Kitiara's wrist and dug the blade into her skin, drawing a little drop of blood.

Kitiara never stirred.

"What a fine assassin I would make," Iolanthe reflected. "But enough foolery. Down to business."

She shifted the blade from Kitiara's throat to her hair. She took gentle hold of a silky black lock that lay tousled on the pillow, and, tugging it to its full length, placed the knife at the roots and sliced it off. She cut off another curl and yet another and was going to take a fourth, when Kitiara gave a deep sigh, frowned, and rolled over.

Iolanthe froze, not daring to move, not daring to even breathe. She was in no danger. The words to a sleep spell were on her lips and a requisite pinch of sand was in her hand, ready to be tossed over the slumberer. She didn't want to have to resort to the use of magic, however, for Kitiara might wake the next morning, and, finding sand in her bed, deduce she'd been ensorcelled during the night. She must suspect nothing. As for the cut on her wrist, warriors were always cutting themselves on their armor or their weapons. She would think nothing of such a small mark.

Kit wrapped her arms around the pillow, and murmuring a word that sounded like "tanning," she sighed, smiled, and drifted back to sleep. Iolanthe couldn't imagine why Kit would be dreaming about tanning leather hides, but one never knew. Tucking the lock of hair in a velvet bag, Iolanthe tied the bag to her belt and left Kit's bedside.

The snail-slime trail of silver gleamed faintly on the wall, marking the exit. Iolanthe walked through the silver doorway and stepped into the curtained alcove of her own home, her night's work a success.

4

A Dragon and his Rider.

itiara's mount, a blue dragon named Skie, waited for her in a secret location outside of the city. Stalls for dragons were provided near each of the military quarters of the Highlords in Neraka, but just as Kitiara preferred to stay in an inn rather than the cramped quarters of military housing, Skie liked his privacy and comfort too well to live in the crowded conditions of the dragon stables. He did pay his fellow dragons a visit, however, and he was ready with the latest gossip and news of dragonkind for Kitiara when she arrived.

The blue dragon had spent a comfortable evening. He'd gone out hunting that morning and brought down a fat deer. After dining, he'd found a patch of autumn sunlight, and lying down, he extended his blue wings. Resting his head on the warm rocks, he basked in the warmth. When Kitiara arrived, he roused himself, shaking his head with its blue mane and flicking his long scaly tail.

The greeting between Highlord and dragon was warm. Skie was the only being Kitiara truly trusted and the dragon was devoted to his rider, something rare for dragons, who generally disdained all lower forms of life. Skie admired Kitiara's courage and her cool-headed skill in battle, and thus he was willing to overlook her defects, putting them down to the fact that she had been born, lamentably, a human.

"What a dragon she would have made!" Skie often commented regretfully.

Kitiara patted the blue's long scaled neck with her hand and asked if he had eaten. Skie indicated the remains of a deer carcass nearby. Few other human riders ever bothered to check on the welfare of their dragons, but Kitiara never forgot. She nodded and then, instead of mounting, as he expected, she stood by his side, her hand resting on his neck, staring at her boots.

Skie saw at once that something was wrong.

"What did the emperor think of your plan to attack the High Clerist's Tower?" Skie asked.

Kitiara sighed. "He thinks it is too reckless, too risky, so he did not approve it. That is true, I suppose, but to my mind we risk far more by curling up all snug and complacent in our dens."

"The man is a fool," Skie remarked.

"No, if Ariakas were a fool, I would not mind so much," said Kitiara somberly. "He is a brilliant commander. Witness the fact that his armies control almost all of Ansalon. But those very victories will be his downfall. Back at the start of the war, when he had nothing to lose, he would have taken my advice and attacked the High Clerist's Tower. Since then, he has grown too fond of victory. He is afraid of defeat so he bets only on the sure thing. Hazarding little, he wonders why his winnings decrease."

Skie shook his head. His belly rumbled. He'd eaten too fast and the deer wasn't sitting well.

"Did you visit the dragon mews?" Kitiara asked. "What news did you hear?"

"As you say, the emperor's war is going well," Skie returned in grudging tones. "The Black Dragon Highlord, Lucien of Takar, has strengthened his hold on the eastern lands, putting down minor uprisings and rebellions, though his greatest achievement appears to have been forcing those lay-about slugs of black dragons to crawl out of their swamps and fight. Lucien has joined with the Highlord of Icereach, Feal-Thas, and his white dragons to conquer the Goodland

Peninsula. Feal-Thas is putting it about that he was the one responsible for the victory, but all know the pointy-eared elf was merely following Lucien's order."

"Of course, no human thinks an elf has a brain in his head, so they discount Feal-Thas," Kitiara remarked, "probably at their peril. We will see for ourselves. We are to pay this elf Highlord a visit. I should learn more about him."

"What, travel to Icereach!" Skie snorted. Sparks of lightning sizzled from between his teeth. "If you go there, you go without me. Nothing but snow and ice. Why anyone would want to travel to such a dreadful place is a mystery to me!"

He didn't mean it, of course. Skie would never think of entrusting Kit's welfare to another mount. Still, let her worry a little.

Kitiara dragged the heavy leather harness out of the brush where she had stashed it for safekeeping. Skie detested the harness, as did all self-respecting dragons. "Harness" equated to "horse" in Skie's mind, and he wore one only because it ensured the safety of the rider. Some riders mounted their dragons with the mistaken idea that they could use the harness to guide and control the dragon. Every dragon soon disabused his rider of that notion.

Dragon and rider worked best as a team. Dragon and rider had to trust each other implicitly, for their lives depended on each other. Such trust was difficult for most dragons and riders to acquire, especially the chromatic dragons who were not given to trusting anyone, not even each other. The blue dragons had turned out to be the best mounts thus far. Blue dragons tended to be more gregarious and outgoing than their fellows and worked better with humans. That said, there always came a time in the relationship of every dragon and his rider when the dragon would have to teach the rider who was really in control. This was often done by the dragon flipping over in midair and dumping his offending rider in a lake.

Skie still recalled with an inward chuckle the time he had done that to Kit. She'd been wearing full plate armor and she'd sunk like a boulder. Skie had been forced to plunge in after her and drag her out, half-drowned. He had thought she would be furious, but once she'd quit spewing up water, she had started to laugh. She had admitted that he'd been right and she'd been wrong and she never again sought to impose her will on him.

The first thing Kitiara had learned from Skie was that aerial combat was far different from battles fought on land. In the air, a human had to learn to think and fight like a dragon. Thinking of this made Skie recall the rest of his news.

"The rumor is that soon the metallic dragons will enter the war," the blue dragon said. "If that happens, Ariakas's victories may dry up. These metallics are our equals, armed with deadly breath weapons and powerful magicks."

"Bah! I don't believe it," said Kit, shaking her head. "The metallics have sworn an oath promising not to enter the war. They don't dare, not while we are holding their precious eggs hostage."

"You and I both know what's happening to those eggs, and some-day the metallics will figure it out. Some are already starting to grow suspicious. Word is that one named Evenstar is going about asking questions about the draconians. When the golds and silvers discover the truth, they will enter this war—with a vengeance!"

"Which reminds me, I suppose you heard Verminaard is dead," Skie added offhandedly.

"Yes, I heard," said Kitiara.

Skie assisted her in putting on the harness, which fit around his neck and chest and forelegs. At least Kitiara did not insist on using one of the awkward and uncomfortable dragon saddles. She rode bareback, settling herself in front of his wings.

"Did you hear the truth of how he died?" Skie asked chattily. "Not battling dwarves in the dwarven kingdom, as we were led to believe, but ignominiously, at the hands of slaves!"

"The draconian commander said he was killed by assassins," said Kit, adding with a chuckle, "At his death, an aurak masqueraded as Verminaard. Quite clever of him."

"The dragons who served under the scaly little bastard were not fooled," said Skie disparagingly.

"You don't like draconians," Kit observed, climbing up on Skie's back.

"No dragon does," said Skie, glowering. "They are a perversion, an abomination. I cannot believe Her Dark Majesty sanctioned such a heinous act."

"Then you do not know Her Dark Majesty," said Kitiara. She glanced about then said quietly, "I suggest we change the subject. You never know who might be listening."

Skie grunted in agreement. "Where are we bound? Back to our camp?"

"Why?" Kitiara asked bitterly. "We have nothing to do there but drink and belch and scratch ourselves. We're not going to be allowed to fight."

She sighed again then said, "Besides, Lord Ariakas has other assignments for me. First, we go to Palanthas . . ."

"Palanthas?" Skie repeated, amazed. "That's in enemy territory. What business do you have in Palanthas?"

"I'm going shopping," said Kitiara with a laugh.

Skie craned his neck to stare at her. "Shopping? What for?"

"A man's soul," Kit replied.

5

The Oath and the Measure.
An assignation.

ir Derek Crownguard did not like being a guest at Castle Wistan, but the knight did not have much choice in the matter. His own holdings—a border castle north of Solanthus—had been overrun by the forces of the Dark Queen and was, so he heard, being occupied and rebuilt by enemy troops, now in control of all of eastern Solamnia. Derek's younger brother had died in the assault. When it became apparent that the castle would fall, Derek had faced the choice of dying in a hopeless cause or staying alive to one day return and reclaim his family's holdings and their honor. He had fled, along with those of his friends and troops who had survived. He sent his wife and children to Palanthas to live with her relatives, while he had traveled to Sancrist Isle, there to spend weeks discussing with his fellow knights how best to recruit and organize the forces that would drive the enemy from his homeland.

Derek had recently returned to Palanthas, frustrated and irate, his plans having been thwarted at every turn by men who, in his opinion, lacked courage, conviction, and vision. In particular, Derek

Crownguard despised his host.

"Gunthar has become an old woman, Brian," Derek said grimly. "When he hears the enemy is on the march, he cries 'Alack-a-day!' and dives under the bed!"

Brian Donner knew this was a ridiculous charge, but he also knew that Derek, like some gnomish device, needed to release steam or else blow up and do damage to those around him.

The two knights were similar in build and in coloring and were sometimes mistaken for brothers by those who did not know them— a relationship Derek was quick to refute, for the Crownguards were a noble family of long lineage and the Donners came of more common stock. Both were blonde and blue-eyed, like many Solamnics. Derek's hair was a darker blonde, now graying, as were his mustaches—the traditional long and flowing mustaches of a Solamnic knight—for he was in his late thirties. The main difference lay in their eyes. Brian's blue eyes smiled. Derek's blue eyes glinted.

"I don't agree with Gunthar's views, but he's not a coward, Derek," Brian said mildly. "He's cautious. Perhaps too cautious . . ."

"His 'caution' cost me Castle Crownguard!" Derek returned angrily. "If Gunthar had sent the reinforcements I asked for, we could have held off the onslaught."

Brian wasn't sure about that either, but he was Derek's friend and a fellow knight, so he conceded the point. The two refought the battle for the hundredth time, with Derek detailing what he would have done if only the requested troops had arrived. Brian listened patiently and agreed, as always, to everything Derek said.

The two were exercising their horses in the meadows and forests outside the city walls of Palanthas. They were alone, or Derek would not have been talking as he did. Though Derek might despise Lord Gunthar, the Measure required that a knight support a superior in word and deed, and Derek, who lived and died by the Measure, never spoke out against Gunthar in public. The Measure said nothing about respecting and supporting a superior in one's private thoughts, however, so Derek could vent his anger alone to a friend and not be guilty of breaking the code of conduct that was meant to govern the lives of the Knights of Solamnia.

Derek and his friend had ridden out for a gallop some distance from the city. The two had returned only yesterday from the meeting of the Knightly Council on Sancrist Isle, a meeting that had devolved into a shouting match. Derek and his supporters advocated sending troops into battle against the dragonarmies immediately, while Gunthar and his faction proposed waiting until their troops were better trained and better equipped and suggested that perhaps they should make some attempt to forge an alliance with the elves.

Neither side proved strong enough to prevail. The knighthood was splintered; no decisions could be made, no action undertaken. Derek believed Lord Gunthar wanted a knighthood divided, since that meant nothing would get done, and he had walked out of the meeting in a rage, choking back words a man must never say to a fellow knight. Though Brian did not entirely agree with Derek, he had supported his friend, and they had boarded the first ship to make the channel crossing from Sancrist to Palanthas.

"If I were Grand Master—" Derek began.

"—which you're not," Brian pointed out.

"I should be!" Derek declared vehemently. "Lord Alfred thinks so, and my lords Peterkin and Malborough . . ."

"But only one of those knights is a member of the Grand Circle and eligible to vote—even *if* a Grand Circle could be convened, which it can't, due to the fact that there are not enough members."

"The Measure provides the means to form a Grand Circle in such dire circumstances as we now find ourselves. Gunthar is deliberately blocking the formation because he knows that if a Grand Circle was convened this day, I would be elected Grand Master."

Brian wasn't so certain about this. Derek had his supporters, but even they had their doubts about Derek, just as they had doubts about Gunthar. The elder knight could not have blocked the formation of a Grand Circle unless other knights were content to let it be blocked. The reason? Caution. Everyone was cautious these days. But Brian wondered whether caution was just a more palatable word for fear.

Fear—the stench of it had been rank in the meeting hall. Fear that Solamnia would fall to the force of the dragonarmies. Fear that the ruler of Solamnia would no longer be the Knights who had governed this land since the days of their founder, Vinus Solamnus. Fear of the man who was now calling himself "Emperor of Ansalon". Most of all, fear of the dragons.

The dragonarmies had a distinct and terrible advantage over the knights—dragons. Two red dragons could wipe out a force of a thousand men-at-arms in a matter of moments. Brian knew that even if Lord Gunthar had sent those reinforcements, Castle Crownguard would have fallen. Derek probably knew it, too, but he had to keep denying it or be forced to face the bleak truth: no matter what the knights did, Solamnia would eventually fall. They could never win against such overwhelming odds.

The two men rode in silence for a long while, letting their horses graze on the late autumn grass that, blessed by the warmth of the sea breezes, was still green, though the trees were losing their fall colors.

At length, Brian said, "I find something about this war very strange."

"What is that?" Derek asked.

"They say the dragonarmies go into battle with prayers and hymns to their dark goddess. I find it strange to think the forces of evil march under a banner of faith, while we, who are on the side of good, deny the gods even exist."

"Faith!" Derek snorted. "Superstitious claptrap is nearer the mark. False 'priests' perform a few flashy tricks they term miracles, and the gullible moan and wail and fall on their ugly faces in worship."

"So you don't believe the goddess Takhisis has returned to the world and brought this war upon us?"

"I believe men brought this war on us," said Derek.

"Then you don't believe there were ever gods," Brian said. "Back in the old days. Gods of Light such as Paladine and Kiri-Jolith?"

"No," said Derek shortly.

"What about the Cataclysm?"

"A natural phenomenon," said Derek, "like an earthquake or a cyclone. Gods had nothing to do with it."

"Huma believed in the gods—"

"Who, these days, believes in Huma?" Derek asked with a shrug. "My little son does, of course, but he is only six."

"We never used to believe in dragons either," Brian remarked somberly.

Derek grunted, but made no reply.

"The Measure speaks of faith," Brian continued. "The role of the High Clerist is as important as that of the High Warrior. Knights of the

Rose, such as yourself, could once cast divine spells, or so history tells us. The Measure speaks of how knights of old could use their prayers to heal those wounded in battle."

Brian was curious to see how Derek would respond to this argument. Derek was devoted to the Measure. He knew many parts of it by heart. He lived his life based on it. How could he reconcile the Measure's admonition that a knight should be faithful to the gods with his avowed lack of faith?

"I have read the Measure very carefully on this," said Derek, "and I have also read the writings of the eminent scholar Sir Adrian Montgomery, who points out the fact that the Measure says simply a knight must have faith. The Measure does not say that a knight must have faith in *gods*, nor does the Measure speak of any god by name, which those who codified it would certainly have done if they thought the gods were an important aspect of a knight's life. Sir Adrian contends that when faith is mentioned in the Measure, it refers to having *faith in oneself*, not in some omnipotent, omniscient, immortal being."

"What if there is no naming of gods in the Measure because it did not occur to the writers that the gods needed to be named?" Brian argued.

Derek frowned. "Are you being flippant?"

"No, of course not," said Brian hastily. "What I mean is this: what if the knowledge of the gods and belief in the gods was so pervasive that the writers never imagined a day would come when the gods would not be known to the knights? There was no need to mention the gods by name, because everyone knew them."

Derek shook his head. "That seems unlikely."

Brian wasn't so sure. "What about healing? Does Sir Montgomery explain—"

He was interrupted by a shout coming from behind them.

"My lord!"

Both men turned in their saddles to see a rider galloping down the road, yelling and waving his hat in his hand.

"My squire," said Derek, and he rode to meet him.

"My lord," said the young man, "I was bidden seek you out to give you this."

The squire reached into his leather belt, drew out a folded missive, and handed it to his master. Derek took the note, read it through swiftly, and looked up.

"Who gave you this?"

The squire flushed, embarrassed. "I am not quite certain, my lord. I was walking through the marketplace this morning when this was suddenly thrust into my hand. I looked about immediately to see who had given it to me, but the person had vanished into the crowd."

Derek handed the note to Brian to read. The message was short. *I can make you Grand Master. Meet me at the Knight's Helm at the hour of sunset. If you are distrustful, you may bring a friend. You should also bring 100 steel. Ask for "Sir Uth Matar" and you will be directed to my room.*

Brian handed back the note to Derek, who read it again, his brow creased in thought.

" 'Uth Matar'," Brian repeated. "I know that name. I can't think why."

He glanced at his friend.

"You don't intend to go!" Brian said, astonished.

Derek folded the note carefully and thrust it into his glove. He started riding back in the direction of Palanthas. The squire fell in behind them.

"Derek," said Brian, "it's a trap—"

"With what purpose?" Derek asked. "To assassinate me? The note says I may bring a friend to ensure against that. To rob me? Relieving me of my purse could be accomplished far more easily and efficiently by accosting me in a dark alley. The Knight's Helm is a reputable establishment—"

"Why arrange a meeting in a tavern at all, Derek?" Brian asked. "What knight would do such a thing? If this Sir Uth Matar has an honest proposition for you, why doesn't he come to call upon you at your dwelling place?"

"Perhaps because he wants to avoid being seen by Gunthar's spies," said Derek.

Brian could not allow such an accusation to go unremarked. He glanced back at the squire, to make certain the lad was out of ear-shot, then said with quiet intensity, "Lord Gunthar is man of honor and nobility, Derek. He would as soon as cut off his hand as spy on you!"

Derek made no comment. He said instead, "Will you accompany me tonight, Brian, or must I seek elsewhere for a true friend to watch my back?"

"You know I will go with you," Brian said.

Derek gave him what passed for a smile, which was nothing more than the creasing of the firm, tight lips, barely visible beneath long blonde mustaches. The two rode back to Palanthas in silence.

The Knight's Helm was, as Derek stated, a reputable establishment, though not as reputable now as it had once been. The tavern was located in what was known as the Old City and its current owner liked to boast that it was one of the original buildings in Palanthas, though that claim was doubtful. The tavern was built underground, extending back into a hillside, and was snug and warm in the winter, cool and pleasantly dark in the summer months.

Patrons entered through a wooden door set beneath a gabled roof. Stairs led down into the large common room that was lit with hundreds of candles burning in wrought iron candle holders and by the light of a fire blazing in an enormous stone fireplace.

There was no bar. Drinks and food were served from the kitchen, which was adjacent. In back, cut deeper into the hillside, were the ale and wine cellars, several small rooms for private parties, and one large room called the "Noble Room". This room was furnished with a massive oblong table surrounded by thirty two high-backed chairs, all of matching wood, carved with birds and beasts, roses and kingfishers—the symbols of the knighthood. The tavern owner bragged that Vinus Solamnus, founder of the knights, used to hold revelries in this very room at this very table. Although no one really believed him, anyone using this room always left an honorary place vacant at the table for the knight's shade.

Prior to the Cataclysm, the Knight's Helm was a popular meeting place for knights and their squires and did a thriving business. Following the Cataclysm, when the knighthood was in shambles, and knights were no longer welcome in Palanthas, the Knight's Helm fell on hard times. The tavern was forced to pander to more common folk in order to pay the bills. The owner continued to welcome the knights, when few other places would do so, and the knights repaid his loyalty by frequenting the tavern when they could. The current owners kept up the tradition, and Knights of Solamnia were always treated as honored guests.

Derek and Brian walked down the stairs and into the common room. This night, the tavern was bright with light and filled with good smells and laughter. Seeing two knights, the tavern owner himself came bustling up to greet them, to thank them for the honor they did his establishment, and to offer them the best table in the house.

"Thank you, Master, but we were told to ask for Sir Uth Matar," said Derek. He glanced keenly about the room.

Brian stood behind his friend, his hand on his sword's hilt. Both were cloaked and wore heavy leather vests beneath. It was supper time and the tavern was crowded. Most of the patrons were members of the burgeoning middle class: store owners, lawyers, teachers and scholars from the University of Palanthas, Aesthetics from the famed Library. Many in the crowd gave the two knights friendly smiles or acknowledged them with nods, then went back to their eating and drinking and talking.

Derek leaned over to Brian to say dryly, "Looks like a den of thieves to me."

Brian smiled, but he continued to keep his hand on his sword.

"Sir Uth Matar," said the tavern owner. "Right this way."

He handed them each a candle, saying the hallway was dark, and directed the knights to the back part of the tavern. When they arrived at the room indicated, Derek knocked on the door.

They heard booted feet cross the floor, and the door opened a crack. A lustrous brown eye framed by long dark lashes peered out at them.

"Names?" the person asked.

Brian gave a start. The voice was that of a woman.

If this startled Derek, he gave no outward sign. "I am Sir Derek Crownguard, milady. This is Sir Brian Donner."

The brown eyes flashed. The woman's lips parted in a crooked smile. "Come in, Sir Knights," she said and opened the door wide.

The two knights cautiously entered the room. A single lamp stood on the table. A small fire flickered in the fireplace. Used for private dining, the room was furnished with a table and chairs and a sideboard. Brian glanced behind the door before shutting it.

"I am alone, as you see," said the woman.

Both men turned to face her. Both were at a loss for words, for they had never seen a woman quite like her. First and foremost, she was dressed like a man in black leather pants, a black leather vest over a long-sleeved red shirt, and black boots. She wore a sword and looked as though she was accustomed to wearing a sword and was probably skilled in its use. Her black curly hair was cut short. She faced them boldly, like a man, not demurely, like a woman. She stood staring at them, hands on her hips. No curtseying or shy lowering of the eyes.

"We are here to meet Sir Uth Matar, Madame," Derek said, frowning.

"He would have come tonight," said the woman, "but he couldn't make it."

"He has been detained?" asked Derek.

"Permanently," the woman said, her crooked smile broadening. "He's dead."

She pulled off her gloves and threw them on the table, then sat down languidly in a chair and gestured. "Please, gentlemen, be seated. I'll send for wine—"

"We are not here to carouse, Madame," said Derek stiffly. "We have been brought here under false pretenses, it seems. I bid you good-night."

He made a cold bow and turned on his heel. Brian was already at the door. He had been opposed to this from the beginning, and he did not trust this strange woman.

"Lord Gunthar's man is due to meet me here at the hour of moonrise," said the woman. Lifting a soft and supple glove, she smoothed the leather with her hand. "He is interested in hearing about what I have to offer."

"Derek, let's go," said Brian.

Derek made a gesture, turned back.

"What *do* you have to offer, Madame?"

"Sit down, Sir Derek, and drink with me," said the woman. "We have time. The moon will not rise for an hour yet."

She hooked a chair with her foot and kicked it toward him.

Derek's lips tightened. He was accustomed to being treated with deference, not addressed in such a free and easy manner. Gripping his sword's hilt, he remained standing and regarded the woman with a grim countenance.

"I will listen to what you have to say, but I drink only with friends. Brian, watch the door. Who are you, Madame?"

The woman smiled. "My name is Kitiara Uth Matar. My father was a Solamnic Knight—"

"Gregor Uth Matar," exclaimed Brian, recollecting where he'd heard the name. "He was a knight—a valorous one, as I recall."

"He was cast out of the knighthood in disgrace," said Derek, frowning. "I do not recall the circumstances, yet I seem to remember it had something to do with a woman."

"Probably," replied Kitiara. "My father could never leave the ladies alone. Yet for all that, he loved the knighthood and he loved Solamnia. He died not long ago, fighting the dragonarmies in the battle of Solanthus. It is because of him—because of his memory—that I am here."

"Go on," said Derek.

"My line of work takes me to the very best houses in Palanthas." Lifting her booted feet, Kitiara placed them on the chair in front of her and leaned back, quite at her ease. "To be honest with you gentlemen, I am not exactly invited into these houses, nor do I enter them to search for information which might help your cause in the war against the dragonarmies. However, sometimes, while looking for such items that are of value to me, I stumble across information which I think may be of value to others."

"In other words," said Derek coldly, "you are a thief."

Kitiara grinned and shrugged, then reached into a bag on the table and brought forth a nondescript wooden scroll case. Removing the lid, she drew out a piece of rolled paper and held it in her hand.

"This is such an item," she said. "I believe it will be quite helpful to the war effort. I may be a bad person," she added modestly, "but, like my father, I'm a good Solamnic."

Derek rose to his feet. "You waste your time, Madame. I do not traffic in stolen goods—"

Kitiara smiled wryly. "Of course, you don't, Sir Derek, so let's assume, as the kender say, that I 'found' it. I discovered it lying in the street in front of the house of a well known Black Robe. The Palanthian authorities have long been watching him, since they suspect he is in league with our enemies. They were going to force him to leave the city, but he forestalled them. Hearing rumors that he was to be run out of town, he left on his own. After I heard of his hasty departure, I decided to enter his house to see if he had left behind anything of value.

"He did. He left this." The woman placed the scroll on the table. "You can see the end is charred. He burned a large number of papers prior to his departure. Unfortunately he didn't have time to insure that they were consumed."

She unfurled the scroll and held it to the light. "Since I assume you gentlemen are not the sort to buy a pig in a poke, I will read you a portion of it. The missive is a letter addressed to a person who resides in Neraka. I assume, from the tone of the letter, this person is a fellow Black Robe. The interesting part reads, 'Due to Verminaard's ineptness, I feared for a time that our enemies had discovered our greatest secret, one that would encompass our downfall. You know that dread object of which I speak. If the forces of Light were ever to find out that the *blank* were not destroyed in the Cataclysm, but that the *blank* still exist, and furthermore, that one is in the possession of *blank*, the knights would move heaven and the Abyss to lay their hands on the prize.'"

Kitiara rolled up the parchment and smiled charmingly at Derek. "What do you think of that, Sir Knight?"

"I think it is useless," said Derek, "since he does not name the object, nor does he say where it may be found."

"Oh, but he does," said the woman. "*I* was the one who did not." She tapped the piece of parchment on her pointed chin. "The name of the object is written here and also the name of the person who has it in his possession. One hundred steel buys this letter."

Derek regarded her grimly. "You ask payment for it. I thought you said you were a good Solamnic."

"Not *that* good," Kitiara replied with a grin and a twitch of her eyebrow. "A girl has to eat."

"I am not interested," said Derek shortly. He rose to his feet and started walking toward the door. Brian was already there. He had his hand on the handle and was about to open it.

"Now that surprises me," said the woman. She shifted her feet on the chair to a more comfortable position. "You are locked in a bitter struggle with Lord Gunthar for the position of Grand Master. If you were to recover this prize and bring it back, I guarantee that every knight in the Council would back you. If, on the other hand, Lord

Gunthar's man is the one to find this . . ."

Derek halted in midstep. His fingers clenched and unclenched on his sword's hilt. His face was set in grim lines. Brian saw his friend seriously considering this, and he was appalled.

"Derek," Brian said in a low voice, "we have no idea whether or not this letter is genuine. She could be making all this up. We should at least do some investigating, go to the authorities, find out if this tale of hers is true—"

"And, in the meantime, Gunthar will buy the letter."

"So what if he does?" Brian demanded. "If there is truth in this letter, the Knighthood will benefit—"

"*Gunthar* will benefit," Derek countered.

He reached for his purse.

Brian sighed and shook his head.

"Here is your one hundred steel, Madame," said Derek. "I warn you. My reach is long. If you have cheated me, I will not rest until I have hunted you down."

"I understand, Sir Derek," said the woman quietly. She took the bag of steel coins and thrust it in her belt. "You see? I don't even bother to count it. I trust you, Sir Knight, and you are right to trust me."

She placed the paper in his hand. "You will not be disappointed, I assure you. I bid you gentlemen a good evening."

She gave them her crooked smile and raised her hand in farewell. Pausing in the doorway, she said, "Oh, when Lord Gunthar's man arrives, tell him he's too late."

She left, shutting the door behind her.

"Read it swiftly," said Brian. "We can still go after her."

Derek was already perusing the letter. He drew in a breath and let it out in a whistle.

"Well, what does it say?" Brian asked impatiently.

"The object is said to be in Icereach, in the possession of a wizard called Feal-Thas."

"What is this object?"

"It is something called a 'dragon orb'."

"A dragon orb. I've never heard of such a thing," Brian said. He sat down. "Now that we're here, we might as well order dinner."

Derek rolled up the paper, tucked it carefully into his glove. "Don't get comfortable. We're leaving."

"Where are we going?"

"To see if you're right, my friend. To see if I have been a fool."

"Derek, I didn't mean—"

"I know you didn't," said Derek, and he almost smiled. He clapped his friend on the shoulder. "Come along. We're wasting time."

6

The WRONG ENTRANCE. DEREK'S DEMAND.
BERTREM'S REFUSAL.

ight had fallen by the time Derek and Brian left the Knight's Helm. The streets were mostly deserted, for the shops were now closed; merchants and customers alike were either home with their families or making merry with friends in the taverns. Those few people walking about carried torches to light their way, though that was hardly necessary, for Solinari, the silver moon, was bright in the heavens.

Rising over the buildings of New City, the moon looked like a bauble caught and held by the finger-like spires reaching into the sky, or at least so Brian fancied. He watched the moon as he and Derek hastened through streets gilded with silver light. He watched the fingers play with the moon like a conjurer plays with a coin until the fingers let loose and the moon was free to drift among the stars.

"Mind where you are walking," said Derek, catching hold of Brian and jerking him away from a large pile of horse manure.

"These streets are a disgrace!" Derek added in disgust. "Here, sirrah, what do you think you're doing? Go clean that up!"

A gully dwarf street sweeper, his large broom tucked in the crook of his arm, was ensconced comfortably in a doorway, sound asleep. Derek shook the wretched creature into sullen wakefulness and sent him on his way. The gully dwarf glared at them and made a rude gesture before sweeping up the muck. Brian guessed the moment they were out of sight, the gully dwarf would go back to his slumbers.

"What were you staring at anyway?" Derek asked.

"The moon," Brian answered. "Solinari is beautiful tonight."

Derek grunted. "We have more important things to do than stare at the moon. Ah, here we are." Derek laid a cautionary hand on Brian's arm. "Let me do the talking."

Emerging from a side street, they entered the street known as Second Ring, so called because the streets of Old City were laid out in concentric rings and were numbered accordingly. All the major buildings of Palanthas were located in the second ring; the largest and most famous of these was the great Library of Palanthas.

White walls, rising three stories into the sky, gleamed in the moonlight as if illuminated by silver fire. Semi-circular marble steps led to a columned porch sheltering large double doors made of thick glass set in bronze. Lights burned in the upper windows of the library. The Aesthetics, an order of monks dedicated to Gilean, God of the Book, worked here day and night—writing, transcribing, recording, filing, compiling. The Library was a vast repository of knowledge. Information on any subject could be found here. Admittance was free. The doors were open to almost all—so long as they came at the appointed hours.

"The Library is closed this time of night," Brian pointed out as they climbed the stairs.

"They will open for me," stated Derek with cool aplomb. He beat on the doors with an open palm and raised his voice to be heard through the open windows above him. "Sir Derek Crownguard!" he shouted. "Here on urgent business of the Knighthood. I demand entrance."

A bald head or two poked out a window. Novices glad for a break in their work peered down curiously to see what all the ruckus was about.

"You're at the wrong entrance, Sir Knight," called one, gesturing. "Go around to the side."

"What does he take me for? A tradesman?" Derek said angrily, and he beat on the bronze and glass door, this time with his closed fist.

"We should come back in the morning," Brian suggested. "If the information the woman gave you is a hoax, it's too late to catch her now anyway."

"I will not wait for morning," Derek returned, and he continued to shout and beat on the door.

"I'm coming, I'm coming!" called a voice from within.

The words were accompanied by the slap of sandals and the sounds of huffing and puffing. The doors opened, and one of the Aesthetics—a middle-aged, shaved-headed man clad in the gray robes of his Order—stared out at them.

"The Library is closed," he said severely. "We open again in the morning, and next time, come to the side entrance. Hey, there! You can't come in—"

Paying no heed, Derek shoved past the pudgy man, who spluttered in indignation and fluttered his hands at them, but did nothing else to try to stop him. Brian, embarrassed, entered along with Derek, muttering an apology that went unheard.

"I want to see Astinus, Brother . . ." Derek waited for the man to provide his name.

"Bertrem," said the Aesthetic. He glared at Derek in indignation. "You came in the wrong door! And keep your voice down!"

"I am sorry, but the matter is urgent. I demand to see Astinus."

"Impossible," Bertrem stated. "The Master sees no one."

"He will see me," said Derek. "Tell Astinus Sir Derek Crownguard, Lord of the Rose, wishes to consult with him on a matter of the utmost importance. It is not too much to say the fate of the Solamnic nation may well rest on this meeting."

Bertrem didn't budge.

"My friend and I will wait here while you carry my message to Astinus," Derek said, frowning. "Why do you dawdle, Brother? Didn't you hear what I said? I need to speak to Astinus!"

Bertrem looked them up and he looked them down. He was obviously disapproving. "I will go inquire," he said. "You will remain *here*, and you will remain quiet!"

He indicated with a jabbing finger the alcove in which they were standing, then he raised that finger to his lips. Finally he departed, walking off with an air of injured dignity, his sandals slapping the floor.

Silence settled over them, soothing and tranquil. Brian glanced into one of the large rooms. It was lined floor to ceiling with books and filled with desks and chairs. Several Aesthetics were hard at work, either studying or writing by candlelight. One or two glanced in the direction of the knights, but seeing that Bertrem apparently had the situation under control, they returned to their work.

"You could have been more polite," Brian said to Derek in a whisper. "Vinegar and flies and honey and all that."

"We are at war for our very survival," Derek returned, "though one would not think it to judge by this place! Look at them, scratching away, undoubtedly chronicling the life cycles of the ant while good men fight and die."

"Isn't this *why* we fight and die?" Brian asked. "So that these harmless souls can keep on writing about the ant and not be forced to mine ore in some slave camp?"

If Derek heard, he paid no heed to Brian's words. He began to pace the floor, his booted feet ringing loudly on the marble. Several of the Aesthetics raised their heads and glared and one said loudly, "Shush!" Derek glowered, but he ceased his pacing.

The sound of slapping sandals on marble heralded the return of Bertrem, looking harried.

"I am sorry, Sir Derek, but the Master is not at liberty to speak to you."

"My time is valuable," said Derek impatiently. "How long am I to be kept waiting?"

Bertrem grew flustered. "I beg your pardon, Sir Derek, you misunderstand me. There is no need to wait. The Master will not see you."

Derek's face flushed, his brows constricted, his jaw tightened. He was used to snapping his fingers and watching people jump and lately he'd been snapping his fingers only to find people turning their backs on him.

"You told him who I am?" Derek asked, seething. "You gave him my message?"

"There was no need," said Bertrem simply. "The Master knows

you and why you have come and he will not see you. He did, however, ask me to give you this."

Bertrem handed over what appeared to be a crude map drawn on a bit of paper.

"What is this?" Derek demanded.

Bertrem looked down at it and read aloud the notation at the top. "It is a map to the Library of Khrystann."

"I can see that! What I meant is what in the Abyss do I want with a map to some blasted library?" demanded Derek.

"I do not know, my lord," said Bertrem, shrinking from the knight's fury. "The Master did not confide in me. He said only that I was to give it you."

"Perhaps that's where you'll find the dragon orb," suggested Brian.

"Bah! In a library?"

Derek reached for his purse. "How much money will Astinus take to see me?"

Bertrem drew himself up to his full height, which put him about level with Derek's chin. The Aesthetic was deeply offended.

"Put away your money, Sir Knight. The Master has refused to see you and his word is final."

"By the Measure, I will not be treated in this manner!" Derek took a step forward. "Stand aside, Brother. I do not want to do you an injury!"

The Aesthetic planted his sandaled feet firmly. Though clearly frightened, Bertrem was prepared to make a valiant stand to block their way.

Brian felt a sudden desire to burst out laughing at the sight of the pudgy, anemic scholar facing down the furious knight. He swallowed his mirth, which would only make Derek angrier, and rested his hand on Derek's arm.

"Think what you are doing! You can't go barging in on this man when he has refused to see you. You put yourself in the wrong. If all you seek is information about the dragon orb, then perhaps this gentleman could assist you."

"Yes, certainly, Sir Knight," said Bertrem, wiping sweat from his brow. "I would be glad to help in any way I can—despite the fact that the library is closed and you came in the wrong door."

Derek wrenched his arm free. He was still furious, but mastered himself. "Whatever I say to you must be kept secret."

"Of course, Sir Knight," Bertrem replied. "I swear by Gilean that I will hold all you say in confidence."

"You ask me to accept an oath to a god who is no longer around?" Derek demanded in scathing tones.

Bertrem smiled complacently and folded his hands over his pudgy belly. "The blessed Gilean is with us, Sir Knight. You need have no worries on that score."

Derek shook his head, but he wasn't about to be drawn into a theological discussion. "Very well," he said grudgingly. "I seek information regarding an artifact known as a 'dragon orb'. What can you tell me about it?"

Bertrem blinked his eyes as he thought this over. "I fear I can tell you nothing, my lord. I have never heard of such a thing. I can, however, do some research on the subject. Can you tell me in what context the artifact is mentioned, or where and how you heard of it? Such information would help me know where to look."

"I know very little," said Derek. "I heard of it in connection with a Black Robe wizard—"

"Ah, then it is a magical artifact." Bertrem nodded his head sagely. "We have little information on such things, Sir Derek. The wizards tend to keep their knowledge to themselves. But we do have a few resources I can consult. Do you need this information right away?"

"If you please, Brother," said Derek.

"Then make yourselves comfortable, gentlemen. I will see what I can find. Oh, and please *do* keep quiet!"

Bertrem pattered off, making his way over to a large section of shelves. He rounded those, and they lost sight of him. They sat down at a table and prepared to wait.

"This is why I wanted to speak to Astinus," muttered Derek. "He is said to have the knowledge of all things at his fingertips. I wonder why he won't see me?"

"From what I hear, he doesn't see anyone—ever," said Brian. "He sits at his desk, day and night, recording the history of every living being in the world as it passes before his eyes. That's how he knew you were here."

Derek gave a loud snort. Heads raised, pens ceased their writing.

He made a motion of his hand in apology and the Aesthetics, shaking their heads, returned to their work.

"Some say he's the god Gilean," Brian whispered across the table.

Derek gave him a disgusted glance. "Not you as well! The monks foster such nonsensical beliefs so they can collect more donations."

"Still, Astinus did give you that map."

"To a library! Useless. It must be some sort of joke."

Derek drew out the scroll he'd purchased to read it over again. Brian sat quietly, afraid to move for fear of drawing down the ire of the scholars. He heard the street crier call out the hour, and then, putting his head down on the desk, he went to sleep.

He woke to Derek's hand shaking him and the sound of slapping sandals—two pairs of sandals. Bertrem came hastening toward them, accompanied by another monk, who bore a scroll in his hands.

"I hope you do not mind, Sir Knight, but I consulted Brother Barnabus, who is our expert on magical artifacts. He recalled having read a reference to a dragon orb in an old manuscript. I will let him tell you."

Brother Barnabus—a taller, thinner, younger version of Brother Bertrem—unfurled the scroll and laid it down in front of Derek. "This was penned by one of our monks who was in Istar about a year prior to the Cataclysm. It is an account of his time there."

Derek looked down at the scroll, then looked back up. "I cannot decipher these chicken scratchings. What does it say?"

"Brother Michael was Ergothian," Brother Barnabus explained, "and thus he wrote in that language. He writes that the soldiers of the Kingpriest were given lists of magical artifacts and sent to raid mageware shops in search of objects that were on these lists. He obtained one of these lists and copied down the objects. One of these is a dragon orb. A description was provided to the soldiers, so they'd know what to look for: 'A crystal orb, ten inches in diameter, filled with a strange swirling mist.' Brother Michael writes that the soldiers were ordered to handle the orb with caution for no one knew exactly what the orb did, though, as he writes here, 'It is believed that it was used during the Third Dragon War to control dragons'."

"Control dragons," Derek repeated softly. His eyes gleamed, but he took care to hide his rising excitement. "Were any found?" he asked in a careless tone.

"Brother Michael does not say."

"And this is the only information you have on these dragon orbs?" Derek inquired.

"That is all we have here in our library," said Brother Barnabus. "However, I did find a cross reference." He pointed to a small notation placed in the margin of the scroll. "According to this, another book said to provide more information on dragon orbs can be found in an ancient library in Tarsis—the lost Library of Khrystann. Unfortunately, as the name implies, few now remember where the library is located. Only we Aesthetics know and we do not give out—"

Derek regarded the monk in astonishment. Then he drew out the map he had so angrily crumpled up and smoothed it out on the table. "Is this it?" he asked, pointing.

Brother Barnabus looked down. "The Library of Khrystann. Yes, that is it." He regarded Derek in suspicion. "How did you come by this map, my lord?"

Bertrem plucked Barnabus's sleeve and whispered something to him. The brother listened then relaxed and smiled. "Ah, of course. The Master."

"Strange," Derek muttered. "Damn strange." He folded the map, treating it with much greater care, and placed it along with the letter in his belt.

"You might want to leave a donation," suggested Brian, having trouble keeping a straight face.

Derek glanced at him sharply, then fumbled in his purse for several coins and handed them to Bertrem. "Put this toward some worthy cause," he said gruffly.

"I thank you, my lord," Bertrem said. "Can I be of further service to your lordship this night?"

"No, Brother," said Derek. "Thank you for your help." He paused then said stiffly, "I apologize for my behavior earlier."

"No need for that, my lord," said Bertrem kindly. "It is already forgotten."

"Maybe Astinus is the god Gilean after all," Brian said, as he and Derek were descending the moonlit steps of the Great Library.

Derek muttered something and continued walking at a rapid pace down the street.

"Derek," said Brian, almost running to keep up, "could I ask you a question?"

"If you must," Derek said shortly.

"You hate wizards. You hate all things having to do with wizards. You cross the street to avoid passing a wizard. This dragon orb was made by wizards. The orb is *magic*, Derek. Why do you want to have anything to do with it?"

Derek kept walking.

"I have an idea," Brian continued. "Send a message to the wizards at the Tower of Wayreth. Tell them you've received this information about one of their artifacts. Let them decide what to do about it."

Derek halted and turned to stare at his friend.

"Are you mad?"

"No more than usual," said Brian wryly. He guessed what Derek was going to say.

"You're suggesting we turn over this powerful artifact to wizards?"

"They made it, Derek," Brian pointed out.

"All the more reason to keep it out of their hands!" Derek said sternly. "Just because wizards made this orb doesn't mean they should be permitted to make use of it. If you must know, it is because I distrust wizards that I am going to seek out the dragon orb."

"What will *you* do with it if you find it?"

Derek gave a tight-lipped smile. "I will bring it to Sancrist Isle and drop it in Lord Gunthar's soup. Then, when they make me Grand Master, I will go out and win the war."

"Of course," said Brian. He had more to say on the subject, but he knew any further argument would be futile. "You'll have to write to Lord Gunthar, tell him you're proposing to go on this quest, and ask his permission."

Derek scowled. He couldn't very well get around this, however. According to the Measure, a knight could not depart on such a long journey—three-quarters of the way across the continent—without receiving sanction from his superior, who happened to be Lord Gunthar.

"A mere formality. He will not dare refuse me."

"No, I don't suppose he will," said Brian softly.

"He will send one of his men along to keep an eye on me," Derek added. "Aran Tallbow most likely."

Brian nodded. "I hope so. Aran is a good man."

"He used to be a good man. Now he's a drunkard who lets Gunthar lead him around by the nose. But I will have you along to watch my back," Derek stated.

Brian wished for once Derek would ask him if he wanted to do something rather than telling him, not that it would make any difference. Brian would go with his friend now as he'd done in the past.

"Just think, my friend. This could be the making of you. You might even be made High Clerist!"

"I don't think I want to be High Clerist," said Brian mildly.

"Don't be ridiculous," said Derek. "Of course you do."

7

The Fewmaster sweats.
Iolanthe entertains the emperor.

o the knight took the bait," said Skie the next morning. He and Kitiara were preparing to leave the dragon's hiding place, a heavily forested area far from the walls of Palanthas.

"It is a good thing he did not ask for a sample of my handwriting," said Kit, grinning. "He not only took the forged letter, he paid me one hundred steel for it. It is not every man willing to pay so handsomely for his own destruction."

"If the orb *does* destroy him," muttered Skie. "It could just as likely destroy us. I mistrust wizards. If this knight is a threat, why didn't you just stick a knife in him?"

"Because Ariakas wants to please his new mistress," said Kit dryly. "What do you know of these 'dragon orbs'?"

"Very little," Skie grunted. "That's what worries me, and it should worry you. Why did you tell him your real name? What if he finds out that Kitiara uth Matar is not a thief, she's a Dragon Highlord?"

"He would not have come to the meeting without hearing the name. These knights are snobs," Kitiara said scornfully. "The fact that my father was a knight, even though he was a disgraced knight, helped convince Sir Nincompoop that I really did have the good of Solamnia at heart. I even told him my dear father died fighting for Solamnia." Kit laughed. "The truth is, my father probably died at the end of some outraged husband's sword!"

She shrugged. "As for Sir Derek finding out I am a Highlord, that is unlikely. My own troops do not know my true name. Kitiara uth Matar means nothing to them. To my soldiers and to the rest of the world, I am the 'Blue Lady', the Blue Lady who will one day rule over them."

"One day," the dragon grumbled. "Not now."

Kitiara reached down to pat Skie on the neck. "I understand how you feel, but for the time being, we must obey orders."

"Where do we go, Blue Lady," the dragon asked bitterly, "since we're not allowed to fight?"

"We fly to Haven, where the Red Dragonarmy has made their headquarters. We are going to try to find a suitable candidate for Dragon Highlord."

"Another waste of time and effort," said Skie, crashing through the brush and trampling scrub trees underfoot in search of a cleared space in which to spread his wings.

"Perhaps," said Kitiara, and a smile played on her lips unseen beneath the helm, "but then again, perhaps not."

The dragonarmy camp near Haven was really nothing more than a small outpost. Most of the Red Dragonarmy troops were scattered across Abanasinia, maintaining their grip on conquests they had already taken. Prior to her arrival, Kitiara had met with her spies inside the dragonarmy. They reported that the army, spread out over a wide area, from Thorbardin to the Plains of Dust, was in disarray; the officers quarreling among themselves, the troops grumbling and discontented, and the dragons furious.

Several officers were vying to become Highlord. Kitiara had a list of likely candidates, with detailed information on each.

"I will be here for several days," Kitiara told Skie. The dragon had landed her in an area some distance from the camp. "I need you to speak to the reds."

"Brainless behemoths," Skie snarled. "Muscle-bound ninnies.

Talking with them is a waste of time. They barely know words of more than one syllable."

"I understand, but I need to know what they think—"

"They don't," Skie retorted. "That's the problem. I can sum up their thought processes in three words: burn, eat, loot, and they're so stupid that most of the time they do it in that order."

Kitiara laughed. "I realize I'm asking a great deal, my friend, but if the reds are truly unhappy and threatening to depart, as I have heard, Ariakas needs to take action. I want you to find out if they are belly-aching or if they are serious."

"Odds are they don't know themselves." Skie shook his mane in irritation. "We should be back in the north fighting battles."

"I know," said Kit quietly. "I know."

Still grumbling, Skie flew off. Kitiara watched the dragon climb among the clouds. His neck craned downward. He was searching for food. He must have spotted something, for he made a sudden diving descent, clawed feet outstretched to snag his prey. Kitiara watched until she lost sight of the dragon among the trees. Then she took a look at her surroundings, got her bearings, and set off walking through the brush, heading in the direction of the camp, which she had seen from the air. She could not see the camp itself, but could tell its location by the haze of smoke rising from cook fires and the blacksmith's forge.

Kitiara walked at her leisure, taking time to look over some dispatches she had received before she'd left. She read again the one from Ariakas stating the red dragons were complaining to their Queen that they were bored. They had entered this war to loot and burn, and if they didn't get orders to do either, they were going to do it anyway on their own. The Queen reminded Ariakas that she had far more important matters to deal with than this and if he couldn't handle this situation, she would find someone who could. Ariakas handled it by dumping it in Kit's lap.

"I'll do what I can, but I wasn't the one responsible for this mess, my lord," Kitiara muttered. "That was your boy, Verminaard. Maybe you'll think twice next time about putting a cleric in charge of fighting a war!"

She opened the next dispatch, a missive she'd received just as she was leaving. This letter came from a spy in Solamnia, one of Lord

Gunthar's squires who was in her pay. The letter was long, and Kit paused beneath a tree to give it her full attention.

Derek Crownguard and two other knights set sail this date from Sancrist, heading for the city of Tarsis.

"Tarsis," Kitiara repeated to herself. "Why do they waste time going to Tarsis? I told the fools the dragon orb was in Icereach."

Reading farther, she found the explanation.

They were told they can find out more information in Tarsis about the dragon orb. Since that city lies not far from Icereach, they decided to stop there. Crownguard is considered a hero for having learned about this artifact. There is general consensus that if he returns with the orb and it allows them to control the dragons, as the knights believe, then Derek will be made Grand Master.

Lord Gunthar argued that they knew nothing about these orbs and so should leave them alone. He did not want Derek to undertake this quest, but he was powerless to stop him. Derek was very clever. He spoke of his discovery of the whereabouts of the dragon orb in open session. All the knights who heard about it were fired with enthusiasm. If Gunthar had tried to prevent Derek from going, there would have been rebellion. These fools are desperate, my lady. They hope for some sort of miracle to save them and they think this is it.

"Your witch's plan appears to be working, my lord," said Kitiara grudgingly. She went back to reading.

Gunthar did venture to suggest that he should consult Par-Salian of the White Robes, master of the Tower of Wayreth, and ask about this orb, so that they would have an expert's opinion of its powers. Derek argued against this, stating that if the wizards learned of the whereabouts of this artifact, they would go after it themselves. Lord Gunthar could not help but admit this argument was valid. All the knights were subsequently sworn to secrecy about the nature of this quest, and Derek and his two companions were sent on their way with loud cheers.

Lord Gunthar did manage to send one of his own men on this quest along with Derek—Sir Aran Tallbow. Sir Aran is an old friend of Derek's and knows him well. Lord Gunthar hopes Aran will act as a moderating influence on Derek. Aran could be a danger to your plans, my lady. The other knight who accompanies Derek is also one of his longtime friends. His name is Brian Donner, and so far as I can judge, he is of no consequence.

Derek and his friends set sail on a fast ship and as the weather is generally good this time of year, it is predicted he will have a swift voyage and a safe one.

Kitiara finished the letter and then thrust it in the pouch with the other dispatches. She would forward the letter on to Ariakas, who would be extremely pleased to hear that all was going even better than expected.

She kicked a rock in the road, sending it flying. The knights were "divided, desperate, searching for a miracle." Now was the perfect time to attack them! And here she was, far from Solamnia, trying to find someone to replace a man whose arrogant folly had brought about his own downfall.

Ariakas had recommended she interview a Fewmaster known as Toede for the position of Dragon Highlord. The Fewmaster, a hobgoblin, had been sending in a flood of reports on the war in the west. These reports were deemed by Ariakas to be works of military genius.

"First he wants a draco as Highlord, now a hob," Kitiara muttered. She kicked at another rock and missed. Halting, she kicked angrily at the rock again and this time connected. "I guess that makes sense. Now that the war is close to being won, Ariakas is beginning to see his human commanders as a threat. He fears that once we have no enemy to fight, we will turn on him."

Kitiara smiled grimly. "In this, he might well be right."

Kitiara carefully avoided entering the city of Haven. Abanasinia was her homeland. She had been born and raised in the tree-top town of Solace located nearby. There might be people in Haven who would recognize her, perhaps even remember that she'd visited the city several times before in company with Tanis and her twin brothers, all of whom were also known there.

Tanis Half-elven. Kitiara found herself thinking of him a lot these days, ever since she'd heard Grag tell Ariakas that a half-elf from Solace had been involved in the slaying of Verminaard. Half-elves were not that common in Ansalon, and Kit knew of only one who came from Solace. She had no idea how Tanis could have managed to get himself tangled up with slaves and Highlords, but if there was any man who could have bested Verminaard, it would be Tanis. Kit's thoughts went back to him, recalling days filled with laughter and adventure, nights spent in his arms.

She became so lost in her memories that, not watching where she was going, she stumbled into a pothole and nearly broke her neck. Picking herself up, she scolded herself.

"What are you doing, wasting time thinking about him? That's over and done with. In the past. You have more important matters to consider."

Kitiara booted Tanis from her mind. It wouldn't do for her to be connected with the local "heroes" who had, according to rumor, dispatched Verminaard. Ariakas was suspicious of her already.

Too bad, Kit sighed. She would have been very comfortable in one of Haven's fine inns. As it was, she resigned herself to staying in the dragonarmy's camp, where she would at least have the satisfaction of demanding that she be given the finest accommodations available.

Kit's unexpected arrival in the headquarters of the Red Dragonarmy threw everyone into a panic. Soldiers rushed about in confusion, falling over themselves and each other in an effort to please her. Some chaos was only to be expected, however, since she'd come on them unannounced. For the most part, Kit found the camp well-run and well-organized. Draconian sentries were at their posts and doing their jobs. She was challenged no fewer than six times before she reached the camp.

Kitiara began to think she had underestimated the hobgoblin. Perhaps Toede *was* a military genius.

Kitiara looked forward to meeting the Fewmaster, but the pleasure was delayed. No one, it seemed, knew where he was. A draconian dispatched a messenger to fetch the Fewmaster, telling Kitiara the Fewmaster was either perfecting his skills with the bow on the firing range, or drilling soldiers in the parade yard. The draconian said all this in the mixture of Common and military argot typically used by soldiers of mixed races. The draco added a comment in his own language to another draco, apparently under the assumption she would not understand, because both grinned widely.

As it happened, Kitiara's own personal bodyguard was made up of sivak draconians. She considered it would never do to have subordinates—especially those on whom her life depended—talking in an unknown tongue behind her back, so she had learned their draconic language.

Kitiara heard, therefore, that the draconians had not sent a messenger to either the parade ground or the archery range. The draconians had sent the messenger to the Red Slipper, one of Haven's most notorious bawdy houses.

Kitiara was escorted to the Fewmaster's headquarters. Inside, she found half the tent jammed with pieces of furniture, rugs, and knick-knacks that had probably been stolen. The other side of the tent was neat and orderly. Weapons of various types were stacked along one side. A large map, spread out on the dirt floor, showed the positions of the different armies. Kitiara was standing over the map, studying it, when a draconian lifted the tent flap and entered. She recognized the draconian officer she had met in Ariakas's office.

"Commander Grag," she said.

"I am sorry I wasn't on hand to welcome you properly, Highlord," the bozak said, standing rigidly at attention, eyes forward. "We were not informed you were coming."

"I did that deliberately, Commander," she said. "I wanted to see the army when it wasn't dressed up for show. Warts and all, so to speak, which terms seems appropriate when speaking of your Fewmaster."

The commander's eyes flickered, but he did not shift his gaze. "We have sent for the Fewmaster, Highlord. He is out in the field—"

"—practicing his thrusts and parries," suggested Kitiara slyly.

Commander Grag finally relaxed. "You could say that, Highlord." He paused, regarded her intently. "You speak draconic, don't you?"

"Enough to get by. Please, sit down."

Grag cast the fragile chairs of elf make a disparaging glance. "Thank you, Highlord, but I prefer to stand."

"It's probably safer," Kitiara agreed wryly. "You know why I'm here, Commander."

"I have a good idea, yes, my lord."

"I'm to recommend someone to become the new Highlord. You impressed the emperor, Grag."

The draconian bowed.

"Would you like the job?" Kitiara asked.

Grag did not hesitate. "No, Highlord, but thank you for considering me."

"Why not?" Kitiara asked with genuine curiosity.

Grag hesitated.

"You may speak freely," she assured him.

"I am a fighter, Highlord, not a politician," Grag answered. "I want to lead men in battle, not spend my time groveling to those in power. No offense intended, Highlord."

"I understand," said Kitiara, and she sighed. "Believe me, I do understand. So you do the soldiering and this Fewmaster Toede does the groveling."

"The Fewmaster is quite good at his job, Highlord," said Grag with a straight face.

At this moment, the Fewmaster came blundering through the tent opening. Catching sight of Kitiara, Toede rushed up to her. The first words out of his yellow mouth proved the truth of Grag's assessment.

"Highlord, forgive me for not being here to welcome you," the hobgoblin gasped. "These dolts"—he cast a furious glance at the commander—"did not inform me you were coming!"

Kit had encountered hobgoblins before. She'd even fought a few before the war began. She had no use for goblins, who could be counted on to turn tail and run the minute the fighting got tough, but she'd come to respect hobgoblins, who were bigger, uglier, and smarter than their cousins.

The bigger and uglier part applied to Toede, who was short and lumpish with a flabby belly; grayish, yellowish, greenish skin; red, piggy eyes; and a thick-lipped, cadaverous mouth that tended to collect pockets of drool at the corners. It was the smarter part that appeared to open to question. Toede's wildly grandiose, self-styled uniform bore no resemblance to any uniform Kitiara had ever seen. His clothes had evidently been thrown on in haste, for the buttons of the coat were in the wrong buttonholes and he had neglected to lace up his pants, leaving a huge gap between pants and shirt—a gap filled by his warty, yellow belly. He had run most of the way, apparently, for he was covered in dust and sweating profusely.

Kitiara had a strong stomach. She'd walked countless battlefields, stinking with the stench of rotting corpses, and been able to eat a hearty meal afterward. The reek of the perspiring Toede in the closed-in tent was too much for her to take. She moved closer to the entrance for a breath of fresh air.

Toede crowded beside her, practically tripping on her heels with his flapping feet. "I was out on a particularly dangerous scouting mission, Highlord, so dangerous I could not ask any of my men to undertake it."

"Did you grapple with the enemy, Fewmaster?" Kitiara asked, glancing sidelong at Grag.

"I did," said Toede with magnificent aplomb. "The battle was ferocious."

"No doubt, since I suppose the 'enemy' would not take your assault 'lying down'," said Kitiara.

Grag made a gurgling sound in his throat and covered it with a cough.

Toede appeared slightly confused. "No, no, the enemy was not lying down, Highlord."

"You had them up against the wall?" Kitiara asked.

At this, Commander Grag was forced to excuse himself. "I have my duties, Highlord," he said and made good his escape.

Toede, meanwhile, was starting to grow suspicious. His pink eyes narrowed as he glared at the departing draconian. "I don't know what that slimy lizard has been telling you, Highlord, but it is not true. While I might have been at the Red Slipper, it was in the line of duty. I was—"

"—under cover," suggested Kitiara.

"Exactly," said Toede. He heaved a relieved sigh and mopped his yellow face with his sleeve.

Having by now come up with a pretty good idea of the wit and wisdom of the Fewmaster, Kitiara thought he would make a perfect Highlord—one who would certainly never become a dangerous rival. While Toede continued his "battles" at the Red Slipper, the real work of running the war would be done by the capable Commander Grag. Besides, promoting this fool would serve Ariakas right.

Kitiara did not intend to apprise Toede of her decision yet. "I must say I admire you for your courage in taking on such a perilous assignment. I have been sent by Lord Ariakas to advise in the selection of a new Highlord, one to take the place of Lord Verminaard—"

She got no farther. The Fewmaster had seized hold of her hand. "I hesitate to put myself forward, Highlord, but I would be highly honored to be considered for the highly coveted high post of Highlord—"

Kitiara wrenched her hand free and wiped it on her cloak. She glanced down. "My boots need polishing," she said.

"They *are* somewhat muddy, Highlord," said Toede. "Allow me."

He dropped down on his knees and began to scrub assiduously at her boots with the sleeve of his coat.

"That will do, Fewmaster," said Kit when she could see her reflection in the leather. "You may get up now."

Toede rose, grunting. "Thank you, Highlord. Could I offer you some refreshment?" He turned around and bellowed. "Cold ale for the Highlord!"

"I do have to ask you some questions, Fewmaster," said Kitiara. Finding a camp stool, she seated herself.

Toede stood hovering over her, wringing his hands.

"I will be glad to assist you with anything, Highlord."

"Tell me about these assassins of Lord Verminaard. I understand they have thus far escaped you."

"That wasn't my fault," said Toede promptly. "Grag and the aurak bungled the job. I know where the felons are. I just . . . er . . . can't seem to find them. They're in the dwarven kingdom, you see. I will tell you—"

"Not interested," said Kitiara, holding up her hand to halt the flow. "Neither is the emperor."

"Of course not," said Toede. "Why would he be?"

"Back to the assassins. Do you know their names? Something about them? Where they came from—"

"Oh, yes," said Toede happily. "I had them in custody!"

"You did?" Kitiara stared at him.

"What I mean to say," Toede gabbled, "is that I didn't actually have them in custody. I had them locked up in cages."

"But not in custody," said Kit, her lips twitching.

Toede gulped. "I thought they were like all the rest of the slaves we were rounding up at the time. I didn't know they were assassins. How could I, Highlord?" Toede spread his hands pathetically. "After all, when I apprehended them, they hadn't assassinated anyone yet."

Kitiara struggled to contain her mirth. She waved her hand.

Toede again mopped his brow. "I was taking the slaves to Pax Tharkas to work in the iron mines when the caravan was attacked by an army of five thousand elves."

"Five thousand elves!" Kitiara marveled.

"Due to my brilliant leadership, Highlord, my small force—there were only six of us—held out against the elves for several days," said Toede in modest tones. "Despite the fact that I was wounded in fourteen places, I was prepared to fight to the death. But sadly, I lost consciousness and my second-in-command—the cowardly bastard—gave the order to retreat. My men carried me from the field. I was near death, but Queen Takhisis herself healed me."

"How fortunate for our cause that Her Majesty loves you so much," said Kitiara dryly. "Now, in regard to the assassins—"

"Yes, let me see if I can recall them." Toede squinched up his face. Presumably this hideous grimace denoted some sort of thought process. "I first encountered these miscreants in Solace when his lordship sent me there in search of a blue crystal staff. If you could just excuse me one moment—"

Toede dashed off. Kitiara saw him running hither and thither around the camp, accosting the troops, asking questions. Apparently, he got his answers, for Toede came dashing back, his big belly flopping, his jowls jiggling.

"I have remembered, my lord. They were impossible to forget. There was a mongrel half-elf by the name of Tanis, a sickly wizard known as Raistlin Majere and his brother, Caramon. There was a knight. Something Brightblade. And a dwarf known as Flint and a foul little beast of a kender going under the name of Hotfoot—"

Kit muttered something.

Toede interrupted himself to ask, "Do you know these felons, Highlord?"

"Of course not," said Kitiara sharply. "Why should I?"

"No reason, Highlord," Toede said, blanching. "None at all. It's just I thought I heard you say something—"

"I coughed, that was all," she said, adding irritably, "The smell in this place is foul."

"It's the draconians," said Toede. "Stinking reptiles. I'd get rid of them, but they have their uses. Now, where was I? Ah, yes, the assassins were traveling in company with some barbarians . . ."

Kitiara was only half-listening. When she had first begun to question Toede, it had all been a game. She had wanted to find out for certain if the assassins had been Tanis, her brothers, her old friends. She hadn't thought hearing their names, discovering the truth, would affect her so profoundly. The feelings she experienced were mixed. She took a perverse pride in her friends for having slain the powerful Highlord and she was dismayed and uneasy because she might well be connected to them. Above all, she had a sudden strong desire to see them all again—particularly Tanis.

"—the half-breed and his friends arrived in Pax Tharkas," Toede was saying when she began to listen to him again, "where I was myself at the time, acting as advisor to Lord Verminaard. The felons were traveling in company with a couple of elves, brother and sister. His name was Gilthanas and her name was, let me see"—Toede's face wrinkled deeply—"Falanalooptyansa or something like that."

"Lauralanthalasa," Kitiara said.

"That's it!" Toede slapped his hand on his thigh, then he regarded her in amazement. "How did you know, Highlord?"

Kitiara realized she had almost given herself away.

"Everyone with a brain knows," she retorted caustically. "The woman you had in your grubby hands is an elf princess, daughter of the Speaker of the Suns."

Toede gasped. "Truly?" he quavered.

Kitiara fixed Toede with a stern glare. "You had the daughter of the king of the elves in your grasp and you did nothing!"

"Not me, Highlord!" Toede squeaked, his voice rising in panic. "It was Lord Verminaard. I just remembered. I wasn't anywhere near Pax Tharkas at the time! I'm sure if I had been in Pax Tharkas I would have recognized the princess at once because, as you say, everyone knows this Lauralapsaloosa . . . this, this . . . princess, and I would have advised Lord Verminaard to . . . uh . . . uh . . ." Toede hesitated.

"You would have advised him to hold her hostage. Use her to demand the elves surrender or you would kill her. You would collect a fortune in ransom for her."

"Yes!" Toede cried. "That's *exactly* what I was going to advise his lordship to do. Verminaard often begged me for counsel, you know. They tell me his dying words were: 'If I had only listened to Toede' . . . Where are you going, Highlord? Is everything all right?"

Kitiara had risen abruptly to her feet.

"I grow weary of this discussion. Where is my tent?"

Toede leapt up. "I will escort you there myself, Highlord—"

Kitiara rounded on the hobgoblin. "I don't need a bloody escort! Just tell me where the damn tent is!"

Toede quailed. "Yes, Highlord. You can see it from here." He pointed meekly to one of the larger tents in the camp. "Over there—"

Kitiara stormed off. She kicked aside a keg and knocked down a draconian who was slow to move out of her way. Ducking thankfully into the cool darkness of the tent, she sat down on the crude bed. She almost immediately got back to her feet again and began to pace.

Lauralanthalasa, known affectionately as Laurana; elf princess, daughter of the Speaker of the Suns—and the betrothed of Tanis Half-Elven.

Tanis had told Kitiara all about that old childhood romance. He had also told her it was forgotten. He loved only one woman in the world, and that was Kitiara.

When she had asked him to travel north with her five years ago, he'd refused. He had made some lame excuse about inner turmoil, the need to think some things over, to come to know himself, try to find some inner peace between the warring halves of his being. He'd heard some rumors of the return of the true gods. He was going to go investigate . . .

"Investigate gods, my ass!" Kitiara fumed. "He went off to investigate his old girlfriend—the lying bastard!"

Never mind that in the intervening years, Kitiara had herself known a score of lovers, including Tanis's close friend, Sturm Brightblade, who had journeyed north with her. That liaison had lasted one night only. She'd seduced the young man mainly because she was angry at Tanis. After Sturm there was Ariakas, and now her handsome second-in-command, Bakaris. She didn't love any of them. She was not sure she loved Tanis, but she was damn sure he should be in love with her—not some spindly-limbed, slant-eyed, pointy-eared elf bitch.

Kitiara no longer cared why or how her friends had come to assassinate Lord Verminaard. All she could think about was Tanis and the elf girl. Was she still with him? What had happened when they were in Pax Tharkas together? Kitiara needed more information, and she regretted having walked away from Toede before he had finished his story. But then, he hadn't been in Pax Tharkas. He'd said so himself. She needed to find someone who had.

She would ask Commander Grag. But she had to find an excuse for asking him about her friends. He must not suspect. No one must suspect. Ariakas was already suspicious, and if he ever found out that Tanis had been Kit's lover . . .

Kitiara collapsed on the bed. She gazed, frowning, up at the canvas ceiling and berated herself.

"What am I doing? Why do I care? Tanis is a man just like every other man I've ever known. Except he isn't," Kitiara added softly, grudgingly.

All those men in her life since she'd been with Tanis. Kitiara realized now that she'd taken these men into her arms and into her bed in hopes that each new lover would make her forget the old one. The only lover who had spurned her, rejected her, turned his back on her and walked out of her life.

As Kitiara drifted off to sleep she saw Tanis's face—just as she saw his face every time some other man made love to her.

———————————

Far away in Neraka, the fire in the brazier blazed brightly. The flames were reflected in Ariakas's eyes, but he wasn't seeing the flames. He was seeing the images within the magical firelight. He was watching and listening with frowning displeasure.

At length, the magical fire consumed the few strands of black curly hair Iolanthe had placed carefully into the brazier. The images of the hobgoblin, Toede, and Kitiara disappeared just as Kitiara stormed off to her tent.

This was the third time Iolanthe and Ariakas had used her scrying spell to spy on Kitiara and the first time they'd ever discovered something interesting. Prior to that, she and Ariakas had observed Kitiara speaking with Derek Crownguard, and the other time she'd been riding Skie. Ariakas had been pleased to discover that Kit was loyal to him, perhaps the only one of his Highlords he could truly trust. He was now being forced to face the truth.

Iolanthe said quietly, "You note, my lord, how she brought the conversation around to those people from Solace. Among those named were her half-brothers, were they not, my lord? Raistlin and Caramon Majere?"

"They were," said Ariakas grimly. He shifted his baleful gaze from the brazier, from which curls of smoke were rising, to Iolanthe. "Kitiara told me about them. I think she once hoped they would join her, but if so, nothing ever came of it. If she did hire these men, why would she ask questions about them? It seems to me she would avoid mentioning them at all, so as not to draw suspicion to herself."

"Unless she fears she might be implicated, my lord. She could be trying to find out if they said or did anything that would point the finger back at her."

Ariakas grunted and shoved back his chair. He rose to his feet and with a flip of his cape, stalked off without a word. He was angry with her for having revealed to him what he didn't want to know. Iolanthe should have tried to appease him, but she was too drained by the spellcasting to go after him. The scrying spell was a powerful one, requiring immense focus and concentration. She was feeling dizzy and nauseous and the stench of burnt hair wasn't helping.

Ariakas halted when he reached the door to her chambers.

"I am not convinced," he told her. "We will do this again."

"I am yours to command, my lord," Iolanthe said wearily, and she managed to find the strength to rise to her feet and bow.

When he was gone, she sank back into the chair and stared at the smoking brazier. She pondered what she was doing. In betraying Kitiara to Ariakas, she was undoubtedly winning Ariakas's favor, but what would happen if Kit found out? Having watched Kitiara, Iolanthe was impressed with her. She was strong, resolute, intelligent. True, she was playing a dangerous game—though just what that game was, Iolanthe could not tell.

The people of Khur love horses. They breed the best in the world, and in order to prove which tribe breeds the finest, tribes race the horses, one against the other, with wagers placed on the outcome.

Iolanthe was starting to wonder if she'd bet her money on the wrong horse.

Iolanthe had noticed something Ariakas had not, something only a woman would see. Kitiara had been in an excellent humor, toying with the imbecile hobgoblin, even as she extracted the information she desired. She had taken pleasure in what Toede had been saying until he had mentioned the name of the elf princess. In an instant, Kitiara's mood had altered. She had been snickering at Toede one moment, flying into a raging fury the next. The moment she'd felt the piercing bite of jealousy's sharp tooth. Kitiara was jealous of the elf woman. This meant that one of those assassins was not only in Kitiara's pay. He was also in her bed.

Iolanthe could have mentioned this to Ariakas. She had no proof, but she did have a quantity of black curls. She decided she would let the horses race on, see how they handled themselves over the distance before she put her money down on one or the other.

8

The spy. The Rival.

Kitiara did not sleep well that night. She spent half the night lying awake, thinking of Tanis with pleasure one moment and the next cursing his name. When she finally fell asleep, Queen Takhisis visited her dreams, urging her to leave Haven and set off immediately for Dargaard Keep, there to challenge the death knight, Lord Soth. Kit fended off the Queen as best she could and woke with a raging headache. Afraid to fall back asleep, lest her Queen once more accost her, Kit rose early and sought out Commander Grag.

The dawn was gray and raw and cold. A chill drizzling rain had fallen during the night and, though it had stopped, water dripped from the trees, stood in puddles on the muddy ground, and trickled down the sides of the tents. The human soldiers grumbled and complained. The draconians complained, too, but not about the weather. They were angry because they were stuck here doing nothing when they wanted to be out fighting. Kit found the commander making his rounds of the sentry posts.

"Commander," said Kitiara, falling in alongside the draconian officer, "the Emperor has tasked me with investigating the death of Highlord Verminaard—"

Grag made a face.

"I don't much relish the assignment either," said Kitiara. "To my mind, Verminaard brought about his own downfall. Still I have my orders."

Grag nodded to indicate he understood.

"I spoke to the Fewmaster last evening. What can you tell me about the assassins?" Kitiara asked.

Grag glanced at her sidelong. All this interest in the assassins. Was she trying to cover her tracks? Grag considered the matter. He liked her and he had thought Verminaard a boorish lout. If the Blue Lady was involved, it wasn't any of his business. Grag shrugged his scaly shoulders.

"Not much, I'm afraid, Highlord. They were slaves and, as such, I had little to do with them. I didn't take any notice of them until they attacked us. Even then, things happened so fast and there was such confusion—dragons battling and half the mountain falling down on top of us—that I paid little attention to the slaves—except to order my men to slay them, of course."

Kitiara was about to walk off, go in search of food, when Grag added, almost as an afterthought, "There is a man who might be able to tell you more. He was one of Verminaard's spies. He managed to worm his way into the confidence of these people and he warned Verminaard they would likely make an attempt on his life. At least, that's what the man claims."

"I could use such information," said Kit. "Where is this man?"

"Take a walk into Haven," said Grag. "You'll find what's left of him by the side of the road."

Kitiara shook her head, not understanding. "You make it sound like he's dead in a ditch."

"He probably wishes he was. The wretch was buried in the rock fall at Pax Tharkas. We thought he was dead when we pulled him out, but he was still breathing. The leeches saved his life, though not his legs. If the beggar's not in his usual spot, go into Haven and ask around. Someone will know where to find him. His name is Eben Shatterstone."

You'll find what's left of him by the side of the road.

Grag's description was accurate.

A good many beggars had taken up positions outside the city, hoping to catch travelers before they spent their money in the marketplace. Most of the men were casualties of the war—most of them missing limbs. Looking at these men, many still clad in the rags of their uniforms, Kit felt a knot in her gut. She saw herself by the side of the road, hand out, begging for scraps.

"Not me," Kit vowed. "Not so long as I have the strength to use my sword."

Opening her purse, she began dispensing coins and asking for a man called Shatterstone. The beggars mostly shook their heads; they were too absorbed in their own misery to care about anyone else. But one pointed with a maimed hand to what appeared to be a bundle of rags dumped beneath a tree.

Kitiara walked over to the bundle and, as she drew closer, she saw it was a man—or rather, the crushed remnants of a man. He had no lower limbs—both legs had been amputated—and he had strapped what was left of himself to a small cart on wheels, using his hands to pull himself over the ground. His face was so badly disfigured it was difficult to tell what he had once looked like, but Kitiara thought he might once have been a handsome young man. His unwashed hair fell over his brow and straggled down around his shoulders.

As she came near, he held out a grubby hand.

"I'm looking for Eben Shatterstone," said Kit, squatting down to put herself on his level.

"Never heard of him," the man said promptly. His eyes were fixed on the purse.

Kitiara drew out a steel piece and held it up. "I have this for Eben Shatterstone. If you happen to run into him—"

He made a grab at the steel piece. Kit was too quick for him. She snapped it back, out of reach. "This coin is for Eben Shatterstone."

"I'm Shatterstone," he said, looking at her with no very friendly eye. "What do you want?"

"Information." Kitiara handed over the coin. He bit it, to make sure it was good, then slid it in a sack he wore suspended from a leather thong around his neck. "There's another one like it if you tell me what I need to know."

"About what?" Eben was suspicious.

"An elf woman. She was traveling with some adventurers who came to Pax Tharkas—"

Eben's lips parted in an ugly leer. "Laurana."

Kitiara seated herself on one of the tree's exposed roots. "That might be the name. I'm not sure."

"She was the only elf woman in Pax Tharkas," said Eben. "And she was a beauty. Too bad she had eyes for only one man—or perhaps I should say half a man. The other half was elf." He laughed at his little joke.

Kitiara laughed, too. "Tell me what you know about this elf. How did she come to be there? Was she traveling in company with this half-elf? Was she his lover, perhaps?" She spoke in casual tones.

Eben took a good look at her for the first time. Kitiara could guess what he must be thinking. She had dispensed with the trappings of a Dragon Highlord and was dressed in ordinary traveling clothes, the kind a sellsword might wear—leather vest, wool cloak, shirt, boots. Her clothes were of fine quality, however, as was the sword on her hip. An air of command and authority clung to her like expensive perfume. He knew she was someone important, he just didn't know who. All of which suited Kitiara.

Eben began to talk. Kit sat with her back against the tree and listened.

The half-elf, whose name was Tanis, and the rest of the group—a mixed bunch of ne'er-do-wells—had been taken prisoner in Solace and were en route to Pax Tharkas when their slave caravan was attacked by a small party of Qualinesti elves (nowhere near five thousand!). The minute the elves had fired their arrows, the caravan's guards, led by Fewmaster Toede, had beat a hasty retreat. The elves had freed the slaves and sent most of them on their way. One of the elves named Gilthanas, whom Eben had known before, recognized the half-elf. Apparently the two had been raised together or something like that. The half-elf and his friends accompanied the elves back to Qualinesti, which at the time was about to come under attack by the dragonarmies.

This Laurana had apparently been engaged to marry the half-elf, an arrangement her father would have opposed had he known anything about it. The elves convinced Tanis and his bunch to go to

Pax Tharkas to start a slave revolt which would presumably keep the dragonarmies occupied and allow the elves time to evacuate their people.

The group set off for Pax Tharkas, accompanied by Laurana's brother, Gilthanas, and Laurana, who sneaked after them and refused to go back home.

Eben Shatterstone knew all this because he had insinuated himself into the group, spying on them for Lord Verminaard. He had warned Verminaard about these dangerous people, but the Highlord, in his arrogance, had paid no heed.

As for Laurana, she was a pretty thing, though she was a spoiled brat who spent most of her time mooning over the half-elf.

"How did this half-elf react to that?" Kitiara asked.

"Tanis claimed he didn't like her hanging all over him and following him around, but of course he was lapping it up like sweet cream," said Eben, sneering. "What man wouldn't? She was a beauty. The most beautiful woman I've ever seen."

"For an elf," said Kitiara.

"Elf, human . . ." Eben gave an ugly grin. "I wouldn't have kicked her out of bed. And I bet that half-elf didn't kick her out either. Who knows what those two were doing when the rest of us were asleep? Oh, sure, Tanis had to pretend he didn't want to have anything to do with her, what with her brother watching him like a hawk. All of us could see the truth, though. Those two weren't fooling anybody."

Kitiara rose abruptly to her feet. She'd heard enough. More than enough. Her insides were twisted up like a tangle of snakes.

Eben looked at her purse. "Don't you want to hear about what they did to Lord Verminaard?"

"Like I give a damn," said Kit. She was in an ill humor. "I don't suppose you know what happened to the elf woman after the fall of Pax Tharkas?"

Eben shrugged. "I heard from some dracos they all ended up in the dwarf kingdom."

"The dwarven kingdom?" Kit repeated.

"Thorbardin. Seems they went there to hide out from the dragonarmies. If the half-elf is in Thorbardin, then I'll bet Laurana's there with him."

Kitiara turned to leave.

"Hey!" Eben shouted wrathfully. "Where's my money?"

Kitiara grabbed a coin from her purse and tossed it into the dirt, then stomped down the road, heading back to the dragonarmy camp. She had never been so angry. Tanis had sworn he loved no one but her and only a few weeks later, he was having a fling with another woman. And a filthy elf, no less! If Kit had met Tanis at that moment, she would have struck him down and stomped all over him.

Skie was still out on his errand and Kitiara had no way to reach him, so she was forced to stay in the dragonarmy camp, doing her best to avoid the imbecile Fewmaster. She kept herself occupied participating in training exercises, for Commander Grag insisted that his troops be kept in top fighting condition. Practicing against the draconians, who were excellent swordsmen, Kit worked out her frustrations and honed her own skills.

But when she wasn't trading jabs with Grag or going along on raids into the surrounding territory, she was alone in her tent, brooding. Or rather, she wasn't alone. An elf woman with golden hair and slanting blue eyes was always with her, sitting on the end of Kit's bed, laughing at her.

Kitiara could not banish Laurana from her mind. Kit needed to find out more about her rival. After all, a good general required knowledge of the enemy in order to conduct a successful campaign. Kitiara sent her own spies into the territory around the dwarven kingdom. They would not be able to enter the mountain fastness, but they could keep watch, let her know if any humans, elves, or half-elves (especially half-elves) were sighted leaving the realm beneath the mountain.

"If I know Tanis," she remarked to herself, as she wrote her directives, "he won't stay cooped up underground with a bunch of dwarves for long. For one, he hates being in confined spaces. Living in a giant hole in the ground must be driving him crazy. For another, there's a war going on and he'll want to be in the thick of it."

Kit was now actually looking forward to traveling to Icereach. Not only was she growing bored here, but it occurred to her that Highlord Feal-Thas, being an elf, must know Laurana, who was also an elf. Of course, this made about as much sense as saying that because Kitiara was human, she must know the Lord of Palanthas, but Kit wasn't thinking straight. She kept close watch on the clouds and rejoiced the day she saw the sun sparkle off Skie's blue scales as he circled overhead.

His report on the red dragons was not good. They were angry and discontented. They heard rumors of the spoils being garnered by dragons in other parts of Ansalon and they wanted the same. If the Red Wing didn't attack something soon, the reds were going to go out on their own and they didn't much care who the target was. In their mood, they'd just as soon attack a friend as a foe.

Kitiara duly reported this to Ariakas, adding her opinion that Fewmaster Toede was just what his lordship was seeking in a Dragon Highlord. When she told Toede she had recommended him, his gratitude and his stench were both overwhelming; apparently pleasure caused the hob's sweat glands to go into a frenzy. When Kitiara finally managed to wipe the hobgoblin slobber off her boots, she went to say farewell to Grag.

She told him she had recommended Toede as Highlord and she told him why she had done it. "You'll be the one in charge," Kit said.

Commander Grag grinned; his long tongue flicked from between his teeth. The two shook hand and claw and Kitiara departed on the grumbling Skie, who did not at all relish the thought of traveling to Icereach.

"Don't worry," said Kit, as she took her place on the dragon's back. "You won't have to stay. I'm sending you back north."

"To fight?" Skie asked eagerly. Though he had small use for his red cousins, he commiserated with them in their disgust over the current lull in the action.

"No," said Kitiara. "I want you to bring part of the Blue Wing south—the draconians and dragons."

Skie twisted his head to stare at her, wondering if she was serious.

"South?" he repeated, astonished and disapproving. "Why south? Our war is in the north."

"Not at the moment," Kitiara said. "Just bring the wing with you when you return. You'll find out the reason soon enough."

And with that, Skie had to be content, for Kit would not tell him anything else.

9

The Winternorn.
The Ice Palace.

he white wolf padded along the snow-carpeted hallway unheard, practically unseen, his snowy pelt blending with his icy surroundings. The wolf trotted past translucent columns of crystal clear ice that lined the long hall and supported the arched ceiling of ice. The sinking sun, a shimmering red orb visible through the full-length arched windows of crystalline ice, caused the ice columns and the snow-block walls to glow with the fire of the day's dying.

The walls of ice changed color a hundred times during the day—flame red and orange with the sunrise, sparkling white during the day when the snow fell, eerie blue starlight at night. The ever-shifting beauty of the crystal hall was remarkable, breath-taking, except to the wolf. For him, all was gray. He pattered down the hall looking neither left nor right, intent upon his mission.

The wolf had come from Ice Wall Castle, some few miles distant, its ruins visible through any of the numerous crystal windows. Ice Wall Castle was not truly a castle. Originally constructed as a fortress lighthouse prior to the Cataclysm, it had been located on a now-forgotten island south of the famous port city of Tarsis. Beacon fires atop its towers had once guided ships through fog and darkness to safe harbor or warned the city of the approach of enemy sails.

When the Cataclysm struck, the upheaval of the earth had swallowed the sea and caused it to recede, leaving Tarsis and its white-winged ships stranded in the sand. The lighthouse and the island on which it stood were overtaken by an enormous glacier encroaching from the south. Shoved about and mauled by the grinding ice, the walls of the fortress broke and crumbled. A single tower of stone survived, and it leaned at a perilous angle, propped up by shoals of ice. The original stonework of the rest of the fortress was no longer visible, having been long since buried beneath the layers of ice.

The inhabitants of this part of the world—fishermen who lived in huts made of animal hides—dubbed the fortress Ice Wall Castle and considered it a curiosity, nothing more. Nomads who made a harsh living following the fish in their swift ice-skimming boats, the Ice Folk had no interest in the castle. After exploring it and taking from it anything they could find that might help them in the daily struggle to survive in a cruelly altered landscape, they left it empty.

Other residents of the region—the bestial thanoi, also known as the walrus-people and long-time enemies of the Ice Folk—took over the castle for a year or so, using it as an outpost from which to launch raids on the Ice Folk. After that, the thanoi left it, driven out by a person they fearfully claimed was the embodiment of winter.

Feal-Thas had returned.

When the War of the Lance commenced, Ariakas needed a Dragon Highlord in this part of the continent. But he ran into trouble finding anyone to take on this onerous task. The climate was horrible, there was little fighting going on in the south and therefore no opportunity for glory and advancement, and nothing in the way of loot unless one had an interest in smoked fish. Ariakas was thinking he would have to order someone to take over Icereach, and then he'd have to put up with a discontented Highlord, listen to him sulk and whine and complain. Ariakas was fortunate, however. He found Feal-Thas.

An elf, even a dark elf, would not have been the emperor's first choice, for Ariakas disliked and distrusted all elves. He agreed with his Queen that the only good elf was a dead elf and he was doing his level best to see to it that Her Majesty's wishes on this score were being carried out. Feal-Thas was the only person who expressed any interest in going to Icereach, however. At that, Ariakas gave Feal-Thas a test of loyalty, ordering him to return to his native Silvanesti to spy out and report on the elven defenses. Feal-Thas provided Ariakas with an accurate account and also gave him valuable information regarding a dark secret held fast in the heart of King Lorac—the secret of the dragon orb that proved to be Lorac's undoing.

Ariakas still did not trust the elf. Feal-Thas was arrogant and sarcastic, and he did not give the emperor the respect Ariakas felt he deserved. But since he could not find another candidate willing to live in Icereach, Ariakas grudgingly handed over the ice-bound wasteland to the elf. Takhisis sent her white dragon, Sleet, to Icereach to keep an eye on the Highlord, and then both the Queen and the Emperor promptly forgot about him.

As for Feal-Thas, he was a mystery to all who knew him. Why would an elf, whose race was known to love and revere all green and growing things, choose to live in a region where all plant life had been frozen to death, all memory of its very existence eradicated, buried under snow and ice?

No one could answer this question, for none of the Silvanesti now remembered Feal-Thas except King Lorac, and he had gone mad. Some record of Feal-Thas could be found in the Tower of High Sorcery at Wayreth, where the wizard had once lived and worked, had anyone cared to look. There seemed no reason why anyone should.

The wolf certainly could not answer any question about the Highlord. All the wolf knew was that the Highlord was his master. Reaching the door to the master's chambers, the wolf shoved it open with his nose and trotted inside.

Feal-Thas, wrapped snugly in a long cloak of white fur, was seated at his desk, which was carved of ice, as were almost all the furnishings of his Ice Palace. When the wolf entered the chamber, the elf was engaged in writing a report to the Emperor. Feal-Thas wrote with a quill pen, dipping it in the ink that would have frozen had he not cast a spell on it. The Highlord's handwriting was small and cramped and delicate, and it irritated Ariakas whenever he saw it, for it smacked of elf.

Ariakas rarely took the time to try to decipher the elf's scratchings. He would give the missive to one of his aides to read and condense Feal-Thas's reports, which were never that interesting anyhow. When the dragonarmies extended their reach into southern Abanasinia and the Plains of Dust, Feal-Thas would be tasked with protecting the supply lines. Until then, he was supposed to stay holed up in his frozen wasteland and keep out of the way of those doing the truly important work of the war.

Feal-Thas was well aware the emperor disliked and distrusted him. Feal-Thas knew this because he knew the secrets of Ariakas's soul, just as he knew the secrets held locked in the souls of others. Feal-Thas had secrets of his own—dangerous secrets, the most closely guarded of which was that he was a winternorn, a rare kind of wizard who possessed, among other powers, the magical ability to "freeze" the River of Time for a brief period (a tenth of a tenth of a second). In that time he could gain a flash of insight into a person's innermost feelings and thoughts, as though a blast of icy wind flowed between himself and the target, carrying with it all manner of impressions that were seared in burning cold into his brain. He did not gain all this information at once. He had to take time to sort through the rubbish that littered people's hearts to glean something of true value to him. Once he did, he stored it away for later use.

The winternorn magic gave Feal-Thas power over others, but it also proved to be a curse. As an elf, an outsider, Feal-Thas should have never been taught the secrets of a winternorn.

Feal-Thas had been proclaimed a dark elf—one who is cast out of the light—and banished from his homeland over three hundred years ago for the crime of murdering his young lover. He had been taken in chains by elven warriors to the land in the south known now as Icereach. Though not the frozen wasteland it would become after the Cataclysm, Icereach was a barren and unforgiving land, with short summers and extremely long winters. The elven warriors left Feal-Thas to die and he might have, but he was rescued by the native humans, who took pity on the handsome young elf (he was only eighteen at the time) and saved his life.

Angry and embittered at his exile to this terrible land, he had taken a human lover, who was a winternorn. He persuaded her to take him as her pupil. Though it was forbidden to teach outsiders the magic, she succumbed to his persuasion, to her everlasting regret.

His soul's own darkness cast a shadow over what he saw in the souls of others. When he looked inside their hearts, he looked to the very darkest corners, and thus he came to believe his fellow men were self-serving, conniving liars. Believing he could trust no one, he had abandoned his lover. And, armed with his power he traveled to the Tower of Wayreth, there to take the dread Test and continue his studies. He had fled the Tower shortly before the Cataclysm, when it seemed likely that the Kingpriest would attack. Returning to Icereach, he had, eventually, made himself useful to Ariakas and had, at the same time, taken his revenge upon the elves by betraying them. Now he lived alone in his Ice Palace, his only trusted companions his white wolves.

Feal-Thas smiled sourly to himself as he wrote a report he knew the emperor would never read. Still, writing these monthly reports was part of his duties as a Highlord, and he would never let it be said that he was remiss in his duty.

The wolf trotted to him and dropped the canvas bundle it carried at his feet. Feal-Thas glanced down at it without interest and went back to his work.

The wolf pawed at the bundle. The wolf made a daily run to Ice Wall Castle, picking up dispatches and messages and relaying orders from Feal-Thas to the commander of the small force of kapak draconians who had taken up unwilling residence.

Feal-Thas smiled at the wolf and rewarded the animal with a ruffling of its fur and a strip of caribou meat. The wolf accepted the treat and swallowed it in a gulp, then sat back on his haunches, waiting to see if the master had further need of him.

Feal-Thas ceased writing. He unwrapped the bundle and removed the message. He glanced through it, frowned, and perused it more closely. His thin lips twisted in anger. He crumpled the message and tossed it across the room.

The wolf, thinking this was a game the two of them often played, went to fetch the "ball," and, bringing it back to Feal-Thas, dropped it at his feet.

Feal-Thas could not help but smile. "Thank you, friend," he said to the wolf. "You remind me that I, too, serve at the pleasure of my master. Shall I tell you what my master wants of me? Listen to this."

He spread the missive out on the desk, smoothed the wrinkles, and began to read aloud. He had fallen into the habit of speaking to his wolves, holding one-sided conversations with them, imparting his thoughts and discussing his plans. Feal-Thas liked to say he found wolves far more intelligent than people, mainly because they never answered him.

"'The Emperor Ariakas sends his respects to Dragon Highlord Feal-Thas of the White Dragonarmy . . .' and so on and so forth."

The wolf regarded the winternorn with bright eyes and fixed attention.

"'Dragon Highlord of the Blue Wing, the Blue Lady, will arrive shortly to meet with you to discuss certain plans I deem vital to the war effort. This is to let you know that the Blue Lady has my complete trust and confidence. You will obey her in all things as you would obey me.' Signed *Ariakas*, Emperor of Ansalon, etc., and so forth."

The wolf gave a great, gaping yawn, then leaned his head down to lick his private parts.

"My thoughts exactly," Feal-Thas muttered.

He picked up the second missive, opened it, glanced at the contents. The writing was large and scrawling. The signature was bold and dashing and almost illegible.

I am here. I look forward to our meeting—soon!
Kitiara

The word "soon" was underlined three times.

Feal-Thas rose to his feet and began to pace the snow-covered floor. His long white furs, worn over thick white woolen robes, brushed the snow behind him. Although he was a Black Robe wizard, the winternorn always dressed in white: white robes, white furs, white leather boots. He was tall and slender with delicate features; his skin was pale, almost as translucent as ice. With his white clothing and his white hair and his eyes the gray color of snow-laden clouds—Feal-Thas viewed himself as the living embodiment of winter, at one with the icy realm to which he had been unjustly banished as a youth and which he had unexpectedly and most astonishingly come to love.

"This bodes ill for us, my friend," Feal-Thas remarked to the wolf. "Ariakas wants something from me, something he believes I will be loathe to give. Thus he sends this Highlord to bully me. I know of this Blue Lady. He thinks I will allow her to walk all over me because I am a lowly elf and she is human and therefore a superior being.

"As to what Ariakas wants, that question is easy enough to answer. He wants the one thing I value. Drat the dragon anyway—meddling, ass-kissing beast. She was the one who told Takhisis the orb was here and Takhisis told Ariakas. It was just a matter of time, I suppose, before he decided he wanted it."

Feal-Thas glanced around his surroundings and sighed in annoyance. He had been anticipating a quiet evening, drinking hot spiced wine and studying his spells. Now he would have to travel to Ice Wall Castle, there to meet with this Highlord and listen to one of Ariakas's inane schemes.

"Fetch the team," he ordered the wolf, who left immediately, ears pricked and tail wagging.

The winternorn, cloaked in fur, left the palace. His wolf team awaited him, all the wolves standing in front of the sled, each wolf in his or her own place. A she-wolf was the leader and she ranged up and down the row, exerting her dominance over them and snarling at a couple of young males who were snapping at each other instead of concentrating on business.

Feal-Thas harnessed the team, then settled himself comfortably in the sled. Bundled warmly in furs and hides, he practically disappeared from sight. He gave the command, and the she-wolf broke into a loping run, setting the pace; the other wolves dashed along behind her. The team pulled the sled rapidly across the snow and ice. Feal-Thas had no need to guide the wolves. They knew where they were bound.

The dying sun's claws raked the sky, leaving long, bloody streaks above his destination—the ice-coated walls and lone standing tower of Ice Wall Castle.

Far above, a blue dragon circled the tower several times; then, dipping its wings, it took off, heading north.

10

A case of frostbite.
Hip deep in wizards.

he journey to Icereach had to be one of the worst either Kitiara or Skie had ever experienced. Kitiara had never been so cold in her life. She had never known such cold as this existed. The air was painful to breathe, lancing her lungs with sharp needles. The very hairs in her nose froze, as did the moisture of her breath, coating her lips and mouth with ice. She knew now what the term "frozen stiff" meant. When Skie finally landed, Kit might yet be sitting on the dragon's back, shivering, unable to move, if she had not been discovered by several kapaks out hunting. The draconians hauled her off the dragon's back and carried her into Ice Wall castle. Kit could not walk. Her feet were so numb with cold she could not feel them.

Kit had heard of people who had lost toes and fingers to the nipping teeth of the cold. She remembered the crippled beggars outside of Haven and she pictured herself among them. She cursed Ariakas bitterly for having sent her to this horrible place, forgetting that she had been eager to come here herself to find out more about Laurana.

Love and jealousy were both frozen solid. Kit was afraid to pull off her boots, fearful of what she might see.

She managed to control her shivering long enough to scrawl a message to Feal-Thas. He did not live in Ice Wall Castle as she had expected, but had built himself a palace some distance away. Considering the condition of this so-called castle, she was not surprised.

The kapaks carried her to a room known as the Highlord's Chamber, though no Highlord was currently in residence. Feal-Thas had lived here once, upon his return from Wayreth, while he constructed his Ice Palace. A fire burned in a large stone bowl filled with some sort of oil and gave off a modicum of warmth. Kitiara huddled close to the flames. The kapak assisted her in removing her armor, but she was still afraid to take off her boots, for she still could not feel her feet. She was growing truly frightened when the door opened and a tall, thin elf clad in furs walked inside.

Kitiara would have berated the elf for not knocking before he entered, but she was too miserable and her teeth were chattering. All she could manage was an angry look. The elf regarded her in silence some moments then turned and left. He came back accompanied by a kapak who bore in his clawed hands a bucket of steaming water.

The kapak set the bucket down in front of Kitiara, who regarded it and the elf with suspicion. Clamping her teeth together, she managed to mumble, "What the hell am I supposed to do? Take a bath?"

The elf's thin lips creased in a smile as chill as the surroundings. "Soak your feet and your hands in the warm water."

Kitiara cast the elf an incredulous look and, growling something unintelligible, edging closer to the oil fire.

"The water has healing properties," the elf continued. "We have not yet been introduced. I am Highlord Feal-Thas. You, I assume, are the Highlord known as the Blue Lady?"

He knelt in front of her and before she knew what he was doing, he had seized hold of one of her boots and yanked it off. Kitiara looked and closed her eyes in despair. Her toes were dead white with a horrid tinge of blue. Feal-Thas felt them and shook his head and looked up at her.

"It seems you live up to your name, Blue Lady."

Kit opened her eyes to glare at him.

"The damage is severe," he continued. "Your blood has frozen, turned to ice. If you do not do as I suggest, your toes will have to be amputated. You might even lose your foot."

Kitiara would have continued to refuse, but she couldn't feel his touch and that scared the wits out of her. She permitted him to remove her other boot, then gingerly, flinching, she thrust first one foot into the warm water and then the other.

The warm water felt good, soothing, until the feeling in her toes started to return. Prickles of liquid fire shot through her flesh. The pain was excruciating. She gave a low moan and tried to snatch her feet out of the water. The elf put his hands on her legs.

"You must keep them there," he ordered.

His voice was melodic, like that of all elves. His hands on her legs were slender and looked delicate, yet kick at him as she might, she could not break his strong grip. She rocked to and fro in agony, her legs twitching. Then she saw color returning to her feet. The terrible cold that had seemed to strike clear through to her bones started to recede, the pain subsided.

Kitiara relaxed, leaned back in the chair.

"You say this water has healing properties. Is it holy water? Your doing, Highlord?"

"Do not be disingenuous, Highlord," Feal-Thas responded. He removed his hands from her legs and stood upright before her, tall and thin, clad all in white. "You are here either to demand something from me or wheedle something out of me. Either way, you needed to learn about me and you have made inquiries. I'm guessing you did not find out much"—his gray eyes glittered—"but you would have learned I am a wizard, not a priest."

Kitiara opened her mouth and shut it again. She was taken aback. Everything he said was true. She had come here to demand that he give up the dragon orb and she had asked questions about him, and she had learned very little. She knew only that he was a dark elf and a wizard.

"As for the water, Highlord—" Feal-Thas began.

"Oh, let us cease with the Highlording," said Kitiara, giving him her best charming, crooked smile. "I am known as the Blue Lady to my troops. To my friends, I am Kitiara."

"The water comes from a fountain inside the castle, *Highlord*," he said, emphasizing the word, an ironic glint in his eye. "Not being a priest, I do not know what god blessed the water, though I might hazard a guess. Before the ice claimed it, the castle was once a fortress in the middle of the sea. The fountain has the symbol of a phoenix on it and thus I assume it was a gift of the Fisher God, Habakkuk."

Kitiara wiggled her toes in the bucket. She didn't really give a damn which god it was, as long as said god healed her. She'd only been making conversation anyway, trying to get a feel for this elf.

"I don't see how any sane person would want to live in this horrible place," she remarked, removing her feet and drying them off. She rose gingerly and began to walk about the room, helping to restore her circulation. "And you an elf. You people spend days composing sonnets to grass. You weep when you cut down a tree. You must truly hate it here, Feal-Thas."

"*Highlord* Feal-Thas," he coolly corrected her. "On the contrary, I have lived in this land since before the Cataclysm. I am at home here. I have become acclimated to the harsh conditions. Not long ago I returned to my homeland, to Silvanesti. I found the heat stifling, oppressive. The thick vegetation began to close in around me. The stench of flowers and plants clogged my nose. I could not breathe. I came away as swiftly as I could."

"Why were you in Silvanesti, Highlord Feal-Thas?" Kitiara spoke the title with her own ironic twist.

"I had unfinished business with King Lorac," Feal-Thas replied.

Kitiara waited expectantly for him to tell his story, but the elf said nothing further. He stood watching her and Kitiara was forced to carry the conversation.

"You heard, I suppose, that your king has been ensnared by a dragon orb he had in his possession," she said. "Lorac lives in thrall to the orb, caught in a terrifying web of nightmares that are twisting and deforming your homeland."

"I believe I have heard something of this," said Feal-Thas, "and you are mistaken, Highlord. Lorac is not my king. I serve the Emperor Ariakas."

His eyes were hard as a frozen lake. Kit's penetrating stare struck the ice and skidded off.

She tried again. "Dragon orbs. Dangerous artifacts," she said ominously. "Unsafe to have around."

"Indeed?" Feal-Thas arched a thin, white brow. "Have you made a study of dragon orbs, Highlord?"

Kit was startled by the question. "No," she was forced to admit.

"I have," he said.

"What have you learned?" Kitiara asked.

"That dragon orbs are dangerous artifacts," Feal-Thas replied. "Unsafe to have around."

Kitiara's palm itched and not from the cold. She longed to use it to smack the elf across his pale, fine-boned face. By arriving here half-frozen, she had placed herself at his mercy. She'd lost control of the situation and she had no idea how to regain it. She had bungled this from the start. She should have been better prepared to meet this Highlord, but she had discounted him because he was an elf. She had expected him to be weasely and sly, fawning and ingratiating, tricky and cunning. Instead he was dignified, straightforward, unafraid and obviously unimpressed.

Kit paced the room, pretending to be absorbed in her thoughts, all the while watching the elf from beneath her dark lashes. He was a male and she might try to seduce him, but she guessed she'd have better luck seducing an iceberg. Like the cruel land in which he lived, he was frozen, dispassionate. No flame warmed him. She noted that he stood far from the fire, in the coldest part of the room.

"Why have you come to Icereach, Highlord Kitiara?" Feal-Thas asked suddenly. "Certainly it was not to enjoy our climate."

Kitiara was about to say that she had important matters of war to discuss with him, but he interrupted her.

"Ariakas sent you here to take my dragon orb."

"Wrong!" said Kitiara, triumphant. "I have not come to take the dragon orb—"

Feal-Thas made an impatient gesture. "Very well, you have tricked a foul Solamnic into taking it. That is much the same thing, for the orb will destroy him and the emperor will take possession of the orb himself. A clever plan on the part of his lordship, though I question what right he has to lay claim to *my* dragon orb."

"I did not know Ariakas had already spoken to you of this, Highlord," said Kitiara, nettled.

"Ariakas speaks to me as little as possible," said Feal-Thas dryly.

He tossed the Emperor's letter onto the floor at her feet. "You can read what his lordship writes if you want."

Kitiara picked it up, glanced at it, and frowned. "You are right, but if he didn't mention it, how did you know about the knight—Wait!" she called out, startled. "We're not finished talking. Where are you going?"

"To my palace," said Feal-Thas, moving toward the door. "I grow weary of this conversation."

"I haven't explained his lordship's orders yet!"

"No need. I understand them well enough," said Feal-Thas. "I will have food and drink sent to you."

"I'm not hungry," she said angrily, "and we're not finished."

He opened the door. Pausing, he glanced back to say, "Oh, and about the elf woman, Lauralanthalasa. I know the name, but I do not know her or anything about her. She is, after all, a *Qualinesti.*" He spoke the word with distaste, as though it soiled his lips, and left the room, quietly shutting the door behind him.

"Qualinesti!" repeated Kit, dumbfounded. "What the deuce does he mean by that? Qualinesti! And how did he know I was even going to ask about the elf woman? How did he know about the dragon orb and the knight if Ariakas didn't tell him?"

Kit dragged a fur blanket off the bed and wrapped it around her shoulders, muttering to herself. "This blasted plot is mired in magic. I'm hip deep in wizards—first that witch, Iolanthe, and now this elf. Wizards sneaking around, chanting and whispering and wiggling their fingers. Give me a fair fight with cold steel."

She toyed with the idea of leaving Icereach. Let Ariakas deal with his elf. Ariakas was himself a user of magic. He would put this Feal-Thas in his place.

A tempting idea, but one she was forced to discard. Returning empty handed would mean admitting failure. The emperor had no tolerance for those who failed. She would certainly lose her command. She might lose her life. Then, too, Kitiara was uneasy over how much the elf knew and what he might do with the information. If Feal-Thas knew about Laurana, he might know about Tanis. And if Ariakas ever found out that she was involved with those who had slain Verminaard . . .

Kitiara broke out in a cold sweat.

She flung herself on the bed. She couldn't leave, not until all this was resolved. She had to crush this Feal-Thas, break him, bend him to her will. Except for Tanis, she'd never yet met the man she couldn't conquer. This elf would be no different. She just had to find his weakness.

Kitiara ate a hearty meal of caribou stew and drank a couple of warming mugs of some sort of potent liquor cooked up by the kapaks. Confident in herself, she crawled beneath layers of furs and hides and slept soundly.

By the time she woke in the morning, she had decided that Feal-Thas must have spies in Toede's camp—maybe Toede himself. Someone must have heard her asking about Laurana and had reported it to Feal-Thas, and, like a shady fortune teller, the elf had dressed it up to fool her into thinking he'd done something special.

This morning she would give Feal-Thas his orders regarding the dragon orb. If the elf didn't carry out his orders, that was no fault of hers. She had done as her lord had commanded. When Skie returned, she would leave this icebound land and its frozen wizard.

Dragging one of the fur blankets off the bed, Kitiara wrapped herself in it and set forth in search of Feal-Thas. She was immediately lost in a maze of frigid hallways. After blundering about, she encountered a kapak, who informed her that if the wizard was in the castle, he was likely to be in his library, which was located next door to the room in which she had spent the night.

Kitiara found the room. The door was closed, but not locked, apparently, for it opened a crack when she gave it a shove. Recalling how he had barged in on her last night, Kitiara thrust the door open and strode boldly into the room.

A large white wolf lying on a rug beside a chair leaped to its feet. The wolf's red eyes fixed on Kitiara. A growl rumbled in the wolf's throat. Its head went down, its ears went back. It bared its teeth in a snarl. Kitiara clapped her hand to her sword.

"He will be at your throat before you can draw your weapon," Feal-Thas murmured.

He was reading a large leather-bound book and did not look up. He said something in his own language to the wolf and, reaching out his hand, lightly touched the beast on its head. The wolf settled down, but the red eyes remained fixed on Kitiara. She kept her hand on her sword's hilt.

She was fuming. Once again, he'd caught her at a disadvantage, put her on the defensive, made her look a damn fool.

"Please, sit down, Highlord," Feal-Thas said, gesturing to another chair.

"I'm not going to be here that long," she told him curtly. "I have been sent to give you the emperor's orders regarding the dragon orb—"

"*My* dragon orb," said Feal-Thas.

Kitiara was ready for this argument. "When you became a Dragon Highlord, you swore an oath to the Queen. You pledged to serve her. The emperor is her chosen representative in the world. He has need of the dragon orb and he has the right to claim it."

The elf's gray eyes flickered. "I could question that, but let us say for the sake of argument I agree." He sighed and closed the book. "Explain this scheme."

"I thought you knew all about it?" Kit said disdainfully.

"Indulge me," the elf returned.

Kitiara related how she had lured the knight, Derek Crownguard, into traveling to Icereach to find the orb. Feal-Thas frowned at this. The elf wore his long white hair smoothed back from his forehead and the dark line of his displeasure was clearly visible on his brow.

"I should have been informed that you were going to reveal the secret of the dragon orb to another. You have placed the orb in great danger. Not from this knight." Feal-Thas waved away Derek as inconsequential. "The Tower wizards have been searching for this orb for centuries. If the Wizard's Conclave were to hear about it—"

"They won't," said Kitiara. "The knights want the orb for themselves. They are doing all in their power to keep it secret. They don't want the wizards to have it any more than you do."

Feal-Thas thought this over and appeared to concede the point, for he made no further argument.

"You will give the dragon orb to the white dragon, Sleet. When this Derek Crownguard arrives," Kitiara continued, "you will allow him to find the dragon orb. Takhisis will give orders to the dragon. Sleet will be told she can kill off any companions, if she wants, but she mustn't harm Crownguard. Once the knight has the orb and it has him—however that works—he will be allowed to depart with it. He will carry it back to Solamnia and that realm will fall, just as Silvanesti fell."

The elf's response was unexpected.

"You don't like this plan, do you, Highlord?"

Kitiara opened her mouth to say that she considered the plan sheer genius, one of Ariakas's finest, but the lie stuck in her throat. "It is not for me to like it or dislike it," she said with a shrug. "I am pledged to serve my Queen."

"I, too, try to obey Her Dark Majesty in all things," said Feal-Thas in mock humility. The elf reached his hand down to scratch the wolf behind his ears. "There is one problem, though. I can provide the knight, Crownguard, with access to the dragon orb, but I cannot guarantee he will survive long enough to claim it. His death will not be my doing, I assure you," he said, seeing Kitiara glower. "I will not touch a hair of his mustache."

Kitiara was exasperated. "As I told you, Highlord, Sleet will receive orders from Takhisis—"

"I can't, unfortunately, give the orb to the dragon."

"You won't, you mean," said Kitiara heatedly.

"Hear me out," said Feal-Thas, lifting a delicate hand. "As I told you, I made a study of the dragon orbs. You are right when you say they are dangerous. Few have any idea *how* dangerous. I know the danger. Lorac's fate might have been mine. The orb has been in my possession for over three hundred years, ever since the wizards asked me to take it from Wayreth in order to hide it from the Kingpriest. Many times I have been tempted to try to gain control of the orb. Many times I have longed to do battle with the essences of the dragons imprisoned inside. I wondered, 'Am I strong enough to make the orb serve me?'"

"And I wonder if I'm supposed to give a damn about any of this," Kit said scathingly.

Feal-Thas went on as if he hadn't heard. "I know myself. One doesn't live for three hundred years without searching one's soul. I know my strengths and my weaknesses. It takes a remarkable person to dare to try to control a dragon orb—a person with absolute confidence in himself, who, at the same time, cares nothing for himself, for his own personal safety. Such a person is willing to risk all—his life, his soul—on a gamble.

"I am conceited. I admit that. I care too much about myself. I came to realize I was probably not strong enough to survive an encounter with the dragon orb. Note that I say 'probably'. There is always, you see, that one small scintilla of doubt. I found myself waking in the night, hearing its voice, feeling myself drawn to it. I would go to it, stare into it, feel the urge to put my hands on it. In a moment of weakness, I might succumb to the temptation. I couldn't take the risk."

Kitiara tapped her boot on the floor. "Get to the point."

"Hundreds of years ago," said Feal-Thas, "I created a magical guardian and placed it in a specially built chamber along with the dragon orb. I gave orders to the guardian to slay anyone who tries to take it. That includes myself. I have slept much better ever since."

The elf went back to his reading.

Kitiara's jaw dropped. She stared at him in disbelief. "You're lying."

"I'm not, I assure you." Feal-Thas spoke matter-of-factly.

"Then . . ." Kitiara floundered. "Remove the guardian. Tell it to go away."

Feal-Thas smiled slightly and shook his head and continued reading his book. "It wouldn't be much of a guardian if I could control it that easily."

Kitiara took a step toward him.

The wolf rose swiftly and silently to his feet and Kitiara halted.

"What do you mean, you can't control it? You have to!" she said. "Those are Ariakas's orders!"

"Ariakas ordered me to permit this Derek Crownguard to enter my castle. I will do so. He ordered me to let Derek Crownguard find the dragon orb. I will do so—"

"And he will be slain by the guardian," said Kitiara.

"That will be up to the knight. Crownguard can battle the guardian or not, as he chooses. If he slays the guardian, he can have the orb. If the guardian slays him, well, there's always some risk involved in questing after valuable artifacts. These loathsome knights wouldn't do it otherwise."

"You're not in the least worried about losing your orb," Kit said accusingly. "You *know* the guardian will slay Crownguard."

"The guardian *is* quite formidable," Feal-Thas admitted gravely. "It has protected the orb for many, many years and during that time it has, I fear, become extremely possessive. When I say I am unable to remove it, I am not being coy. I assure you, it would kill me on sight."

"I still don't believe you," Kitiara said.

"What does that matter to me?" Feal-Thas said as he turned a page.

"When my lord Ariakas comes to pay you a visit, it will matter," Kitiara threatened.

"The emperor will not leave his precious war to travel all this way to upbraid me, Highlord." Feal-Thas glanced up at her, amusement lighting the gray eyes. "*I* am not the one who will face his displeasure."

Clutching the furs about her shoulders, Kitiara glared at the elf in impotent fury. He was right, curse him. Kitiara had never come across such an infuriating man, and she had no idea what to do.

"Takhisis will not look kindly upon this," Kitiara said at last.

Feal-Thas shrugged. "My god is Nuitari, Takhisis's son. He has little love and less respect for his mother—feelings to which you can undoubtedly relate, Kitiara uth Matar, considering how you despised your own mother."

Kitiara opened her mouth, then shut it again. The blood pounded in her temples. Dealing with this elf was like fighting a will-o-the-wisp, one of those fiendish swamp denizens. He kept flitting about her, trying to confuse her, jabbing her in places where she least expected it.

Kitiara dug her nails into her palms. He was trying to lure her into a bog of confusion. She had to concentrate on the issue at hand, ignore everything that did not relate to it, such as the fact that she had hated her mother.

"You want our side to win this war—" she began.

"Ah, the appeal to patriotism," said Feal-Thas. "I was wondering when you would resort to that. I have lived in this world for several centuries and barring something unforeseen occurring I am likely to live a few more. I have seen emperors come and emperors go. I will be here long after you and Ariakas and all the rest of his vaunted Highlords lie moldering in the ground. I will be here long after this great empire he is building has crumbled into dust. In other words, Highlord, I don't give a damn about your war."

"Then why go to all the trouble to became a Highlord? From what I heard, you risked your life to return to Silvanesti and spy on your own people. You betrayed your own king—"

"*That* was personal," Feal-Thas remarked coldly.

"Why did you do it? Because like all of us you're ambitious! You want power. You want to rule. My guess is that you plan to challenge Ariakas—"

"Don't get your ambition confused with mine, Highlord," said Feal-Thas, still perusing his book. "The only thing I want is to be left in peace to pursue my studies."

Kitiara gave a scornful laugh.

The elf lord shut his book and set it aside. He reached out to fondle the wolf, calming the animal, who did not like Kitiara's loud laughter or her abrupt movements.

"I was born and raised in Silvanesti. Like all elves, I loved my homeland more than life itself. For reasons I will not go into because they no longer matter, I was unjustly banished from my lush green paradise and sent to a land where nothing lived, nothing grew. A land of death and desolation. My death, or so I thought.

"It was the dead of winter. The people of this region found me dying, almost frozen to death. They had never seen an elf before. They did not know what I was, but that didn't matter. They took me into their homes and warmed me, fed me and sheltered me. They brought me back to life. I learned their secrets, secrets they had never revealed to any outsider. One woman gave those secrets to me out of love for me, for a handsome elf youth.

"I stole her secrets. I stole her love, and I betrayed her and the people who had saved me to the ogres who once dwelt in this land. My lover and her people were all slain, and when they were dead, I took their land and their possessions. My palace stands now on the byre where I burned the bodies.

"I am this land, Highlord. I am ice. Feelings such as pity, love, compassion skate off my frozen surface. If I were to somehow find a way to touch the sun, I doubt if even its flames could thaw me.

"What do I want? Peace. Solitude. I want to live here in my palace with my winter wolves and my books for the remaining years of my life (and I come of a long-lived family, even for elves), and I do not want to be disturbed. I do not want to rule anyone. Ruling people means dealing with people. It means instituting laws and collecting tribute and fighting wars, because there is always someone who wants what you have got and will try to take it from you.

"I became Highlord because I saw this was the means to my end. I intend to remove all trace of life from this part of the world. The thanoi will destroy the Ice Folk. The kapaks will destroy the thanoi. My wolves and I will destroy the kapaks. My land will fall blessedly silent as only the land can be silent when it lies empty and still beneath the trackless snow.

"So you ask what I want, Highlord? I want silence." Feal-Thas picked up another book and opened it.

"You can find silence in death, you know," said Kitiara grimly.

"Try it," he said. "With a gesture and a word, I could freeze you into a solid block of ice. Then I would place your statue in the hallway—a lasting monument to stupidity."

He resumed his reading.

Kitiara glared at the elf, but the glare was wasted, for he never once looked up at her. She considered her options. She could go back to Ariakas and complain about Feal-Thas, but that would only make Ariakas angry with her. She could leave Icereach altogether and let the fool knight come here and get himself killed, but again, Ariakas would blame her. Or she could just deal with the problem herself.

"You have no objection, I suppose, if I kill this guardian?" Kit asked.

Feal-Thas turned a page. "Be my guest. I can always create another."

"That won't be necessary," said Kit caustically. "I'll give the orb to Sleet and order her not to let you have the orb. That way, you can sleep at night. What sort of guardian is it?" She considered the wizard's likely talents, the probable location. "A frost giant? Ice wight?"

Feal-Thas's lips twitched, as close as he'd come to laughter in a couple of centuries.

"Nothing so trite, Highlord," he replied. "The guardian is my own creation. Quite unique, or so I should imagine."

Kitiara turned on her heel and banged out the door.

Feal-Thas smiled and scratched the wolf behind his ears and continued his reading.

II

Death on ice. The Dragon Orb.

eaving Feal-Thas, Kitiara went in search of the commander of the kapak forces. She emerged from the building where the Highlord had his library and was half-blinded by the dazzling glare of the sun on the ice. She shaded her eyes and when she could finally see, she discovered that she hadn't missed much. All that remained of the fortress was a courtyard of ice, several tumble-down outbuildings made of ice, and a stone tower jutting up out of the ice. In the center of the courtyard, a fountain carved in the shape of a phoenix sent clear water shooting upward in a sparkling jet and cascading into a pool below. Kitiara had been skeptical of the elf's tale of magical holy water, but the fact that the fountain was not frozen solid in the bitter cold was in itself some sort of miracle.

She did not stay to marvel at the fountain. A frigid wind blowing off the glacier seemed likely to freeze her face. Seeing draconians coming and going from one of the outbuildings, Kit assumed this was their headquarters. Winding herself in the furs, she made a dash across the courtyard. She slipped and slithered on the icy pavement and envied the draconians their clawed feet.

A wooden door stood barred against the cold. Kit was unwilling to release her hold on her fur coverings in order to knock. She kicked at the door with her boot and mumbled curses through cold-stiffened lips until someone came to open it.

Warmth from two oil burners enveloped her. Several kapaks were inside; one of them was issuing orders while the others rounded up gear. Apparently, the commander and his troops were preparing to go on a hunting expedition. The kapaks wore thick fur hides over their scales, the fur turned to the inside. With fur and hide and scales, the draconians looked like some sort of freakish crossbreeds.

The kapaks glanced at her as they worked, but did not appear particularly interested in her. Kit thought about Feal-Thas's remark that he planned to destroy the kapaks, and she wondered if she should warn the kapak commander that he could not trust his master. She decided the warning would not be necessary. Draconians never trusted anyone.

She asked the commander if she could speak to him. He sent his men on their way, then turned to her. His copper-colored scales shone in the fire light. He was quite willing to talk with her, seemed glad of the company.

Life here must be boring as the Abyss, Kit thought. They first discussed the dragon orb.

The commander knew about the orb, though he'd never seen it or had anything to do with it.

"Where is it?" Kitiara asked.

"In the ice tunnels below," the kapak answered. He gestured with his claws at the floor to indicate the level beneath their feet. "Near the dragon's lair."

"I hear the orb has a guardian," said Kit. "Can you tell me what it is?"

"Damned if I know," said the kapak.

"You've never seen it?"

"No reason to. The elf told me about the dragon orb and ordered me and my troops to keep away from that part of the castle. I obey orders."

"My! What a good little draco you are," said Kitiara, annoyed.

The kapak grinned, showing all his teeth. "Oh, I went to see for myself, just to make certain Her Dark Majesty's interests were being looked after, of course."

"Of course," said Kitiara dryly. "Were they?"

"From what I saw they are," said the commander.

"So you did see the guardian?"

"No, but I saw what it had done to those who had seen it—a group of thanoi, or what was left of them, which wasn't much. Blood and bones, hair and blubber smeared all over the ice."

"Were these thanoi after the orb?"

"I doubt it. Thanoi aren't bright enough. They probably blundered into the orb's chamber by accident on their way to the food pantry."

"Just because you saw some bones doesn't mean there's a guardian," Kitiara stated. "Feal-Thas could have killed them himself, then made it look like some horrible monster slaughtered them."

The kapak made a hooting sound. "Have you ever seen a thanoi leg bone?"

"I've never seen a thanoi," said Kit impatiently, "much less its leg bone. What are they?"

"Walrus-people, the Ice Folk call them. They're huge, blubbery beasts that walk upright like men, and they have tusks and a hide like a walrus. They're big and they're strong. A thanoi could tuck me—tail and wings, armor and all—under one arm and never notice the weight. They have leg bones that are as thick as tree stumps. Maybe thicker." The kapak's tail twitched and thumped the floor. "Those tree stumps had been snapped into two and scattered like twigs. Feal-Thas didn't do that. Not with those delicate hands of his."

Kitiara was still not convinced. "Sounds like the work of the dragon," she suggested.

"The thanoi were attacked long before Sleet arrived. What's left of them is well preserved in the ice, and if you ask me, even the dragon's afraid of the guardian. Sleet won't go near the chamber where the orb's hidden."

Kitiara shook her head. She stomped her feet on the floor to warm them and began to pace the room, not so much out of anxiety as the need to keep from freezing.

"Why all the questions about the guardian?" the commander asked.

"Because I have to fight it," said Kit glumly.

The kapak's tongue flickered out of his mouth in astonishment. "You're going to steal the orb from Feal-Thas?"

"No, I'm not going to steal it," Kitiara said testily. "What would I want with a dragon orb? I wish I'd never heard of the damn thing. It's cost me nothing but trouble."

She halted in her pacing, turned to face the kapak. "If I had soldiers with me—"

The commander shook his head. "Not on your life, lady."

"I'm a Dragon Highlord," Kit said, scowling. "I could order you to assist me."

"I take my orders from Highlord Feal-Thas," said the commander, grinning again, "and I don't think he's going to order me to help you steal his dragon orb."

"I'm not stealing it!" Kitiara protested. "I'm going to give it to the dragon for safe-keeping."

"Trust me, it's being safely kept now," the kapak said.

"I'm under orders," said Kitiara. "Just tell me how to get there."

The kapak shrugged. "It's your funeral."

He gave her instructions on how to find her way through the maze of tunnels, which he likened to the labyrinthine sewers of Palanthas, then he set out after his men. Kit saw him and his troops, armed with bows and arrows, trekking off.

Kitiara resumed her pacing and her thinking.

All right, so there was a guardian. How bad could it be? She didn't for one minute believe the kapak's nonsense about the dragon being afraid of it. Dragons are at the top of the food chain. They aren't afraid of anything. The commander was just trying to scare her. That wild tale about snapped leg bones! He was probably out with his men having a good laugh over her gullibility.

Trying to guess what the guardian could be, so she could determine what weapons to use to fight it, Kit called to mind all the stories she'd ever heard of guardians set to watch over valuable treasure. Was it undead? A ghoul or a ghost? Certainly it was magical. Maybe a golem. It could be a frost giant, even though Feal-Thas had said it wasn't. But the castle's inhabitants would certainly know if there was a giant chained up in the basement. Kit thought of this monster and she thought of that, and suddenly she came to the realization that thinking wasn't accomplishing anything except giving her a throbbing pain in her temples.

"Bugger it!" she said to herself wrathfully.

Clutching the furs around her, she went to rummage through the kapak's weapon stash. She had her own sword, but she wanted a kapak weapon and she found one that suited her—a small, curve-bladed weapon that would fit into her belt—a couple of daggers and a spear. She was careful to keep from touching the blades of the draconian weapons, for kapaks licked the blades with their tongues to coat them with their poisoned saliva, which was the reason Kit wanted to use them. She picked up a shield on her way out.

Kit crossed the courtyard again to return to her room, first stopping in the library to have a few choice words with Feal-Thas. The elf was not there, however. The wolf was, and Kitiara did not linger. She found someone had brought food to her room in her absence. She ate a good meal and washed it down with a couple of swigs of dwarf spirits from her flask to warm her blood, then dumped the rest of the spirits onto the floor.

She put on her armor, cinched on her own sword belt holding her short sword in its sheath. She shoved the extra sword into the belt, along with the empty flask. She wrapped herself in the furs and went back out to the courtyard and filled up the flask with the presumably-holy waters of the fountain.

Feeling ready for anything from giants to zombies, Kitiara headed for the lower levels of the castle.

———

Kitiara had no fear of this guardian. She knew she would defeat it. She found it annoying she had to waste her time and energy on it. It was all stupidly ironic. She should be back in Solamnia slaughtering knights, and here she was, fighting a monster in order to keep some fool knight alive.

According to the kapak, glacial springs had carved out the first tunnels in the ice below the ruins of the castle. Feal-Thas had further enhanced the natural tunnels with his magic to carve out the chamber of the dragon orb. Upon her arrival, Sleet had established residence in a lair dug magically by some white dragon eons ago. Sleet had expanded the lair to her own liking, adding new entrances and exits and digging even more tunnels.

Kit would have no trouble finding her way down, according to the kapak. Portions of the glacier routinely broke off, exposing the tunnels to the open air.

She found one such entrance leading into what looked like a mole-run bored through solid ice. She started to make her cautious way down, walking gingerly, but almost immediately her feet slid out from underneath her. She dropped her shield and spear trying to break her fall, and ended up sliding half-way down the tunnel on her backside. The shield went clear to the bottom and crashed up against a wall with a clatter and bang that could have been heard in Flotsam.

Cursing all wizards everywhere, Kitiara crawled the rest of the way down the icy tunnel on her hands and knees. She retrieved her shield at the bottom and managed to regain her feet. The bright sun shone through the ice, illuminating the tunnels with an eerie green light. She stared at the walls.

Tired of losing his men in the maze, the kapak commander had told her he'd come up with a system for marking the tunnels so that anyone venturing down there stood a reasonable chance of finding his way back to the surface. The marks were carved into the ice and could be found at every intersection. Crude arrows showed the way back. A drawing with wings and a tail indicated the dragon's lair. Tunnels leading to the orb's chamber were marked with an ominous X.

Kitiara headed off in the direction of the dragon. Despite what the kapak had told her about the dragon fearing the guardian, Kit considered it would be worth her while to try to enlist the dragon's aid. Kit had devised a lie about why she needed to destroy the guardian of the dragon orb. The lie was lame, not very convincing, but white dragons were not all that intelligent. Skie referred to whites as the gully dwarves of dragons. Kit figured that if the lie failed, she could bully the white into helping her.

As it turned out, she'd gone to the trouble for nothing.

Kit found Sleet's lair, but no Sleet. The dragon had been here quite recently, to judge by a half-eaten caribou carcass. She was gone now, however. Disappointed, Kitiara turned to leave and bumped into Feal-Thas, who was standing right behind her.

"Quick reflexes," remarked Feal-Thas, eyeing the dagger that seemed to leap into Kit's hand.

"You're lucky I didn't slit your fool throat!" Kit snarled, angry that she'd let him sneak up on her like that. She wouldn't have said it was possible for someone to break out in a sweat in these freezing temperatures, but she was proof it could be done.

"Were you looking for the dragon?" Feal-Thas asked mildly. "She's not here. I sent her off with a message to our fellow Highlord in Khur. Sleet will be gone some time, I should think." Feal-Thas smiled, tight-lipped. "I'm not convinced she knows where Khur is."

He turned to leave, then turned back.

"Don't be too disappointed. The dragon wouldn't have been any use against the guardian, as you will soon find out. Good luck, Highlord."

He walked off, moving with soundless ease over the slick floor. Kit's hand clenched on the dagger's hilt. She had to fight to resist the urge to bury it between the Highlord's shoulder blades. She thrust the dagger back in her boot.

She left the dragon's lair and made her way cautiously through the tunnels, following the X's that were meant to warn people away. She wondered how she would know the chamber when she found it, but as it turned out, she had no trouble.

She came to an intersection where a narrow tunnel slanted off from the main one. There was no X here. No need. A rivulet of blood frozen in the ice ran from the small tunnel into the main one. Kit followed the grisly trail and found the scene of violent death that was just as the kapak commander had described it.

Kit swiftly drew her sword and raised her shield. She had seen many horrible sights in her lifetime. She'd killed her share of both men and monsters and was not one to flinch at the sight of smoking entrails or severed limbs. This was not the worst she had ever seen, but it was certainly the most bizarre—a massacre frozen in ice.

Blood was smeared over the icy walls and made a gruesome carpet on the floor. It had dripped from the ceiling, freezing to form strange pinkish icicles. Globs of frozen flesh with fur attached and hunks of blubber were scattered about in hideous piles throughout the corridor. She found a broken tusk and several cracked bones.

What truly gave her pause and made her draw her sword was the sight of bloody claw marks scratched in the ice. She had found a severed paw on the floor, which she assumed belonged to a thanoi, and she could tell that whatever claw had made these marks were not the short and stubby claws of the thanoi. The bloody tracks were far apart, yet evenly spaced, which meant that the clawed hand or foot that had made them was extremely large.

Glancing around the tunnel, Kit had a pretty good notion of what had happened. The thanoi had entered the tunnel either by accident or design. They'd encountered the guardian, and there had been a desperate battle. The heat of many bodies fighting for their miserable lives had raised the temperature in the corridor, so that the blood and gore had sunk into the melting ice, which had then refrozen after the battle was over. As to what had happened to the rest of the thanoi— the heads were missing—Kit didn't like to think.

She looked down the length of the tunnel and saw that she had come to the right place. The tunnel opened into a chamber carved out of ice. In the center of the room, beneath the domed ice ceiling was an object, presumably the dragon orb, mounted on a pedestal of ice. The chamber was wide open, no door, no locks to protect the orb. Only the guardian.

Whatever it was. Wherever it was.

From her vantage point in the tunnel, Kit had a view of the entire chamber, and it was empty, save for the dragon orb.

Holding her sword before her, keeping her shield up, Kitiara crept slowly down the corridor. *A little fear is good for you,* her father always told her. *Keeps you alert, on your toes. Just never let fear master you.* Kitiara was more determined than fearful. She wanted to see this guardian, this monster. She wanted to slay it and take its dripping head to Feal-Thas and throw it at his delicate feet.

Drawing closer, she noted that the chamber in which the dragon orb stood was unblemished. Not a drop of blood defaced the walls or marred the pristine white of the walls, ceiling, or floor. Either the guardian kept the chamber clean or it took care to do its killing in the tunnel. Mindful of this, Kit put her back to the icy wall and edged along, stepping over bloody remnants of the thanoi, keeping a sharp look out all around her.

She listened as hard as she looked, but she heard nothing and the silence made her nervous. She had never heard such awful quiet. It was as if the world had ended and all life had been swept away except for her. Every tiny sound she made—her foot crunching on the ice, the rattle of her armor, the jingle of her chain mail, her breath whistling inside the helm of the Dragon Highlord—seemed to resound to the heavens. She was continuing to sweat despite the cold, and she wished irritably that the guardian would attack and end the suspense. Kitiara had never been known for her patience.

It suddenly occurred to her that the dragon orb might be its own guardian, and she cast a sharp glance at it. She wished, a little belatedly, that she'd thought to do some research on dragon orbs, for she had no idea what this thing did or didn't do or even what it looked like. Maybe this wasn't really a dragon orb at all. Certainly it was an orb. It was made of crystal and appeared very fragile, as if a loud shout could shatter it. Mist swirled inside it, shifting colors—pale reds and blues, greens, blacks, with streaks of white.

She edged nearer. The colors inside the orb were beautiful, shimmering, swirling. She felt a sudden longing to touch the orb. Its crystal looked so smooth. She lowered her sword and her shield and was about to drop them to the floor when a voice startled her.

I am afraid.

Kitiara whipped around, immediately on guard.

The chamber was empty. No one there. She turned irresistibly back to the orb and realized the voice came from the orb. It was the speaker.

I rest on the golden pedestal and people pass by, never noticing me, for I have been in the Tower so long I am nothing now to them but another artifact collecting dust. I am part of the furniture. They stand near me, talking in low and fearful tones, and I listen to them with the minds of dragons, and I hear what they say. What they say frightens me.

They don't think I can hear them or understand them. So many years have passed since my creation that they have forgotten my powers.

But I do understand. I hear about the rise of a man known as the Kingpriest. I hear he fears all who practice magic, for he cannot control them. He has threatened their annihilation. He has lately sent an army to attack the sister Tower of High Sorcery at Daltigoth. The wizards destroyed that Tower rather than allow it to fall into the hands of those who have no understanding of the awful power of magic. They fear our Tower at Wayreth is next. His army is on the march, and many wizards who make their homes here have already decided to flee.

And I must flee, as well. A dragon orb must never fall into the hands of the Kingpriest. They say he will destroy me or, worse, he might try to gain control of me and use my power to his own ends.

So they have decided to use their magic to carry me into the ethers, to walk the roads of magic that are hidden in time and space, bearing me to a realm far away. The journey will be fraught with peril, for there are rumors that the clerics of the Kingpriest have grown so powerful that they can stalk the paths of magic, waiting to pluck traveling wizards from the ethers and slay them in the name of righteousness.

Feal-Thas the Winternorn has volunteered to transport me to a place of safety, a land cold and barren, the land to which he was exiled when his crime was judged and sentence passed on him by the Silvanesti king, Lorac Caladon.

The wizards believe I will be safe there, for the Kingpriest cares little for this land that has no wealth and few people to worship him.

I will go with Feal-Thas, not because I want to, but because I am afraid of remaining here. For I see dark clouds gathering and a terrible wind rising and the seas boiling and fire raining down from the heavens. I see the wrath of the gods falling like a hammer upon Krynn. I see the people cry to the gods, and I hear no answer.

If I remain here, I am doomed, and though I chafe against my exile, I accept it. I will travel in the safekeeping of this wizard to the land of Icereach, and I will remain hidden in this loathsome wasteland until the time comes when the power of the gods returns to the world.

Then I will find a way to escape.

The mists swirled and the color was beautiful, entrancing. Kit thought she could see hands reaching out to her.

Time was. Time is. The gods have returned. You are god-sent. Come closer. Touch me. Help me escape.

Kit listened enthralled. She edged closer. "Who are you?" she breathed. "What are your powers? If I help you, will you give them to me . . ."

She felt more than saw something enter the chamber.

12

The Guardian.

itiara stood perfectly still. Her eyes narrowed. She fell back on the defensive. Only moments before the chamber had been empty, then this man had materialized inside, standing near the dragon orb. The man was human. He was clad in armor that had seen its share of battle, for it was dented and scratched, yet he'd kept it in good repair. Kit recognized the armor. It was the armor of a Solamnic knight.

The knight did not see her. He had his back to her and he was staring up at the ceiling. Something about him, about his stance, about the way he moved— graceful and light on his feet, yet powerful, like a mountain lion—was familiar. The knight wore a sword, but he was not wearing a helm. He had black curly hair, cut short. He appeared to be waiting for something, for he shifted his gaze from the ceiling to the walls, and then he started to turn around.

"Hold there!" Kitiara ordered. "Keep your hands away from your weapons and turn around slowly."

The knight did as she ordered, moving with a lithe, almost lazy ease that she knew well. Her heart constricted, then thudded painfully. The knight turned to face her. She knew the movement, knew the black curling hair, the jaunty mustache, the dark good looks . . . He stared at her, trying to see her face through the eyeslits of the elaborate horned helm of the Dragon Highlord.

"Is that you inside that bucket, Kit?" he asked. She had not heard that rich, hearty voice in many years, yet she knew it as well as the sound of her own. "Don't you know me? Put your sword down. I'm your father, girl."

Kitiara held fast to her sword and didn't answer. This was a trick.

"You're all grown up, Kit," Gregor uth Matar continued in admiring tones. "I didn't expect that. I guess I thought you'd be the teenage girl I left behind. I'm sorry about that, by the way," he added with a shrug. "I meant to come back for you like I promised. I started to return to Solace half a dozen times, but I never made it. There was always a war to fight or a woman to love . . ."

He smiled the warm, off-kilter smile that had charmed so many hearts. "I guess there was no harm done. You didn't need me after all. You've obviously done well for yourself. A Dragon Highlord. I'm proud of you, Kit—"

He took another step forward.

"Don't move!" Kitiara ordered in a choked voice. She coughed to clear her throat. "Stay where you are. This doesn't make any sense. My father is dead."

"Did you ever find my body?" Gregor asked cheerfully. "Locate my grave? Meet anyone who saw me die?"

The answer was no, but Kitiara didn't answer. "I'm asking the questions. What are you doing in the chamber with the dragon orb? Are you the guardian?"

"Me! The guardian!" Gregor chuckled. "I'm one of the best swordsmen in Krynn, but let's face it, daughter dear, would *you* hire me to guard something this valuable?"

"Then where is the guardian?"

Gregor shrugged, a gesture so similar to Kit's own she might have been watching herself in a mirror. "I banished it. Sent it packing."

Gregor took another step. He grinned. "I see you've got your flask with you. Would you happen to have a drop of dwarf spirits in that flask, Kit? Forget orbs and guardians and such. Let's share a dram and talk about what you've been doing all these years."

Kit hesitated, then she said, "All right, but don't come any closer. I'll toss the flask to you.

Gregor shrugged and smiled, but he did as he was told. He halted a few feet from her.

Kitiara kept her sword raised and lowered her shield, slinging it by the strap over her arm. With her free hand, she reached down to her belt and took hold of the flask. She uncorked it with her teeth, spit out the cork, then flung the water into Gregor's face.

He gasped in astonishment as the water hit him and stood there staring at her. Water dripped from his nose and chin and mustache.

"Gods' breath, girl, what did you do that for?" Gregor demanded, wiping water from his eyes. He looked at her, standing tense and taut, sword ready, and then he burst out laughing.

The chamber shook with his laughter that was as big, raucous and careless as himself. Kitiara had always loved to hear her father laugh.

"Holy water!" Gregor could scarcely talk for his guffaws. "You think I'm a ghost! Ha, ha, ha!"

"I don't know what you are!" Kitiara said through clenched teeth. Tears stung her eyes and froze on her cheeks. "But you're not my father. My father is dead. That's why he never came back for me. He's dead!"

She lunged at the guardian with her sword.

A horrible stench made her gag. A savage roar cut off the sound of her father's laughter. One moment Gregor was there and the next she was enveloped by the stench, confronting an enormous being covered in filthy gray-white hair with huge arms and mauling paws. If it had eyes, she could not see them in the tangle of the hair. It had teeth, though, sharp fangs and a long, slavering tongue. She stabbed at the thing desperately and felt her sword bite into flesh. The thing roared again, this time in pain. Claws as long as swords slashed at her, raked across her.

Kitiara gasped as the razor-sharp claws cut through the dragon armor, sliced neat as a razor into the flesh of both her forearms and across her midriff. She staggered back, blood dripping from the gashes. Fumbling at the shield that she'd slung over her arm, she lifted it up to protect herself and held her sword ready. She couldn't feel the pain, not yet, but she knew it would come any moment now and she braced herself. She gathered her strength and was prepared to lunge again . . . at Tanis.

He stood in front of her, regarding her with loving concern.

Kitiara blinked and squinched her eyes shut against the phantom and it was then the pain hit her. She bit her lip to keep from crying out. Opening her eyes again, she saw Tanis still standing there.

"Kit," he said gently. "You're hurt."

He was as she remembered him—tall and muscular, with the strong arms and hands of a skilled bowman. He wore his hair long, to cover the pointed ears that gave away his elven heritage. His smile was warm and wide, his chin strong and clean-shaven.

"Kit," said Tanis sadly, "you didn't come to the inn. You broke your oath. We were all there. Your brothers, Caramon and Raistlin, and Tasslehoff and Flint. Sturm came, too, and I came. I came because of you, Kit. I came back for you, to tell you I'd made a mistake. I love you. I want to be with you always . . ."

"No," cried Kitiara, choking from the burning pain. She watched her own blood dribble down her legs and drip off her arms and splatter on the icy floor. "I don't believe you." She shook her head angrily. "I don't believe *in* you—whatever you are."

"Since you weren't at the inn as you promised," said Tanis, "I assume that means you don't care about me."

"I care about you," said Kit, knowing this wasn't real, yet wanting it to be. "It's just . . . I was busy. Ariakas made me a Dragon Highlord. I command an army. I've conquered nations. I have a war to fight . . ."

"When you didn't come, I decided to love another," Tanis continued, as though he hadn't heard her, "an elf woman named—"

"Laurana. I know!" Kitiara cried angrily. "You told me about her, remember? You called her a spoiled little girl. You said she was immature. You wanted a woman . . ."

"I want you, Kitiara," said Tanis, and he held out his arms to embrace her.

"Get back!" Kit warned.

The holy water. She had dropped the flask when the apparition attacked. The flask lay on the blood-covered floor at her feet. She made a grab for it, keeping her gaze on Tanis, holding out her sword. She lifted the visor of her helm and swallowed a gulp of the healing water. Her pain eased. Her blood stopped dripping.

She had to attack it again. She'd hurt the thing once. She didn't know how badly, but she guessed that not all the blood covering the ice was her own. Attacking it meant she would have to go in close and brave the terrible raking claws again. She dropped the flask and lowered her visor and raised her shield. Gripping her sword, she ran at Tanis.

The thing roared. The stench made her gag. She hacked at it with her sword and the filthy white fur was drenched with blood. Flaming black eyes glared at her. Claws raked across her shoulders and her chest and down her thighs. The claws dug deep, piercing flesh. She heard and felt claw scrape against bone and she shuddered from the rending pain, but she kept stabbing at the creature with her sword and finally she felt the blade strike something hard and solid. Putting all her weight behind it, she drove the blade into the thing's hairy body, thrusting the blade deep, twisting it.

The creature roared in pain and fury and slashed at her violently with the cutting claws. Blood sprayed across the visor and got into her eyes, half blinding her. Kit yanked her sword free. She stumbled backward, and her feet slipped and she fell.

Her hand struck the ice, knocking loose her sword. The weapon slid out of her reach. She tried desperately to stand, but the pain was bad, very bad, and it was hard to breathe. Claws slashed down at her, and Kit rolled out of the way. She remembered the kapak's sword and she fumbled at it, yanking it out of her belt. She waited until the hairy beast roared down on her and then, blindly, she drove the sword into its body, drove it through hair and flesh and bone. Blood flowed over her hands. A horrible bellow deafened her and a gigantic fist struck, driving her to the floor.

Kitiara found herself lying on her belly. She blinked her eyes, trying to clear the blood, and saw the flask, just out of reach. She crawled toward it, reaching for it with a shaking hand.

There was her mother. Rosamun lay on the floor, her hand on the flask. She gazed at Kitiara with her large doe eyes that never seemed to quite focus on the present, but stared out at some hazy horizon no one could see but her.

"Your father didn't come home last night," Rosamun said accusingly.

Kitiara cringed. Not again. The pain of her wounds was terrible, but it was nothing to the pain of the torture rack on which her parents had strapped her, pulling her between them whenever they fought.

"He was with that woman, wasn't he?" Rosamun's voice rose shrilly. "The one with the red hair I saw him flirting with at the market yesterday."

"He was at the Trough, Mother, drinking with his friends," Kit mumbled. She had to reach the flask. She crawled nearer, holding her sword, ready to strike.

"Don't lie for him, girl," Rosamun shouted, her voice rising to a shriek. "He hurts you as much as me with his philandering. Someday he'll leave us both. Mark my words . . ."

Kitiara sank down on the floor. Her eyes closed in exhaustion. She saw her father with the red-haired bar wench. The woman had her back against the outhouse, her legs spread, her skirts hiked up. Gregor crowded close to her, nuzzling bare breasts. Kit heard the woman squeal and her father grunt and the squeals blended with her mother's hysterical ravings.

Kit pushed herself painfully off the red ice. She staggered to her feet. Lifting her sword, she plunged it into her mother's body, then drove into her father's body. She kept stabbing and hacking at both of them until the roaring and the sobbing ceased and the thing quit twitching.

Kitiara collapsed.

She lay on the ice, staring at the blood-spattered ceiling. Her hand closed over the flask, and she tried to bring it to her mouth.

"I meant to come back, Tanis," she told him. "The truth is . . . I forgot . . ."

Her hand fell, limp, to the icy floor.

13

Recovery. Fewmaster Toede surpasses expectations.

itiara fought on. Clawed hands had hold of her, and she lashed out in fury, kicking and hitting, and screaming curses.

"Hold her down!" a guttural voice ordered angrily.

"I'm trying, sir!" panted another.

"Belek, sit on her feet. Rult, pour more water down her throat!"

A heavy weight immobilized Kit's lower limbs. Strong hands seized her wrists and prized open her jaws. Someone poured water into her mouth.

The water went down the wrong way, and Kitiara choked. Gasping for air brought her back to consciousness. She opened her eyes and saw monstrous faces leering at her. She couldn't move and she tensed to fight, then the mists cleared and she realized the faces were covered in scales, not fur, and none of them were faces from her past.

They were kapak faces, and the lizard-men had never looked so wonderful to her as they did now.

"You can let go of me," she mumbled.

The commander regarded her warily, then gave a nod of his head.

The kapak who had been sitting on her legs got up, groaned and limped off—apparently she had kneed him in a sensitive spot. The two kapak soldiers who held her wrists backed off.

"What about the guardian?" Kit asked.

"Dead," said the commander.

Kit nodded thankfully and closed her eyes to let the dizziness pass.

"What was it?" she demanded.

"Hard to tell," said the kapak. "You hacked it to bits. Whatever it was, none of us had ever seen one before."

"Some foul creation of the wizard's," said Kit, shuddering. "You're *sure* it's dead?"

"Very," replied the commander.

Kitiara sighed and relaxed. She was not in pain, but she felt weak and trembly and her brain wasn't working right. Her father had been there . . . and Tanis. But that wasn't possible, and the dragon orb, talking to her . . .

Kit's eyes flared open. "The dragon orb! I have to go save it—"

"No, you don't," said the commander. "Sleet's guarding the orb. Takhisis's orders. You should rest. You've earned it."

"How long have I been out?" Kit wondered confusedly.

"A week," said the kapak.

"A week!" Kitiara repeated, staring at him disbelief.

"The healing water closed your wounds, but you lost a lot of blood, then a fever set in. We thought you were dead a couple of times. Her Dark Majesty must think highly of you."

"And you went to all this trouble to save me." Kit shook her head and noticed even that small motion exhausted her. "Why didn't you just let me die? You dracos don't have much love for humans."

"We don't like humans," the kapak agreed, "but we don't like elves more."

Kit smiled weakly. "Speaking of elves, I'm surprised Feal-Thas didn't kill me."

"He hasn't been here with flowers," said the kapak dryly. "In fact, he hasn't been here at all. He's holed up in that ice palace of his."

"Perhaps he doesn't know his guardian's dead."

"Oh, he knows," said the kapak. "The winternorn knows everything. They say he can read minds. He's cunning, that one. He has as many twists and turns as a snake. If you want my opinion, he set you up to die. He wants you out of the way. One less rival."

Kitiara thought this over. It made sense, as much as anything made sense around here.

"I'll guess I'll have to kill him," she said. "Give me my sword—"

She tried to sit up. The kapak gave her a shove and Kit fell back on the bed with a groan.

"Maybe I'll wait until tomorrow . . ." she mumbled.

The commander chuckled. "I can see why you're a Dragon Highlord. And speaking of dragons, a blue has been hanging about, worried sick about you. He threatened to tear down the castle if anything happened to you. I never saw a dragon in such a stew."

"It must be Skie. Good old Skie." Kitiara sighed deeply and contently. "Tell Skie I'm all right, will you? And thanks, Commander. For everything."

She rolled over on her side, hugged the fur blankets around her, and went to sleep.

———————————————

Two days and several caribou steaks later, Kitiara felt well enough to leave her bed. The first thing she did was to see for herself that the guardian was truly dead. She ventured cautiously into the narrow tunnel, sword in hand. The blood—her blood—was frozen in the ice, but no corpse. The kapak had told her there wasn't much left of the monster, and now there was nothing at all.

Feal-Thas must have removed the remains. Either that or they'd disappeared on their own.

Kit left the chamber where she'd almost died and continued down the tunnel to the dragon's lair, intending to discuss Ariakas's plan for the dragon orb. This did not go well, for Sleet proved to be every bit as dull and obtuse as Skie had predicted. The white dragon blinked at Kit with heavy eyelids, scratched her ear with a clawed foot, and tilted her head to the side, as if viewing Kitiara from that angle somehow made her instructions clearer. At length Sleet yawned, lay her head down on the ice, and closed her eyes.

"Do you understand what you're supposed to do?" Kitiara asked, exasperated.

"I'm to guard the dragon orb," Sleet muttered.

"Guard it from Feal-Thas," said Kit.

"I hate Feal-Thas." The dragon's lip curled back over her teeth.

"When the Solamnic knight comes, you—"

"I hate Solamnic knights," the dragon added, and rolling over on her back, she fell asleep with her legs in the air and her tongue lolling out of her mouth.

Kit gave up and walked out. She hoped they all killed each other.

———————◆———————

Kit was ready to leave Icereach. She had decided against seeking revenge on Feal-Thas. Ariakas more than half-suspected her of being complicit in the death of Lord Verminaard. She didn't want the emperor to think she was going about Ansalon on a quest to murder his Highlords. She would have her revenge on the elf, but in a time and place of her choosing, not his.

She sent a message to Feal-Thas in his Ice Palace, saying she was leaving. His message back to her read, *I didn't know you were still here.*

"The emperor was a fool to put a dark elf in charge of anything," Skie remarked when Kitiara told him her tale. "Good elves are bad, but bad elves are worse."

The two stood on a wind-swept ice field outside the castle walls. Kitiara was bundled in furs and held her hand over her eyes to protect against the blinding glare of the sun off the ice. She wondered irritably how a sun this bright could shed such little heat.

"You should go inside," Skie added. "Your teeth are chattering."

"So are yours," said Kit, fondly stroking the neck of the blue dragon. Icicles hung off Skie's chin, making it look as if he had grown a hoary beard.

"I'm cold inside and out," said the dragon glumly. "When do we leave this horrible place?"

"I have to read those dispatches Ariakas sent first, see if he has any orders for me."

She left the dragon stomping about the glacier, flapping his wings, trying to keep warm.

———————◆———————

The first dispatch she read was from Emperor Ariakas, informing her of victories in the eastern part of Krynn. The Highlord Lucien of Takar now had half the continent under his control, or so Ariakas claimed. Kitiara ground her teeth as she read this. Solamnia would be under her control now if Ariakas had permitted it. As for Lucien, what had he conquered? Kender, elves, and goat herders. Bah!

Ariakas said he hoped her meeting with Highlord Feal-Thas was going well. Kitiara growled deep in her throat at this. He expected her to send him a full report.

Kitiara sat for a long while, pondering the message. Something was wrong. Ariakas had never before written her anything as formal and stiff as this. The letter was not even in his handwriting. He had dictated it. Always before he had written to her personally.

There were many reasons why Ariakas might have dictated this message—he was fighting a war, trying to govern a large region, searching for the Green Gemstone man, dealing with an impatient goddess. Small wonder if he did not have time to write her a personal note.

Still, Kit was bothered by this and by other small details. She had expected him to ask for her report in person and he had instead told her to write it. He had said nothing about future orders. He had said nothing about Solamnia. Kitiara decided she would leave the blue wing to search for Tanis around Thorbardin. She would travel immediately to Neraka to find out what was going on.

She rolled up the missive in a tight twist and held it to the flame floating atop the seal oil. She watched the fire consume it, dropping it only when the flame was about to burn her fingers.

The next thirty or so dispatches were all from Fewmaster Toede. Kit glanced over them, grinning. They were copies of dispatches sent to commanders of the forces of the Red Dragonarmy containing orders that contradicted his former orders that countermanded his previous orders. Kitiara figured the commanders simply tossed these away, which is what she was prepared to do when she noticed that one was addressed to her.

Kitiara settled down and prepared to enjoy it, figuring the inanities of the hobgoblin would at least give her a good laugh.

The opening salutation did just that. Written in a hand certainly not belonging to the hobgoblin, it took up half a page and began by addressing Kitiara as: "Most Exalted, Revered and Esteemed Highlord, Honored Among Men and Gods and Nations," and it went on from there. She skipped over most of it to reach the main body of the missive, which began by describing the pleasure the Fewmaster had received from meeting her and expressing his ardent desire that he be permitted to polish her boots again the next time they met, which he hoped and prayed to Her Dark Majesty would be soon.

Then Kitiara's chuckles ceased. She sat bolt upright and reread the paragraph.

My spies in Thorbardin report that those persons in whom you most graciously expressed an interest, these being those assassins who murdered our much beloved and deeply lamented Lord Verminaard (may Chemosh embrace him) have left the mountain fastness of the dwarves and are reportedly en route to Tarsis, trying to flee the justice they so richly deserve.

"Tarsis . . ." murmured Kitiara, interested. She read on.

Immediately upon receiving this news, I put out a bounty on these criminals and I fully expect they will be captured soon. Knowing that your most gracious lordship was interested in seeing these miscreants brought to account and for your lordship's further edification, I have included here within a copy of the bounty notice I drew up, complete with the names and descriptions of these assassins. I have sent these notices to the commanders of our illustrious forces in the region. I confidently expect to have these criminals under lock and key at any moment.

Kitiara doubted if any of the commanders had even bothered to look at it.

Of course, "these criminals" might not be Tanis and his friends. There were, by report, eight hundred human refugees holed up in Thorbardin. She fished out the notice that had been rolled up in the center of the Highlord's letter and, her heart beating fast, scanned over the names.

Her past seemed to leap out at her, as it had done in the chamber with the guardian. Faces rose from the mists of time.

Tanis Half-elven. Bearded half-elf. Thought to be the leader. Of course, Kit thought to herself. As always.

Sturm Brightblade. Human. Solamnic Knight. Her tryst with Sturm had certainly not gone as planned.

Flint Fireforge. Dwarf. Grumpy old Flint. He'd never liked her much.

Tasslehoff Burrfoot. Kender. Hard to believe that little nuisance was still alive.

Raistlin and Caramon Majere. Human. Wizard, warrior. Her little brothers. Half-brothers, really. They had her to thank for their success.

Tika Waylan. Human. The name sounded familiar, but Kit couldn't place her.

Elistan. Human. Cleric of Paladine. Dangerous rabble-rouser. How dangerous could the cleric of a weak god like Paladine be?

Gilthanas, elf; Goldmoon, cleric of Mishakal . . . yes, yes . . . Kit scanned past them impatiently. Where was the name she sought . . .

Laurana. Elf princess. Capture alive! The elf female is the property of Fewmaster Toede and is not to be harmed, but should be sent back immediately under heavy guard to the Fewmaster. Reward offered.

"So here you are," Kit said, displeased. "Still with him."

She stared hard at the name as though she could conjure up a picture of her: blonde, slender, beautiful.

Friends, family. Lover. Rival. Heading for Tarsis. So, presumably, was Derek Crownguard! Her spies had told her he was going to Tarsis in search of some library. What if they met? Sturm and Derek were fellow knights. They undoubtedly knew each other. Perhaps they were friends. What would be the consequences if they encountered one another in Tarsis? Would Derek mention her name?

Kit thought it over and didn't see why he should, yet the possibility that he might reveal he had seen her and talked to her was troubling. She wished she hadn't told him her real name. That had been a bit of bravado.

Tarsis—a day's journey by dragon.

Kitiara sat for a long time gazing at the flames flickering in the bowl of seal oil, making plans. She did not forget Ariakas. Those who forgot Ariakas tended to live very short lives. He had to be appeased, kept happy. He had to be made to think that what she was about to do was being done for him.

She smiled and shook herself from her scheming and went back to finish Toede's letter, expecting to be entertained by more evidence of the hob's stupidity. Unfortunately, his stupidity did not prove to be that entertaining. Kitiara sucked in an angry breath that exploded in a curse.

"You bloody fool!"

She bounded to her feet, crumpling the letter in her hand. She started to hurl it into the flames, then checked herself. She made herself read it again, but it didn't improve the second or third time. She then threw it into the flames and watched it and all her plans go up in smoke.

The idiot hobgoblin was going to attack Tarsis!

She knew why. The red dragons were putting pressure on Toede to take them into battle, and although the hob's guts spilled out over his belt he apparently didn't have enough to stand up to the dragons.

Toede should be massing his forces to attack Thorbardin, concentrating on that. Instead he was committing his forces to an assault on a city that had no military value and little wealth, a city he could not hope to keep. He simply did not have troops enough to occupy it. Once, Tarsis might have been a worthy prize, back before the Cataclysm when the city was a seaport. After the fiery mountain struck, the sea departed, leaving Tarsis landlocked, its merchants bankrupt.

She had no idea what Toede was thinking. The answer was—he wasn't. Kitiara was on her feet, prepared to fly to Haven to try to put a stop to this when she realized, suddenly, that she might be able to use this inane decision on the part of the hob to her advantage.

She recalled the date he'd given for the attack—a fortnight from now. She did not have much time and there was a lot to be done—and done circumspectly. Not even Skie must suspect her true motives. She tucked the sheet of parchment with the names and descriptions of the assassins of Lord Verminaard beneath her shirt, took a couple of swigs of dwarf spirits to enable her to endure the freezing cold of the journey, and, bundled in furs, she gathered up her gear and went out to meet the dragon.

"Where are we bound?" Skie asked. He was in a hurry to leave.

"Thorbardin to fetch the blue wing," said Kitiara. "Then we're going to Tarsis."

Skie snaked his head around to stare at her. "Tarsis! What are we doing in Tarsis?"

"I'll explain later," Kit said, her voice resounding hollowly from inside the horned helm.

Skie wanted to hear more about this crazy decision to bring the blue wing to Tarsis, but he decided to wait to discuss it some place where his tail wasn't stuck to the ice. He spread his wings, wrenched his tail loose, gave a great leap off his powerful hind legs, and soared thankfully into the crystalline blue sky.

BOOK II

1

AN OffERING to ZEboim.
DEREk quotes the Measure.

erek Crownguard and his fellow knights, Brian Donner and Aran Tallbow, stood at the rail of a merchant ship, watching their entry into the harbor of Rigitt, a port city located about seventy miles from Tarsis. The ship, known as the *Marigold*, named for the captain's daughter, had encountered fair weather and smooth seas the entire way.

Aran Tallbow stood head and shoulders over his fellow knights. Aran was a large man and he lived large, being jovial, good-natured, and fun-loving. He had sandy red hair and his mustaches—the traditional mustaches of a Solamnic knight—were long and flowing. He was fond of a "wee dram" as the dwarves say and carried a small flask in a leather holder attached to his sword belt. Inside the flask was the finest brandywine, which he sipped continually. He was never drunk, just always in a good humor. His laughter came from his belly and was as large as himself. He might seem an unlikely knight, but Aran Tallbow was a fierce warrior, his courage and skill in battle renowned. Not even Derek could fault him for that.

As the ship sailed into the harbor of Rigitt, the knights watched with amusement as the sailors offered up gifts of thanksgiving. The gifts ranged from necklaces made of shells to small wooden carvings of various monsters of the deep, all handmade by the sailors during the voyage. Chanting and singing their thanks for a safe journey, they tossed the gifts into the water.

"What is that word they keep repeating, sir?" Aran asked the captain. "Sounds like 'Zeboim, Zeboim'."

"That's it exactly, sir," said the captain. "Zeboim, goddess of the sea. You should make an offering to her yourselves, my lords. She doesn't take kindly to being slighted."

"Despite the fact there has been no sign of this goddess for over three hundred years?" Aran asked, with a wink at his friends.

"Just because we've heard no word from her, nor seen a sign, doesn't mean Zeboim's not keeping her eye on us," said the captain gravely.

He leaned over the rail as he spoke to drop a pretty bracelet made of blue crystals into the green water. "Thank you, Zeboim," he called out. "Bless our journey home!"

Derek watched with stern disapproval. "I can understand ignorant sailors believing in superstitious nonsense, but I can't believe that you, Captain, an educated man, take part in such a ritual."

"For one, my men would mutiny if I did not, my lord," said the captain, "and for another"—he shrugged—"it's better to be safe than sorry, especially where the Sea Witch is concerned. Now, if you gentlemen will excuse me, as we are coming into port, I have to attend to my duties."

The knights stood beside the railing, observing the sights and sounds of the port. With winter fast closing in, the port was almost empty except for the fishing vessels that braved all but the fiercest winter gales.

"Beg pardon, m'luds," came a voice behind them.

The three knights turned to see one of the sailors bowing and bobbing to them. They knew this man well. He was the oldest aboard ship. He claimed to have been a sailor for sixty years, saying he had gone to sea as a lad at the age of ten. He was wizened and bent, his face burnt brown by the sun and wrinkled with age. He could still climb the ropes as fast as the young men, however. He could predict the coming of a storm by watching the way the gulls flew, and he claimed he could talk to dolphins. He had survived a shipwreck, saying he had been rescued from drowning by a beautiful sea elf.

"For you both, m'luds," the old man said, gumming the words, for he was missing most of his teeth to scurvy. "For to give to the Sea Witch."

He held in his hands two carved wooden animals, and these he presented with a bob and a bow and a toothless grin to Aran and Brian.

"What is it?" Brian asked, examining the small hand-carved wooden animal.

"It looks like a wolf," Aran remarked.

"Yes, m'lud. Wolf," said the old man, touching his hand to his forehead. "One fer both." He pointed a gnarled finger first at Aran, then to Brian. "Give 'em to the Sea Witch. So she'll take kindly to you."

"Why wolves, Old Salt?" Aran asked. "Wolves are not very sealike. Wouldn't a whale suit her better?"

"I was told wolves in a dream," said the old man, his shrewd eyes glinting. He pointed to the sea. "Give 'em to the goddess. Ask 'er for 'er blessing."

"You do and I'll bring you up on charges before the Council," Derek stated.

Derek was not noted for his sense of humor, but he did sometimes indulge in small dry jokes (so dry and so small they often went unnoticed). He might be teasing, but then again, he might not. Brian couldn't tell.

Not that it mattered with Aran, who was quick to turn anything into a jest.

"You frighten me. What would be the charges, Derek?" Aran asked with mock concern.

"Idol worship," said Derek.

"Hah! Hah!" Aran's laughter went rolling over the water. "You're just jealous because you didn't get a wolf."

Derek had kept to their cabin during the voyage, spending his time reading the copy of the Measure he carried with him, making notations in the margins. He left the cabin only to take daily exercise on the deck, which meant that he walked up and down it for an hour, or to dine with the captain. Aran had roamed the deck from morning to night, mingling freely with the sailors, learning "the ropes" and dancing the hornpipe. He had undertaken to scramble up the rigging and had nearly broken his neck when he fell from the yardarm.

Brian had spent most of his time at sea trying to restrain the high spirits of Aran.

"So I just toss this into the water . . . " said Aran to the old man, prepared to suit his actions to his words. "Do I say a prayer—"

"You do not," said Derek sternly. He reached out and plucked the wolf carving from Aran's hand and gave it back to the old man. "Thank you, mate, but these knights have their swords. They don't need a blessing."

Derek looked pointedly at Brian, who, muttering his thanks, handed his wolf to the old man.

"Are you certain sure, m'luds?" the old man asked, eyeing them intently. His shrewd scrutiny made Brian uncomfortable, but before he could respond Derek cut him off.

"We have no time for fairy tales," Derek said tersely. "Gentlemen, we will be going ashore soon and we have our packing to finish."

He left the railing and went striding across the deck.

"You give it to the goddess for me," said Aran to the old man, clapping him on the shoulder, "with my thanks."

Glancing back, Brian saw the old man still standing there, still watching them. Then the captain's voice rang out with an order to all hands to prepare to drop anchor. The old man tossed the wolf carvings overboard and dashed off to obey.

Derek disappeared below decks, heading to the small cabin the three knights shared. Aran followed after him, taking a pull from his flask as he went. Brian lingered to gaze out to sea. The breeze blew off the glacier that was far to the south and carried with it the nip of winter. The waves were sun-dappled gold on top, blue below. The wind plucked at the hem of his cloak. Sea birds wheeled in the sky, or bobbed up and down placidly on the surface of the water.

Brian wished he'd taken the old man's wolf carving. He wished he'd made an offering to the sea goddess, whoever she was. He imagined her: beautiful and capricious, dangerous and deadly. Brian lifted his hand to salute her.

"Thank you for a safe voyage, my lady," he said, half-mocking and half-serious.

"Brian!" Derek's irate voice echoed up from down below.

"Coming!" Brian called.

———————————

The knights did not stay long in Rigitt. They hired horses for the journey north to Tarsis that would take them across the Plains of Dust. The road was still passable, though there had been snow up north around Thorbardin, or so Aran heard from a drinking companion, a mercenary who had just traveled that route.

"He advised us not to stay inside Tarsis," Aran told them, as they were loading supplies onto the horses. "He suggests we make camp in the hills and enter the city during the day. He said we should keep the fact that we're Knights of Solamnia to ourselves. The Tarsians have no love for us, it seems."

"The Measure states: 'A knight should walk openly in the sunshine, proudly proclaiming his nobility to the world'," Derek quoted.

"And if the Tarsians toss us out of the city on our noble posteriors, what of our mission to find the dragon orb?" asked Aran, grinning.

"They won't toss us out. You have this information on the authority of some rag-tag sellsword," said Derek disparagingly.

"The captain told me much the same, Derek," Brian said.

"Prior to the Cataclysm, the knights made Tarsis a Lord City of Solamnia, despite the fact that the city was hundreds of miles away. That way, the knights could protect the city from enemies. Then came the Cataclysm and the knights couldn't protect themselves, much less a city far from Solamnia. The knights who had lived in Tarsis—those who survived—returned to Palanthas, leaving the Tarsians to fight their battles alone."

"The Tarsians have never forgiven us for abandoning them," Brian concluded.

"Perhaps we could find a loophole—" Aran began.

Brian shot him a warning glance, and Aran, rubbing his nose, rephrased his suggestion.

"Perhaps the Measure makes some provision for such a delicate political situation."

"You should be better versed in the Measure," said Derek reprovingly, "otherwise you would know what it says. We will not enter Tarsis under false pretenses. We will present our credentials to the proper authorities and receive their permission to enter the city. There will be no trouble if we behave honorably, whereas there would be trouble if we were caught sneaking into the city like thieves."

"You make it sound like I'm suggesting we enter the city dressed in black with sacks over our heads," said Aran, chuckling. "There's no need to flaunt the fact that we're knights. We don't have to lie—just pack up our fancy tabards and the hand-tooled leather armor, replace our ornate helms with plain, take off the badges that mark our rank, remove our spurs, and wear ordinary, serviceable clothing. Maybe trim our mustaches."

That last was absolutely the wrong thing to say. Derek did not even deign to respond. He made a final adjustment to the horse's bridle, then left to go settle the bill with the innkeeper.

Aran shrugged and reached for his flask. He took a couple of sips, then offered the flask to Brian, who shook his head.

"Derek does talk sense, Aran," Brian argued. "It might go badly for us if we were caught trying to hide our true identities. Besides, I can't imagine the Tarsians would still hate us after three hundred years!"

Aran looked at him and smiled. "That's because you can't imagine hating anyone, Brian." He sauntered over to look out the stable door, then, seeing Derek was out of earshot, he returned to his friend. "Do you know why Lord Gunthar asked me to come on this mission?"

Brian could guess, but he didn't want to. "Aran, I don't think—"

"I'm here to make certain Derek doesn't screw it up," Aran said flatly. He took another drink.

Brian winced at the crudeness of the expression. "Derek's a Knight of the Rose, Aran. He's your superior and mine. According to the Measure—"

"Piss on the Measure!" said Aran sharply, his jovial mood evaporating. "I'm not going to allow this mission to fail because Derek cares more about adhering to some moldy old code of antiquated laws than he does about saving our nation."

"Perhaps without those laws and the noble tradition they represent, the nation wouldn't be worth saving," Brian remarked moodily.

Aran rested his hand affectionately on his friend's shoulder.

"You're a good man, Brian."

"So is Derek," said Brian earnestly. "We've known him a long time, Aran. We've both been his friends for years."

"True," said Aran, shrugging again, "and we've both seen how much he's hardened and changed."

Brian sighed. "Be patient with him, Aran. He's suffered a lot. The loss of castle, his brother's terrible death . . . "

"I will be patient," said Aran, "up to a point. Now I'm going to indulge in a stirrup cup. Join me?"

Brian shook his head. "Go on. I'll wait for Derek."

Aran mounted his horse and rode off to enjoy a final mug of ale and to refill his flask before starting out.

Brian remained in the stable, adjusting the horse's bridle. Damn Aran anyway! Brian wished Aran hadn't told him the true reason he'd come. Brian didn't like to think Lord Gunthar trusted Derek so little he'd set a friend to spy on him, and Brian didn't like hearing Aran had accepted such a demeaning assignment. Knights did not spy on each other. That must be in the Measure somewhere.

If so, Derek didn't quote those parts, for he had his own spies in the court of Lord Gunthar. Perhaps Derek's spies had told him that Aran was a spy. Brian leaned his head against the horse's neck. He could almost believe Queen Takhisis had returned to the world, planting the seeds of discord among those who had once been the champions of honor and valor. The seeds had taken root in fear and were now flourishing into noxious weeds of hatred and mistrust.

"Where is Aran?" Derek's voice roused Brian from his dark reflections.

"He went to get some ale," Brian said.

"We're not on a kender outing," Derek said grimly. "He takes nothing seriously, and now I suppose we must go haul him out of some bar."

Derek was wrong. They found Aran, wiping foam from his mouth, waiting for them on the road that led to Tarsis.

The three set out, with Aran in the middle, Derek on his right, and Brian on his left. He recalled with sudden vividness another quest, their very first.

"Do you remember when the three of us were squires, and we were tired of tilting at the quintain and whacking each other with wooden swords. We decided to prove ourselves and so we—"

"—decided to go to Nightlund to seek the death knight!" Aran began to chuckle. "By my soul, I had not thought of that in a long time. We rode three days into what we fancied was Nightlund, though in truth we never got close, and then we came to that empty castle. It was deserted. The walls were cracked, the battlements crumbling. One of the towers was charred and burned, and we knew we'd found it—Dargaard Keep. The accursed home of the dread Lord Soth." Aran's chuckles turned to laughter. "Do you remember what happened next?"

"I'm not likely to forget," said Brian. "I lost five years of my life that night. We camped out near the keep to keep watch on it, and sure enough, we saw a strange blue light flickering in one of the windows."

"Ha, ha! The blue light!" Aran guffawed.

"We girded on our armor—"

"—that didn't fit us, because it was stolen from our masters," Aran recalled. "All of us were scared out of our wits, but we would none of us admit it and so we went forth."

"Derek was our leader. Remember, Derek? You gave the signal, and we charged inside and"—Brian could barely speak for mirth—"we were met by a dwarf—"

"—who'd set up an illegal spirit distillery inside the keep . . ." Aran roared with laughter. "The blue light we saw was the fire cooking his mash! He thought we were there to steal his brew and he came roaring at us from the shadows, waving that bloody great ax. He looked ten feet tall, I swear!"

"And we gallant knights ran off in three different directions with him chasing after us, shouting he was going to chop off our ears!"

Aran was doubled over the pommel of his saddle. Brian was laughing so hard, he could barely see. He wiped his streaming eyes and glanced over at Derek.

The knight sat bolt upright on his horse. He gazed straight ahead, slightly frowning. Brian's laughter trailed off.

"Don't you remember that, Derek?" he asked.

"No," said Derek. "I don't."

He spurred his horse to a gallop, making it clear he wanted to ride alone.

Aran brought out his flask, then fell into line behind Derek. Brian chose to bring up the rear. There were no more stories, no more laughter. As for singing songs of heroic deeds to enliven the journey, Brian tried to recall one, but found he couldn't.

Singing would only annoy Derek anyway.

The three rode north in silence, as the gray clouds massed and the snow began to fall.

2

Abrupt end of a peaceful journey.
The Measure reconsidered.

 he journey to Tarsis was long, cold and miserable. The wind blew incessantly across the Plains of Dust and was both a curse and a blessing; a curse in that its chill fingers plucked aside cloaks and jabbed through the warmest clothing, a blessing in that it kept the road clear of mounding snow drifts.

The knights had brought firewood with them, figuring there would be little chance of finding wood on the way. They did not have to make use of it, however, for they were invited to spend the first night with the nomads who lived in this harsh land.

The Plainsmen gave them shelter consisting of a hide tent and food for themselves and their horses. All this, yet they never spoke a word to them. The knights woke in the gray of dawn to find the Plainsmen dismantling their tent around them. By the time the knights had made their morning ablutions, the nomads were ready to depart. Derek sent the affable Aran to give the Plainsmen their thanks.

"Very strange," Aran commented on his return, as Brian and Derek were readying the horses.

"What is?" Derek asked.

"The man we took for their leader seemed to be trying to tell me something. He kept pointing north and frowning and shaking his head. I asked him what he meant, but he didn't speak Common or any other language I tried. He pointed north three times, then he turned and walked off."

"Perhaps the road to the north is blocked by snow," Brian suggested.

"Could be what he meant, I suppose, but I don't think so. It seemed more serious than that, as if he were trying to warn us of something bad up ahead."

"I was thinking to myself last night it was odd to find the Plainsmen traveling this time of year," said Brian. "Don't they usually make permanent camp somewhere during the winter months?"

"Maybe they're fleeing something," said Aran. "They were in a hurry this morning, and the chief certainly looked grim."

"Who can tell what such savages do or why," said Derek dismissively.

"Still, we should be on our guard," Brian suggested.

"I am always on my guard," returned Derek.

◆━━━━━━━━━━━━━━━━━▸▸◀◆━━━━━━━

The snow let up and a freshening wind whisked away the clouds. The sun shone, warming them and making their journey more pleasant. At Derek's insistence, they still wore the accoutrements of knighthood: tabards marked with the rose, the crown, or the sword, depending on their rank; their ornate helms; tall boots with the spurs each had won; and fine woolen cloaks. They had covered many miles the day before and hoped that by hard riding and stopping only long enough to rest the horses they would reach Tarsis before nightfall.

The day passed uneventfully. They did not find any places where the road was blocked. They met no other people, nor did they see signs anyone else had traveled this way. They gave up trying to puzzle out what the Plainsman had meant.

Toward late afternoon, the clouds returned and the sun disappeared. The snow started, falling furiously for a time, then the squall lifted and the sun came back. This continued on the rest of the afternoon, the knights riding from patches of snow into patches of sunlight and back to snow, until the weather grew so confused—as Aran quipped—they could see the snowflakes glitter in the sun.

During one of the flurries, the knights topped a slight rise and found, on their way down, the vast expanse of the plains spread out before them. They could see bands of snow glide across the prairie, and during a break in one of the small storms, a walled city.

The city disappeared in a sudden burst of blowing snow, but there was no doubt that it was Tarsis. The sight cheered them, as did the thought of an inn with a blazing fire and hot food. Aran had said no more about camping in the hills.

"The captain of the ship recommended an inn known as the Red Dragon," Brian said.

"Not exactly a propitious name," Aran remarked dryly.

"You can throw salt over your shoulder and turn around in a circle thirteen times before you go inside," said Derek.

Aran looked at him in astonishment, then he caught Derek's smile. The smile was stiff, as if not much used, but he was smiling.

"I'll do that," Aran said, grinning.

Brian breathed a sigh of relief, glad to feel the tension between them ease. They rode on, climbing yet another gentle rise. Topping this one, they saw ahead of them a deep, rock-strewn gully spanned by a wooden bridge.

The knights halted as a sudden snow squall enveloped them in white, obscuring their vision. When the snow lessened and they could see the bridge again, Aran started to urge his horse forward. Derek raised a warding hand.

"Hold a moment," he said.

"Why?" Aran halted. "Did you see something?"

"I thought I did, before that last squall. I saw people moving on the other side of the bridge."

"No one there now," said Aran, rising in his saddle and gazing ahead.

"I can see for myself," said Derek. "That's what bothers me."

"This *would* be a good place for an ambush," observed Brian, loosening his sword in its scabbard.

"We could find another place to cross," Aran suggested. He was one of the few knights skilled in archery, and he reached for the bow he wore slung on his back.

"They've seen us. If we turn back, it will look suspicious. Besides," Derek added coolly, "I'd like to see who is lurking about this bridge and why."

"Maybe it's trolls," Aran said, grinning, recalling the old child's tale, "and we're the billy goats."

Derek pretended he hadn't heard. "The bridge is narrow. We'll have to cross in single-file. I will go first. Keep close behind me. No weapons, Aran. Let them think we haven't seen them."

Derek waited until another flurry of snow descended on them then touched his horse lightly on the flanks and started forward at a slow pace.

As his horse reached the bridge, Aran said in a low voice, "'It's only I, Billy Goat Gruff!'"

Derek half-turned in the saddle. "Damn it, Aran, be serious for once!"

Aran only laughed and urged his horse forward, falling in behind Derek. Brian, keeping watch over his shoulder, brought up the rear.

The knights rode slowly across the bridge. Though the snow concealed them, the horse's hooves clattered on the wooden planks, effectively announcing their coming. They kept their ears stretched, but could hear nothing. Brian, peering behind them through the intermittent flurries, saw no one following them. He might have concluded Derek was jumping at shadows, but he knew the man too well for that. Derek might be a prize ass at times, but he was an excellent soldier—intuitive and keenly observant. Even Aran, though he'd joked about billy goats, was not joking now. He had his hand on his sword's hilt and was keeping close watch.

Derek was about half-way across the bridge. Aran was coming along behind him, his horse clattering over the wooden slats, and Brian's horse was behind Aran's, when three strangers suddenly reared up out of the snow and began walking toward them. The strangers were enveloped in long cloaks that trailed over the snowy ground. They kept their hoods drawn over their heads, making it impossible to see their faces. Large leather gloves covered their hands, and they wore heavy boots.

Whoever they were, the horses didn't like them. Derek's horse snorted and laid back its ears. Aran's horse danced sideways, while Brian's nervously backed and shied.

"Well met, fellow travelers!" one of the strangers called out as he ambled toward the bridge. "Where are you bound in such foul weather?"

Brian stirred in the saddle. The stranger spoke Common well enough and was trying to sound friendly, but Brian tensed. He had detected a faint sibilant hissing at the end of the word "travelers." Thus might a draconian speak the word. And draconians had been known to try to disguise their scaly bodies in long cloaks with hoods. Brian wondered if his companions had heard the hiss too and if they were likewise on their guard. He didn't dare turn to look at them or act as if anything was out of the ordinary.

Then Aran, riding ahead of him, said softly in Solamnic, "Not trolls. Lizards."

Brian shifted his hand beneath his cloak to grasp the hilt of his sword.

Derek eyed the strangers warily, then said, "Since we are on the road to Tarsis and that city lies directly ahead of us, it would seem safe to say that Tarsis is where we are bound."

"Mind if we ask you a few questions?" the draconian inquired, still friendly.

"Yes, we do," said Derek. "Now stand aside and let us cross."

"We're looking for some people," the draconian continued, as if he hadn't heard. "We have a message for them from our master."

Brian caught movement out of the corner of his eye. A fourth draconian was off to the side of the road, half-hidden behind a signpost. Hooded and cloaked like the others, the draconian was far shorter than his three companions. He was moving about inside his cloak, and Brian thought perhaps the creature was about to draw a weapon. Instead, the draconian brought forth a document of some sort. The creature consulted the document, then called out something to his comrades and shook his head.

The leader glanced over at the draconian with the paper and then, shrugging, said affably, "My mistake. A good journey to you gentlemen," and turned to walk off.

The knights stared at each other.

"Keep riding," Derek ordered.

The knights rode on. Derek's horse made it across the bridge, and Aran's was close behind when a gust of wind swirled down the gully, seized the corner of Derek's cape and blew it back over his shoulder. The rose of his Order, embroidered on his tabard, flared bright red, the only color in the white, snow-covered landscape.

"Solamnics!" The word hissed from the short, squat draconian by the sign post. "Kill them!"

The draconians whipped around. They flung back their cloaks, revealing themselves as baaz draconians, the footsoldiers of the dragonarmies. Snatching off their gloves, they drew long, curve-bladed swords. Their bodies might be covered in scales and they held their weapons in clawed hands, but they were fierce and intelligent fighters, as the three knights had reason to know, for they had fought against them in Vingaard and at Castle Crownguard.

Sword in hand, Derek spurred his horse directly at the lead draconian, trusting that the beast's stamping hooves would force the attacking draconian to retreat or be trampled. Unfortunately, Derek's horse was a hired nag, not a trained war horse. The horse was terrified by the strange-smelling lizard-man and it reared back on its hind legs, whinnying frantically and nearly dumping Derek out of the saddle.

Derek struggled to calm the horse and keep his seat, and for the moment he could pay attention to little else. Seeing one knight in trouble, a draconian came at him, sword raised. Aran rode his horse between Derek's plunging steed and his attacker. Slashing at the draconian with his sword, Aran cut the monster across the face.

Blood sprayed. A large chunk of bloody flesh sagged loose from the creature's jaw. The draconian hissed in pain, but he kept coming and tried to jab the curve-bladed sword into Aran's thigh. Aran kicked at the blade with his booted foot and knocked it from the draconian's hand.

Brian spurred his horse off the bridge, heading to block off the third draconian, who was running to join the others. As he rode, he kept an eye on the short, squat draconian near the signpost and saw in amazement that the creature appeared to be growing! Then Brian realized the draconian was not growing; he was merely standing upright. A bozak draconian, he had been squatting comfortably on his haunches. Now he rose up to his full seven-foot height.

The bozak did not reach for a weapon. He lifted his voice in a chant and raised his hands, fingers extended toward Aran.

Brian bellowed, "Aran! Duck!"

Aran did not waste time asking why but flung himself forward, pressing against his horse's neck. An eerie pinkish light flared through the falling snow. Balls of fire shot from the draconian's fingers. The missiles whistled harmlessly over Aran's back, showering sparks as they passed.

Shouting challenges, Brian drew his sword and galloped his horse toward the bozak, hoping to stop the creature from casting another spell. He heard, behind him, the clash of steel and Derek yelling something, but Brian did not dare lose sight of his enemy long enough to see what was happening.

The bozak coolly ignored Brian. The draconian did not believe he was in any danger, and Brian realized there must be a good reason for this. Brian looked about. A draconian was running alongside his horse, ready to spring at him and try to drag him to the ground.

Brian made an awkward, back-handed slash with his sword, and he must have hit the draconian, for blood spurted and the creature dropped out of sight. Brian tried to stop his horse's forward motion, but the beast was terrified by the smell of blood and the shouts and the fighting and was completely out of control. Wild-eyed, spittle flying, the horse carried Brian closer to the bozak. The draconian raised his clawed hands, fingers splayed, pointing at Brian.

Brian flung his sword into the snow and leaped off the maddened horse, hurling himself at the bozak. Brian slammed into the draconian, taking the bozak completely by surprise. The fiery missiles shot off in all directions. The bozak, arms flailing wildly, toppled over backward with Brian on top of him.

Brian scrambled to his feet. The bozak, jarred by the fall, was fumbling for his sword. Brian snatched the knife at his belt and stabbed it with all his strength into the bozak's throat. The draconian gurgled and choked as blood welled around the knife, and the creature glared at him in fury that rapidly dimmed as death took him.

Remembering just in time that bozaks were as dangerous dead as they were alive, Brian shouted a warning to his friends, then turned and hurled himself as far from the creature as he could manage. He landed belly-first on the snow-covered ground, bruising his ribs on a rock, just as an explosion sent a wave of heat washing over him. He lay still a moment, half-stunned by the blast, then looked back.

The bozak was charred bone, smoldering flesh, and fragments of armor. Aran, swearing loudly, stood over his dead foe, trying to wrench free his sword encased in the stony statue that had been a baaz. Aran gave his sword a mighty yank. The stone crumbled to ash and he nearly went over backward. He caught his balance, and, still swearing, wiped blood from a cut on his chin.

"Anyone hurt?" Derek called out. He stood beside his shivering horse. His sword was wet with blood. A pile of ashes lay at his feet.

Aran grunted in response.

Brian was looking about for his horse, only to see it galloping madly across the plains, heading for home. He whistled and shouted, all in vain. The horse paid no heed, kept running.

"There goes my gear!" Brian exclaimed in dismay. "The rest of my armor, food, my clothes . . ."

He'd been wearing his breastplate and helm, but he was sorry to lose the remainder: grieves and bracers, gloves . . .

Shaking his head, Brian bent to retrieve his sword and saw the document the bozak had been consulting lying in the snow. The draconian must have tossed it down in order to concentrate on his spellcasting. Curious, Brian picked it up.

"What in the Abyss are draconians doing camped out by a bridge in the snow?" Aran demanded. "This doesn't make any sense."

"Ambushing travelers makes sense for them," said Derek.

"They weren't going to ambush us. They were going to let us go until they saw that bright red rose of yours and realized we were Solamnic knights," Aran returned.

"Bah! They would have jumped us from behind no matter what," said Derek.

"I'm not so sure," said Brian, rising to his feet, the document in his hand. "I think they're bounty hunters. I saw the bozak consulting this as we rode up. He saw that we didn't match the descriptions, and he ordered the baaz to let us go."

The document contained a list of names, accompanied by descriptions, and amounts to be paid in reward for their capture. Tanis Half-elven was the first name on the list, Flint Fireforge was another with the word "dwarf" written alongside. There was a kender, Tasslehoff Burrfoot, two elves, a wizard, Raistlin Majere, and a man listed as a cleric of Paladine.

"And look at this." Brian indicated a name. "An old friend of ours."
Sturm Brightblade. Beside his name was written, *Solamnic knight.*

"Huh! Brightblade is not a knight," said Derek, frowning.

Aran looked at him in astonishment. "Who cares if he's a knight or not?" He jabbed at the document. "This is why the draconians were keeping a watch on this bridge. They were looking for these people, one of whom happens to be a friend of ours and a Solamnic."

"A friend of yours, perhaps," said Derek. "Brightblade is no friend of mine."

"I don't think we should stand here arguing," Brian pointed out. "There could be more draconians around. Tarsis might have fallen into enemy hands for all we know." Folding the paper carefully, he thrust it into his belt.

"Not likely," said Derek. "We would have heard news of that in Rigitt, and these draconians were in disguise. If they were in control of Tarsis, they would be swaggering about letting everyone know they were in charge. They were here in secret, acting on their own."

"Or on orders from their master," Aran commented. "Did you notice—they were wearing blue insignia like the draconians that attacked us in Solamnia."

"That is odd, come to think of it," Brian said. "According to reports, the red wing of the dragonarmy is nearer to Tarsis than the blue."

"Blue or red, they are all our foes, and Brian is right," said Derek. "We have already been here too long. Brian, you ride with Aran. His horse is the largest and strongest. We'll transfer his gear to my horse."

They shifted the saddlebags from Aran's horse to Derek's, then Aran mounted and pulled Brian up behind him. Brian's horse had long since disappeared.

Aran and Brian started to canter off down the road.

"Where are you going?" Derek demanded.

"Tarsis," said Aran, halting. "Where else?"

"I don't think we should enter Tarsis openly," said Derek. "Not until we know more about what is going on."

"You mean, not announce our noble presence?" Aran exclaimed in mock horror. "I'm shocked, Derek, shocked that you would even suggest such a thing! I may never recover." He drew out his flask and took a consoling drink.

Derek gave him an angry look and did not answer. Brian glanced at the sky. The clouds were swirling, gray over white. A pale light gleamed from beneath them. If the clouds cleared, the night would be frigid.

"Where do we go?" he asked.

"According to the map, there is wooded hill country west of Tarsis. We will camp there for the night, keep watch on the city, and decide what to do in the morning." Derek turned his horse's head, striking off across the plains.

Aran, chuckling to himself, followed along behind him.

"Interesting to see Brightblade's name on a bounty list," Aran said to Brian. "And keeping strange company from the looks of it—elves, dwarves and the like. I suppose that's what comes of living in a cross-roads town like Solace. I've heard it's a wild place. Did he ever say anything to you about his life there?"

"No, he never discussed it. But then, Sturm was always a very private man. He rarely spoke about himself at all. He was more concerned about his father."

"Too bad about that." Aran sighed. "I wonder what sort of trouble Sturm's in now?"

"Whatever it is, he's in this part of Ansalon—either that, or someone thinks he is," said Brian.

"I'd like to see Brightblade again. He's a good man, despite what *some* think." Aran cast a dour glance at Derek. "I don't suppose it's likely, though."

"You never know who'll you'll meet on the road these days," said Brian.

"That's true enough," Aran stated, laughing, and he dabbed at his chin to see if it was still bleeding.

———————

The three knights spent a cold and cheerless evening huddled around a fire in a shallow cave in the hills above Tarsis. The snow-storm had blown itself out and the night was clear, with both Solinari and Lunitari shedding silver and red light.

From their camp, the knights could see one of the main gates, closed and barred until morning. Guards manned the walls, pacing off the watch in slow, measured tread. The city was dark; most people were in their beds.

"The city seems quiet enough," said Brian, when Aran came to relieve him, taking his turn at watch.

"Yeah, and draconians not ten miles from here," said Aran, shaking his head.

The knights were up early to see the gates open. No one was waiting to enter and only a few people departed (mostly kender being escorted out of town). Those who left took the road to Rigitt. The gate guards remained in their towers, venturing out into the cold only when forced to do so by someone wanting admittance. The guards walking the battlements did so in bored fashion, pausing often to warm themselves at fires burning in large iron braziers and to chat companionably. Tarsis was the picture of a city at peace with itself and all the world.

"If draconians were watching for these people on a bridge leading to Tarsis, you can bet they're also keeping an eye out for them in Tarsis itself," said Brian. "They'll have someone lurking about near the gates."

Aran winked at Brian. "So, Derek, are we going to march into Tarsis wearing full knightly regalia and carrying banners with the kingfisher and the rose?"

Derek looked very grim.

"I have consulted the Measure," he said, bringing out the well-worn volume. "It states that fulfillment of a quest of honor undertaken by a knight with sanction from the Council should be the knight's first priority. If the fulfillment of the quest of honor requires that the knight conceal his true identity, succeeding at the quest takes precedence over the duty of the knight to proudly proclaim his allegiance."

"You lost me somewhere around precedence and fulfillment," said Aran. "In words of one syllable, Derek, do we disguise ourselves or not?"

"According to the Measure, we may disguise ourselves without sacrificing our honor."

Aran's lips twitched. He caught Brian's warning glance, however, and swallowed his glib comment along with a gulp from the flask.

The knights spent the rest of the day removing all their badges and insignia. They cut the embroidered decorations from their clothes and stowed away their armor in the back of the cave. They would wear their swords, and Aran would keep his bow and quiver of arrows. Weapons were not likely to cause comment, for no one went forth unarmed these days.

"All that's left of our knighthood is our mustaches," said Aran, tugging at his.

"Well, we're certainly not going to shave," said Derek sternly.

"Our mustaches will grow back, Derek," Aran said.

"No." Derek was adamant. "We will pull our hoods low and wrap scarves around our heads. As cold as it is, no one will pay any attention."

Aran rolled his eyes, but he accepted the ruling meekly, much to Derek's surprise.

"You owe Derek," said Brian, as he and Aran were arranging the screen of brush over the cave.

Aran grinned sheepishly. The knight's long, luxurious red mustache was his secret pride. "I guess I do. I would have shaved my mustache, mind you, but it would have been like cutting off my sword arm. Don't tell Derek, though. I'd never hear the end of it."

Brian shrugged. "It seems strange to me that we risk imperiling our mission for the sake of some fuzz on our upper lips."

"This is not to be termed 'fuzz'," said Aran severely, fondly smoothing his mustache. "Besides, it might actually look worse if we shaved. Our faces are tan from the sea voyage, and the white skin on our lips would look very suspicious, whereas, if we don't shave . . . well . . . I'm sure we won't be the only men in Tarsis with mustaches."

They decided to enter the city separately, their reasoning being that three armed men entering alone would cause less stir than three trying to enter together. They would meet at the library of Khrystann.

"Though we have no idea where this library is or how to find it," Aran remarked lightly. "Nor do we know what it is we're looking for once we get there. Nothing I like better than a well organized fiasco."

Bundled in their cloaks, their hoods pulled low and scarves wrapped around their faces from nose to neck, Aran and Brian watched Derek ride down out of the hills, heading for the main city gate.

"I don't see what we could do differently," Brian said.

Aran shifted restlessly in his saddle. His customary cheerfulness had left him suddenly, leaving him moody and edgy.

"What's wrong?" Brian asked. "Your flask empty?"

"Yes, but that's not it," Aran returned gloomily. He shifted again on his saddle, glancing around behind him. "There's a bad feel to the air. Don't you notice it?"

"The wind's changed direction, if that's what you mean," said Brian.

"Not that. More like a goose walking across my grave. Only in this case the goose has built a nest on it and hatched goslings. I felt the same way before the attack on Castle Crownguard. You'd better go, if you're going," Aran added abruptly.

Brian hesitated. He regarded his friend with concern. He'd seen Aran in all sorts of moods from wild to reckless to merry. He'd never seen him in a black mood like this.

"Go on." Aran waved his hand as though he were shooing the aforementioned geese. "I'll meet you in the library that was probably destroyed three hundred years ago."

"That isn't funny," Brian growled over his shoulder as he walked down the hill, heading for the gates of Tarsis.

"Sometimes I'm not," said Aran quietly.

3

The bargain.
The Library of Khrystann.

efore the Cataclysm, Tarsis had been known as Tarsis the Beautiful. When she looked into her mirror, she saw reflected there a city of culture and refinement, wealth, beauty, and charm. She spent money lavishly, and she had money to spend, for ships brought rich cargos to her ports and laid them at her feet. Lush gardens of flowering plants adorned her like jewels. Knights, lords, and ladies walked her tree-lined streets. Scholars came from hundreds of miles away to study at her library, for Tarsis was not only elegant and refined and lovely, she was learned, too. She looked out over her glittering bay and saw nothing but joy and happiness on her horizon.

Then the gods hurled the fiery mountain on Krynn, and Tarsis was forever changed. Her glittering bay vanished. The water receded. Her ships were stranded in the mud and muck of a wrecked harbor. Tarsis looked in the mirror and saw her beauty ruined, her rich clothes soiled and torn, her jewel-like gardens withered and dead.

Unlike many who suffer tragedy and adversity and have the

grace and dignity and courage to rise again, Tarsis let tragedy sink her. Wallowing in self-pity, she blamed the Knights of Solamnia for her downfall and drove the knights from their homes into exile. She blamed wizards, too, and dwarves and elves and anyone who was not "one of us." She blamed the wise men and women who had come there to study in the ancient Library of Khrystann, and she drove them out. She left the library in ruins and forbade anyone from entering it.

Tarsis turned mean and mercenary, covetous and grasping. She took no joy in beautiful things. The only beauty in her eyes was the glitter of steel coins. Her seaport was gone, but she still maintained overland trade routes and used her wiles to foster trade with her neighbors.

At last, more than three hundred years later, Tarsis could look in the mirror once again. She would never regain her former beauty, but she could at least dress herself up in her borrowed finery, rouge her cheeks and paint her lips. Sitting in the shadows where no one could see her clearly, she could pretend that she was once more Tarsis the Beautiful.

The city of Tarsis had been guarded by a twenty-foot-high stone wall, pierced by towers and gates at intervals, and by the sea. The wall ended at the harbor where the sea took over. Where the sea ended, the wall resumed. The wall remained, but the sea's absence left an unfortunate gap in the city's security.

A reduction in the population caused by the departure of sailors and ship builders, sail makers and merchants and all those who had depended on the sea for their living meant a drastic drop in tax revenues. Tarsis went from wealth to poverty literally overnight. There was no money to build a new stretch of twenty-foot-high wall. Five feet was about as much as could be managed. Besides, as one Tarsian lord said gloomily, they didn't need protection anyway. Tarsis had nothing anyone wanted.

That had been years ago. Tarsis was more prosperous now. The Tarsians had heard rumors of war in the north. They knew Solamnia had been attacked ("Snooty knights! Serves them right!"), and they had heard that the elves had been driven out of Qualinesti ("What could you expect of elves? Simpering cowards, all of them!"). There was talk that Pax Tharkas had fallen ("Pax what? Never heard of it.") Tarsis paid little heed to any of this. With prosperity had come complacency. Tarsis had been at peace forever, and her people saw no threat on their horizon, so why waste money on something as dull and prosaic as a wall when they could build fine houses and showy municipal structures? Thus the five-foot-wall remained.

The wall had two main iron-clad gates located in the north and the east. Derek was to enter by the northern gate, where traffic was deemed to be heaviest. Aran rode in through the eastern gate, and it fell to Brian to try to make his way on foot through the gate at the southern part of the city—the Harbor Wall, as it was known.

Being the weakest part of the city's defenses, the knights assumed the Harbor Wall would be the one most closely guarded. Derek's choice of Brian for this route was something of a back-handed compliment. He cited Brian's calm and unruffled demeanor, his quiet courage. He also mentioned that, of the three of them, Brian looked the least like a knight.

Brian accepted the truth of Derek's statement and was not offended. Although of noble birth, Brian had been raised to hard work, not privilege, as had the wealthy Derek. Brian's father had not inherited his bread; he'd been forced to earn it. An educated man, he had been hired as Derek's tutor, and he and his family were given housing at Castle Crownguard. Aran, son of a neighboring lord, was invited to come study with the other boys, and thus the three friends became acquainted.

Brian's lineage was not as long or as noble as Derek's and Aran's, and Brian felt the difference between them. Aran never alluded to it or thought anything about it. If Brian had been a fishmonger's son, Aran would have treated him the same. Derek never mentioned his background, never said an unkind or uncivil word to Brian or demeaned him in any way, yet, perhaps unconsciously, Derek drew a line between the two of them. On one side was Derek Crownguard and on the other side the son of the hired help. When Derek said that Brian didn't have the look of a knight, Derek wasn't being arrogant. He was just being Derek.

The day was sunny and cold, the air calm. Brian walked across the plains at an easy, measured pace, taking note of all who came and went. Each gate was guarded by two or three men, and these were all members of the Tarsian guard. He saw no signs of draconians.

Brian approached the gate cautiously, searching the shadows of the tower for anyone taking an unusual interest in people entering the city. A few loiterers were standing about, all of them bundled up against the cold. If one was a draconian, he would be difficult to spot.

The Tarsian guards stood huddled near a fire in an iron brazier and seemed reluctant to leave it. Brian continued walking toward the gate, and no one challenged him. The guards looked him over from a distance and didn't appear much interested in him, for they continued to hold their hands over the blaze. When Brian reached the gate, he came to a halt and looked at the guards.

Two of the guards turned to a third. Apparently it was his turn to deal with those who wanted to enter. Annoyed at being torn away from his warm place by the fire, the guard pulled a fur cap down about his ears and walked over to Brian.

"Name?" the guard asked.

"Brian Conner," said Brian.

"Where from?"

"Solamnia," said Brian. The guard would be able to tell as much by his accent.

The guard scowled and shoved the fur cap away from his ear to hear better.

"You're not one of them knight-fellows?" the guard demanded.

"No," said Brian. "I am a wine merchant. I heard there was the possibility of obtaining some very fine wines in Tarsis these days. What with the fall of Qualinesti and all," he added nonchalantly.

The guard frowned and said loudly, "No elf wine here. Nothing like that going on in Tarsis, sir." In a low voice, the guard added, "I've a cousin deals in that sort of 'hard-to-find' merchandise. Go to Merchant's Row and ask for Jen. She'll fix you up handsome."

"I will, sir, thank you," said Brian.

The guard gave him directions to find Merchant's Row and said, "Remember Jen," and told him he could enter. Brian tried, but the guard continued to stand in the gate, blocking his way.

Brian wondered what was going on, then he saw the guard surreptitiously rub his thumb and two fingers together. Brian reached into his purse and brought out a steel coin. He handed it to the guard, who snapped his hand shut over the coin and then stepped to one side.

"Have a pleasant stay in our fair city, sir," said the guard, as he touched his hat.

Glad that the scarf over his face hid his smile, Brian walked through the gate. He headed toward Merchant's Row, just in case the guard was watching him. The streets were crowded, despite the cold, with people going to work or to market or simply out for a walk now that the snow had ceased falling.

Once there, he'd make his way to the Upper City which, according to the Aesthetic Bertrem, was the last known location of the lost library. Brian glanced back over his shoulder occasionally to see if anyone was following him, but as far as he could tell, no one seemed the least bit interested in him. He hoped his companions had entered the city with similar ease.

The three knights met up with each other in the old part of the city. Derek and Aran had each gained access to the city without difficulty, though Derek had discovered, as had Brian, that entry came with a cost. The guard at the main gate had demanded two steel in payment, terming it a "head" tax. Aran had not been "taxed" at all, so perhaps there were still honest people in Tarsis, or so he said. He was the last to arrive; he'd stopped on the way to refill his flask and he was in a much better mood.

Both Aran and Derek had seen people standing about the gates, but they might have been nothing more than the usual idlers curious to see who came and went. That led them to talk of Sturm Brightblade and his strange companions.

"I never understood why you dislike Sturm Brightblade so much, Derek," Aran said, as they sat down on a crumbling garden wall to eat bread and meat, washed down—for Aran's part—with brandywine. "Or why you opposed his candidacy for knighthood."

"He did not have the proper upbringing," said Derek.

"You could say that about me," said Brian. "My father was your tutor."

"You were raised in my father's house among your peers," said Derek, "not in some border town on the edge of nowhere among outlandish folk. Besides, Brian, your father was a man of honor."

"Angriff Brightblade was honorable. He was just unfortunate," said Aran, shrugging. "According to Lord Gunthar—"

Derek snorted. "Gunthar was always an apologist for the Brightblades. Would you seriously recommend for knighthood a man who never knew his father? If Angriff *was* Sturm's father . . ."

"You have no right to say that, Derek!" stated Brian angrily.

Derek glanced at his friend. Brian was generally easy-going, slow to anger. He was angry now, and Derek realized that he'd gone too far. He had, after all, impugned the reputation of a noblewoman and that was very much against the Measure.

"I didn't mean to imply that Sturm was a bastard," Derek said gruffly. "I just find it damn odd that Sir Angriff suddenly packed off his wife and child to some place where he knew they would never have contact with anyone from Solamnia, as if he were ashamed of them."

"Or as if he were trying to save their lives," suggested Aran. He offered the flask around, got no takers, and so enjoyed it himself. "Angriff Brightblade had made some very bad enemies, poor man. He did what he thought he was best by sending his family away. I think it is to Sturm's credit that he made the journey all the way back to Solamnia to find out what happened to his father—"

"He came to find his fortune," said Derek scornfully, "and when he discovered there was nothing left, he sold the family property and went back to live in his tree house."

"You put everything into the worst possible light," said Brian. "Sturm sold the family property to pay off the family's debts, and he went back to Solace because he found a harsh welcome in Solamnia."

"Give it up, Brian," said Aran, grinning. "Sturm Brightblade could be another Huma and single-handedly drive Queen Takhisis back into the Abyss and Derek would still think he was not worthy of his spurs. It all goes back to that feud between their grandfathers—"

"That has nothing to do with it!" said Derek, growing angry in his turn. "Why are we even discussing Sturm Brightblade?"

"Because if there is a chance that he is in Tarsis and he needs our help, we are bound to help him," said Brian. "Whether he is a knight or not, he is a fellow Solamnic."

"To say nothing of the fact that our enemies are eager to get their scaly hands on him," added Aran. "The friend of my enemy is my friend . . . or is it my enemy? I can never remember."

"Our mission comes first," said Derek sternly, "and we should end this conversation. You never know who might be listening."

Brian glanced at their surroundings. The old city was a dump. The pavement of the street was cracked and broken, littered with chunks of stone and rubble. Mounds of rotting leaves lay in odd corners of broken stonework, all that remained of abandoned buildings that were either wholly or partially demolished. Large oak trees growing from the crevices in the middle of the shattered streets were evidence that this part of the city had been lying in ruins for many years, perhaps ever since the Cataclysm.

"Unless the dragonarmies have found a way to recruit rats, I'd say we're pretty safe," commented Aran, dislodging one of the creatures with a chunk of a stone. "We haven't seen another living thing in the last hour."

Brian stood with his hands on his hips and looked up and down the dusty street. "I think Bertrem sent us on a wild kender chase, Derek. There's no sign of a library anywhere around here."

"Yet this is valuable property," Aran remarked. "You'd think the good people of Tarsis would either rebuild or at least clear out the rubble and turn it into a park or something."

"Ah, but then that would mean they'd have to remember what they once were. Remember the beauty, remember the glory, remember the white-winged ships, and Tarsis can't let herself do that," said a woman's voice coming from behind them.

The knights grasped the hilts of their swords, though they did not draw them, and turned to face the eavesdropper. The woman's voice was high-pitched, bright and effervescent, and her looks matched her voice. She was slender, short and brown-skinned, with a pert smile and russet-colored hair that fell about her face and shoulders in a wild and haphazard manner.

Her movements were quick and quiet, and she had a wide, ingenuous smile enhanced by a roguish dimple in her left cheek. Her clothes were plain and nondescript and appeared to have been put on without much thought, for the color of her blouse clashed with her skirt and her thick cloak was at odds with both. Judging by her speech, however, she was well-educated. Her accent was Solamnic. She was somewhere between twenty and thirty years of age, or so Brian guessed.

She stood in the shadows of an alleyway, smiling at them, not in the least disconcerted.

Derek made a stiff bow. "I beg your pardon for not giving you proper greeting, Mistress." He spoke politely because she was a woman, but coldly because she had been eavesdropping on them. "I had no idea of your presence."

"Oh, that's all right," said the woman with a laugh. "You must be Sir Derek Crownguard."

Derek's jaw dropped. He stared at her in astonishment, then he frowned.

"I beg your pardon, Mistress, but you have the advantage of me."

"Didn't I introduce myself? I'm so forgetful. Lillith Hallmark," she replied and held out her hand.

Derek regarded her in shock. Well-bred Solamnic women curtsied. They did not offer to shake hands like a man. He eventually took her hand in his—to do otherwise would insult her. But he did not seem to know what to do with her hand and released it as soon as possible.

"Would you by any chance be related to the Hallmarks of Varus?" Aran asked her.

"I'm Sir Eustace's daughter," Lillith said, pleased. "His fourth daughter."

Derek raised an eyebrow. He was certainly not having much luck with knights' daughters these days. First the Uth Matar woman in Palanthas, who'd turned out to be a thief. Now this young woman, the daughter of a knight, walking about in garb she might have stolen from a kender, and talking and acting as boldly as a man.

"How is my father, sir?" Lillith asked.

"I have the honor to report that the last time I saw him, your noble father was well," said Derek. "He fought bravely at the battle of Vingaard Keep and left the field only when it was apparent we were heavily outnumbered."

"Dear old Daddy," said Lillith, laughing. "I'm surprised he had sense enough to do that. Usually he stands around like a big dummy just waiting to get hit on the head."

Derek was shocked beyond words at such disrespectful talk, especially from a woman.

Aran laughed loudly and shook hands jovially with Lillith, and

Brian kissed her hand, which caused her to laugh again. He noted, as he held her hand in his, that the index finger and thumb were stained dark purple and there were similar purple splotches, both faded and fresh, on her woolen blouse and her skirt. Brian let go her hand reluctantly. He thought he'd never seen anything so enchanting as the dimple in her left cheek. He wanted to make her laugh again, just to see the dimple deepen, see the gold flecks in her hazel eyes.

Derek frowned at his cohorts, considering they were encouraging bad behavior. He had to speak to this lady, but he would speak coldly, to express his disapproval.

"How did you know me, Mistress Hallmark?" he asked.

"Bertrem sent word to me to keep watch for a Solamnic knight searching for the fabled Library of Khrystann," Lillith answered. "You're the first, last, and only knights I've seen in these parts for years, and then I heard you mention Bertrem's name, so I assumed you must be Sir Derek Crownguard."

"I did not give the Aesthetic Bertrem leave to proclaim our coming," said Derek stiffly. "Indeed, I ordered him to maintain the strictest secrecy."

"Bertrem didn't tell anyone except me, and I haven't told anyone else, Sir Derek," said Lillith, her dimple flashing. "It's a good thing he did. You would have spent years searching for the library and never found it."

"You're an Aesthetic!" Aran guessed.

Lillith winked at him; something else highly improper for a well-bred Solamnic woman. "Do you gentlemen want me to take you to the library?"

"If it's not too much trouble, Mistress," said Derek.

"Oh, it's no trouble at all, sir," returned Lillith, folding her arms across her chest. "But in return, you must do something for me. I need a favor."

Derek scowled. He did not like this young woman and he certainly did not like being blackmailed into serving her. "What would you have us do, Mistress?"

Lillith's dimple vanished. She seemed troubled and suddenly motioned them to come near and, when she spoke, she kept her voice low. "Something is very wrong in this city. We've heard rumors—"

"Who is 'we?' Derek interrupted.

"Those of us who have the interests of the world at heart," Lillith replied, meeting his gaze steadfastly. "We're on the same side in this war, Sir Derek, I assure you. As I was saying, we've heard rumors that draconians have been seen inside the city walls."

The three knights exchanged glances.

"Outside the city walls, too," said Aran.

"So the rumors are true. You've seen them?" Lillith said, looking grave. "Where?"

"On the road to Tarsis. They were camped out by a bridge. They were watching those who crossed . . ."

"That makes sense," said Lillith. "Someone is circulating a bounty list for the assassins of Dragon Highlord Verminaard. I happened to get hold of a copy." She reached to her waistband and drew out a document similar to the one they had taken from the draconians.

"I've been searching for a person a long time, only to find him at last on this list. I want you to apprehend him and bring him to me." Lillith held up a warning finger. "You must do this without anyone's knowledge."

"You have the wrong people, Mistress," said Derek. "You should speak to the local Thieves Guild. They are experts at kidnapping—"

"I don't want him kidnapped! And I certainly don't want thieves to get hold of him, or the draconians." Lillith flushed in her earnestness. "He carries something of great value and I'm very much afraid he doesn't appreciate its importance. He might give this object to the enemy out of sheer ignorance. I've been trying to think of some way to get hold of him ever since I saw his name on this list. You gentlemen are a godsend. Give me your word of honor as knights that you will do this for me and I will show you how to find the library."

"That is blackmail—unworthy of the daughter of a knight!" said Derek, and Brian, regretfully, couldn't help but agree with him. This was all very vague and shadowy.

Lillith was not daunted. "I think it's unworthy of a knight to refuse to help a knight's daughter!" she said spiritedly.

"What is the object this person carries?" Aran asked curiously.

Lillith hesitated, then shook her head. "It's not that I don't trust you. If it were my secret, I would tell you, Sir Knight, but the secret is not mine to share. My information came from one who would be in great peril if he were discovered. He's not supposed to be talking to us. He risked a great deal revealing this much, but he's worried about this valuable object and also the person carrying it."

Derek continued to look grim.

"Which person on this bounty list do you want us to find?" Brian asked.

Lillith put her finger on a name.

"Out of the question!" barked Derek.

"Derek . . ." said Brian.

"Brian!" said Derek, glowering.

"I'll just leave you gentlemen to discuss this among yourselves." Lillith walked off out of ear-shot.

"I do not trust this hoyden," said Derek, "even if she is the daughter of a knight, and I have no intention of kidnapping a kender! She is playing some sort of prank on us."

"Derek, we've tramped up and down this blasted street most of the morning and we haven't seen hide nor hair of a library," Aran said, exasperated. "We could spend the rest of our lives searching for it. I say we agree to do this little errand of hers in return for her helping us locate the library."

"Besides, if the draconians are keen to get their claws on the kender, that alone should give us reason enough to want to save him," Brian pointed out. "He was one of those who killed the Highlord, apparently, along with Sturm."

"He might be able to tell us where we could find Sturm," said Aran.

Brian shook his head, signaling to Aran that this argument was the last one to use to induce Derek to go along with Lillith's plan. Quite the opposite, in fact. For his part, Brian was eager to help Lillith regardless, if only to see her smile again.

Derek was obviously not happy about the situation, but he had to face facts: they could not find the library and, with draconians lurking about the city there was no time to waste.

He called to Lillith. "We will undertake this task for you, Mistress. Where do we find this kender?"

"I have no idea," she said brightly. Seeing Derek's brows come together, she added, "My fellow Aesthetics are keeping an eye out for him. They'll let me know. In the meantime, I will show you the library. See there? I can be honorable, too."

"What are draconians doing in Tarsis, Mistress?" Brian asked. She was leading them down an alleyway that appeared to be a cul-de-sac, with no library in sight.

Lillith shook here head. "Maybe nothing more than searching for these people. We don't know."

"Have you reported this to the authorities?"

"We tried," said Lillith, making a face. "We sent a delegation to see the lord. He scoffed at us. He claimed we were imagining things. He termed us rabble-rousers, said we were trying to start trouble."

Lillith shook her head. "There was something odd about him, though. He used to be a gracious man, always taking his time to listen to supplicants, but when we saw him this time, he was brusque, almost rude." She sighed deeply. "If you ask me, trouble's already started."

"What do you mean?"

"We think the enemy has him in their control. We can't prove it, of course, but it would make sense. They have some sort of hold over him. That's the only reason our lord would allow those monsters to even get near our city."

The alley ran between a large building which had fallen into such decrepitude it was hard to tell that it had once been an elegant mansion. The walls looked as if they would tumble down if someone breathed on them and they kept clear, though Lillith assured them the building had been standing for hundreds of years. She continued down the alley, pausing every now and then to glance over her shoulder, to make sure they were not being followed.

"Mind the sewer grate," she said, pointing. "The bolts are rusty, and it's not to be trusted. You could take a nasty tumble."

Aran, who had been about to step on the grate, hopped nimbly over it.

"Why don't the Tarsians clean all this up?" he asked, gesturing. "It's been over three hundred years, after all."

"At first they were too busy just trying to survive to rebuild what was lost," Lillith answered. "They took the bricks and granite and marble blocks from ruined structures and used them to construct houses. I think they meant to rebuild their city at first, but what with hardship, danger and people leaving the city to find work other places, there was always a lack of money and, perhaps more important, a lack of will."

"In later years, as they grew more prosperous, they must have considered rebuilding this part as they did other parts," said Brian. "I saw some magnificent structures on my way here."

Lillith shook her head. "It's because of the library. This part of the city came to be associated with those the people blamed for their woes—wizards, clerics, scholars, and Solamnic Knights like yourselves. The citizens feared that if they rebuilt the library and universities troublemakers like us would come back."

"I'm surprised they didn't destroy the library," said Aran.

"The Aesthetics feared the worst. When word of the trouble occurring in Tarsis reached our Order, they were deeply concerned. They sent a group to the city—a dangerous journey back then, what with the lawlessness in the land—with instructions to either save the books or, if they were too late, salvage what they could.

"When they arrived, the Aesthetics found that the clerics of Gilean working here prior to the Cataclysm had received warnings that something terrible was about to occur. The clerics could have left Krynn safely with the clerics of the other gods, but they chose to remain to guard the books. Fortunately the library had been built below ground, so that when the fiery mountain struck, the library was spared. All they had to fear now was men.

"When the mobs came to burn and loot the library, they found the Aesthetics guarding it. Many of them were slain in the battle, but they kept the mobs at bay until they could seal up the library entrance. After that, they concealed the entrance so that no one could find it or open the door unless they knew the secret. The books have thus remained safe all these centuries, guarded by those who love them."

"Such as yourself," said Brian admiringly. He took hold of her hand, indicating her ink-stained fingers.

Lillith blushed, but she gave a matter-of-fact nod. Brian kept hold of her hand, as if by accident. Lillith smiled at him, the dimple flashed, and she gently slid her hand out of his grasp.

"What book or reference are you looking for, Sir Brian? Perhaps I can help you find it. I'm familiar with most of what's down here, though not all, mind you. That would take several lifetimes."

Derek gave Brian a sharp glance, silencing him.

"It is not that we do not trust *you*, Mistress Hallmark," Derek said coolly. "But I believe we should keep this information to ourselves. We might put you in danger otherwise."

"Just as you choose," said Lillith. She came to a halt. "Here we are."

"A blank wall," Aran stated.

They walked through a shadowy archway that led to a dead end. A wall made of multi-colored stones, rounded and weathered and set in mortar, butted up against a hillside covered over with long grass.

"The Library of Khrystann," said Lillith.

She placed her boot on a flagstone in front of the wall and pressed on it. To the knights' amazement, the solid stone wall gave a sudden jolt and slid off to one side.

"It's not stone at all," exclaimed Aran, reaching out his hand to touch it. "It's wood painted to look like stone!" He laughed. "What a masterpiece! It fooled me completely!"

The knights looked back down the alley and saw it in a far different light.

"The alley is part of the library's defenses," said Brian. "Anyone trying to reach the library *has* to walk down it."

"And the sewer grate I almost stepped on—it's a trap!" Aran regarded Lillith with more respect. "You and your Aesthetics appear ready to fight and die to defend the library. Why? It's only a bunch of books."

"A bunch of books that contain the bright light of wisdom of past generations, Sir Aran," said Lillith softly. "We fear that if this light is quenched, we will plunge into a darkness so deep we might never find our way out."

She shoved aside the wooden door painted to look like stone. Behind it was another wooden door, this one of very old workmanship. Carved into the wood were the scales of balance resting on a book.

"The symbol of Gilean, God of the Book and Keeper of the Balance." Lillith reached out her hand to touch the scales.

"You speak of him with reverence," said Brian. "Do you believe the gods have returned?"

Lillith opened her mouth to reply, but Derek cut her short. "We have no time for such nonsense. Please proceed, Mistress."

Lillith gave Brian a sidelong glance and a secret smile.

"We will speak of that later," she said.

She pressed on one of the scales twice, then the other scale three times, then pressed four times on the symbol on the book. The second door slid open. A long staircase extended straight down into darkness. A lantern hung on a hook on the wall near the door. Lillith removed the lantern and, opening a glass panel, lit the stub of a candle inside. The flame burned clear. She shut the glass panel carefully and lighted their way down the stairs.

The air grew warmer. The stairway smelled of old leather and sheepskin and the dust of time. At the bottom of the stairs was another door, again decorated with the scales and a book. Lillith pressed on each again, only in a different order. The door slid into the wall. She entered the room, holding her lantern high.

The room was enormous. Long and wide, it extended far beyond the reach of the lantern light. And it was filled, floor to ceiling, with books. Shelves of books lined the walls. Shelves of books marched in long rows across the floor, row after row, on and on into the darkness. It was a veritable forest of shelves, and the books on those shelves were as numerous as the leaves on a forest of trees.

The three knights stared at the books in awe mingled with growing dismay.

"Are you *sure* you don't need my help, Sir Derek?" Lillith asked serenely.

4

A hopeless search.
The riot. Kender-snatching.

here are thousands!" Aran gasped.

"Thousands of thousands," said Brian in hopeless tones.

Derek turned to Lillith. "There must be a catalog of the books, Mistress Hallmark. The Aesthetics are known for their meticulous record-keeping."

"There was," said Lillith. "The books were catalogued and cross-referenced by title, author, and content."

"You're speaking in the past tense," Aran noted ominously.

"The catalog was destroyed," Lillith told them gravely.

"Who would do such a thing? Why?" Brian asked.

"The Aesthetics themselves destroyed it." Lillith gave a deep sigh. "Right before the Cataclysm, during the time that the Kingpriest handed down the Edict of Thought Control, he threatened to send his Enforcers to the library to search the catalog of books so that his Enforcers could remove and burn all those deemed 'a threat to the faith'. The Aesthetics could not allow this, of course, so they burned the catalog. If the Enforcers wanted to know what was in the books, they were going to have to read them. *All* of them."

"And so, it seems, are we," said Brian grimly.

Brian pointed to Lillith's ink-stained fingers. "Not necessarily. You've been recreating the catalog, haven't you, Mistress Hallmark?"

"I wish you would all just call me Lillith, and, yes, I've been trying to recreate the catalog. I haven't gotten very far. It's an enormous task."

"Derek, we must tell her why we're here," murmured Aran.

Derek was determined to keep the orb a secret, and for a moment he looked obstinate. Then his gaze went to the shelves of books, shelf after shelf after shelf of books. He pressed his lips together a moment, then said tersely, "We're looking for information concerning dragon orbs. All we know for certain is that they were created by wizards."

Lillith gave a low whistle. "Wizards, eh? I don't recall coming across any information on dragon orbs, but then, I haven't started work on the books that deal with magic."

Derek and Brian looked at each other in dismay. Aran, shaking his head, reached for his flask.

"I can show you the section where books on the arcane are shelved," Lillith offered. "They're all the way in the back, I'm afraid."

The shelves were stacked closely together; the aisles between them were so narrow that occasionally Aran had to turn sidewise to fit. They moved cautiously, for the lantern light didn't go very far. Brian fell over a crate in the dark and almost knocked down an entire shelf.

"Sorry about the mess," Lillith said, as they edged their way around several shelves that had toppled over, spilling their contents onto the floor. "I haven't started to work on this section yet and I didn't want to disturb anything. Though it may not look it, there is order in this chaos.

"Which reminds me, gentlemen," Lillith added in severe tone, "if you take a book down from a shelf, *please* put it back in exactly the same place you found it. Oh, and if you could make a note of the contents, that would be a big help to me. By the way, how many different languages do you speak?"

"Solamnic," Derek answered impatiently, not understanding the reason for the question, "and Common, of course."

Lillith paused, holding the lantern high. "Nothing else? Elvish? Khurian?"

The knights all shook their heads.

"Ah, that's a shame," she said, biting her lip. "We Solamnics assume everyone in the world speaks our language, or if they don't, they should. Wizards come in all races and nationalities. Their writings are in many different languages, including the language of magic. Given the way our people feel about wizards, I doubt you'll find many books written in Solamnic."

"This just keeps getting better and better!" Aran remarked cheerfully. "We could take weeks to find a scroll on dragon orbs, only to discover it's written in some obscure dwarvish dialect and we can't understand a word! Here's a toast to our quest!" He took a pull from his flask.

"Don't borrow trouble," Derek admonished. "Fortune might smile on us."

Lillith clapped her hands together. "By Gilean's Book! Fortune *has* smiled on you. I just thought of something. That kender you're going to rescue might be able to help you!"

"A kender?" Derek repeated in disgust. "I most seriously doubt it!"

"How could he help us?" asked Brian.

Lillith flushed. "I can't tell you that, but he might."

"The kender again! When do we go in search of this kender?" Derek asked in resigned tones.

"Whenever my friends tell me he's arrived in Tarsis, if he comes here at all. I'm just hoping he will because of that list." Lillith hiked up her skirts to climb over another shelf. "This way. I'll show you where to look and I'll give you what help I can."

The knights spent two days in the library in what proved to be a frustrating and fruitless search. They decided against returning to their camp, for that would mean passing in and out of the city gates, and once inside, they deemed it wise to stay, particularly if there were draconians about. Lillith suggested they sleep in the library—an ideal hiding place, since no one in Tarsis ever came there. Brian took the two horses to a stable near the main gate, in case they had to make a hasty departure. Lillith brought them food and drink.

They made their beds on the floor among the shelves.

Dusk to dawn, they searched through books, manuscripts, treatises, scrolls, collections of notes, and scribbles on scrap paper. They sat at long wooden tables hemmed in and blocked off by a maze of shelves that Aran swore shifted position when they weren't looking, for if they left, they always seemed to lose their way back. They worked by lantern light, for the library had no windows. Lillith pointed out the old skylights located high in the lofty ceiling that had once let in the sunlight. The skylights were covered over with earth and debris and rubble.

"We thought it best to leave them hidden like that," she said, and added wistfully, "Someday, perhaps, we can uncover them and light will once again shine on us. Now is not the time, however. Too many people in this world consider knowledge a threat."

The library was not only dark, it was eerily silent. All sound was absorbed and swallowed up by the books. The world could end in an explosion of fire outside and they would be none the wiser.

"I tell you honestly," said Aran on the morning of the third day, "I'd rather be fighting death knights." He opened a book. Dust flew up his nose and he gave a violent sneeze. "An entire legion of death knights with a hundred drunken dwarves thrown in!"

He glanced dispiritedly through the discolored pages. "This appears to have been written by spiders who dipped their legs in ink and ran across the vellum. There *are* pictures of dragons, though, so this might have something to do with orbs."

Lillith peered over his shoulder. "That's the language of magic. Put it here with the other books on dragons." She shoved her hair out of her eyes, leaving a smear of dirt on her forehead. "Be sure to mark its place on the shelf."

"This book also has pictures of dragons," said Brian, "but the pages are so brittle I'm afraid they'll disintegrate if I continue examining it, and I can't read it anyway."

Lillith took the book from him, handling it carefully, and added it to the small pile.

"Perhaps there is a wizard is the city who could translate this writing for us—" Brian began.

"We're not telling the wizards about this," Derek stated flatly.

"There aren't any wizards in Tarsis, anyway," said Lillith, "or at least any who'd openly admit to it. We'll wait for the kender. I'm not promising anything, mind you, but—"

"Lillith?" A male voice called out her name. "Are you here?"

Derek rose to his feet.

"Don't be alarmed," said Lillith hurriedly. "It's one of the Aesthetics." She raised her voice. "I'm coming, Marcus!"

She hurried off toward the front of the library.

"Brian, go with her," Derek ordered.

Brian did as he was told, wending his way through the shelves, trying to remember the twists and turns that would take him to the front and not strand him on some remote literary island. He kept the light of Lillith's lantern in sight and eventually caught up with her.

"What's the matter? Don't you trust me?" Lillith asked, dimpling.

Brian felt his cheeks burn and was thankful it was so dim she couldn't see him flush.

"It's just . . . it might be dangerous," he said lamely.

Lillith only laughed at him.

A man stood in the doorway. He was wrapped up in cloak and scarves and it was difficult to tell anything about him. Lillith hurried over to him and the two conferred together in low voices. Brian hung back, though he knew quite well Derek had sent him to spy on her. The two didn't speak long. Marcus left and Lillith came back to Brian. Her eyes were shadowed in the lantern light. She looked troubled.

"What's wrong?" Brian asked.

"You should alert the others," she said.

Brian gave a halloo that echoed off the walls and shook the dust from the ceiling. He heard Aran swear and the sound of heavy objects falling.

Lillith winced. "Be careful!" she called out anxiously.

"Oh, I'm all right," Aran answered.

Lillith muttered something, and Brian grinned. It wasn't the knight she was worried about. It was her precious books.

"The kender is in Tarsis," she reported when Derek and Aran emerged from the gloom into the lantern light. "He and his friends entered the city through one of the gates this morning. They're staying in the Red Dragon, but there's going to be trouble. The guards at the gate saw that one of the men was wearing a breastplate with the markings of a Solamnic knight and reported him to the authorities.

They've sent guards to the inn to arrest them."

"That would be Brightblade," said Derek irritably, "and he is not a knight. He has no right to wear such armor!"

"That's not really the point, Derek," said Aran, exasperated. "The point is that Brightblade and his friends are about to be arrested, and if the draconians find out that these are the people they've been searching for—"

"They can't find out!" said Lillith urgently. "They mustn't! They'll search the kender's belongings, and they'll discover what he's carrying. You have to save him."

"From the Tarsian guards? In broad daylight? Mistress, I don't care what mysterious thing this kender is supposed to be carrying. A rescue attempt would only end in our joining the kender in prison," said Derek.

"My friends are going to create a diversion," Lillith said. "You'll be able to grab the kender in the confusion. Bring him straight here. I'll be waiting for you. Now hurry!" She started to herd them up the stairs.

"How will we find this inn?" Brian asked. "We don't know our way around town!"

"You won't have any trouble," she predicted. "Keep to the main road out front. Go back through the Central Plaza, the way you came. After that, just follow the shouting."

———————◆———————

Brian blinked and rubbed his eyes as he walked into the bright winter sunlight. He'd been living in the library in perpetual night, and he had no idea what time of day it was. From the position of the sun, he guessed it must be about midmorning. The knights hastened along the main street as Lillith had told them, meeting no one until they came to the Central Plaza. Here, they found crowds of people, all in a state of excitement. Those who had been inside the shops and stalls were pouring out into the streets, while others were breaking into a run. The knights could hear a low roaring sound, as of waves breaking on a shore.

"What's happening, my good man?" Aran asked, stopping to talk to a shopkeeper gloomily watching his customers stream out of his store. "Has the sea come back?"

"Very funny," the shopkeeper growled. "Seems there's some sort of riot going on over by the Red Dragon Inn. A Solamnic Knight made the mistake of showing his insignia in our city. The guards tried to haul him off to the Hall of Justice, but they may not get that far. We don't take kindly to his kind in Tarsis. He'll get justice, all right."

Aran raised his hand to make sure the scarf he had wound around his nose and mouth had not slipped. "A pox on all Solamnic Knights, I say. I think we'll go have a look. Good day to you, sir."

"Here," said the shopkeeper, handing Aran a rotting tomato. "I can't leave the store, but throw this at him for me."

"I'll do that, sir, thank you," said Aran.

The three ran off, joining the throng of people heading in one direction. They found their way blocked by people yelling insults and tossing the occasional rock. Judging by the craning heads, the prisoners were coming in their direction. Brian peered over the shoulders of those in front of him and saw the small procession come into view. The Tarsian guards had their prisoners surrounded. The crowds fell back and grew quiet at the sight of the guards.

"There's Brightblade, all right," Aran announced. He was the tallest of them and had the best view. "And to judge by his ears, that man with him is the half-elf. There's a true elf and a dwarf, and *that* must be Lillith's prize kender."

"Where's the diversion?" Brian wondered.

"We can at least get closer," said Derek, and they shoved their way through the mob that was milling about indecisively. The crowd had grown bored yelling at the knight and it seemed they might disperse when, suddenly, the kender lifted his shrill voice and yelled at one of the guards, "Hey, you! Adle-pated pignut! What happened to your muzzle?"

The guard went red in the face. Brian had no idea what an adle-pated pignut was, but apparently the guard did, for he lunged at the kender, who dodged nimbly out of the guard's grasp and swatted him over the head with his hoopak. Some in the crowd jeered, others applauded, while others began throwing whatever came to hand—vegetables, rocks, shoes. No one was particular about his aim, and the Tarsian guards found themselves under fire. The kender continued to taunt anyone who caught his fancy, with the result that several in the crowd tried to break through the guards' defenses to get to him.

The commander of the guard started yelling at the top of his lungs. The elf was knocked off his feet. Brian saw Sturm halt and bend protectively over the fallen elf, fending off people with his hands. The dwarf was kicking someone and punching with his fists, while the half-elf was trying desperately to make his way to the kender.

"Now!" said Derek. He commandeered a gunny sack he found lying in front of a vegetable stand and shouldered his way through the crowd. Brian and Aran followed in his wake.

The half-elf was about to grab hold of the kender. Not knowing what else to do, Aran tossed his tomato and struck the half-elf full in the face, momentarily blinding him.

"Sorry about that," Aran said ruefully.

Derek swooped down on the kender and clamped his hand over his mouth. Brian and Aran grabbed the kender's feet. Derek popped the sack over his head and carried him, wriggling and squeaking, down the street.

Someone yelled to stop them, but the knights had acted so rapidly that by the time those watching realized what had happened, they were gone.

"You take him!" Derek shouted to Aran, who was the strongest among them.

Aran tossed the kender over his shoulder, keeping one arm clamped over his legs. The kender's topknot had fallen out of the sack and straggled down Aran's back. Derek ran down an empty side street. Brian came last, keeping an eye on their backs. With only a vague idea of where they were, they feared getting lost and they made their way back to the main road as quickly as possible.

The bagged kender was emitting muffled howls and wriggling like an eel. Aran was having difficultly hanging onto him and people were stopping to stare.

"Keep quiet, little friend," Aran advised the kender, "and quit kicking. We're on your side."

"I don't believe it!" shrieked the kender.

"We're friends of Sturm Brightblade," said Brian.

The kender ceased to howl.

"Are you knights like Sturm?" he asked excitedly.

Derek cast Aran a stony glance and seemed about to launch into one of his tirades. Aran shook his head at him.

"Yes," he said, "we're knights like Sturm, but we're in hiding. You can't tell anyone."

"I won't, I promise,' said the kender, then he added, "Can you take me out of the sack? It was fun, at first, but now it's starting to smell of onion."

Derek shook his head. "Once we reach the library. Not before. I've no mind to go chasing a kender through the streets of Tarsis."

"Not just yet," Aran said conspiratorially. "It's too dangerous. You'd be recognized."

"You're probably right. I'm one of the heroes of the battle of Pax Tharkas, and I helped find the Hammer of Kharas. When are we going to rescue the others?"

The three knights looked at each other.

"Later," said Aran. "We . . . uh . . . have to think up a plan."

"I can help," the kender offered eagerly. "I'm an expert at plan-thinking. Would it be possible for you to open a small hole so that I could breath a little better? And maybe you could not jounce me around quite so much. I ate a big breakfast and I think it's starting to turn on me. Have you ever wondered why the same food that tastes so good going down tastes really horrible when it comes back up—"

Aran dropped the kender on the ground. "I'm not going to have him puke on me," he told Derek.

"Keep a firm grip on him," ordered Derek. "He's your responsibility."

Aran removed the bag. The kender emerged, red in the face from being dangled upside-down and out-of-breath. He was short and slender, like most of his race, and his face was bright, inquisitive, alert, and smiling. He twitched a fur-lined vest and garishly colored clothes into place, felt to make sure his topknot of hair was still on top of his head and checked to see that all his pouches had come with him. This done, he held out his small hand.

"I'm Tasslehoff Burrfoot," he said. "My friends call me Tas."

"Aran Tallbow," said Aran, and he gravely shook hands, then offered his flask. "To make up for the onion."

"Don't mind if I do," said Tas, and he took a drink and almost took the flask, quite by accident, of course, as he told Aran in apology.

"Brian Donner," said Brian, extending his hand.

Tas looked expectantly at Derek.

"Keep moving," said Derek impatiently, and he walked off.

"Funny sort of name," muttered the kender with a mischievous gleam in his eye. "Sir Keep Moving."

"He's Derek Crownguard," said Aran, getting a tight grip on the kender's collar.

"Humph," said Tas. "Are you sure he's a knight?"

"Yes, of course, he is," said Aran, grinning at Brian and winking. "Why do you ask?"

"Sturm says knights are always polite, and they treat people with respect. Sturm is always polite to me," said Tas in solemn tones.

"It's the danger, you see," Brian explained. "Derek's worried about us. That's all."

"Sturm worries about us a lot, too." Tas sighed and looked back over his shoulder. "I hope he and the rest of my friends are all right. They always get into trouble if I'm not with them. Of course," he added on second thought, "my friends get into lots of trouble when I *am* with them, but then I'm there to help them out of it, so I think I should go back—"

The kender made a sudden jerk, gave a twist and a wriggle, and before Aran knew what was happening the knight was holding an empty fur vest, and the kender was dashing off down the street.

Brian leaped after him and was finally able to catch him. Fortunately, Derek was far ahead of them and hadn't seen what had happened.

"How did he escape like that?" Aran demanded of his friend.

"He's a kender," said Brian, unable to help laughing at the bewildered expression on Aran's face. "It's what they do."

He assisted Tas in putting his fur vest back on, then, said, "I know you're worried about your friends. So are we, but we've been sent on a very important mission to find you."

"Me?" Tas said, astonished. "An important mission to find me— Tasslehoff Burrfoot?"

"There's someone who wants to meet you. I promise," Brian added gravely, "on my honor as a knight that when I have taken you to talk to our friend, I will help you rescue your friends."

"Derek's not going to like that," Aran predicted with a grin.

Brian shrugged.

"An important mission!" breathed Tasslehoff. "Wait until I tell

Flint. Yes, sure, I'll come with you. I wouldn't want to disappoint your friend. Who is your friend anyway? Why does he want to see me? Where are we going? Will he be there when we arrive? How did you know where to find me?"

"We'll explain everything later," said Aran. "We have to hurry."

Aran took hold of Tas by one arm, Brian grabbed him by the other, and they hustled him down the street.

5

Magical Glasses. The word "chromatic".
Love amid the dust.

illith was waiting for them at the entrance to the library. Her face brightened when Aran and Brian deposited the kender on the ground in front of her.

"You found him! I'm so glad," Lillith said, relieved.

"Tasslehoff Burrfoot," said the kender, reaching out his hand.

"Lillith Hallmark," she returned, taking his hand in hers and pressing it warmly. "I am so very honored to meet you, Master Burrfoot."

Tas flushed with pleasure at this.

"We should not be standing out in the open," Derek warned. "Take him into the library."

"Yes, you're right. Come inside." Lillith led the way. The kender followed her, delighted with the wonder of this unexpected adventure.

"A library! I love libraries. I'm not usually permitted inside them, however. I tried to visit the Great Library of Palanthas once, but I was told they don't allow kender. Why is that, Lillith, do you know? I thought maybe they had made a mistake and what they meant to say was that they didn't allow ogres, which I can understand, and I tried to crawl in through a window, so as not to bother anyone at the door, but I got stuck, and the Pathetics had to come help me—"

"Aesthetics," Lillith corrected, smiling.

"Yes, them, too," said Tas. "Anyway, I found out the rule doesn't say anything about ogres, but it does say 'no kender'. I'm very glad *you* admit kender."

"We don't as a general policy," said Lillith, "but in your case, we'll make an exception."

By this time, they'd descended the stairs into the library proper. Tasslehoff stood quite still, staring around in awe. Lillith kept her hand on his shoulder.

"Thank you very much, gentlemen, for bringing him, and now, if you could excuse us, I must speak with Master Burrfoot in private." Lillith added in apologetic tones, "As I told you, this is not my secret."

"Secret?" said Tas eagerly.

"Of course, Mistress," said Derek. He hesitated then added, "You mentioned something about Burrfoot being able to assist us—"

"I will let you know if he can or not," Lillith assured him. "That's part of the secret."

"I'm extremely good at keeping secrets," Tas announced. "What secret am I keeping?"

Derek bowed in acknowledgement, then headed for the back of the library. Aran and Brian accompanied him, and Lillith soon lost sight of them among the shelves. The sound of their footfalls grew muffled and faint, though she could still hear Aran's laughter, resounding through the building, shaking the dust from the books.

"Come, sit down," said Lillith, guiding Tas to a chair. She sat down beside him and drew her chair close to his. "I have a very important question to ask you. The answer is very important to me and to many other people, Tasslehoff, so I want you to think very carefully before you reply. I want to know—do you have with you the Glasses of Arcanist?"

"The what of who?" Tasslehoff asked, puzzled.

"The Glasses of Arcanist."

"Did this Arcanist say I took them?" Tas demanded, indignant at the accusation. "Because I didn't! I never take anything that's not mine."

"I have a friend, a very good friend named Evenstar, who says that you *found* the glasses in the floating tomb of King Duncan in Thorbardin. He says you dropped them, and he picked them up and gave them back to you—"

"Oh!" Tas leaped up in excitement. "You mean my Special Magical Glasses for Reading Stuff! Why didn't you say so in the first place? Yes, I think I have them somewhere. Would you like me to look?"

"Yes, please," said Lillith, alarmed at the kender's cavalier attitude, but she reminded herself, he *is* a kender, and the gold dragon knew that when he allowed him to keep the glasses.

"I hope you haven't told anyone about Evenstar," said Lillith, watching in growing concern as Tas started upending his pouches and dumping their contents onto the floor. She knew kender picked up all manner of various and assorted trinkets and treasures, ranging from the valuable to the ridiculous and everything in between. But she hadn't quite realized the vast extent of a kender's holdings until she saw it piling up on the floor. "Our friend could get into a lot of trouble if anyone knew he was helping us."

"I haven't said a word about meeting a golden . . . woolly mammoth," Tasslehoff replied. "You see, we were in Duncan's tomb—my friend, Flint, and I and there was this dwarf who said he was Kharas, only then we found the real Kharas and he was dead—extremely dead. So we wondered who the dwarf was really and I'd found these glasses inside the tomb and I put them on and when I looked through the lenses at the dwarf, he wasn't a dwarf, he was a golden . . . woolly mammoth."

He gave her a pitiful glance. "You see how it is? When I tried to tell anyone that I met a golden . . . woolly mammoth . . . it always comes out . . . woolly mammoth. I can't say . . . woolly mammoth."

"Ah, I see," said Lillith in understanding.

The golden dragon had apparently found a way to keep even a kender's lips sealed on his secret, a secret he had since revealed, but only to the Aesthetics.

Many years ago, the good dragons had awakened to find their eggs had been stolen away from them by the dragons of Queen

Takhisis. Using their eggs as hostages, the Queen forced the good dragons to promise they would not take part in the upcoming war. Fearing for the fate of their young, the good dragons agreed, though there were some among their number who advocated strongly that this was the wrong course. Evenstar had been one of these. He had spoken out forcefully against such appeasement and had vowed that he would not feel bound by any such oath. He had been punished for his rebellion. He had been banished to the Floating Tomb of King Duncan in Thorbardin, there to guard the Hammer of Kharas.

Two dwarves, Flint Fireforge and Arman Kharas, accompanied by Tasslehoff, had recently discovered the sacred hammer and restored it to the dwarves, freeing Evenstar from his prison. While in the tomb, Tasslehoff had encountered Evenstar, who questioned the kender about the situation in the world. What he heard greatly disturbed Evenstar, especially when he learned that an evil new race known as draconians had appeared on Krynn. A terrible suspicion was growing in his mind as to the fate of the young metallic dragons. Evenstar did not yet dare reveal himself. If the forces of darkness knew that a golden dragon was awake and watching the doings of the dark Queen, she would send her evil dragons after him, and, because he was isolated and alone, he would be no match for them. Thus he had found this magical method to make a kender keep a secret.

"The next time I looked through the glasses we were in a great big hall I can't recall the name of and the dwarves were fighting Dragon Highlord Verminaard, only he was supposed to be dead, so I looked at him through the glasses and he wasn't Verminaard at all. He was a draconian!"

Tas had plopped himself down on the floor and was sorting through his valuable possessions as he talked, searching for the glasses. Lillith realized in dismay that this search could take a considerable amount of time, since the kender could not pick up anything without examining it and showing it to her and telling her all about how he'd come by it and what it did and what he planned to do with it.

"Tas," said Lillith, "there are some very dangerous people in the city who would give a great deal to find these magical glasses. If you think you might have left them back in the inn—"

"Ah! I know!" Tasslehoff smacked himself in the forehead. "I'm such a doorknob, as Flint is always telling me." Tas reached his hand into one of the pockets in his bright colored trousers. He pulled out an assortment of objects—a prune pit, a petrified beetle, a bent spoon which he said was to be used for turning any undead he might be lucky enough to encounter, and finally, wrapped in a handkerchief embroidered with the name C. Majere, was a pair of spectacles made of clear glass with wire rim frames.

"They're truly remarkable." Tas regarded them with fond pride. "That's why I'm so careful of them."

"Uh, yes," said Lillith, vastly relieved.

"Does your friend want them back?" Tas asked wistfully.

Lillith didn't know how to answer. Evenstar had told Astinus, the Master of the Great Library, to seek out the kender and make certain Tas had the glasses in his possession. The dragon had said nothing about taking the glasses away from the kender, nor had he said anything about the kender using them to help the knights or anyone seeking knowledge.

As the follower of a neutral god, one who maintained the balance between the gods of Light and those of darkness, Lillith was not supposed to take sides in any war. Her assigned task was to guard the knowledge. If this was done, if the knowledge of the ages was preserved, then no matter whether good or evil prevailed, wisdom's flame would continue to light the way for future generations.

The Kingpriest, though he had revered Paladine, God of Light, had feared knowledge. He feared that if people were permitted to learn about gods other than Paladine and the gods of Light, they would cease to worship those gods and turn to others. That was why Paladine and the other gods of Light had turned against him.

Now Takhisis, Queen of Darkness, was trying to conquer the world. She also feared knowledge, knowing that those who live in ignorance will not ask questions, but will slavishly do what they are told. Takhisis was trying to stamp out knowledge, and Gilean and his followers were determined to oppose her.

Where were the gods of Light in this battle? Had they returned with Gilean? Did Paladine and the other gods of Light have their champions, and if so, would they be like the Kingpriest? Would they want to destroy the books? If they did, Lillith would fight them as she would fight draconians or anyone else who threatened her library.

Perhaps this was the reason Evenstar had turned to Astinus for help and not to Paladine, assuming Paladine was around. Evenstar distrusted Takhisis and her minions, yet he was not certain he could trust the gods of Light.

Now Lillith was confronted with the kender, and although she considered herself open-minded and free from prejudice, she couldn't help but think the dragon might have chosen a more responsible guardian for such a valuable artifact. She considered it a major miracle the kender had kept hold of the glasses all during the long journey from Thorbardin to Tarsis. It was not her place to judge, however, especially when she didn't know all the facts. She had been told to find the kender and ascertain that he had the spectacles on him. She could report back that he did. Her job was done, but should she allow him to help the knights?

"No, Evenstar doesn't want them back," Lillith said to Tas. "You can keep them."

"I can?" Tas was thrilled. "That's wonderful! Thank you!"

"You can thank your friend the golden woolly mammoth," said Lillith, smiling. She took out a small book and began to take notes. "Now, tell me what you see this time when you look through the lenses . . ."

In the back portion of the library, the knights had not resumed their search but were embroiled in an argument.

"You did *what*?" Derek demanded, scowling at Brian.

"I gave the kender my word of honor as a knight that I would help rescue Sturm and the others," Brian repeated calmly.

"You had no right to make such a promise!" Derek returned angrily. "You know the importance of our mission to recover this dragon orb and take it back to Solamnia! You could put it all in peril—"

"I didn't say anything about *you* assisting them, Derek," Brian told him. "You and Aran can continue with your search for the dragon orb. Brightblade is a fellow Solamnic, and though I only knew him a short time, I consider him a friend. Even if I didn't know him, I would do everything in my power to keep him and his companions from falling into the hands of the enemy. Besides," he added stubbornly, "I have now given my word."

"The Measure says it's our duty to thwart and confound our foes,"

Aran pointed out, tilting his flask to his mouth, then wiping his lips with the back of his hand.

"Tell me how we confound our foes by rescuing a half-elf and a dwarf and a counterfeit knight?" Derek retorted, but Brian could see that his argument was having some effect. Derek was at least considering his proposal.

Brian went back to work, giving Derek time to think things through. Their studies were interrupted by Lillith, who came marching the kender along, her hand on his shoulder, giving his hand an occasional slap—in a friendly manner—when he tried to pluck a book off the shelves.

All three knights rose politely to their feet.

"Yes, Mistress, how may we serve you?" Derek asked.

"It's how I can serve you, or rather, how Tasslehoff can serve you." Lillith reached for one of the books in the stack dealing with dragons. Opening the book to a page at random, she moved it near the lantern. "Tas, can you read this?"

Tasslehoff climbed onto a tall stool. He settled himself comfortably and peered at the page. He wrinkled his forehead. "You mean all those squiggly lines? No, sorry."

Derek grunted. "I'd be surprised if he can read at all!"

Lillith said softly, "Tas, I meant for you to put on the special glasses when you read. What we talked about."

"Oh, yeah! Right!" Tasslehoff reached his hand into his pocket and fumbled about.

"I think they're in the other pocket," Lillith whispered.

"Mistress, we are wasting valuable time—"

Tasslehoff dove into the correct pocket and came up, glasses in hand. He placed them on his small nose, pinched the nosepieces together to help them stay on, and looked down at the page.

"It says, 'The red dragons are the largest of the chro . . . chrom . . . "—he stumbled over the word—"chromatic dragons and the most feared. Although they disdain humanoids, red dragons may occasionally ally themselves with those who have the same goals and ambitions, which include a lust for power. Red dragons revere Queen Takhisis—' "

"Let me see that!" Derek snatched the book away from Tasslehoff. He stared at it, then shoved it back. "He's lying. I can't read a word."

"But he can," said Lillith triumphantly, "with the magical Glasses of Arcanist."

"How do you know he's not making it up?"

"Oh, come now, Derek," said Aran, laughing, "would a kender or anyone else for that matter make up the word 'chromatic'?"

Derek eyed Tas dubiously. He held out his hand. "Let me see those glasses."

Tasslehoff glanced at Lillith. She nodded her head and Tas handed him the glasses, though with obvious reluctance.

"They're mine," he said pointedly, "given to me by a golden woolly mammoth."

Derek attempted to put the glasses on his nose, but they were much too small. He peered at the book through the lenses, practically going cross-eyed to try to focus on the words. Lowering the glasses, he rubbed his eyes and regarded the kender with more respect.

"He's telling the truth," Derek admitted, sounding astonished beyond belief. "I can read the words with those glasses, though I have no idea how."

"They're magical," said Tas proudly. He quickly plucked the glasses out of Derek's hand. "They used to belong to some guy named Arachnid."

"Arcanist," said Lillith. "He was a half-elf sage who lived before the Cataclysm. He made several pairs of these glasses and gave them to the Aesthetics to use in research."

"How do they work?" Brian asked.

"We don't really know for certain. It's thought—"

But she didn't have a chance to finish. A shout interrupted her. "Lillith, it's me, Marcus!"

"Excuse me," she said. "I sent Marcus to find out about your friends, Tas. This is probably important news."

"I'll come, too," Tas jumped off his stool.

"You will sit and read, kender," said Derek.

Tas bristled with indignation. "Now, see here, Sir Shinguard, my friends may be in danger and if they are, they need me, so you can take your book and—"

"Please, Master Burrfoot," Brian hastily intervened, "we really need your help. We can't read these books and you can. If you could look through them and find anything at all about dragon orbs, we would be deeply in your debt. You remember that I have pledged to help your friends and I give you my word as a knight that I will do my utmost."

"You can be of vital service to these knights, Tas," Lillith added gravely. "I think the golden woolly mammoth would take it as a personal favor."

"Well . . . I guess," said Tas.

He eyed Derek balefully, then climbed back up on the stool and, putting his elbows on the table, began to read, his lips moving with the words.

Lillith started back to the front of the library to meet with her friend. She had taken only a few steps when she paused, turned back, and gave Brian a dimpled smile. "You can come with me, if you like. Just to make sure I'm not selling your secrets to the enemy."

Brian glanced at Derek, who looked very annoyed, but gave a nod.

"I'm sorry about the way Derek's acting," he said in a low voice as he trailed Lillith. "I hope you know that I don't suspect you—"

"I am deeply offended, sir," said Lillith, stopping. "I may never get over it."

"Please, Mistress." Brian took hold of her hand. "I am truly sorry . . ."

Lillith burst out laughing. "I was teasing! Do you knights always take everything so seriously?"

Brian flushed deeply. He let go of her hand and started to turn away.

"Now I'm the one who is sorry," Lillith said. "I didn't mean to make sport of you, sir."

She found his hand in the shadowy darkness and squeezed it tightly.

"I'm not 'sir'," he said. "I'm Brian."

"I'm Lillith," she said softly, pulling him nearer.

Tall bookshelves surrounded them, fenced them in and cut them off, separating them from everyone else in the world. Dust clung to them. They had only Lillith's lantern for light, and she set it on the floor in order to take both his hands in both of hers. The two seemed to stand in a pool of candle-lit radiance, even as they remained hidden in sweet darkness.

Neither was ever sure quite how it happened, but their lips met and touched and kissed and parted and touched again and kissed again.

"Lillith!" Marcus again called out for her. "It's important!"

"Just a minute!" she called breathlessly, then added softly, "We should go . . . Brian . . ."

"Yes, we should, Lillith . . ."

But neither moved.

They kissed again, and then Lillith, with a little sigh, picked up the lantern. Holding hands, they wended their way through the bookshelves, taking their time, warmed by each other's touch. When they neared the front, they paused for one last, quick kiss.

Brian smoothed his mustaches, Lillith smoothed her tousled hair, and both tried very hard to look perfectly innocent. Rounding a corner of a shelf, they came suddenly upon Marcus, who had grown tired of waiting and started down an aisle in search of her.

"Oh, there you are," Marcus said, raising his lantern.

Marcus was not at all what Brian had come to expect of an Aesthetic. His head wasn't shaved and he wore ordinary breeches, shirt and coat, not robes and sandals. He wore a sword and he had the look of a soldier, not a scholar. Still, Lillith wasn't what Brian had expected in an Aesthetic either.

"Did the knights rescue the kender?" Marcus asked.

"Yes," said Lillith, "we have him safe and sound. What about his friends, the others on the bounty list?"

"The half-elf, the dwarf, the elf, and the knight have been taken before the lord in the Hall of Justice. I stayed to listen to some of the trial. The lord seemed surprised to see a Solamnic knight, but I think he was pleased as well. He tried to do what he could to help them, but that strange fellow—the one in the cloak—intervened, and started whispering in the Lord's ear."

"You say they're on trial? What crime are Sturm and the others supposed to have committed?" Brian asked curiously.

"Remember the bounty list," said Lillith.

"Ah, right," said Brian. "Killing Highlord Verminaard."

"No one's supposed to know that, of course," Marcus said. "But a couple of bounty hunters got drunk in a bar down by the old docks and told the tale and now the story's all over town. There's other news, too."

"Not good, I take it," said Lillith.

"According to Alfredo—"

"—his lordship's clerk," Lillith explained for Brian's edification. "Alfredo's also one of us."

"His lordship has been secretly slipping out of the city by night to meet with someone. Add to this the way his lordship has been acting—nervous and edgy and unhappy—and Alfredo decided to follow him, find out what was going on."

"He took an enormous risk," said Lillith.

"To give Alfredo credit," said Marcus wryly, "he suspected his lordship of doing nothing more terrible than cheating on his lordship's lady wife. Our friend found out different. His lordship went to meet with representatives of a Dragon Highlord."

"Blessed Gilean!" Lillith gasped in horror, her hand over her mouth. "We were right!"

"From what Alfredo could gather, our lord is negotiating with the new Highlord of the Red Wing—a hobgoblin named Toede. If Tarsis surrenders peacefully, the city will not come under attack—"

"The Highlord is lying," said Brian bluntly. "They made the same false promise at Vingaard. They pretend to negotiate, but it's just a ruse they use until their forces are in place. When they are, they will break off negotiations and attack."

Brian turned to Lillith. "The attack could be only a matter of days away, hours maybe. You are a Solamnic and the daughter of a knight. You will be in grave danger. Come with us. We will take you to a place of safety."

"Thank you, Brian," said Lillith gently, "but I cannot leave the library. You have your mission, and I have mine. The library has been given into my trust. I have vowed to protect the books, and as you say, I am the daughter of a knight, one who keeps her vows."

Brian started to press the issue, but she shook her head with a smile and turned back to her friend. Brian saw that nothing he could say would sway her, and he loved her more for her courage and her honor, even as he wished with all his heart she were not so honorable, nor so courageous.

Lillith and Marcus were discussing Brightblade and his friends. "Half the group is still in the Red Dragon Inn, including a cleric of Mishakal and a cleric of Paladine."

"Those old gods of long ago? People are claiming to be their clerics?" Brian asked.

Lillith and Marcus looked very solemn, and Brian realized suddenly they were serious.

"Oh, come now. You don't think they are— I mean, you can't believe—"

"—in the true gods? Of course we do," Lillith said crisply. "After all, we worship one of those gods ourselves. We Aesthetics are clerics of Gilean, pledged to his service."

Brian opened his mouth and shut it again, not knowing what to say. Lillith seemed a sensible young woman and here she was, going on about serving gods who had abandoned humanity three hundred years ago. Brian would have liked to question Lillith about her faith, but now was hardly the time for a theological discussion.

"I saw cloaked and hooded figures hanging about the inn," Marcus added. "I'm certain they're draconians and they're keeping watch on these people. If the Highlord gets hold of a cleric of Paladine and a cleric of Mishakal—"

"We can't let that happen," said Lillith firmly. "We must bring the others here to the library. If the city is attacked, this is the one place they might be safe. Marcus—go outside, see if the library is being watched."

Marcus nodded and raced up the stairs.

Lillith turned back to Brian. Resting her hand on his arm, she looked up into his face.

"You must try to save the knight and his friends. The draconians won't take them to prison. They'll take them to their deaths."

Brian put his arm around her and drew her close.

"I will do anything you ask of me, Lillith, but first, answer me this. Do you believe in love at first sight?"

"I didn't," Lillith said softly, smiling up at him, "until now."

They held each other close for a long, sweet moment, then Lillith sighed deeply and said, "You'd better go. I'll stay here to keep on eye on the kender."

"I'll stay in the library with you, help you defend it. Derek and Aran can go on this dragon orb mission without me—"

Lillith shook her head. "No, that wouldn't be right. You have your duty, and I have mine." She smiled. Her dimple flashed. "When this is over, we will share war stories. You'd better hurry," she added.

Knowing it was hopeless, Brian gave up trying to persuade her. He shouted for Derek and Aran, and they made their way through the stacks of books. Tasslehoff accompanied them, despite Derek's repeated orders for the kender to return to his reading.

"My friends *are* in trouble, aren't they?" Tas heaved a deep sigh. "I suppose I'll have to go save them—*again*. Did I tell you about the time I rescued Caramon from a vicious man-eating Stalig Mite? We were in this wonderful haunted fortress known as Skullcap—"

"You are not going, kender," said Derek.

"Yes, I am, human," said Tas.

"We can't chain him to the stool. He'll only run off if you leave him," Lillith pointed out. "You might as well take him with you. That way, at least you'll know where he is."

Eventually Derek was persuaded, though he wasn't happy. "Once we return, Burrfoot," Derek said, "you will continue searching for information on dragon orbs."

"Oh, I found that already," said Tas nonchalantly.

"You did?" Derek exclaimed. "Why didn't you tell me?"

"Because you didn't ask me," said Tas with grave dignity.

"I'm asking now," said Derek, glowering.

"Not very nicely," Tas admonished.

Lillith leaned down to whisper something in his ear.

"Oh, all right, I'll tell you. Dragon orbs are made of crystal and magic and they have something inside them . . . I forget . . ." He thought a moment. "Essence . . . that's it. Essence of chromatic dragons."

Tasslehoff enjoyed the way these words rolled off his tongue, and he repeated them several times with relish until Derek ordered him sharply to get on with it.

"I don't know what the essence of a chromatic dragon is," Tas said, gleefully taking advantage of the chance to say it all one more time, "but that's what's in them. If you can gain control over one of these dragon orbs, you can use it to order dragons to do your bidding, or summon them, or something."

"How does it work?" Derek asked.

"The book didn't give instructions," Tas replied, irritated at being asked all these questions when his friends were in danger. Seeing

Derek frown, he added, "I have a friend who probably knows all about them. He's a wizard. His name is Raistlin and we can ask him—"

"No," said Derek, "we can't. Did the book say where to find these dragon orbs?"

"It says one was taken to a place called Icereach—" Tas began.

"You should really hurry," Lillith interrupted urgently. She had been fidgeting near the door the entire time, glancing nervously up the stairs. "We can talk about this when you come back. Your friend the knight has been arrested and it's likely he's going be killed."

"He's not a knight," insisted Derek. "But," he added in a more subdued tone, "he is a fellow Solamnic. Brian, you're in charge of the kend—Master Burrfoot." He and Aran started up the stairs. Tasslehoff hung about at the bottom, waiting for Brian.

"One more kiss," Brian said to Lillith, smiling. "For luck?"

"For luck!" she said and kissed him, then she added wistfully, "Have you ever found something you've searched for all your life, only to know that you're bound to lose it and maybe you'll never find it again?"

"That happens to me all the time," exclaimed Tasslehoff, crowding close to the two of them. "I once found this extremely interesting ring that belonged to an evil wizard. It kept jumping me all over the place—first here, then there, then back to here again. I was quite fond of it, only I seem to have misplaced it—"

Tasslehoff stopped talking. His story about the ring and the evil wizard was extremely exciting, very interesting and mostly true, but he'd lost his audience. Neither Lillith nor Brian were listening.

Derek called his name impatiently. Brian gave Lillith one last kiss then got a firm grip on Tasslehoff, and the two ran up the stairs.

Lillith sighed and went back to her dusty books.

6

The Rescue.
Sturm settles an argument.

he knights and the kender emerged from the library's secret entrance to find themselves in a snow storm, a startling change in the weather, for the day had been sunny when they went underground.

Large, heavy snowflakes were plummeting down from the sky, obscuring their vision and making walking on the stone streets slippery and treacherous. Though Marcus had been gone only a few moments, his footprints were already being covered up by the fast-falling snow. As Tas said, the snow was so thick they could barely see their noses in front of their faces, and they were startled when a figure suddenly loomed out of the white curtain.

"It's me, Marcus," he said, raising his hands as he heard the rattle of steel. "It occurred to me you'll need a guide to the Hall of Justice."

Derek muttered his thanks as he sheathed his sword, and they hurried on through the storm, blinking the snow out of their eyes and slipping on the icy pavement. Though the rest of the world had gone still and silent beneath a snowy blanket, their little part of it was quite lively, for the kender talked incessantly.

"Have you ever noticed how snow makes everything look different? I guess that's why it's really easy to get lost in a blizzard. Are we lost? I don't remember seeing that tree before—the one that's all humped over. I think we've taken a wrong turn—"

Eventually they came to a street corner and a building the kender did recognize, though this didn't stop his flow of talk.

"Look at all the gargoyles! Hey, I saw one of them move! Brian, did you see that very fierce-looking gargoyle move? Wouldn't it be exciting if it flew off its perch on that building and swooped down on us and gouged out our eyes with its sharp talons? Not that I want to have my eyes gouged out, mind you. I like my eyes. I couldn't see much without them. Say, Marcus, I think we're lost again. I don't remember going past that butcher—oh, wait, yes, I do—"

"Can't you keep him quiet?" Derek grumbled.

"Not without cutting out his tongue," Aran returned.

Derek seemed to be considering this as a viable option. By this time, however—fortunately for Tas—they had arrived at the Hall of Justice, a large, ugly brick structure. Despite the storm, a crowd had gathered out front, some of them shouting for the detested Solamnic to quit skulking about behind the lord's skirts and show himself.

"These people truly hate us," said Derek.

"You can't really blame them," said Marcus.

"*They* were the ones who turned on us," returned Derek. "Many Solamnics died in this city after the Cataclysm at the hands of the mobs."

"That was a tragedy," Marcus admitted. "And after the riot was over, some of the people here were genuinely ashamed of themselves. The Tarsians sent a delegation to Solamnia to try to make peace. Did you know that?"

Derek shook his head.

"Their overtures were rebuffed. They were not even permitted to leave their ship to set foot on Solamnic soil. If the Solamnics had been forgiving to those who wronged them, as the Measure states they should," Marcus added with a sidelong glance at Derek, "the knights would have been welcomed back to Tarsis and perhaps the city might not find itself about to be attacked by the dragonarmy."

"Much of Solamnia is now in the hands of the enemy," said Derek.

"Yes, I know," Marcus replied. "My parents live in Vingaard. I have not heard from them in a long time."

The knights were silent a moment, then Brian asked quietly, "You are from Solamnia, then?"

"I am," said Marcus. "I am one of the 'Pathetics' as the kender terms us." He smiled through the snow at Tasslehoff. "I was sent here with Lillith and several others to protect the library."

"There's no way you can protect it!" said Brian, suddenly and unreasonably angry at the man. "Not from the dragonarmies. The library's safely hidden. You and Lillith should just lock it up and leave it. You're putting your lives in danger over a few books."

He paused, flushing. He had not meant to speak with such passion. They were all staring at him in astonishment.

Marcus was gentle, sympathetic, but resolute. "You forget, Sir Knight, that our god is with us. Gilean will not leave us to fight alone, if fight we must. Wait here a moment. I see one of my colleagues. I'll go ask him what's going on."

He hastened through the snow to speak to a man who had just come out of the Hall. After a moment's conference, Marcus came hurrying back.

"Your friends are going to be taken to prison—"

"I hope it's a nice prison," Tasslehoff said to no one in particular. "Some are and some aren't, you know. I've never been in the Tarsis jail before, so I haven't any idea—"

"Silence, Burrfoot!" Derek ordered peremptorily. "Aran, put that damn flask away!"

Tasslehoff opened his mouth to give the knight a piece of his mind, but he sucked in a gigantic clump of snowflakes and spent the next few moments trying to cough them back up.

"The constable won't risk bringing them within sight of this mob," Marcus continued, "not after what happened when he tried to arrest them. He'll take them round by an alley in the back."

"Luck is on our side, for once," said Derek.

"Not luck," said Marcus gravely. "Gilean favors us with his blessing. Hurry! This way!"

"Perhaps it was Gilean who choked the kender," suggested Aran.

He had put the flask back in his belt and was patting the coughing Tasslehoff on the back.

"If he did, I may become his disciple," said Derek.

———————————

Marcus led them around the side of the Hall to an alleyway that ran behind the building. As if the storm delighted in playing tricks, the snow shower ended, and sunlight sparkled on the new fallen snow. Then more clouds scudded across the sky and the sun began to play at peek-a-boo, ducking in and out of the snow showers, so that one moment the sun shone brightly and the next snow was falling.

The building cast a shadow over the alley that was dark and gloomy. Just as they entered it, Brian saw two cloaked and hooded figures detach themselves from the wall at the far end and walk off in the opposite direction.

"Look there!" he said, pointing.

"Draconians," said Aran, sneaking a drink when Derek wasn't looking. "They're dressed exactly like those who stopped us at the bridge."

"Do you think they saw us?"

"I doubt it. We're in shadow. I wouldn't have seen them but they walked into the sunlight. I wonder why they left so quickly—"

"Hush! This must be them!" Marcus warned.

A door opened and they could hear voices.

"Take the kender," Derek told Marcus.

Tasslehoff tried to insist they would need his help in the upcoming battle, but Marcus clapped his hand over Tas's mouth and that ended that.

The constable emerged from the Hall. He was leading five prisoners, one of whom, they were astonished to see, was a woman. Three guards marched alongside. Brian recognized Sturm walking protectively near the woman, and they had been told correctly: Sturm was indeed wearing a breastplate on which was engraved the rose and the kingfisher, symbols of the knights.

Whatever Derek might say of Sturm Brightblade, Brian had always found the man to be the personification of a Solamnic knight—gallant, courageous and noble—which made it strange that Sturm would do something so dishonorable as to lie about being a knight, wear armor he had no right to wear.

Brian drew his sword, sliding it slowly and silently from its sheath. His friends had their weapons in hand. Marcus drew the muzzled kender back further into the shadows.

The door slammed shut behind the prisoners. The constable marched them down the alleyway. Brian saw Sturm exchanging glances with one of the other prisoners, and he guessed that they were going to try to make a break for freedom.

"I'll take the constable," said Derek. "You take the other guards."

The constable could hear the shouts of the mob in the front of the building, but he believed they were safe in the alley. He wasn't looking for trouble and consequently wasn't keeping a very good watch. The first he knew of trouble was when he caught a flash of steel. Seeing three cloaked figures rushing toward him, he put his whistle to his lips to sound the alarm. Derek clubbed him with the hilt of his sword, knocking the man unconscious before he could summon help. Aran and Brian menaced the three guards with their swords, and they ran off down the alleyway.

The knights turned to the prisoners, who were blinking in astonishment at their sudden rescue.

"Who are you?" demanded the half-elf.

Brian regarded the man curiously. He was tall and muscular, clad in leather and furs, and he wore a beard, perhaps to conceal his elf features, though they weren't that noticeable that Brian could see, except for his pointed ears. He appeared no older than his mid-thirties, but the expression in his eyes was that of someone who has lived long in the world, someone who knew life's sorrows as well as its joys. Of course, the elf blood in him would give him a life-span far longer than most humans. Brian wondered how old he really was.

"Have we escaped one danger only to find a worse?" the half-elf demanded. "Unmask yourselves."

It wasn't until that moment that Brian realized they must look more like assassins than saviors. He pulled down his scarf, turned to Sturm, and spoke swiftly in Solamnic, *"Oth Tsarthon e Paran,"* meaning, "Our meeting is in friendship."

Sturm had placed himself in front of the female prisoner, keeping her protectively behind him, shielding her with his body. The woman was heavily veiled and wore a thick cloak, so that Brian could gain no clear impression of her. She moved with flowing grace and her hand, resting on the knight's arm, was remarkable for its delicacy and alabaster purity.

Sturm gasped in recognition.

"*Est Tsarthai en Paranaith*," he replied, meaning, "My companions are your friends." He added in Common, "These men are Knights of Solamnia."

The half-elf and the dwarf both looked at them suspiciously. "Knights! Why—"

"There is no time for explanation, Sturm Brightblade," Derek told him, speaking in Common out of politeness, since he assumed the others could not speak Solamnic. "The guards will return soon. Come with us."

"Not so fast!" stated the dwarf.

He was an elder dwarf, to judge by the gray in his long beard, and like most dwarves Brian had known, he appeared to be irascible, obstinate, and headstrong. He snatched up a halberd one of the guards had let fall, and grasping it in his large, strong hands, he slammed it down on his bent knee, snapping off the handle so that he could wield it more easily.

"You'll find time for explanations, or I'm not going," the dwarf told them. "How'd you know the knight's name and how came you to be waiting for us—"

Tasslehoff had, by this time, managed to escape Marcus's grasp.

"Oh, just run him through," the kender cried cheerfully. "Leave his body to feed the crows. Not that they'll bother; there's few in the world who can stomach dwarf—"

The half-elf relaxed and smiled. He turned to the red-faced dwarf. "Satisfied?"

"Some day I'll kill that kender," the dwarf muttered into his beard.

All this time, Sturm had been staring hard at Derek, who had removed his scarf from his face.

"Brightblade," Derek acknowledged coldly.

Sturm's lips tightened, his face darkened, and his hand clenched over the hilt of his sword. Brian tensed, foreseeing trouble, but then Sturm glanced at those with him, especially at the veiled woman. Brian could guess what Sturm was thinking. Had he been alone, he would have refused to accept any aid from the man who had publicly insulted him and his family.

"My lord," said Sturm, his voice equally cold. He did not bow. If either had been going to say more, they were cut off by the sound of whistles and shouts heading in their direction.

"The guards! This way!" called Marcus.

Sturm's friends looked to him and he gave a nod. Marcus led them into a maze of streets and alleyways that twisted and turned back in on themselves like a drunken serpent. They soon lost the guards, and when they could no longer hear the whistles, deemed they were safe from pursuit and slowed their pace to mingle with the people in the street.

"Are you glad I rescued you, Flint?" asked Tasslehoff, walking alongside the scowling dwarf.

"No," he answered, glowering, "and you didn't rescue me, you doorknob. These knights did." He cast Brian, who was keeping near the kender, a grudgingly grateful glance.

Tasslehoff grinned and winked conspiratorially at Brian, then said, "That's a fine halberd you have there, Flint!"

Flint had been about to toss away the broken weapon, but at the kender's teasing, he held onto it firmly. "It suits my purpose," he said, "and besides, it's not a halberd. It's a hauberk."

"No, it isn't!" Tasslehoff gave a smothered giggle. "A hauberk's a shirt made of chain mail like the one Sir Brian is wearing. A halberd's a weapon."

Flint snorted. "What would a kender know about weapons?" He shook it at Tasslehoff, who was now so overcome with laughter he was having difficulty keeping up with his friends. "This is a hauberk!"

"Oh, yes! Just like that helm you're wearing has the mane of a griffon! All of us know it's horse hair," Tasslehoff retorted.

Flint was already red in the face and puffing from the running. At this accusation, he went purple. He put his hand to the white tail that dangled down from his helm. "It is not! Horse hair makes me sneeze! This is the mane of a griffon!"

"But griffons don't have manes!" Tasslehoff protested, skipping alongside the dwarf, pouches bouncing and spilling their contents. "Griffons have an eagle's head and a lion's body, not the other way around. Just like that's a halberd, not a hauberk—"

"Is this or is this not a hauberk?" Flint demanded. He shoved his weapon practically in Sturm's nose.

"That is what we knights know as a halberd," said Sturm, moving the point away from the mysterious woman, who continued to hold onto his arm.

Tasslehoff gave a whoop of triumph.

"However," Sturm added diplomatically, seeing Flint look chagrined, "I believe the Theiwar dwarves have a word for 'halberd' that sounds similar to 'hauberk'? Perhaps that is what you were thinking, Flint."

"That's true!" stated Flint, his dignity upheld. "I . . . er . . . can't rightly recall the word right at this moment, not being fluent in Theiwar, you understand, but it sounds like hauberk, which is what I meant."

Tasslehoff grinned and seemed about to comment, but the half-elf, exchanging smiles with Sturm, put an end to the discussion by seizing hold of the kender and hustling him up to the front of the group so fast that his boots skimmed the street.

Brian was impressed by the good fellowship among this oddly assorted group of friends. He was particularly impressed with Sturm. He kept fast hold of the woman he had taken under his protection, and though clearly concerned with her, he had the patience to end the argument between the kender and the dwarf, while managing to maintain the dwarf's dignity.

As if aware of what Brian was thinking, Sturm met his eye and gave a half-smile and a slight shrug of the shoulders.

They continued moving through the side streets, avoiding the major roads. Tanis Half-elven had hold of the kender and was keeping hold of him. The kender wriggled and squirmed in his friend's grasp, his shrill voice raised in pleading. Whatever Tas wanted, Tanis was obviously having none of it.

They came to the marketplace, and here they would have to leave the side streets and move out into the open, taking the main road that led to the library. A few guards could be seen searching for them, but finding a handful of people amidst the throng of shoppers was going to be difficult and the guards were obviously not all that interested in capturing the escaped prisoners.

Brian recalled Lillith saying that something was wrong in this city. The guards apparently thought so, for they looked dour and unhappy. Ordinary citizens were still going about their business, but now that he paid attention, he saw people huddling together in knots, talking in hushed voices and glancing nervously over their shoulders. Sturm and the others kept their heads down, their eyes lowered, and did nothing to call attention to themselves. Obviously they've been in tense situations like this before, Brian realized. The half-elf even managed to squelch the kender.

They made their way safely through the market and came at last to the road that led to the old part of the city and the library. Here Tanis called a halt. Kender in tow, he came to speak to the knights.

"I thank you, sirs, for helping us," Tanis said. "We must take our leave of you. We have friends in the Red Dragon Inn who have no idea what has happened—"

"You can't, Tanis!" Tasslehoff cried. "I keep telling you! You have to come to the library to look at what I've found. It's really, really important!"

"Tas, I don't need to see another petrified frog," Tanis said impatiently. "We have to go back to tell Laurana—"

"Oh, tell *Laurana*!" Tasslehoff said through a smothered giggle.

"—*and* Raistlin, Caramon, and the others that we are safe," Tanis continued. "The last they saw of us, we were being taken off to prison. They will be worried." He held out his hand. "Sir Derek, thank you—"

Tas took advantage of his friend's distraction to give a wrench and a leap, and managed to twist himself out of Tanis's grasp. Derek made a grab for the kender, but he missed, and Tas ran off down the alleyway.

"I'll meet you in the library!" Tas called over his shoulder, waving his hand. "The knights know where!"

"I'll go fetch him," Flint offered, though he was so winded he stood doubled over, his hands on his knees. He seemed to be having difficulty breathing.

"No!" said Tanis. "We're already split in two. I won't have us going off in three directions. We keep together."

Marcus volunteered to go after him, and he set off in pursuit.

"I say leave the kender and good riddance," stated Flint.

"Actually, he *has* found something of vital importance," said Derek. "I think you should come see what we have discovered."

Brian and Aran exchanged startled glances.

"What are you doing?" Aran asked Derek, drawing him to one side. "I thought this dragon orb was a secret."

"I'm going to need the half-elf's cooperation," Derek said in a low voice. "I intend to take the kender with us to Icereach—"

"You're joking!" Aran exclaimed, horrified.

"I never joke," said Derek sternly. "He's the only one who can translate these magical writings for us. We will need him."

"He won't go," said Brian. "He won't leave his friends."

"Then Brightblade must persuade him, or better yet, I will order Brightblade to accompany us."

"He's not a knight, Derek, as you keep reminding us," said Brian. "He doesn't have to obey your orders."

"He will unless he wants me to tell his friends the truth," said Derek harshly. "He can make himself useful on the journey minding the horses and the kender."

They had kept their voices low, but Sturm must have heard his name mentioned for he looked over at them to see Derek's disapproving gaze fixed on his breastplate. Sturm flushed, then turned away.

Derek, don't do this, Brian begged his friend silently. *Just let it be. Let them go their way and we'll go ours.*

He had the unhappy feeling that wasn't going to happen.

"Come with us, Brightblade," Derek called, making it sound like an order.

The half-elf and the dwarf exchanged troubled glances, then both looked at Sturm, who had not heard, for he was talking in low and reassuring tones to the veiled woman.

"Mark my words—this isn't going to end well," the dwarf predicted "and it's all the fault of that rattle-brained kender!"

The half-elf gave a deep sigh and nodded his head in gloomy agreement.

"They don't know the half of it!" Aran remarked.

He took out his flask, hefted it, found it was empty. He shook it. Nothing came out.

"Great," he muttered. "Now I have to put up with Derek while I'm sober."

7

A last kiss. Fire and blood.

he knights and their newfound companions arrived back at the library without incident. Marcus had returned to report that Tas was safely back at the library, regaling Lillith with his tale of how they had fought off six hundred Tarsian guards and a wandering giant.

"Brian," said Derek, "before we enter the library, go fetch Brightblade. Tell him I want to speak with him."

Brian sighed deeply, but went to do as he was told.

Sturm Brightblade came of an honored family and he had the backing of Lord Gunthar, who was an old and valued friend of the family. When Sturm had asked that he be considered for knighthood, Lord Gunthar had supported the young man. It was Derek who had opposed Sturm's nomination to enter the knighthood on various grounds: Sturm had not been raised in Solamnia; he had been raised by his mother, his father having been absent during his formative years; Sturm was not properly educated; he had not served as a squire to a knight; and most damning, Derek had hinted that Sturm's parentage was subject to question.

Fortunately Sturm had not been present to hear all that Derek had said about him and his family, or there would have been bloodshed in the council hall. As it was, Lord Gunthar had answered the charges, arguing vehemently in favor of his young friend, but Derek's charges had been enough to sink Sturm's candidacy.

Rumor had it that when Sturm heard rumors of what Derek had said, the young man had tried to challenge Derek to a contest of honor. That was not possible, however. A mere nobody, such as Sturm Brightblade, could not challenge a Lord Knight of the Rose to mortal combat. Feeling himself disgraced, Sturm had determined to leave Solamnia. In vain, Lord Gunthar had tried to persuade Sturm to remain. Gunthar urged him to wait a year, and his name could be submitted again. In the meantime, Sturm could refute Derek's charges. Sturm refused. He left Solamnia shortly after, taking with him his inheritance—his father's sword and armor, part of which he was now wearing, though he had no right to do so.

Two proud and stubborn men, Brian thought, both at fault.

"We need to talk to you, Sturm," said Brian. "In private. Perhaps the lady would like to take some time to rest," he concluded awkwardly.

Sturm escorted the veiled woman to a stone bench near what had once been a marble fountain. He gallantly brushed off the snow, removed his cloak, and spread it out on the bench, then graciously assisted her to seat herself. The true elf, whose name was Gilthanas, had not spoken a word to any of them this entire time. He sat protectively beside the woman. Tanis stood fidgeting, looking about. He nodded in acquiescence when Sturm told him he was going to speak with his friends.

Derek led the way to a place where they could talk in private and not be overheard. Brian, who had the dread feeling he knew what was coming, found a chance to say a quick word to Sturm, holding him back when he would have followed Derek.

"I just wanted to tell you I'm sorry for what happened to you—in regard to the knighthood. Derek's my friend and there's no man I love and honor more," Brian smiled ruefully, "but he can be a horse's rear end sometimes."

Sturm made no reply. He kept his gaze fixed on the ground. His face was dark with anger.

"All of us have our failings," Brian continued. "If Derek would ever take off his armor, we'd find a human being underneath, but he can't take off that armor, Sturm. He's just not made that way. He expects perfection of everyone, especially himself."

Sturm seemed to soften at this. He looked less grim.

"When the dragonarmies overran Castle Crownguard," Brian continued, "a dragon killed his younger brother, Edwin. That is, we assume he is dead." He paused a moment, thinking back to that terrible time, and said quietly, "We hope he is dead. Derek's wife and child are now forced to reside with her father, because Derek cannot provide a house to shelter her. How must any man feel about that, especially a man as proud as Derek? He has nothing left, except the knighthood, this quest of his—" Brian sighed "—and his pride. Remember that, Sturm, and forgive him, if you can."

Having said this, Brian walked away, lest Derek should suspect he'd said anything. Sturm was silent, stiff and formal when he joined Derek. Aran, peering over Derek's helm, looked at Brian and lifted his eyebrows in a question. Brian could only shake his head. He had no idea what Derek was doing.

"Brightblade," said Derek abruptly, "we have had our differences in the past . . ."

Sturm's body trembled, his hands clenched. He said nothing, but gave a stiff nod in acknowledgement.

"I remind you that according to the Measure, in time of warfare, all personal animosities must be set aside. I am willing to do so," Derek added, "if you are. I prove it by taking you into our confidence. I am going to reveal to you the nature of our quest."

Brian was astonished, as all of a sudden he realized what Derek was doing. He felt himself growing so angry he had to choke back the harsh words; Derek was being conciliatory to Sturm because he needed the kender.

Sturm hesitated, then gave a great sigh, as though letting go a heavy burden, and said quietly, "I am honored by your trust, my lord."

"You have leave to tell your friends of our mission," Derek said, "but this must go no further."

"I understand," said Sturm. "I answer for their honor as for my own."

Considering that he was speaking for outlandish folk, such as dwarves and half-elves, Derek raised an eyebrow at this, but he let it go. He needed the kender.

Derek was about to proceed when Aran interrupted.

"Is it true you killed a Dragon Highlord in Pax Tharkas?" he asked with interest.

"My friends and I assisted in a slave uprising in Pax Tharkas that resulted in the death of the Highlord," Sturm replied.

Aran was impressed. "No need to be modest, Brightblade. You must have had more to do with it than that, for your name to be on the Highlord's bounty list!"

"Is it?" Sturm asked, startled.

"It is. Your name and those of your companions. Show him, Brian."

"We can do that another time. We have more important matters to discuss now," said Derek, casting Aran an irate glance. "We have been sent by the Knight's Council to find and bring back to Sancrist a valuable artifact called a dragon orb. We heard rumors that this orb might be found in Icereach, and we have stopped here at the ancient library to try to gain more information. The kender has been of valuable assistance to us in this."

Sturm smoothed his mustaches, embarrassed and uneasy. "I do not like to speak ill of anyone, my lords, especially Tasslehoff, whom I have known for many years and whom I consider a friend—"

Derek frowned at the thought of anyone considering a kender a friend, but fortunately, Sturm didn't notice.

"—you should be aware, however, that Tas, while a very good-hearted person, is known to sometimes . . . er . . . fabricate—"

"If you are trying to say that the kender is a little liar, I am aware of that," stated Derek impatiently. "The kender is not lying now. We have proof of the veracity of his claims. I think you and your friends should come see for yourselves."

"If Tasslehoff has been able to help you, I am glad. I'm sure Tanis will want to speak to him," Sturm added wryly. "Now, if there is nothing more to discuss—"

"Just one thing—who is the woman in the veil?" Brian asked curiously, glancing over his shoulder.

The woman was still seated on a bench, speaking to the true elf and the half-elf. The dwarf stumped about nearby.

"Lady Alhana, daughter of the King of Silvanesti," Sturm answered. His gaze warmed as it fell upon her.

"Silvanesti!" Aran repeated, amazed. "She is far from home. What is a Silvanesti elf doing in Tarsis?"

"The reach of the Dark Queen is long," said Sturm gravely. "The dragonarmies are about to invade her homeland. The lady has risked her life to travel to Tarsis in search of mercenaries to help the elves fight off their foes. It was for that she was arrested. Mercenaries are not welcome in this city, nor are those who seek to hire them."

"Do you mean to say the dragonarmies have moved so far south that they threaten to attack Silvanesti?" asked Brian, aghast.

"So it would seem, my lord," Sturm replied. He glanced at Derek and said in tones of sympathy and regret, "I hear war has come to Solamnia as well."

"Castle Crownguard fell to the dragonarmies, as did Vingaard," said Derek stolidly, "and all the realm to the east. Palanthas yet stands, as does the High Clerist's' Tower, but the fiends may launch an attack at any moment."

"I am sorry, my lord," said Sturm earnestly, and he looked Derek in the eye for the first time. "Truly sorry."

"We do not need sympathy. What we need is the power to drive these butchers from our homeland," Derek replied harshly. "That is why this dragon orb is of such vital importance. According to the kender, it confers upon the one who masters it the ability to control dragons."

"If that is true, it would indeed be good news for all of us who fight for the cause of freedom," Sturm said. "I will go inform my friends."

He walked off to speak to the half-elf.

"Now, I suppose we must be civil to these people," said Derek dourly, and bracing himself, he went to join Sturm.

Aran stared after him. "You know what he's doing, don't you, Brian? He's being nice to Brightblade so he will help us keep hold of the kender. Otherwise, Derek wouldn't give Sturm the back of his hand."

"Maybe," Brian admitted. "though, to do him justice, I honestly believe Derek doesn't think of it like that. In his mind, he's doing this for Solamnia."

Aran tugged on his mustaches. "You're a good friend to him, Brian. I wish he deserved you."

He started to reach for his flask, then remembered it was empty, and with a sigh sauntered off to make the acquaintance of Sturm Brightblade's regrettable friends.

———————————

As it turned out, one was not so regrettable, not even to Derek, who felt no reduction of his dignity upon being introduced to the Lady Alhana. The Solamnics had not been ruled by a king for many centuries, but the knights were still respectful of royalty and charmed by it, especially by such surpassingly beautiful royalty as Alhana Starbreeze.

They proceeded to the library, where they found the kender perusing books with the magical glasses. The half-elf, who had been presented to them as Tanis Half-Elven, was inclined to be severe with Tas for running off, but eventually Tanis relented, when it appeared that Tasslehoff was actually able to read the ancient texts and was not making it all up.

While the knights and the kender and his friends were talking, Brian slipped away to go in search of Lillith. He had been disappointed to find, on his return, that she had left upon some errand. He went back to the entrance and found Marcus peering nervously up the stairs.

"There's a bad feeling in the air," he said. "Do you notice?"

Brian remembered Aran saying the same thing not so long ago. Now that Marcus had called his attention to it, Brian did feel ill-at-ease. As Aran had said, it was as though someone were walking across his grave.

"Where's Lillith?" Brian asked.

"She's praying in our chapel," Marcus replied. He indicated a room off to one side of the main entrance. Another door, marked with the book and the scales, stood partway ajar.

Brian was startled by this. He didn't know what to do.

"It's just . . . we might be leaving soon . . . I wanted to see her . . ."

"You can go in," Marcus said, smiling.

"I wouldn't want to interrupt—"

"It's all right."

Brian hesitated, then he walked over and gently pushed on the door.

The chapel was quite small, large enough for only a few people at a time. At the far end was an altar. On the altar lay an open book and beside it was a scale of balance, perfectly poised so that both sides were equal. Lillith was not kneeling, as Brian had half expected. She sat cross-legged before the altar, very much at her ease. She was speaking in a low voice, but it did not seem that she was praying so much as holding a conversation with her god, for she would occasionally emphasize a point with a gesture.

Brian opened the door a little farther, intending to slip into the back of the room, but the door hinges creaked. Lillith turned around and smiled at him.

"I'm sorry," Brian said. "I didn't mean to disturb you."

"Gilean and I were just talking," she said.

"You speak of him as though he were a friend," said Brian.

"He is," said Lillith, rising to her feet. Her dimple flashed.

"But he's a god. At least, you believe he is a god," said Brian.

"I respect and revere him as a god," Lillith answered, "but when I come to him, he makes me feel welcome as if I were visiting an old friend."

Brian glanced down at the altar, trying to think of some way to change the subject, which made him uncomfortable. He looked at the book, thinking it must be some holy text, and said in astonishment, "The pages of the book are blank. Why is that?"

"To remind us that our lives are made up of blank sheets waiting to be filled," Lillith replied. "The book of life is open when we are born, and it closes with our death. We write in it continually, but no matter how much we write, what joy or sorrow we experience or what mistakes we have made, we will always turn the page, and tomorrow's page is always blank."

"Some people might find that prospect daunting," said Brian somberly, looking down at the page, so starkly white and empty.

"I find it filled with hope," said Lillith. She moved close to him.

He took hold of her hands and clasped them in his own. "I know what I want to write on tomorrow's page. I want to write my love for you."

"Then let us write it on today's page," said Lillith softly. "We will not wait for tomorrow."

A small cut-crystal jar filled with ink stood on the altar; beside it was a feather pen. Lillith dipped the quill in the ink and then, half-serious and half-laughing, she drew a heart on the page, as might a child, and wrote his name, Brian, inside the heart.

Brian picked up the pen and was going to write her name, but he was interrupted by the sound of horn calls coming from outside the library. Though the horns were distant, far away, still he recognized them. His stomach clenched. His heart thudded. His hand jerked and dropped the pen that had been forming the letter "L".

He turned toward the door.

"What is that dreadful noise?" Lillith gasped.

The blaring noise was growing louder by the moment. She grimaced at the discordant, raucous blaring.

"What is it?" she asked urgently. "What does it mean?"

"The dragonarmies," said Brian, striving to be calm for her sake. "What we feared has happened. Tarsis is under attack."

He and Lillith looked at each other. This was the moment they must part, he to his duty, she to hers. They gave each other the gift of a precious moment, a moment to cling to each other, a moment to memorize a loved face, a moment they would each hold in the coming darkness. Then they let go, each turning away.

"Marcus," Lillith called, running out of the chapel. "Fetch the Aesthetics! Bring them here!"

"Derek!" Brian shouted. "The dragonarmies! I'm going out to take a look!"

He was about to race up the stairs when he heard raised voices coming from the library's interior. Brian groaned inwardly. He could guess what was going on. He turned from the stairs and made his way among the bookshelves, moving as rapidly as possible, hoping to head off a dispute.

"Where do you think you are going, kender?" Derek could be heard shouting.

"With Tanis!" Tas yelled back, sounding amazed at the question. "You're knights. You can get along fine without me, but my friends need me!"

"We offer you our protection, Half-Elven," Derek was saying as

Brian arrived. "Are you turning that down?"

"I thank you, Sir Knight," Tanis replied, "but as I told you, we cannot go with you. We have friends in the Red Dragon. We must return to them—"

"Bring the kender, Sturm," Derek ordered, "and come with us."

"I cannot, sir," Sturm replied. He rested his hand on the half-elf's shoulder. "He is my leader, and my first loyalty is to my friends."

Derek was incensed that Sturm Brightblade, a Solamnic, would have the temerity to refuse a direct order from a knight who was his superior by birth, and to add insult to injury, instead proudly proclaim that he obeyed the orders of some half-breed elf.

Tanis understood. He started to say something, perhaps to try to assuage Derek's ire, but Derek intervened.

"If that is your decision, I cannot stop you," Derek said, cold with anger. "But this is another black mark against you, Sturm Brightblade. Remember that you are not a knight. Not yet. Pray that I am not there when the question of your knighthood comes before the Council."

Sturm went livid. He cast a conscience-stricken look at the half-elf, who appeared considerably astonished.

"What did he say?" the dwarf demanded. "The knight's not a knight?"

"Leave it, Flint," said Tanis quietly. "It doesn't matter."

"Well, of course it doesn't matter." Flint shook his fist under Derek's nose. "We're glad he's not one of you stuck-up steel-for-brains knights! It would serve you right if we *did* leave you with the kender!"

"Tanis," Sturm said in low tones, "I can explain—"

"There's no time for explanations!" Tanis was shouting in his urgency. "Listen! They're coming closer. Gentlemen, I wish you success. Sturm, see to the Lady Alhana. Tasslehoff, you're coming with me." Tanis laid firm hands on the kender. "If we get separated, we'll meet at the Red Dragon Inn."

The horn calls were coming closer. Tanis managed to marshal his friends together and they hurried off, following the kender, who knew the path through the bookshelves. Derek glared at the books piled on the table in frustration. There were a number not yet studied.

"At least we know there's an orb in Icereach, and we know what it does," Aran pointed out. "Now let's get out of this city before all hell breaks loose."

"The horses are stabled near the main gate. We can escape in the confusion—" Brian added.

"We need that kender!" Derek stated.

"Derek, be reasonable," Aran said, but Derek was unpacking his armor and refused to heed him.

The time for disguising themselves was past. They might have to fight their way out of the city, and Aran and Derek buckled on their breastplates over chain mail and put on their helms. Brian, who had lost his armor when his horse ran off, had to make do with his leather. They sorted through their gear, took only what they deemed necessary, and left the rest behind. They made their way among the books, back to the entrance.

"I thank you for your assistance, Mistress," Derek said to Lillith, who was keeping guard on the door. "How do we find the Red Dragon Inn?"

Lillith stared at him in astonishment. "This is a strange time to go inquiring for a room, sir."

"Please, Mistress, we don't have much time," Derek stated.

Lillith shrugged. "Go back to the center of the city. The inn's not far from the Hall of Justice."

"You go on ahead," said Brian to the others. "I'll catch up."

Derek cast him an annoyed glance, but made no comment. Aran grinned at Brian and winked, then he and Derek dashed up the stairs.

Brian turned to Lillith. "Shut and seal the door. They won't find it—"

"I will," she said. Her voice trembled a little, but she was composed and even managed a smile. "I'm waiting for the other Aesthetics to come. We have laid in supplies. We'll be safe. Draconians are not interested in books—"

No, thought Brian, despairing, they're only interested in killing.

He gave her a last, lingering kiss, then—hearing Derek bellowing—he tore himself away from her and ran after his friends.

"May the Gods of Light watch over you!" she called after him.

Brian glanced back over his shoulder and waved his hand in

farewell. The last he saw of her, she was smiling and waving, then a shadow passed overhead, blotting out the sun.

Brian looked up to see the red wings and enormous red body of a dragon. The dragonfear swept over him, crushing hope and rending courage. His sword arm faltered. He staggered as he ran, barely able to breathe for the terror that seemed to darken everything around him.

The dragonarmies had not come to conquer Tarsis. They had come to destroy it.

Brian fought against the fear that twisted inside him so that he was nearly physically ill. He wondered if Derek and Aran were watching him, a witness to his weakness, and pride and anger bolstered him. He kept running. The red monster flew by, heading toward those sections of Tarsis where panic-stricken people were thronging into the streets.

Brian found Aran and Derek sheltered in the shadows of a crumbling doorway.

More red dragons came, their wings filling the skies. The knights heard the roaring of the monstrous beasts, saw them wheel and dive down upon their helpless victims, breathing great gouts of fire that incinerated everything and everyone it touched. Smoke began to rise as buildings exploded into flame. Even from this distance, they could hear the horrible screams of the dying.

Aran had gone ashen. Derek maintained his stern composure but only by great effort. He had to lick his lips twice before he could speak.

"We're going to the inn."

They all ducked involuntarily as a red dragon flew overheard, his belly skimming the treetops. Had the dragon looked down, he would have seen them, but the beast's fierce eyes were staring hungrily ahead. He was eager to join in the slaughter.

"Derek, that's madness," Aran hissed. Sweat beaded his lip beneath his helm. "The dragon orb is what is important. Forget the damn kender!" He pointed to the thickening coils of black smoke. "Look at that! We might as well march into the Abyss!"

Derek gave him a cold look. "I'm going to the inn. If you're afraid, I'll meet you back at our campsite."

He started off, running down the street, dodging from one shelter to another, diving from a doorway to a grove of trees to a building, trying to avoid attracting the attention of the dragons.

Brian looked helplessly at Aran, who flung up his hands in exasperation.

"I suppose we'll have to go with him! At least maybe we can keep the idiot from getting himself killed."

BOOK III

1

The Red Dragon Inn. The chase.

Upon leaving Icereach, Kitiara and Skie had met up with her force of blue dragons and her sivak draconian guards, who had been loitering about on the outskirts of Thorbardin, keeping watch on the dwarven kingdom to see if those on the bounty list turned up. Kit had a good excuse for going to Tarsis. Ariakas had recently promoted Fewmaster Toede to the position of Dragon Highlord of the Red Wing, though on a temporary basis. Kitiara could tell the emperor she had gone to view the battle brewing there to see how the hobgoblin conducted himself.

The blue dragons had heard about the possibility of an attack on the city and were eager to get in on the fighting. Skie was the only dragon who was not pleased at the prospect, and this was because he knew the truth. Kitiara wasn't going to Tarsis to fight or to evaluate the hobgoblin. She was going for her own personal reasons. She'd told him as much.

Skie revered Kitiara as few dragons in the history of Krynn had revered a human. He honored Kitiara's courage. He could personally attest to her skill and her intelligence when it came to warfare. He credited her tactics and strategy with having conquered much of Solamnia, and he was convinced that if Kitiara had been in charge of the war instead of Ariakas they would have now been taking their ease in the conquered city of Palanthas. Kitiara was calm and cold-blooded, masterful and courageous in battle. But when it came to her personal life, she gave in to her wayward passions and let desire master her.

She went from lover to lover, using them, then discarding them. She thought she was in control of these affairs, but Skie knew better. Kitiara thirsted for love as some thirst for dwarf spirits. She hungered for it as a glutton does his dinner. She needed men to adore her and even when she no longer loved them they were supposed to continue to love her. Ariakas was perhaps the sole exception, and that was because Kitiara had let him love her simply to achieve advancement. They understood each other, probably because they were alike. He required of women what Kit required of men. He was the only man Kitiara feared, and she was the only woman to daunt Ariakas.

Take this Bakaris, Skie thought. Kitiara's sub-commander and her current lover. Charming, handsome, he was an adequate soldier, but certainly not her equal. Left to his own devices in Solamnia, which is where he was now, he'd make a pig's breakfast of the battle should they be called upon to fight. Skie only hoped that this foray into the south didn't keep her away from the war too long.

Skie didn't know the identity of the man she was chasing after in Tarsis. She hadn't told him that. All he knew was that it was someone she had known in her youth. Skie was confident it would be only a matter of time before Kit told him everything. He was the one being she trusted implicitly. Let her find this long-lost lover, whoever he was, Skie thought, and get him out of her system. Then she could get back to business.

They established their headquarters outside the city, near a hot springs Skie had discovered. Kitiara sent spies armed with Toede's bounty list to Tarsis and other cities in the region and also sent search parties with orders to keep an eye on the major trade routes.

Although the snow hampered their efforts considerably, one of the search parties did come across something, though not what Kit had expected.

"Why haven't Rag and his baaz reported in?" Kitiara asked the sivak commander of her squad of draconians.

The sivak had no idea, and he sent a patrol on dragonback to find out. They returned with unfortunate news.

"Rag and his men are dead, my lord," the sivak reported. "We found what was left of them near a bridge south of Tarsis. The tracks in the snow indicated three men riding horses. They were on the road leading from Rigitt. One of the horses apparently bolted, for its tracks ran off back to the south. Two horses left the bridge together, traveling west, leaving the road and cutting across country.

"We found the runaway horse wandering about the plains," the sivak added, "and on it was this."

He held up a bracer decorated with the kingfisher and the rose.

"Solamnic Knights," Kitiara muttered irritably. She shuffled through reports from her other spies, searching for one of them in particular.

The knight, Derek Crownguard, traveling with two fellow knights, arrived in Rigitt. The three men hired horses, stating they were planning to ride to Tarsis . . .

"Son of a bitch," swore Kitiara.

Of course it had to have been them. Who else but Solamnic knights would have dispatched draconian warriors so handily? She couldn't believe it.

"How long have they been dead?" she asked.

"A couple of days, maybe," the sivak replied.

"Son of a bitch!" Kit swore again, this time with more vehemence. "So the bridge was left unwatched for days. The felons we are after could have crossed unnoticed, entering Tarsis without our knowledge."

"We didn't see any other footprints, but we will find them if they did, my lord," the sivak promised, and that proved to be the case.

"Those you seek are in Tarsis, my lord," the sivak reported a day later. "They entered the gates this morning. All of them." He pointed to the bounty list. "Matches the descriptions perfectly. They are staying in the Red Dragon Inn."

"Excellent," said Kitiara, rising. Her face was flushed, her eyes glinting with excitement. "Summon Skie. I will fly there immediately—"

"There is, um, a slight problem." The sivak gave a deferential cough. "Some of them have been arrested."

"What?" Kitiara glared at him, hands on her hips. "Arrested? Who was the fool who ordered that?"

The moment she mentioned the word "fool" the answer came to her.

"Toede!"

"Not Highlord Toede in person," the sivak said. "He sent a draconian emissary who is conducting the 'negotiations' with the Lord of Tarsis in Toede's name. It seems that one of the gate guards recognized the Solamnic knight—this Sturm Brightblade," added the sivak, consulting the list. "The gate guard told the Lord of Tarsis, who seemed inclined to make nothing of it. The draconian emissary insisted that the guards be sent to bring in the knight and his companions for 'questioning.'"

"I'll wring that hob's neck!" Kit said through her teeth. "Does this emissary know these people are on this bounty list?"

"I don't think he made the connection, my lord. All he knew was that a Solamnic knight had arrived in the city. The reason I say that is because some of the group were allowed to remain in the inn. The half-elf, the knight, the elf, the dwarf and the kender were the only ones taken into custody."

Kitiara relaxed. "So the half-elf and the others are in prison."

The sivak coughed again. "No, my lord."

"By our Queen, what else went wrong?" Kit demanded.

"It seems there was a riot, and in the confusion the kender disappeared. The others appeared in court along with another elf, who turned out to be daughter of King Lorac. They were all being taken off to prison when the guards were attacked by three cloaked men who rescued the prisoners."

"Don't tell me," said Kit in a dangerously calm voice. "The three men who rescued them were Solamnic knights."

"It appears so, my lord," said the sivak after a slight hesitation. "My informant overheard them speaking the Solamnic tongue, and the knight, Brightblade, recognized the others."

Kitiara slumped back down in her chair. "Where are they now?"

"I regret to say the knight and his companions escaped. My men are searching for them. However, the women on the list and the other men, including the wizard and the cleric of Paladine, are still in the inn."

"At least something has gone right," said Kit, good spirits returning. "The half-elf will not abandon these people. They're his friends. He'll be back for them. Keep your spies at the Red Dragon Inn. No, wait. I will go there myself—"

"There's, uh, one more problem, my lord," the sivak said, sidling back a few steps to be out of sword range in case her wrath got the better of her. "Highlord Toede has ordered the attack. As we speak, dragons are flying on Tarsis."

———————————

"I told that fool to wait for my signal!" Kitiara fumed to Skie as the dragon climbed toward the clouds.

She pressed herself close to Skie's body, hunching down low over the dragon's neck so as to add as little possible wind resistance. Taking off was always the most difficult part for the dragons. Even without riders, lifting their ponderous bodies into the air required great strength. Some riders were inconsiderate of their mounts, doing little to aid them and sometimes actually impeding them.

Kitiara understood instinctively how to help Skie, perhaps because she loved flying. When in the air, she and her dragon melded together. She felt almost as if she was the one who had wings. In battle, she knew Skie's every move before he made it, just as he knew by the touch of her knees on his flanks or her hand upon his neck where she wanted to go—always to the fiercest part of the fighting.

A flight of blue dragons soared after them, each dragon leaping into the air, following Skie, their leader. This was always a proud moment for him, and for her, as he knew well.

"The reds will not be pleased to see us," Skie shouted over the rush of cold air.

Kitiara remarked what the red dragons could do with themselves and added a few choice words about what they could do with Toede into the bargain.

"We are looking for an inn called the Red Dragon," she told Skie.

"I think you're a little late!" he called out.

They had just come in sight of Tarsis—or rather what had once been Tarsis.

Smoke and flame billowed into the air. Skie's nostrils twitched and he shook his mane. He enjoyed the stench of destruction, but clouds of thick smoke would make seeing anything on the ground below damn difficult.

Kitiara had anticipated this, however, and had sent scouts into the city. She and Skie waited at some distance for the scouts to return, the dragon wheeling in easy circles just beyond the clouds of smoke. They had not been waiting long when a wyvern-rider came into view, emerging from the pall that covered the doomed city. Sighting the Highlord, the wyvern-rider changed course and flew over to them in haste.

"Slow down," Kitiara commanded her dragon.

Skie's lip curled in a sneer, but he did as he was ordered. Like most dragons, he detested wyverns. He considered them filthy beasts, a mockery of dragons, with their grotesque bird-legs, stunted, scaly bodies, and barbed tails. He glared at the wyvern as it approached, warning it not to come too near. Since the blue dragon could have snapped the wyvern in two with one bite, the wyvern heeded the blue's warning, forcing the sivak rider to shout at the top of his lungs to make himself heard.

"The inn has been hit, my lord! Part of it has collapsed. The Red Wing's troops have it surrounded." The sivak draconian gestured. "That flight of reds you see is going to—"

Kitiara wasn't about to wait to hear what the reds were planning to do. Skie understood her need, and he had altered course and was soaring after the reds before she had given him the command.

"Return to your post!" she shouted at the sivak, who saluted, and the wyvern sped thankfully away.

Blue dragons are smaller and more maneuverable than the hulking red dragons. Skie and his blues easily caught up with the reds, who were, as Skie had predicted, extremely displeased to see them. The reds glared balefully at the blues, who glared just as balefully back.

Kitiara and the leader of the Red Wing held a brief mid-air conference; the red shouting to Kit that he had orders from Toede to kill—not capture—the felons if he found them. Kit shouted back that he would be the one killed, not captured, unless he brought the assassins to her alive and well. The commander of the Red Wing knew Kitiara. He also knew Toede. He saluted Kit respectfully and flew off.

"Locate the inn," Kit ordered Skie and the rest of the blues. "We're searching for three people, remember, a half-elf, a human wizard, and his big, dumb-looking brother."

The dragons flew into the smoke, blinking their eyes and keeping sharp watch to make certain no smoldering cinder landed on the vulnerable membranes of their wings. The blues had to be careful, for the reds, drunk with the joy of killing and burning, were heedless and reckless in their flight, swooping down on hapless people trying to escape, breathing flame on them, then watching them run, screaming, hair and clothes on fire, until they collapsed in the street.

Paying no attention to where they were going, the reds blundered into buildings, smashing them, knocking them down with their tails. They would also blunder into each other in the smoke and confusion, and Skie and the other blue dragons had to do some fancy maneuvering to avoid collisions. A few jolts of lightning breath helped drive away reds who flew too close.

The stench of burnt flesh, the screams of the dying, the rumble of falling towers, was nothing new to Kitiara. She paid little heed to anything going on around her, concentrating instead on peering through the smoke into the occasional patch of clear air created by the flapping of Skie's wings.

She had scouted out the part of the city in which the inn was located and she soon spotted it, for it was—or had been—one of the larger buildings in the area. The inn was under attack by draconian forces, battling those inside.

Kit sucked in her breath. She knew perfectly well who was in there, fighting for his life and the lives of his friends. She imagined herself strolling into the inn amidst the smoke, climbing over the rubble, finding Tanis, reaching out her hand to him, and saying, "Come with me." He'd be astonished, of course. She could picture the look on his face.

"Griffons!" Skie bellowed.

Kitiara blinked away her reverie and peered intently through the eyeslits of her helm, cursing the smoke, for she couldn't see. Then there they were, a flight of griffons flying low beneath the smoke, coming to the rescue of those trapped in the inn.

Kitiara uttered an exclamation of anger. Griffons are ferocious creatures, afraid of nothing, and they fell on the draconians who surrounded the inn, snatching them up in their sharp talons, snapping off their heads with their beaks, as an eagle eats a rat.

"There are elves mixed up in this!" Skie snarled.

Griffons, though fiercely independent, revere elves, and bonded griffons will serve them if their need is great. Griffons on their own would have never flown into a raging battle, risking their lives to save humans. These griffons were here on orders from some elf lord. Those who had been trapped in the ruins of the inn could be seen clambering onto the backs of the griffons, who wasted no time. Having picked up their passengers, they took off, flying north.

"Who escaped?" Kit cried. "Could you see them?"

Skie was about to answer when a red dragon appeared, barreling through the smoke. Catching sight of the fleeing griffons, the red flew after them, intending to incinerate them.

"Cut him off!" Kitiara ordered.

Skie disapproved of Kit involving herself in this fight, but he did enjoy thwarting any red dragon, who, because they were bigger, considered themselves better. Skie swooped in front of the red's nose, forcing the huge dragon to almost flip himself head over tail in order to avoid a crash.

"Are you mad?" the red roared furiously. "They're escaping!"

Kitiara ordered the red to go kill people in some other part of the city and sent her blue dragons off in pursuit of the griffons, reminding them several times that the people the griffons carried were to be taken alive and brought straight back to her.

"Aren't we going after them?" Skie demanded.

"I need to make sure who they were. I don't want to leave until I find out they were the ones who escaped. I couldn't see them. Could you?" she yelled at Skie.

Skie had been able to get a good look at them while Kit was arguing with the red dragon.

"Your wizard and a large human warrior, a human female with red hair and a man clad in leather. He could have been a half-breed. He looked to be the leader, for he was giving the orders. Oh, and a couple of barbarians."

Kitiara asked him sharply, "There was no blonde elf woman?"

"No, lord," said Skie, wondering what this had to do with anything.

"Good," Kitiara said. "Maybe she's dead." Then she frowned. "What about Flint, Sturm and the kender? Tanis would never leave them behind . . . So maybe that wasn't him on the griffon . . ."

"What are your orders, Lord?" Skie asked impatiently.

The dragon was hoping she would think better of this folly and tell him to recall the blues who had gone winging after the griffons. Fast beasts, griffons. They were already nearly out of sight. The blues would be hard-pressed to catch them. He hoped she would tell him they were all going to go back to Solamnia, to forests teeming with deer and glorious battles to be fought and cities to be conquered.

What she told him was not what he had hoped for or expected. Her order confounded him utterly.

"Set me down on the street."

Skie twisted his head around to stare at her. "Are you mad?"

"I know what I am about," she said. "That cleric of Paladine, Elistan, was not among those you mentioned, yet he was staying at the inn. I must find out what has become of him."

"You said the cleric was of no importance! He wasn't the one you were after. Those you were after are disappearing over the horizon."

"I've changed my mind. Set me down!" Kitiara repeated angrily. "You go with the other blues. Continue your pursuit of those on griffon-back, and when you catch them, bring them back to camp. Alive!" she emphasized. "I want them alive."

"Highlord," said Skie earnestly, doing as he was told but not liking it, "you are taking a great risk! This city is going up in flames, and it's filled with draconians thirsting for trouble. They'll kill you first and find out you are a Highlord after!"

"I can take care of myself," Kit told him.

"The one you seek has escaped Tarsis! Why go back? Don't tell me that you're chasing after some foul cleric!"

Kit glared at him as she hoisted herself out of the saddle, but she did not answer. The dragon had no idea what she was scheming. But he knew full well it had nothing to do with the war and everything to do with her current obsession.

"Kitiara," Skie pleaded, "let this go. You risk not only your command, you risk your life!"

"You have your orders," Kitiara told him, and Skie saw by the look in her eye that he continued this argument at his peril.

Skie landed on the only patch of open ground he could find—the marketplace. The area was littered with bodies, the smoldering ruins of stalls and trampled vegetables, terrified dogs howling, and roving draconians, their swords red with blood. Kitiara climbed out of the saddle.

"Remember!" she said to Skie, as he was about to take to the air, "I want them alive!"

Skie grunted that he'd only heard that about six hundred times. He flew up through the smoke that had smelled so good to him at the start, but which he now found annoying, for it clogged his lungs and stung his eyes.

He would obey Kitiara's orders, though the last thing Kit needed was to be caught by Ariakas romping in the bed of a half-elf who had killed Verminaard.

Skie would chase after this half-elf, but he'd be damned if he was going to catch him!

———————————

Iolanthe watched Kitiara make her way through the ravaged city. The smell of burning was in the air here as well, but the smell did not come from smoldering wooden beams or charred flesh. The smell came from the burnt black curls—a few wisps of hair withering in the fire of Iolanthe's spell.

Iolanthe was in her chambers in Neraka, watching Kitiara with intense interest, noting those details she might decide to share with Ariakas when she made her report to him. He no longer sat in on the spell-casting when Iolanthe spied on Kit. He was too busy, he told her curtly.

Iolanthe knew the truth. He would never admit it, but he was deeply hurt by Kitiara's betrayal. It was the winternorn, Feal-Thas, who had placed the last rock on Kitiara's funeral pyre. He had sent Ariakas a detailed report on Kitiara, claiming to have probed the depths of Kitiara's soul to discover she was infatuated with a half-elf who was implicated in the slaying of Verminaard. Iolanthe had been there when he'd read the report, and Ariakas had flown into such a blind, furious rage that for a few moments Iolanthe had trembled for her own life.

Ariakas had eventually calmed down, but though his fury no longer blazed, it continued to smolder. He was convinced that Kitiara was responsible for the death of Verminaard. Ariakas sent his guards to Solamnia in search of Kit, only to be told by her sub commander, Bakaris, that she was not around. She had gone off on some mysterious errand with Skie and had taken a flight of blues with her.

Ariakas had no doubt she was going to meet her half-breed lover, and he began to believe she was in some sort of conspiracy with the half-elf, against him. The fact that she'd taken the blues with her confirmed his suspicions. She was going to establish herself in opposition to him, challenge him for the Crown of Power.

Ariakas had ordered Iolanthe to use her magic to locate Kitiara and report back what she discovered.

So now Iolanthe watched as Kitiara commandeered a squad of draconians roaming through the marketplace. She divested herself of her Highlord helm and armor, wrapped them in her cloak, and stashed them beneath a pile of rubble. Kit snatched a cloak off a corpse and wrapped herself in it. She tied a scarf over her nose and mouth, to protect her from smoke and the stench of death, and also to conceal her identity, for she stuffed her black curly hair into a hat stolen from the same corpse.

This done, Kitiara set off down the street, accompanied by the draconians, heading in the direction of the inn in which Iolanthe had heard her tell the dragon the half-elf had been staying. Meanwhile, the half-elf was escaping on griffon-back. Iolanthe couldn't understand what was going on. Why hadn't Kit gone after him? Iolanthe began to think she'd been mistaken about Kit. Perhaps she had decided to apprehend this cleric of Paladine, in which case, she would return a hero, for half of Ansalon was searching for this cleric, while the other half were looking for the elusive Green Gemstone man.

Iolanthe was intrigued. After watching what Kitiara had been doing so far, witnessing all the foolish mistakes she'd made, Iolanthe had been about to place her money on the emperor, but now she wasn't so sure. This horse was performing much better than anticipated.

2

The wrath of the god. Rivals.

K it walked the bloody, burnt streets of Tarsis. She had with her a squad of draconians, who had been amazed and not terribly pleased to see this Blue Dragon Highlord appear out of the smoke and flame of the dying city and order them to accompany her. Kitiara's untimely arrival had spoiled the draconians' plans for looting, raping, and butchering. Now they had to protect this blasted Highlord, which meant they were missing out on the fun. The baaz did as they were ordered, but they were sullen and inclined to grumble.

Kitiara's own plans for what she intended to do were vague, half-formed, something unusual for the woman who never went into battle without a well-thought-out plan of attack. Her first impulse had been to fly off in pursuit of Tanis and her half-brothers, but it had occurred to her that Skie could chase them down on his own. Kitiara needed to find out what had happened to her rival. Was Laurana dead? Had she and Tanis quarreled, separated, or chosen deliberately to take different paths?

Above all else, Kitiara wanted to see Laurana, to talk to her. One of Kit's father's dictums: know your enemy!

The red dragons continued to fly overhead, though now their enjoyment was dampened; they could not attack anymore, for their own troops had marched into the city. The red dragons dove down now and then to breathe a gout of flame on a building or chase after those who had fled the city and were trying to escape across the plains. The wind rose, fanning the fires that yet burned, picking up sparks and cinders and flinging them about, starting additional blazes.

Draconians and goblins roamed the streets in packs. Some of them were drunk by this time and were engaged in looting or looking to satiate other, more dreadful appetites. They had ceased fighting the few brave or desperate men and women who continued to battle. A lone human, Kitiara might have been menaced, but for her draconian troops. Seeing a commanding-looking man (for such she appeared) striding purposefully down the street, accompanied by a squad of baaz, even the most drunken draconian knew her for an officer, and since officers were to be avoided at all costs, they left her alone.

The streets were filled with the dead and dying. Some victims, caught in the fiery breath of the dragons, had been reduced to lumps of charred flesh, unrecognizable as human. Others had been cut down by swords, shot with arrows, or spitted on spears. Bodies of men, women, and children lay in pools of blood that mingled horribly with the melting snow. The gutters of Tarsis ran red.

Some people were still alive, but to judge by their tortured screams they were the unlucky ones. Some were still fighting, some had managed to escape into the hills, and some had found safe hiding places where they hunkered down in terror, afraid to breathe too loudly lest they be discovered.

Kitiara had seen dead bodies before and she stepped over and around them, feeling neither pity nor compassion, paying them little heed. The baaz who accompanied her had been among those who were in the city prior to the attack and they knew where the Red Dragon Inn was located. They led Kit, who had lost her way in the smoke and the rubble, to her destination, hoping to get rid of her as quickly as possible and get back to their fun.

Arriving at the inn—or what was left of it—Kitiara ordered her troops to halt. This street was oddly quiet compared to other streets. No roving gangs, no looters. The fires had been put out. The inn was in ruins, the upper stories smoldering. No one was about. The spies she'd planted here were nowhere in sight.

Kitiara pulled down the scarf she'd tied over her nose and mouth to keep out the smoke, thinking she'd give a yell to see if anyone answered. Before she could call out, however, smoke flew down her lungs, and she could do nothing for a few moments except cough and curse Toede.

By this time, she had been seen and recognized. A shadow detached itself from a building and came strolling over to her. It was a sivak draconian and at first she thought he was one of hers, but then she noted the sivak wore the insignia of the Red Dragonarmy.

"Where is Malak?" Kit demanded.

"Dead," said the strange sivak laconically. "A red torched him by accident. Dumb-ass dragon," he added in a mutter, then, straightening his shoulders, he saluted. "Malak relayed your orders regarding the assassins to me, Highlord, and since he was dead and there was no one left but baaz"—the sivak made a disdainful gesture—"I took command."

"So what is going on here?" Kitiara asked, looking again around this part of the city that was oddly quiet, a haven of peace in a storm of chaos.

"I deployed the troops at both ends of the street, my lord," the sivak replied. "I figured you'd want the area around the inn cordoned off until you caught the felons, especially since there's money to be made off them," he added, as a seeming afterthought.

"Good idea," Kitiara said, eying the sivak with more interest. "Have you captured any of those on the list?"

"Some escaped on griffons—"

"I know that!" Kit interrupted impatiently. "What of the others? Are they alive?"

"Yes, Highlord," the sivak answered. "Come with me."

The sivak led the way down a street filled with rubble. Not a building was left undamaged. Kit had to climb over heaps of stone and broken beams and shattered glass. She could see, as she went, baaz draconians standing guard, warning away other troops who might have ventured into the area.

"We located the rest of the party," the sivak informed her as they made what haste they could among the rubble. "They're all together. I posted guards around the area to protect them, awaiting your orders. Otherwise they would be dead by now."

"Wait for me here," Kitiara told the baaz who had trailed after her. The baaz squatted down on their haunches, not sorry to have time to rest.

She and the sivak continued on for about a block, arriving at an intersection where the sivak called a halt. He pointed down a street that angled off the one on which they were standing. Kit peered through the swirling smoke. A house had collapsed into the street. A small group of people stood huddled around something lying on the ground. The group seemed nervous, continually glancing over their shoulders in fear of being attacked.

The sivak explained what had happened. "One of them—the kender—was pinned under a large beam. The rest managed to drag him out and now, near as I can tell, that guy with the beard is praying over him, trying to heal him." The sivak gave a disparaging snort. "As if any god would bother himself to heal one of the little squeakers."

The street was dark with smoke and shadows. Kitiara had to draw nearer in order to see. She recognized two of her old comrades—Flint Fireforge and Sturm Brightblade. She could not see the kender from where she stood, but she guessed it must be Tasslehoff. She gazed long at her old friends. She had not thought of them in years, but now, seeing them again, she felt a flicker of interest—Flint because he was Tanis's closest friend and Sturm because . . . well, that was a secret she kept buried deep inside, a secret she had never told anyone, a secret she didn't even trust herself to think about lest somehow it should slip out.

Flint was grayer, but otherwise much the same. Dwarves were long-lived and aged slowly. But she was shocked at the change in Sturm. When they had traveled north together five years ago, he had been handsome and youthful, albeit grave and solemn. He looked to have aged a quarter century in those five years, though, of course, part of his haggard pallor could be due to the fact that they were trapped in a city under enemy attack and his friends might be dead or dying.

Kitiara's gaze glanced off Flint and Sturm and rested on the only female in the group—blonde and obviously an elf.

"Laurana." Kitiara growled the word in her throat.

This woman, like the others, was covered in soot and dirt, her clothes sodden from the rain, filthy and bedraggled, her face streaked with tears. Yet even as Kitiara could look into the sky and see through the clouds of greasy, ugly smoke the bright radiance of the sun, so she could look through the dirt and grime, fear and sorrow and see the bright radiance of the elf woman's beauty.

Kit eyed her, wondering if such a dangerously beautiful rival should be allowed to live. Now was the perfect opportunity to kill her. Tanis would never know Kit had been the cause of his beloved's death. He would think his childhood sweetheart had died in the assault on Tarsis, just one victim among many.

Of course, her other friends would have to perish, too. She could not leave them alive to tell the tale. Kit felt a twinge of regret at that. The sight of Flint and Sturm brought back memories of some of the happiest times in her life. But their deaths couldn't be helped. They might recognize her and tell Tanis she had killed his lover, and she didn't dare run that risk.

What should be her plan of attack? The knight was the only one who was armed. Flint should have been carrying his ax, but he must have dropped it in his efforts to free the kender, for he didn't have it on him. There was another elf—a male, whose resemblance to Laurana made it apparent that he was some relation, perhaps her brother. He was covered in blood, however, and though he was standing, he looked weak and ill. Nothing to worry about there. That left the vaunted cleric of Paladine—a thin, gaunt, middle-aged man, kneeling in the dirt and blood, praying to his god to heal a kender.

"I want them dead," said Kitiara, drawing her sword. "But first I must interrogate the elf maid. While I do that, you slay the others."

"Begging your pardon, my lord," said the sivak, "but Toede's put a bounty on this lot, and he'll pay up only if they're brought in alive."

"I'll pay double what Toede has offered. Here, take this," Kit added, seeing the sivak look skeptical. Reaching to her belt, she detached a purse and tossed it to the draconian. "There's far more in there than what these wretches are worth."

The sivak took a quick glance into the purse, saw the glint of steel coins, hefted the weight of the purse, did some quick mental calculations, then tied the purse securely to his battle harness. The sivak made a motion with his hand, and the baaz left their posts around the street and came to join him, moving silently on their clawed feet.

"Give me time to snatch the elf, then you attack," Kit ordered.

"Kill the knight first," the sivak advised his troops. "He's the most dangerous."

Kitiara did not have much time. Red dragons were still flying overhead, taking their time, pausing on their way out of the city to destroy anything still standing. She could hear screams, shouts and explosions. Any moment, some fool red might knock down a building on top of her. Either that or a squad of goblins, mad with battle lust, could come along and ruin everything. Kitiara slipped from shadow to shadow until she had taken up a position directly across the street from where Laurana stood.

Kit waited. Her moment would come. It always did.

Tasslehoff was sitting up. His head was covered in blood, but he was most definitely alive. The cleric raised his hands into the air. A pity his triumph wouldn't last long, Kit thought. Flint put his hand to his eyes and rubbed his nose. The dwarf would never let the kender see he was touched; he'd be shouting at Tas about something in a minute. Sturm knelt beside Tas and put his arm around him. Laurana stood watching and weeping quietly. She stood apart from the group, seemingly overcome by grief.

Kitiara darted forward. She ran swiftly on the balls of her feet, so that her footfalls made little noise. The sivak watched her bear down on her prey. He gave her a moment's head start, then raised his voice in a gurgling shout. The baaz, swords drawn, surged forward. The sivak, keeping one eye on the Highlord, ran with them.

Kitiara grabbed Laurana from behind. Clamping one hand over her mouth and shoving the point of a knife into her ribs with the other, Kit started to drag her off.

The woman was an elf, lovely and delicate. Kit half-expected her to faint in terror. What she didn't expect was for the delicate elf maid to sink her delicate teeth into Kit's hand and to kick her, hard, in the shin.

Kit grunted in pain, but she didn't let loose. She tried to haul Laurana away, but it was like trying to haul off a half-starved cougar. The elf maid twisted and writhed. She drove her nails into Kit's flesh and lashed out with her feet, almost tripping her. Kit was losing patience, starting to think that she should just knife the bitch and be done with it, when the sivak appeared.

"Need help, my lord?" he asked, and before she could answer, he had grabbed hold of Laurana's feet and lifted her off the ground. Between them, they carried her, kicking and struggling, into a nearby alley.

Here Kit released her. The evening sky was red with the lurid light of flames, and by that light, Kit could see blood welling from bite marks on her palm. She wrung her hand and glared at Laurana, who glared defiantly back at her. The sivak had the elf-maid pinned to the ground. He held his knife at her throat.

"Keep her quiet," Kit said. "I'm going to see what's happened to the rest."

She watched as the baaz bore down on their victims. Sturm was on his feet, holding his sword, as Flint had hold of his axe and stood protectively over Tasslehoff. The elf lord and the cleric were searching about, shouting Laurana's name.

"Elistan, get behind me!" Sturm called out.

The small group faced twenty baaz, eager for blood. Still, Kit knew her old friends. They wouldn't go down without a fight. She sucked on her hand, cursing Laurana, and watched. She had no doubt of the outcome, but the battle should be an interesting one.

Sturm was continuing to shout at the cleric to take cover behind him, but the cleric wasn't listening. He stood his ground and turned to face the baaz draconians, who shouted and slavered with glee at the easy kill. The cleric lifted his hands to heaven and raised his voice in a thunderous exhortation.

"Paladine, I beseech you! Send down your wrath upon the enemies of your most holy light!"

Kitiara chuckled, sucked on her bleeding hand, and waited for the baaz to spit the cleric.

A cascade of flame, white and dazzling and awful, thundered down from the heavens. The wrath of the god engulfed almost half of the attacking baaz. Half blinded, Kit could hear screams and horrible popping and sizzling sounds. When she could see again, she watched in shocked amazement as the scaly flesh melted from their bones, the bones blackened and withered away. The holy flame died, and there was nothing left of the draconians except greasy spots on the pavement.

"Damn!" said Kitiara, impressed.

The wrath of the god gave heart and strength to the others. Sturm and Flint ran to attack the remaining draconians, who, having witnessed their comrades die a horrible death, slowed their rush toward the cleric. Laurana's brother continued to shout her name.

"I'll find her," shouted the cleric, and he turned and looked in Kit's direction.

Kitiara took to her heels, hastening back to where the sivak was still holding fast to Laurana, keeping his knife at her throat. He'd bound her hands with a strip of leather cut from her own tunic.

"What was that bright light and all that screaming?" the sivak asked curiously.

"Your baaz going up in flames. Apparently Paladine is not the weak and sniveling god our Dark Queen claims," said Kitiara.

The sivak shook his scaly head. "Baaz," he muttered in disgust, "what can you expect?" Shrugging, he grinned and patted the purse she'd given him. "Fewer ways to split the take."

"We don't have much time. The cleric's headed this direction, looking for the elf." Kit squatted down to put herself eye-to-eye with Laurana. "Hand me the knife. You keep watch. Let me know if he gets close."

The sivak did as ordered and dashed off to the end of the alley. Laurana made a sudden lunge, tried to struggle to her feet.

Kitiara gave her a light tap to the jaw with her fist, not enough to knock her out, but enough to stun her. Laurana fell back and Kit put her knee on Laurana's chest, holding the knife at her throat. A trickle of red blood ran down the alabaster skin.

"I'm going to kill you," Kitiara said matter-of-factly. She was hoarse from coughing, her voice gruff.

Laurana glared at Kitiara, not in fear, but in defiance.

"I just want you to know I'm not some ordinary cutthroat," Kit continued. "I want you to know why—"

Movement at the far end of the alley caught Kit's eye. She glanced up and saw three men emerging from the smoke. They carried bloody swords in their hands, and one them held a burning torch to light their way through the smoke and gloom of coming night. The torch light shone full on his face. Kitiara recognized him immediately.

She swore almost every curse word she knew.

Derek Crownguard and his two friends were striding purposefully down the alley. She had no idea what they were doing here when they should have been out questing after dragon orbs, but that didn't matter now. What mattered was that he must not see her. If he did, if he recognized her as belonging to the enemy side, he would immediately wonder why the enemy was sending him on a quest for a dragon orb. He'd be suspicious, perhaps even refuse to continue, and that would be the end of Ariakas's pet plan.

As if this weren't trouble enough, the sivak was hissing at her from behind.

"Highlord! Best hurry with your killing. That cleric's coming!"

Kitiara put her knife to Laurana's throat.

"Go ahead, kill me," Laurana said, choking with tears. "I want to die. Then I'll be with him."

Tanis, Kitiara said to herself. She's talking about Tanis. She thinks Tanis is dead! They all think Tanis is dead!

She saw it so clearly then—the inn collapsing, Tanis buried beneath the rubble, these people escaping, the group of friends separated. Of course, each must think the other dead, and Kit would be the last to disabuse her rival of that notion.

Kitiara thrust the knife back in her boot and stood up.

"Sorry, I don't have time to kill you today, Princess, but we'll meet again—you and I."

The sivak's clawed feet scraped on the cobblestones. He skidded to a halt and stared at the knights, who, seeing the draconian, shouted and broke into a run.

A wrathful cleric at one end of the alley. Three Solamnic knights at the other.

"This way!" said the sivak, pointing up.

A balcony from a second-story window extended out over the street. Smoke was rolling off the roof, but fire had not yet engulfed the building. The sivak crouched down below the balcony, then gave a convulsive leap. His strong legs propelled him into the air. He had long, skinny arms, and he grasped hold of the balcony's railing and pulled himself up and over. Leaning down, he extended a clawed hand to Kitiara. She grabbed hold of his wrist and he dragged her up.

The sivak climbed onto the balcony's rail and balanced precariously. Another, shorter leap carried him to the roof. He dug his claws into the wooden shingles, hung a moment, kicking frantically, then managed to get a leg up. Lying on his belly, he hauled Kitiara after him.

Kit looked back down. One of the knights was bending over Laurana. The other two were staring up at the draconian and Kit, wondering if they should give pursuit. Kit didn't think they would, and she was right. With hundreds of enemy soldiers roaming the streets, there was no sense wasting precious time chasing after two of them. The cleric—who might have done some damage to them even from a distance—had stopped to tend to Laurana.

The sivak shouted at her, and Kit began to run along the rooftop. From her vantage point, she saw the remaining draconians haring off down the street, not ready to risk their lives when there were easier pickings in other parts of the doomed city. Among them were the troops Kitiara had brought with her.

"Baaz!" The sivak shook his head.

He and Kit took their time, making their way from one rooftop to the next until they ran out of buildings. The sivak could have jumped off at any point, relying on his short, stubby wings to carry him safely to the ground. He stayed with Kit, however, until he found another balcony only a short distance from the roof. From there, Kit easily jumped down to the street.

Though Kit protested that she would be safe enough, the sivak remained by her side.

"I know my way around. I can show you how to get out of the city," he said, and Kit, who had no idea where she was, accepted his help.

Fires still raged. They would burn until the buildings were consumed, for there was no one to put them out. The red dragons had departed with the coming of night, flying off to rest and gloat over the ease of their victory. Draconians, goblins and human soldiers loyal to the Dark Queen roamed the city, searching for amusement. No one was in command. Highlord Toede had stayed far away from the fighting. He would not come anywhere near Tarsis until he'd been assured there was no danger. If there were officers in the city, no commander would dare try to restrain his forces, who were drunk with liquor and blood, for fear they would turn on him. Not that there were many commanders who would do so. Most were as drunk as, or drunker than, their troops.

"Stupid idea—attacking Tarsis," the sivak commented.

A drunken goblin lurched into their path. The sivak bashed him on the jaw and kicked the crumpled body off to one side.

"We can't hold the city," the sivak went on. "No supply lines. Two days our forces will be here. Maybe three. Then we'll be forced to pull out."

He glanced at Kitiara and said slyly, "Unless, of course, this attack was your idea, Highlord. Then I'll say it was sheer genius."

Kit shook her head. "No, this wasn't my idea. It was hatched from the seething brain of your Highlord."

The sivak looked momentarily confused.

"Toede," said Kitiara. "Highlord of the Red Dragonarmy." She gestured to the insignia the sivak wore on his harness. Then, looking at it more closely, Kit grinned.

The two had reached the city gate. The sivak came to a halt. He was looking back toward the city, probably with an idea of returning to claim his share of what riches remained.

"Except you're not with the Red Dragonarmy, are you?" Kitiara said.

"Huh?" The sivak jerked his head back to face her. "Sure I am," he said, pointing to the insignia.

"It's upside down," Kit said dryly.

"Oh," returned the sivak, and he gave a sheepish grin and righted it. "That better?"

"If they catch you, they'll hang you. That's what they do to deserters."

"I didn't desert." The sivak waved a claw. "My commander and I heard about the attack on Tarsis, thought there might be some profit in it. We decided we'd bring the boys by to take a look, see what we could pick up."

"Who is your commander?"

"You know, in all the excitement, I seem to have forgotten his name," said the sivak, scratching his head and grinning. "Don't get me wrong, Highlord. We do our part for the Queen, but we figure she won't begrudge us making a bit of profit on our own. We're what you might call independent contractors. We make certain we get something more out of this war than maggot-ridden rations and latrine duty."

He cocked an eye at her. "You gonna try to arrest me, Highlord?"

Kitiara laughed. "Not after what we've been through tonight. You have served me well. You can go back to your commander. I'll be safe enough from here on. My camp is not far. Thanks for your help."

She held out her hand. "I hope you don't mind telling me *your* name?"

"Slith, my lord," said the sivak. After some hesitation, he extended his clawed hand.

"Good to meet you, Slith. I am—"

"The Blue Lady. Everyone knows you, ma'am." Slith spoke in admiring tones.

The two shook, hand and claw, then the sivak turned and headed back toward the rubble, blood, and ash that had once been Tarsis.

"Hey, Slith," Kit called after him, "if you ever stop being an independent contractor, come work for me!"

The sivak laughed, turned and waved, but kept on going.

Kitiara started walking. The plains stretched ahead of her. The night was dark and silent here, far from the chaos inside the city. The snow crunching beneath her boots was black with soot and ash. Furtive shadows slipped through the night around her—survivors lucky enough to have escaped Tarsis.

Kit let them be.

3

Saving the Kender.
Escape from Tarsis.

hen he left the library, Brian did not expect to make it out of Tarsis alive. He expected to face a well-organized and determined foe, such as the forces of the Blue Lady they had faced at Castle Crownguard and Vingaard, and he resolved to die bravely and take as many draconians with him as possible. Instead, what he and the other knights found when they went into the streets was a drunken, leaderless mob, far more interested in plundering and looting, murdering and raping, than in conquest.

The red dragons posed the biggest threat, and while they were in the skies, breathing down fire upon the city and its hapless inhabitants, the knights were in danger. They sought shelter from the beasts as best they could, ducking into doorways or diving under rubble as the dragons roared overhead, spewing flame, occasionally snatching up some hapless person in their claws and devouring him in mid-air.

Friend and enemy were both in danger from the dragons, for the reds had no compunction about blistering goblin hide or watching draconians sizzle. At one point, Brian hid beneath a smoldering oak tree alongside a quaking goblin, neither of them daring to move as a red dragon swooped low, searching for more victims. When the dragon had gone, the goblin took a gulp of some liquid from a greasy leather water skin, and, after a moment's hesitation, offered Brian a drink. Brian should have probably slain the creature, but he couldn't bring himself to do it. The two had shared a moment of terror, and both had survived. Brian politely refused the drink and waved his hand, indicating the goblin could depart. The goblin shrugged, and after a wary glance, he gave Brian a nod, then took to his heels. Derek spent the next ten minutes lecturing Brian sternly on his foolish sentimentality.

The knights had fought their way through the streets to the Red Dragon Inn, doing what they could to save people from the brutish enemy or to ease the suffering of the dying. Most of the foes the knights encountered took one look at their grim faces and bloody swords, and unless they were bolder or drunker than most, ran off. It soon became clear to the knights that once the dragonarmy had gutted Tarsis, the soldiers would depart, slinking away into the night, hung-over and loaded down with spoils and slaves. The Highlord had no plans to occupy this city, merely to destroy it.

Derek never lost sight of his goal, which was to find the Red Dragon Inn and find out what had become of the kender. But as they were walking down a side street near the inn, the knights came upon a draconian and a human soldier bending over a fallen woman, obviously with evil intent. The knights hastened to rescue the woman from the two, but before they could reach them, the draconian and the soldier had escaped into the night, climbing over the rooftops.

"Should we go after them?" Aran asked wearily.

They were all exhausted, half-suffocated from the smoke. Brian's throat was raw from coughing and parched from thirst. They dared not drink the water from any of the wells, for it all had a reddish tinge to it.

"Pointless," Derek said, shaking his head. "Brian, see that the woman has come to no harm. Aran, come with me. The inn is in the next block."

Brian hastened over to help and found a middle-aged man helping the woman to her feet. Brian assumed he must be a relative until, getting a good view of the woman, he saw that she was an elf, and even though her face was smeared with dirt, soot, blood and streaked with tears, her beauty made him catch his breath.

The man rose to his feet at the sight of the armed men, and he stood protectively in front of the woman, prepared to defend her. Brian saw the man was bearded and that he wore robes that must have once been white, though they were now gray from the soot and ash raining down over the city. He stood tall, upright and unafraid, though he had no weapons. A medallion on his chest flickered in the lurid light. He was a cleric.

A cleric and an elf woman.

"Have no fear. I am a Solamnic knight, sir," said Brian. He turned around and shouted over his shoulder, "Derek! I've found them. You must be Elistan, I think," Brian added, turning back to the two, who were regarding him in astonishment. "And you must be Laurana of Qualinesti. Are you hurt, Mistress? Did they harm you?"

"No, but they meant to," Laurana said. She seemed dazed, overwhelmed. "It was all so horrible . . . confusing. One of them seemed to know me. He said the strangest things to me . . . but how is that possible?"

Elistan put his arm around her. She leaned against him, shivering. "I couldn't see his face, for he wore a scarf over it, but I saw his eyes . . ." She shuddered.

"How do you know us, sirs?" Elistan asked as Derek and Aran joined them, both coughing as a gust of smoke came swirling down the street.

"Time for questions later, sir," said Derek peremptorily. "You are still in danger. Where are the kender, Brightblade, and the rest of your party?" He looked about. "Where is Tanis Half-elven?"

Laurana gave a sob at the name and put her hand to her mouth. Tears flooded down her cheeks, and she staggered weakly. Elistan held her and an elf male came hastening up to her. Brian recognized the elf as Gilthanas. He'd been with Tanis and the others at the library. Gilthanas glanced at the knights, gave a brief nod, then turned to care for his sister. He spoke gently to Laurana in their own language.

"I'll stay with her," Gilthanas said in an aside to Elistan. "You see to the kender."

"Kender," Derek repeated. "Do you mean Burrfoot? Where is he?"

"Tasslehoff was hurt when a beam fell on him," Elistan explained, leading the knights back down the alley. "He was near death, but Paladine, in his mercy, brought him back to us. He is over here with the others."

Brian glanced at Derek, who shook his head and smiled derisively.

"Hullo again, Sir Knights!" Tasslehoff cried, waving his hand and then coughing himself nearly in two as smoke flew down his windpipe.

"Are you sure he's not hurt?" Brian exclaimed in amazement. "Look at him!'

The kender's clothes were torn and covered with blood. His jaunty topknot was matted with blood. His face and arms were badly bruised, though the bruises seemed to be fading.

Tasslehoff answered Brian's question by jumping gamely to his feet.

"I'm fine!" he announced. "A house fell down, blam, right on top on me! My ribs were all smashed in and I was breathing funny when I was breathing at all, which I wasn't sometimes, and the pain was pretty bad, and I thought I was a goner. But Elistan asked Paladine to save me and he did! Think of that," the kender added proudly, pausing to cough, "Paladine saved my life!"

"Why he bothered is beyond me," stated the dwarf, and he gave the kender a poke in the back. "You wouldn't catch Reorx saving the life of a kender fool enough to let a house fall on top of him!"

"I didn't *let* the house fall on me!" Tas explained patiently. "I was running along, minding my own business, and the house gave a sort of jump and a lurch and the next thing I knew—hey, Laurana! Did you hear? A house fell on me and Paladine saved me!"

"Enough!" said Derek. "We must make haste! This place is still crawling with the enemy. Where is the rest of your party, Brightblade? The half-elf and the Lady Alhana?"

"We were separated in the chaos," said Sturm. He looked exhausted, his face was lined with sorrow and grief. "The inn was hit by dragon-fire. The others . . ."

Sturm couldn't go on. He shook his head.

"I see," said Derek in understanding. "I am sorry for your loss, but we need to get you and your friends to safety."

"Loss!" Tasslehoff cried shrilly. "What loss? What are you talking about? We can't leave yet! What about Tanis? And Raistlin and Caramon?"

Flint covered his face with his hand.

"Tas," said Sturm gently, going down on one knee and putting his hands on the kender's shoulders, "there's nothing we could do. The inn collapsed and he and the others were buried underneath—"

"I don't believe you," Tas cried. Pulling free of Sturm's grasp, he staggered weakly in the direction of the inn. "Tanis! Caramon! Raistlin! Don't give up! I'm coming to save you!"

He did not get far before his knees buckled and he went sprawling. Sturm picked up Tas and carried him back to where the knights were waiting.

"Let go of me! I have to save them! Paladine will bring them back! He brought *me* back!" Tas fought to free himself from Sturm's grip.

"Tas," said Elistan, patting the kender kindly on the shoulder, as Sturm set him on his feet, "our friends are with the gods now. We have to let them go."

Tas shook his head stubbornly, but his shrieks quieted to sobs and he quit struggling.

"I need you, Tas," Laurana added, a quiver in her voice. She put her arm around him. "Now that Tanis is . . . is not here . . ."

Tasslehoff took hold of Laurana's hand and squeezed it tight. "I'll take care of you," he said. "I promise."

Derek gathered the group together and started them moving down the street, heading in the direction of the south gate. Sword in hand, Aran took the lead. Brian brought up the rear, as usual. Derek kept close to the kender.

Two days! Brian thought. Only two days ago, I walked through that very same gate. So much had happened, it seemed more like two years.

Brian was more than half-tempted to run back to the library, back to Lillith. He would let Derek and Aran continue on their hunt for the dragon orb. He stopped in the street, and let the others go on ahead.

Derek and Aran. Brian sighed deeply. The two would never make it to Icereach, not without him to mediate between them, curb Derek's ambition, calm Aran's wilder impulses. He had made a pledge to the Knight's Council to go on this quest, and he could not abandon his leader or go back on his sworn word.

Lillith was keeping her word. Though she laughed about being a knight's daughter, she was a true Solamnic. She would be disappointed in him for breaking his oath. Still, he could not bear to leave, not knowing. He'd seen the horrible things draconians did to women.

A hand touched his arm. Brian looked up to find Elistan standing beside him. "Gilean holds Lillith in his hand," the cleric said to him. "You need have no fear for her or the others. They are safe. The draconians did not find them."

Brian stared at the cleric in bewilderment. "How do you—"

The cleric smiled at him. His smile was weary and wan, but reassuring. Elistan went to join the others, and Brian, after another moment's hesitation, ran after them.

Laurana walked hand in hand with Tas. Gilthanas kept close beside her. Flint came along at their heels; Elistan rested his hand comfortingly on the dwarf's shoulder. Sturm walked behind, watching over all of them protectively.

Brian regarded them in wonder. A more unusual group of friends could not be found: human, dwarf, kender, elves. Yet the friendship and love these people felt for each other was so strong that nothing could break them, not even death.

Their friendship keeps them going on even after such devastating loss, Brian realized. Each puts aside his or her own grief to comfort and give strength to the others.

Brian felt a pang of envy. He, Aran and Derek had been friends since childhood, and while once they had been close like this, they were not any more. Derek had walled himself off from the other two, sealing himself up inside his soul's fortress. Aran no longer trusted Derek. He was there to make certain Derek did not fail, or perhaps, Brian thought bleakly, Aran is here to make certain Derek *does* fail. Aran is Gunthar's man, after all. . . .

Brian was caught in the middle, the only one to see the cracks between them widening, the only one to see that they might all of them fall into those dark crevices and never be able to find their way out.

The knights and those under their protection left Tarsis safely. No enemy soldier attacked them or molested them or even paid much attention to them. Tarsis lay weltering in a pool of her own blood, writhing in her death throes. Her eyes were dimming, closing to the light. Leaving the city through the gate that had been smashed by the dragons, Brian saw the guard who had taken his money lying dead in a pool of blood.

The knights led their charges safely into the hills, to the cave where they had made camp earlier. Brian could not sleep and he offered to take first turn at guard duty. He sat on the hillside and watched the flames flare and roar, then sink to a sputter, and then, when there was nothing left to consume, the fires died.

And so did Tarsis.

4

Iolanthe lies. Skie rebels.

ar from Tarsis, in the city of Neraka, in the small apartment over the mageware store, Iolanthe watched the image of Kitiara vanish, wafting away with the smoke and the wisps of hair.

"That is the last lock of her hair, my lord," Iolanthe said. "Unless I can obtain more, I can no longer cast the spell."

"It is not important." Ariakas planted his hands on the table and leveraged himself to his feet. He stood long moments, still frowning at the last little trails of smoke. "I know all I need to know now."

As he was leaving, he tossed over his shoulder, "I will require your presence at her trial."

Iolanthe lifted her eyebrows. "Trial, my lord?"

Ariakas rarely bothered with such formalities. He made a gesture of resignation. "Kitiara is a Highlord. Her troops, and more importantly, her dragons are fiercely loyal to her. There would be trouble if I simply killed her. Her crimes must be made public. You will testify what your magic has revealed."

"I cannot do that, my lord," Iolanthe replied.

He halted in the door, his face dark with rage.

She added, humbly, "I have sworn on oath to Nuitari, God of the Dark Moon, that I would never reveal the secret of that spell. I may not break such an oath on peril of my life."

"You are in peril of your life right now, Iolanthe," growled Ariakas, clenching his fist.

Iolanthe trembled, but she did not back down.

"I honor and respect you, my lord," she said in a low voice, "but Nuitari is my god."

She was on safe ground. Ariakas believed in the gods, and although he did not serve Nuitari, having chosen to pledge his loyalty to Nuitari's mother, Queen Takhisis, he revered the god of dark magic and feared him. Even the Emperor of Ansalon would be loathe to do anything to arouse Nuitari's wrath.

Ariakas stared at her, trying to intimidate her. She stood impassive under his scrutiny, meeting his gaze. Ariakas gave a snarl and a grunt, then turned and stalked out of the room. He slammed the door behind him with such force the walls shook.

Iolanthe gasped and shuddered with relief and sank down in a chair, too weak and shaken to stand. She poured herself a glass of brandy-wine with a shaking hand, drank the fiery liquid, and felt better.

When her hands ceased to tremble, she reached into the silken bag and took out one more lock of curly black hair. Iolanthe twisted the lock thoughtfully in her fingers, as she gazed into the flames and smiled.

———————◆◆◆———————

Kit arrived back at her camp in the gray dawn. She had been looking forward to finding Tanis here, waiting for her, only to discover Skie had not yet returned with the prize she'd sent him to fetch. Kit went to bed, leaving orders that the guards wake her the moment the dragon appeared. She slept the day through and well into the night. When she finally woke, there was still no sign of Skie.

Several days passed after that with no news of the dragons. Kitiara fumed, fretted and made life hell for the draconians, who kept out of her sight as much as possible. She had plenty of time to think not only about Tanis but also about her rival. Kit decided she was glad she hadn't killed Laurana. Kitiara had always been competitive.

"I didn't want Tanis until I found out another woman might take him from me," Kit realized. "As it is, making him mine again will be that much sweeter." She smiled the crooked smile. "Perhaps when I'm finished with him, I'll send the elf maid whatever's left."

Lying in bed at night—alone—she entertained herself with thoughts of what she would do when Skie brought Tanis back.

"I will be angry with Tanis. I will tell him I have discovered his infidelity. I will accuse him of abandoning me for Laurana. He'll deny it, of course, but I won't listen. I'll rant and rave and work myself into a passion. No tears. I can't abide women who weep. He'll beg my forgiveness. He'll take me in his arms, and I'll fight him. I'll dig my nails into his flesh until the blood runs and he'll stop my curses with his lips, and then I'll relent slowly. Ever so slowly . . ."

Kitiara fell asleep with a smile on her lips, a smile that disappeared when Queen Takhisis paid her yet another visit in her dreams, urging, pleading, cajoling. Lord Soth, it seemed, had yet to enter the war. Kit woke groggy and in a bad temper to find that Skie and the other blue dragons had finally returned.

Kit hurried to meet them, only to discover they had failed utterly.

"We chased the damn griffons for days," Skie told her. "We couldn't catch them and eventually lost them."

The blue dragon was sullen.

"I have no idea where the half-elf is," he added in response to her questions, "and I could not care less."

Kitiara was enraged. The entire mission to Tarsis had been a waste of time, money, and energy. She needed someone to blame, and she settled on Toede. She was writing up a scathing report on the hobgoblin, recommending that he should be relieved of his command *and* his head, when a messenger arrived on dragonback, summoning her to Neraka for an emergency meeting of the Highlords.

"Don't go," Skie said abruptly, as Kitiara was putting on her helm.

"What? Don't be silly. Of course, I'm going. I'll make my charges against Toede in person. Much more effective. What's the matter?" she demanded, seeing Skie lower his head and hunch his shoulder.

"What's this urgent meeting about?" he asked.

Kitiara shrugged. "Ariakas didn't say. Perhaps it will be about the debacle in Tarsis or maybe the matter of the death knight."

Hands on her hips, arms akimbo, Kit stared at the dragon.

"Why shouldn't I go?"

Skie was silent, brooding, then he said, "Because you were wrong. You were wrong to bring us here to chase after your lover. You were wrong to send us off in pursuit of him, and you were doubly wrong to risk your life seeking out your rival like some jealous whore—"

"Shut up!" Kitiara shouted angrily.

Skie kept quiet, but his tail twitched, his claws dug into the dirt, clenched and released and clenched again. He eyed her, then looked away.

"I am going to Neraka," Kitiara stated.

"Then find another dragon," said Skie, and he lifted his wings, pushed off with his hind legs, and soared into the sky, heading north, back to Solamnia.

Kitiara stood on the ground, staring after him. She watched in astonishment until he had finally disappeared. Then she took off her dragon helm, put it under her arm, turned, and walked away.

5

Fleeing Tarsis. Danger from above.
Laurana's decision.

he next morning, the smoke of the burning funeral pyre that was now Tarsis continued to rise into the air. Snow started to fall and this would be forever known as the Day of the Black Snow, for the white flakes were tainted with soot and cinders. The black snow settled on the bodies in the street and on the comatose draconians who had passed out due to a surfeit of dwarf spirits. By the end of the day, their officers had sobered up enough to start rousing their men; the mighty force of the Red Dragonarmy—having no orders to do otherwise— started to straggle back north.

The three knights woke early from a sleep that had been brief, cold, and uncomfortable, and took stock of their situation. They had no horses; the beasts had either run off during the attack on the city, or, more likely, they had been stolen. They had found horse blankets in the stable and appropriated these to use for bedding. Tas had discovered a heavy, fur-lined, hooded coat for Laurana, who had been inside the inn when it was attacked and had been forced out into the cold wearing only a leather tunic of dwarven make over a woolen shirt and leather breeches tucked into leather boots. The rest had clothing suitable to the cold, but no food. They drank melted snow water, and that sparingly, for it tasted like blood.

Derek had spent the hours he was standing watch making plans.

"We travel south to Rigitt," Derek stated. "Once there, we will separate—"

"What if Rigitt was attacked?" Aran interrupted. "We could be walking into another hell just like this one." He jerked his thumb back at the smoldering ruins of the city.

"I don't think Rigitt is in any danger," said Derek. "The dragon-armies don't have the will or the manpower to hold Tarsis. When we reach Rigitt, Aran will book passage on a ship and escort Gilthanas, Laurana and Elistan back to Solamnia. From there, the elves can search out their people and Elistan can do whatever it is he does. Brian and I will take the kender and sail to Icereach—"

Seeing Aran shaking his head, Derek halted his planning.

"What's wrong?" Derek demanded, annoyed.

"There won't be a sailing vessel left in the city, Derek," Aran explained testily. He kept reaching for his flask, only to remember that it was empty, and he was in an uncharacteristic bad mood. "Even if Rigitt hasn't been attacked, its people will be certain they're next and they'll be fleeing the city in anything that floats."

Derek frowned, but he couldn't very well argue against the wisdom of this.

"I'm going to Icereach with you," Aran continued firmly. "You're not getting rid of me that easily."

"I had no intention of 'getting rid of you,'" said Derek. "I am concerned for the welfare of the elf brother and sister. They are royalty, after all. I am also worried about the older gentleman. That is why I proposed sending you with them. I still believe this is a good idea. If we can find a ship—"

Aran began to argue, and Brian hurriedly intervened.

"We might hire a fishing vessel," he suggested. "Fishermen are a hardy lot. They don't scare easily and they've their livelihood to make. They aren't likely to run off in a panic."

Both Derek and Aran agreed his suggestion was sound, though Aran grumbled some. That ended the argument, however, and the three continued to talk of this and consider other options, and, for the moment, the matter of how they would split the party was forgotten.

———————————

Gilthanas stood at the entrance to the cave, listening to the knights. Hearing footsteps behind him, he half-turned. He saw it was Laurana and put his finger to his lips, cautioning her to be silent.

"Why?" she whispered.

"So I can hear what they are plotting," he returned.

"Plotting?" Laurana repeated, bewildered. "You talk of the knights as if they were the enemy."

"And *they* talk of going to Icereach to find a dragon orb," said Gilthanas.

He shushed her when she would have said more and continued to listen. The knights' conversation had ended, however. They had risen to their feet, stretching to ease the kinks in stiff, chilled muscles.

Gilthanas took hold of Laurana and steered her hurriedly away from the entrance, drawing her deeper into the darkness where Flint, Elistan and Tasslehoff were still asleep, huddled together for warmth.

Laurana looked at them enviously.

She was sick with fatigue, yet she had not been able to sleep. Every time she dozed off, she saw those ruthless dark eyes, she felt the knife prick her throat, and the terror returned, jolting her into wakefulness. When she was awake, she remembered Tanis and her grief tore at her so that she bled inside. He was dead, and her soul had died with him. She did not even have the poor comfort of being able to lay him to rest, sing the hymns of praise and love that would guide him on his way to the next stage of his life's journey. If only she could have gone with him . . .

"Laurana, are you listening to me?" Gilthanas demanded. "This is important."

"Yes, Gil," Laurana lied. She dredged up some vague memory of what he had been saying. "You were talking about dragon orbs. What are they?"

Gilthanas saw her pallor. He saw the dark circles that smudged the skin beneath her eyes, and the red-rimmed, swollen eyelids and the tear-streaked grime on her cheeks. He put his arm around her and she leaned against him, grateful for his comfort.

———————————

"I know you don't care about any of this," he said softly, "but you must. It's important—"

Laurana shook her head. "Nothing's important anymore, Gil. Nothing matters."

"This does, Laurana. Listen to me! Dragons orbs are powerful magical artifacts created by wizards long ago. I heard talk of them when I was studying magic. I asked my master about them, but he could tell me little, except that he believed they were either destroyed by the Kingpriest or by the mages themselves during the Lost Battles. All he knew was that those who mastered the orbs were supposed to have the ability to control dragons.

"At that time, we had no idea that dragons remained in the world, so none of us thought much about them." The elf's expression grew dark. "If a dragon orb has been found, it must not fall into the hands of humans! That knight, that Derek, means to be rid of us. He wants to ship us back home, and I know why. The Solamnics plan to use the orb to save themselves. Never a thought for our people!" he added bitterly.

Laurana shrugged. "What does it matter anyway, Gil? What could one of these orbs do to help us even if we did have it? What could hundreds of orbs do? We can't win against the Dark Queen's might. We can only hope to survive for a day or a week or month, knowing all the while that in the end the evil will find us . . ."

She wept in quiet despair. Her brother pressed her close, but even as he soothed his sister, he remained fixated on the dragon orbs.

"Apparently, Tasslehoff knows something about this dragon orb," Gilthanas whispered. "Perhaps you could persuade him to tell you—"

Laurana smiled through her tears. "If the knights are relying on Tasslehoff for information about this orb, I do not think you have anything to fear, brother. Tas has undoubtedly made up this wondrous tale, and the knights have been gullible enough to believe him."

"They are not fools. Say nothing of this!" he warned Laurana, and he walked abruptly out the cave as the knights were entering, bumping his shoulder rudely into Brian as he passed him. The elf's ire was so apparent that Brian stopped to stare after him in wonder.

Laurana sighed softly, despairingly, as she watched the black snow fall outside.

"None of it matters, Gil," she repeated wearily. "We cannot win. We just wait our turn to die."

⚓━━━━━━━━━━━━━━ ▸◂ ━━━

The snow stopped falling, but the gray clouds remained with them all day and into the night. No dragons appeared and no one felt the sense of unease and foreboding that comes with a dragon presence in the area. Derek decided that it would be safe to venture forth, and they set out, traveling south. They avoided the main road, for fear of the dragonarmies, and the going was slow. Tasslehoff, wrapped for extra warmth in a horse blanket, was still weak and though he was game, his legs "let him down," as he stated, going all wobbly.

Laurana walked as in a trance, moving her feet, going where she was told to go, stopping when she was told to stop, but with little idea of where she was or why. She kept reliving those last moments in the inn when they heard the dragon roaring overhead and then the explosion and the thick beams in the ceiling groaning beneath the weight of the top levels caving in and then the cracks that foretold the ceiling about to give way. Tanis had caught hold of her and picked her up and hurled her as far as he could, throwing her clear of the destruction, and perishing beneath it.

She was not alone in her grief. Sturm's sorrow was etched on his pallid face. Flint remained silent and stoic, though his grief over the loss of his long-time friends must run deep as the fathomless sea. Tasslehoff pulled out a handkerchief he thought had once belonged to Caramon and had to fight off a snuffle. Yet they carried on bravely, even finding the strength to murmur a gruff and awkward word of sympathy to her or give her a kind pat on the hand. Elistan tried to comfort her and at his gentle touch, she felt her sorrow ease a little, but when his hand was removed and his voice was silent, she sank back into misery.

Laurana also sensed the mounting impatience of the knights. "At this rate," Derek was heard to state grimly, "we might reach Rigitt by springtime!" She sensed the tension and the fear that kept everyone watching the skies. She felt she should try to crawl out of this well of black despair into which she had fallen, but she did not want to leave the darkness. The light up top was too bright. Voices were too loud, jarring. She found comfort in the silence. She dreamed of pulling the rocks and dirt down on top of her and letting them bury her, as the debris had buried Tanis, and put an end to her suffering.

They walked on until darkness overtook them. Laurana discovered that if the day had been bad, the night was worse, for again she could not sleep. Morning broke, cold and cheerless, and they started out. After a time, night and day began to merge together for Laurana. She walked in a waking dream in one, and dreamed she walked in another. She had no idea what time it was, how far they had come, or how many days they had traveled. She could not eat. She drank water only because someone thrust the water skin into her hands. She walked, numb with grief and fatigue and cold, heedless of all around her. She knew her friends were growing increasingly concerned about her and she wanted to tell them not to bother, but even that called for more effort than she had to give.

Then came the day when shouts of alarm roused her from her somnambulist state.

She saw everyone looking into the sky, pointing and exclaiming. Aran was armed with a bow, and he had nocked an arrow on the string. Derek had grabbed hold of Tasslehoff and tossed him into a snow-filled ditch. Brian was urging the rest of them to take cover.

Laurana stared into the clouds and could see nothing, at first, and then ten enormous winged beasts appeared, spiraling down out of the sky.

Aran raised his bow, taking aim.

Laurana gasped and whispered, "No! Stop!" just as Gilthanas gave a hoarse cry and threw himself against the knight, jostling his aim and nearly knocking the man down. Derek turned on Gilthanas and punched him on the jaw, felling him. Elistan ran to help Gilthanas, who lay limp in the snow. Flint stood alongside Sturm, both of them staring into the sky. Sturm had his sword drawn; Flint was fingering his axe.

Tasslehoff, floundering knee deep in snow in the ditch, was wailing, "I can't see! What's happening? I can't see!"

Aran regained his balance and was once more nocking his arrow. Laurana looked at her brother, but he was still unconscious. She ran forward, seized Aran's arm and gripped him tightly.

"Do not shoot, Sir Knight! They are griffons!"

"Yes, so?" he said harshly.

"Griffons are dangerous," Laurana cried, keeping fast hold of him, "but only to our foes!"

Aran hesitated. He looked at Derek, who scowled and said in Solamnic, "I do not trust her. Shoot them down."

Laurana did not understand his words, but she understood the dark look he gave her and she guessed what he had said. Aran was once more taking aim.

"Can you shoot all of them with one arrow, sir?" Laurana demanded angrily. "Because that is what you will have to do. If you strike one, the others will attack and rip us apart."

Sturm was by her side, adding his own urging. "You can trust her, Aran," he said. "My life on her word."

Since the griffons were almost upon them now, it made little difference whether Aran trusted her or not. The great beasts landed some distance away, their feathery wings extended, powerful leonine hind legs touching the ground, gaining purchase by digging in the sharp claws of their eagle talons. Fierce black eyes glared at them above the curved beaks.

"Lower your bow," Laurana told Aran. "Sturm, Flint, the rest of you—sheathe your weapons."

Sturm immediately did as she asked. Flint put his axe back in its harness, but he kept his hand near the handle. Aran lowered his bow. Brian slowly slid his sword back into the scabbard. Derek shook his head stubbornly and held fast to his weapon.

Watching the griffons, Laurana saw the glint in their eyes. Their beaks snapped. Their lion claws tore at the ground, their lion tails twitched, their eagle talons lifted and flexed.

"Sheathe your sword now, Sir Knight!" Laurana hissed at Derek through clenched teeth, "or you will get us all killed!"

Derek glanced at her, his expression grim. Then, with an angry gesture, he thrust his sword back into its scabbard.

Laurana looked over her shoulder at her brother, hoping he could deal with this dangerous situation. Gilthanas had regained his senses, but he was leaning against Elistan, rubbing his jaw, and peering about dazedly. It was up to her.

Laurana ran her fingers through her hair, doing what she could to comb the golden tangles, and smoothed and straightened her clothing. Picking up a handful of snow, she scrubbed her face. The rest were staring at her as though she had taken leave of her senses, but she knew what she was about. She had dealt with griffons often in Qualinesti.

Noble, dignified beasts, griffons are fond of ceremony and formalities. They are easily insulted and must be approached with the utmost politeness, or they could quite literally fly into a rage. Their attention was fixed on her. They ignored the rest. Griffons dislike and distrust humans, dwarves, and kender, and would just as soon kill them as not. Griffons do not always love elves, but they know elves and sometimes can be convinced to serve them, particularly by the elven royalty, who enjoy a special bond with griffons. Laurana's attempts to make herself neat and presentable before she spoke to them would please the griffons.

She started to walk forward to meet them. Sturm moved to accompany her, but she saw the beasts' black eyes glitter with anger and she shook her head.

"You are human and you carry a sword," she said softly. "They don't like that. I must do this alone."

When Laurana was about six feet from the leader, she stopped and bowed low.

"I am honored to be in the presence of one of such magnificence," she said, speaking Elvish. "How may I and my comrades"—she gestured to those standing behind her—"be of service to you?"

Griffons, unlike dragons, do not have the gift of speech. The story goes that when the gods created the griffons, the gods offered the beasts the ability to communicate with humanoids, but the griffons, seeing no reason to have speech with such lesser creatures, proudly declined. In this and in most other things, griffons consider themselves superior to dragons.

Over the centuries, however, as the griffons and the elves developed their unique bond, members of the elven royal family learned to communicate mind-to-mind with the winged beasts. Laurana had acted often as her father's emissary to those griffons who had made their home near Qualinesti. She knew how to treat them with the courtesy and respect they required, and she could understand the gist of what they were saying, if not their precise words.

The beast's thoughts entered her head. The griffon wanted to know if she was truly Daughter of the Speaker of the Sun of Qualinesti. The griffon was clearly dubious. Laurana couldn't blame the beast. She did not look much like an elf princess.

"I have the honor to be the daughter of my father, the Speaker of the Sun of Qualinesti." Laurana managed the correct reply, though she was considerably startled by the question. "Forgive my asking, Great One, but how do you know me? How did you know where to find me?"

"What is going on?" Derek asked in a low voice. "Does she really expect us to believe she is communicating with these monsters?"

Elistan cast him a rebuking glance. "Like many members of the Qualinesti and Silvanesti royal families, Laurana has the ability to mentally communicate with griffons."

Derek shook his head in disbelief and whispered to Brian, "Be ready to fight our way out of this."

The griffon continued to inspect Laurana, looking her up and down, and apparently decided to believe her. The griffon told her they were sent by Lady Alhana Starbreeze to take the Daughter of the Speaker of the Sun and her brother wherever they wanted to go.

That explained the mystery. Laurana had heard from Gilthanas how he and Tanis and the others had met the Silvanesti princess, and how they had saved Alhana from being thrown into a Tarsian prison. The Silvanesti princess was mindful of her debt to them, it seemed. She had sent the griffons to find them and make certain they were safe.

Laurana clasped her hands. She forgot the formalities in her joy. "You can take us home?" she cried. "To Qualinesti?"

The griffon assented.

Laurana longed for home. To be once more in her father's warm embrace. To see again the green woodlands and the sparkling rivers. To breathe the perfumed air and hear the soft, sweet music of flute and harp. To know she was safe and loved. To lie down among the tall green grass, there to drift into deep and dreamless sleep.

Laurana forgot, in her dream of home, that her people had been driven from Qualinesti, that they were living in exile, but even if she had remembered, it would not have made much difference.

"Gilthanas!" Laurana cried to her brother in Elvish. "They have come to take us home!" She flushed, remembering that the others could not understand her, and then repeated her words in Common. She looked back at the griffons. "Will you take my friends as well?"

The griffons did not appear at all pleased with this. They glared at the knights and looked extremely hostile at the sight of the kender, who had at last managed to climb out of the ditch and was saying excitedly, "Do I really get to fly on a griffon? I've never done that before. I rode on a pegasus once."

The griffons conferred, cawing raucously, and at length agreed to carry the others. Laurana had the vague impression that Lady Alhana had asked them for this favor, though she guessed the griffons would not admit it. They laid down many conditions, however, before they would consent to let the others come near them, particularly the kender and the knights.

Laurana turned to give the others the good news, only to find her words met with grim, dubious, or uneasy looks.

"You and your brother and the rest may fly off with these creatures if you choose, Lady Laurana," Derek said coldly, "but the kender stays with us."

"What if the kender doesn't want to stay with you?" Tasslehoff demanded, but everyone ignored him.

Gilthanas was on his feet. His jaw was swollen, but he had his wits about him. "I'm staying with the knights," he said in Elvish. "I'm not going to let them get hold of this dragon orb, and I think you should stay, too."

Laurana stared at him in dismay. "Gil, this is some tale Tas made up—"

Gilthanas shook his head. "You're wrong about that. The knights discovered confirmation of the orb's existence in the library back in Tarsis. If there is a chance a dragon orb has survived all these centuries, I want to be the one to find it."

"What are you two jabbering about?" Derek demanded suspiciously. "Speak Common, so that we may all understand."

"Stay with me, Laurana," her brother urged, continuing to speak in Elvish. "Help me recover this orb. Do this for the sake of our people instead of wallowing in grief over the half-elf."

"Tanis gave his life for mine!" Laurana cried in a choked voice. "I would be dead if he hadn't—"

But Gilthanas wasn't listening. Glancing at the knights, then turning back to his sister, he said, speaking Common, "Ask the griffons to take us to Icereach."

Derek, Aran and Brian exchanged glances. Although unorthodox, this mode of transportation solved all their problems. The griffons could fly over the sea and thereby take them directly to their destination, saving them days and perhaps weeks of travel, even if they could find a ship, which was not guaranteed.

"Gil, please, let's just go home," Laurana begged.

"We will go home, Laurana, once we have the dragon orb," Gilthanas replied. "Will you desert our friends in this time of peril? Leave them behind? Our friends would not abandon you. Ask Sturm what he intends to do."

None of her friends had spoken yet. They had been watching and listening in silence, not thinking it right to intervene. They regarded her with sympathy, preparing to offer comfort, understanding her need, leaving the decision to her.

"What should I do?" she asked Sturm.

"Tell the griffons to take you home, Laurana," he said gently. "The rest of us will travel to Icereach."

Laurana shook her head. "You don't understand. The griffons will take you humans only if I am with you . . . I'm the only one who can understand them. Gilthanas never had the patience to learn."

"Then we will find our way to Icereach without their help," Flint declared.

"You could come back to Qualinesti with me," Laurana said. "Why don't you?"

"It's the kender," Flint explained. "The knights plan to take him to Icereach."

"I don't understand," said Laurana. "If Tas doesn't want to go, Derek can't make him."

"You tell her," Flint said, nudging Sturm.

Sturm hesitated, then said, "I think Tas should go, Laurana. I agree that this dragon orb may be of great help to us, and if Tas goes . . ." He paused, then said, "Derek would not hesitate to sacrifice his life for his cause, Laurana, and he would not hesitate to sacrifice the lives of others. Do you understand?"

"I go with Sturm and the knights," said Flint, adding gruffly, "After all, someone has to protect them from Tasslehoff." The dwarf reached out, awkwardly patted her hand. "Sturm is right. You go home, Laurana. We'll manage."

Laurana looked last to Elistan, her mentor, her guide. He lightly touched the medallion of Paladine he wore around his neck.

He was saying she should turn to Paladine in her trouble. Laurana had no need to ask the god. She knew what she wanted to do, and she knew what she had to do. She could not fly off to safety and leave her friends to face a long and dangerous trek to Icereach, not when she could provide them with safe, swift transport. Gilthanas was right. She could not desert friends who would never think of deserting her.

Laurana gave one last longing thought to her homeland, then left her friends and walked back the griffons. "I thank you for your offer to take us to Qualinesti," she said. Her voice quivered as she began, but grew stronger as she proceeded. "However, we have urgent business to the south in Icereach. I was wondering if you would take my friends and me to that land."

Derek said loudly, "Tell the beasts that an evil elf wizard named Feal-Thas is Dragon Highlord of Icereach and that we go to destroy him."

The griffons appeared highly amused by this. Several cawed loudly and stomped their hind feet and twitched their lion tails. The leader rubbed his beak with a talon and told Laurana that they knew of this Feal-Thas. He was a dark elf, cast out of Silvanesti before the Cataclysm for murdering his lover, and he was an extremely powerful wizard who would not be taken down by a handful of iron-clad fools. The griffon advised her that her first course of action was wise. The beast told her to return home to her father, where she belonged.

"I thank you, Great One," Laurana said, gently but firmly, "but we will travel to Icereach."

The griffon's admonition to go home "where she belonged"—as though she were some errant, heedless child—stung Laurana. She had been just such a child once, but no more.

"If you will not take us," she continued, seeing the griffons about to refuse, "then we must travel to that land on our own. When you return to Silvanesti, give the Lady Alhana my grateful thanks for her care and concern."

The griffon mulled over her request. The griffon would be forced to tell Lady Alhana that he had refused to carry Laurana and the others to her chosen destination. Griffons do not consider themselves obliged to serve elves they are not bonded to, but they had agreed to this task and the beasts would consider themselves honor-bound to undertake it. Besides, on consideration, Icereach was close to their home, which was near Silvanesti. Qualinesti was far away.

"We will take you," the griffon agreed grudgingly, "for the sake of Lady Alhana."

"I thank you and your brethren with all my heart," said Laurana, bowing. "I will give you rich reward when I am in my own homeland and able to do so."

The griffon grunted. He appreciated the gesture, though the beast obviously doubted that Laurana would live long enough to fulfill her promise.

Flint glowered at the thought of riding a griffon, especially without a saddle.

"It is not much different from riding a horse bareback," Gilthanas told him soothingly.

"Except if you fall off a horse, you get bumps and bruises," Flint pointed out. "Whereas if I fall off that great beast, I will end up splattered over a lot of ground!"

He continued to mutter his protests, even as he allowed Sturm to assist him onto the griffon's back.

Laurana instructed the dwarf to sit forward of the wings and hang on tightly, keeping his arms around the griffon's neck. The last was unnecessary, for Flint had hold of the griffon in a grip that appeared likely to strangle the beast.

"Don't look down. If you feel giddy once you are airborne, close your eyes or bury your head in the griffon's mane," she told him.

At this, Flint looked triumphantly at Tasslehoff. "I told you griffons had manes, you doorknob!"

"But, Flint," Tas returned, "the griffon's mane is made of feathers. The mane on your helm is horse hair—"

"It is the mane of a griffon!" Flint insisted.

He sat bolt upright after that and eased up on his grip, trying to look as though flying on griffon-back was something dwarves did on a daily basis.

The knights were ill at ease. Aran said he feared he was too heavy; the beast could not bear his weight. The griffon only snorted and shook his head and twitched his tail in impatience to be gone. Reluctantly, Aran and Brian mounted their beasts. Sturm took charge of Tasslehoff, who was overheard asking the griffons if they could take him to visit Lunitari after they stopped at Icereach. If Derek had doubts, he resolutely kept them to himself. When everyone was mounted, the lead griffon, bearing Laurana, leapt into the air and the rest followed.

Laurana had flown on griffons before. She was used to flight, and she kept a concerned watch on her companions. Brian had gone deathly pale as they soared into the air, but once airborne he stared down at the ground unrolling beneath him and gasped in awe and delighted wonder. Derek was stern and grim, lips pressed tightly together. He did not look down, but he did not hide his face either. Aran was enjoying himself. He yelled out that they should try to convince the griffons to carry them into battle, as the Dark Queen's minions rode their evil dragons. Sturm had all he could do to keep tight hold of Tasslehoff, who nearly tumbled off in his efforts to grab a cloud.

Beneath them was the Plains of Dust, white with snow. They saw a band of Plainsmen, who halted in their travels and gazed upward as the shadows of the griffons flowed over them. The beasts flew over Rigitt, and though they saw no signs of the dragonarmy, they could see the wharf crowded with people eager to flee. Only a few ships were in the harbor; far too few to carry all those seeking passage.

Leaving Rigitt behind, they flew over the gray-blue sea, and now all of them buried their heads in the griffons' manes, not from fear, but for warmth. The frigid wind blowing off the glacier stung their cheeks and burned their eyes and froze their breath. When the griffons began to spiral downward, Laurana peeped out from the feathers to see beneath her a white land of blue shadows, frozen and empty.

She laid her head among the griffon's feathers and pictured her homeland, where it was always springtime, the air always warm, perfumed with the scents of roses, lavender and honeysuckle.

Her tears froze on her skin.

6

Highlords. High treason.

itiara's journey from Tarsis to Neraka was not a pleasant one. The skies were gray and overcast. A chill drizzling rain mixed with snow fell almost the entire trip. She was chilled and wet all the time. When they stopped at night to rest, she could not build a fire to warm herself, for the only wood she could find was soaked. The blue dragon was respectful to her and deferential, but he wasn't Skie. She couldn't talk to this dragon about her plans and schemes, couldn't visit with him while he crunched beef bones from a stolen cow and she stewed a rabbit.

Kitiara was angry at Skie. He had no right to make such accusations, yet she found herself hoping the dragon would think better of his temper fit and come in search of her, ready to apologize. Skie did not appear, however.

They arrived at Neraka as darkness was falling. Kitiara sent the blue to the dragon stables, telling the beast to be ready to depart the moment the meeting was adjourned. Kitiara made her way through the crowded streets to the Broken Shield Inn. She was cold, hungry, and wanted a warm bed, a blazing fire, and hot, spiced wine. But when she arrived, she was told regrettably that there was no room. The inn was filled to capacity with Highlord Toede's personal staff, retinue, soldiers, and bodyguards.

Kitiara could have slept in her own private quarters in the Temple of the Dark Queen, but those chambers were cold, gloomy, and comfortless, not to say unsettling. The gates were trapped with deadly magicks, and she would have to remember the password and hand over her weapons and answer a lot of fool questions. She got on well enough with the draconian guards, but she couldn't abide the dark priests slinking about in their heavy black woolen robes that always smelt of incense, cheap dye, and damp sheep. The fire in her grate in the temple would be small and feeble, almost as if the Nightlord was wary of any source of light invading his sacred darkness. There would be no spiced wine, for strong drink was forbidden on Temple grounds, and Kitiara believed, as did Ariakas, that while she was there, unfriendly eyes were watching her, ears were listening.

Seeing the rage in Kit's dark eyes when told there was no room, the innkeeper recalled suddenly that there might be one available. He hastily sent his servants to remove two of Toede's henchmen who had drunk themselves into a stupor. It took six men to haul the dead drunk hobgoblins out of their beds; and they woke the next morning to discover, to their bleary astonishment, that they'd spent the night in the stables. Kitiara took over their room, aired it out well, drank several mugs of the warming wine, and fell into bed.

———————

Since this was an emergency meeting of the Dragon Highlords, there was none of the ceremony generally attendant upon such an exalted gathering. Formal meetings of the Highlords were accompanied by parades of soldiers dressed in shining armor marching through the streets with standards flying. As it was, few people in Neraka knew the Highlords were in town. Two, Salah Khan and Lucien Takar, were accompanied by their personal staff and bodyguards. Two others, Kitiara and Feal-Thas, traveled alone.

The newly promoted Highlord Toede was the only one to bring his entourage. Toede had hoped to be able to triumphantly parade his troops, with himself mounted upon a black stallion, through the streets of Neraka. Various difficulties crushed the hob's dreams. The stallion bolted at the smell of him; half his soldiers had deserted during the night, and the other half were too drunk to stand. Toede had to content himself with attending his first meeting resplendent in a suit of dragon armor, the scales of which weighed nearly as much as if they were still on the dragon, causing the poor hob considerable pain and discomfort, and hampering his mobility to such an extent that, in lieu of riding on the black stallion, he had to be hauled to the meeting in a hay wagon. The helm obscured his vision and his sword tangled his legs, tripping him, but Toede thought he looked sublime—every inch the Highlord—and he anticipated making a grand entrance.

The meeting was scheduled for early in the morning. Kit left orders to be awakened at dawn and went to bed early. Takhisis was almost immediately in her dreams again, prodding her to go to Dargaard Keep. Kit refused. The Dark Queen scolded and taunted, sneered at Kitiara, called her a coward. Kitiara pulled her pillow over her head and either the Dark Queen grew weary of badgering her, or Kitiara was so tired that she slipped beneath the dreams into exhausted slumber.

At the appointed hour, someone came banging on her door. Kitiara swore at them and told them to go away. When she finally woke up, it was to bright sunlight and the panicked feeling she was late. Muddle-headed and sluggish, Kit hurriedly dressed herself in her gambeson and put her armor on over that.

She had given orders to have her armor polished and her boots cleaned and this had been done, though the job was not up to her standards. No time to remedy that, however. She was going to be late as it was. Her temples throbbed from lack of sleep and too much wine. She wished her head were clearer so that she could think better.

Accoutered in her blue dragon scale armor and cloaked in a long blue velvet cape that was sadly wrinkled from having been stuffed into her traveling bag, Kitiara placed the helm of the Dragon Highlord on her head and set forth. The meeting was being held in the Blue Quarter, in the headquarters building of the Blue Wing, the same building where Kit had first heard about Tanis, first heard Ariakas's idiot scheme regarding the dragon orb, first met Ariakas's witch whose name she could not recall.

Citizens and soldiers alike made way for Kitiara, and many cheered her. She cut a fine figure, walking tall and proud, her hand on her sword's hilt. Kit enjoyed the walk. The cold air blew away the fumes of the wine, the cheers braced and emboldened her. Kitiara took her time, accepted the crowd's adulation. The other Highlords could wait for her, she decided. She was not going to rush on account of the likes of Toede and that bastard Feal-Thas. She had a few things to say to Ariakas about him, as well.

The Highlords had gathered in the dining hall of the Blue Wing, the only building large enough to hold them and their bodyguards. Since no Highlord trusted the others, the bodyguards were considered indispensable.

Lucien of Takar, Highlord of the Black Army, who was half-human and half-ogre, brought with him two immense ogres, who towered over everyone in the room and gave off the stench of rotting meat. Salah Khan was Highlord of the Green Army. He was human; his people were desert-dwelling nomads with a love for battle. He was accompanied by six human males armed with long, curve-bladed knives thrust into their belts and scimitars on their hips.

Fewmaster Toede came surrounded by thirty hobgoblin guards, all armed to the teeth and all of them clustered protectively around Toede, who could barely be seen in their midst. Ariakas banned all but six of the hobs from entering. Weighed down by his armor, Toede clunked into the meeting room, guided by his guards, for he was having difficulty seeing through his ornate helm.

Toede greeted the other Highlords with much slavering and slobbering. Ariakas ignored him. Lucien regarded him with disgust and Salah Kahn with disdain. Though he could not see all that well, Toede felt the distinct chill in the atmosphere, and he retired precipitously behind his bodyguards. He spent the rest of the time poking his hobs in their backs, urging them to remain alert.

Feal-Thas strode into the room alone, accompanied by a great white wolf that padded silently at his side.

"No men-at-arms tripping on your heels, Feal-Thas?" asked Ariakas, who was himself accompanied by six bozak draconians. One of them, a bozak with a deformed wing, was one of the largest draconians any of them had ever seen.

"Why should I bring guards, my lord?" Feal-Thas asked with a look of feigned surprise. "We are all friends here, are we not?"

"Some more than others," growled Lucien.

Salah Kahn grunted his agreement, and Ariakas chuckled. Neither of the other Highlords liked or trusted the dark elf. They would have turned on him in an instant, their knives out for blood, except for Ariakas. The emperor himself had no great love for the elf, nor did Queen Takhisis. They tolerated him because, for the moment, he was useful to them. Let him cease being useful and their support would end.

"Besides," Feal-Thas added, wrapping his fur robes around him, "I see so little in this room to fear."

Salah Kahn, whose temper was legendary, bounded to his feet, drawing his sword. Lucien, fists clenched, was rising from his chair, and Toede was eying the nearest exit. The bent-wing bozak drew a sword as large as some humans were tall and took his place in front of the emperor.

Feal-Thas sat unperturbed, his long, thin-fingered hands folded on the table. The white wolf growled menacingly and put its head down, tail twitching.

"Sheathe your sword, Salah Kahn," ordered Ariakas good-humoredly, a fond parent separating quarreling children. "Sit down, Lucien. We are here on important business. Feal-Thas, bring that beast of yours to heel."

When order had been more or less restored, he added with a grimace. "We're all a bit irritable. If you're like me, you got little sleep last night."

"I slept fine, Your Lordship," said Toede loudly. No one answered him, and, thinking they could not understand his words, he managed, with the help of two of his guards, to extricate himself from his helm.

"I worship and respect Her Dark Majesty," Salah Kahn was saying, treading cautiously. "No one more. But it is impossible for me to leave the war in the east to travel to Dargaard Keep. I wish Her Majesty could be made to understand this. If you were to have a word with her, Emperor—"

"What's this about Dargaard Keep?" Toede asked, mopping his brow.

"She plagues me as she does you, Salah Khan," Ariakas returned. "She is obsessed with this notion of bringing Soth into the war. She talks of nothing *else*, except that and finding the Green Gemstone man."

"Lord Soth?" Toede asked. "Who is Lord Soth?"

"Personally I do not want this death knight anywhere near me. Consider his arrogance. He sets *us* a test?" Feal-Thas shrugged. "He should be honored to serve any one of us. *Almost* any one of us," he amended.

"Oh, *that* Lord Soth," said Toede with a knowing wink. "He approached me, offered to work for me. I turned him down, of course. 'Soth' I said. I call him 'Soth', you see, and he calls me—"

"Where the devil is Kitiara?" Ariakas demanded, slamming his hands on the table. He turned to a servant. "Go fetch her!"

The servant departed, only to come back to say that the Blue Lady was at that moment entering the building.

Ariakas exchanged a few words with the bent-wing bozak. He and several baaz draconians took up positions on either side of the door. Lucien and Salah Kahn glanced at each other, wondering what was up. Though neither knew, they both sensed trouble and kept their hands near their weapons. Toede was having some difficulty seeing over the heads and shoulders of his bodyguards, but he had the uncomfortable feeling that something dire was about to happen, and the only exit was now being blocked by six large bozaks. The hob gave an inward groan.

Feal-Thas, who had written the letter betraying Kitiara, was able to guess what was about to happen. He waited with anticipation. He had never forgiven her for killing his guardian.

Booted footsteps rang in the hallway, then Kitiara's raised voice, calling jocular greeting to the guards. Ariakas's dark, baleful gaze was fixed on the entrance. The bozaks flanking the door tensed.

Kitiara strolled inside, her sword clattering at her hip, her blue cape flowing after her. She carried her helm beneath her arm.

"My lord, Ariakas—" she began, about to raise her hand in salute.

The bent-wing bozak seized hold of her, pinning her by the arms. A second bozak grabbed her sword and yanked it from its sheath.

"Kitiara uth Matar," said Ariakas in sonorous tones, rising ponderously to his feet, "you are under arrest on a charge of high treason. If you are found guilty, the penalty for your crime is death."

Kitiara stood frozen, staring, open-mouthed and confounded, so astonished she made no attempt to resist. Her first thought was this was some sort of jest; Ariakas was noted for his perverted sense of humor. She saw in his eyes, however, that he was serious—deadly serious.

Kitiara looked swiftly around the room. She saw the other Highlords—three of them as astonished as herself—and she realized they had not been brought here for a meeting. This was a trial. These men were her judges, each one of whom coveted her position as Highlord of the Blue Dragon Army. Even as she realized this, she saw each man's shock give way to pleasure, saw each cast dark glances at his compatriots, plotting and scheming how best to attain her position. In their minds, she was already dead.

Kitiara's impulse then was to fight, but that came a little too late. Her sword was gone. She was in the firm and painful grasp of an enormous bozak, who was armed with both a sword and powerful magicks. The thought crossed Kit's mind that it would be better to fight a hopeless battle to the death now than face whatever torment Ariakas had in mind for her. She restrained herself, however. The Solamnics have "My honor is my life" as their credo. Kit's was "Never say die."

She recovered her composure. She had not always obeyed Ariakas's orders. She had gone off on raiding parties when she should have been laying boring siege to some castle. She had appropriated for the use of her troops certain tax revenues meant to go to the emperor. None of these offences could be termed crimes of high treason, however, though of course the emperor could call stealing a meat pie from his table high treason if he chose. Kit had no idea what all this was about. Then she saw the faint smile upon the lips of Feal-Thas, and Kit immediately recognized her enemy.

She stood tall and straight, fearless and dignified in the grasp of her captors, and faced Ariakas.

"What is the meaning of this, my lord?" Kitiara demanded with an air of injured innocence. "What act of high treason have I committed? I have served you faithfully. Tell me, my lord. I do not understand."

"You are charged with plotting the murder of Dragon Highlord Verminaard and hiring assassins to carry it out," said Ariakas.

Kitiara's jaw dropped. The irony was chilling. She was being charged with the one crime of which she was innocent. She glanced at Feal-Thas, saw the faint smile broaden, and she snapped her jaw shut with a click of her teeth.

Her voice trembling with rage, Kitiara stated, "I utterly refute and deny that charge, my lord!"

"Lord Toede," said Ariakas, "did Highlord Kitiara ask you in a most suspicious manner for information regarding the felons who assassinated Verminaard?"

Toede managed to worm his way through the forest of his body-guards and said with a gasp and many moppings of his brow, "She did, my lord."

"I did not!" Kitiara retorted.

"Did she talk to a man called Eben Shatterstone, also seeking information about these people?"

"She did, my lord," Toede said, proud of being the center of attention. "The wretch told me so himself."

Kitiara would have liked to choke the hobgoblin until his beady little eyes popped out of his yellow head. But the bent-wing bozak had a grip of steel on her and she could not break free. She contented herself with shooting Toede a look so threatening and malevolent that Toede shriveled up and shrank back, terrified, among his bodyguards.

"She should be in manacles, my lord!" the hob quavered. "Put her in leg irons!"

Kitiara turned to Ariakas. "If you have no other evidence besides the word of this quivering mound of goo—"

"The emperor has my evidence," said Feal-Thas. Gathering his robes about him, he rose gracefully to his feet, his motion slow and unhurried. "As many of you know," he said, speaking to the group at large, "I am a winternorn. I will not go into detail explaining this magical skill to the uninitiated. Suffice it to say, a winternorn has the power to delve deep into the heart of another.

"I looked into your heart, Highlord Kitiara, when you were gracious enough to visit me in my ice-bound solitude, and I saw the truth.

You sent these assassins to kill Lord Verminaard, hoping to succeed him as Highlord of the Red Dragonarmy."

"Lies! Liar!" Kitiara lunged at Feal-Thas in such fury that the bozak holding her was nearly dragged off his clawed feet. "I should have killed you at Icereach!"

Feal-Thas glanced at Ariakas as much as to say, "Do you require any more proof, my lord?" and sat down, undisturbed by Kit's ravings.

Realizing she had only made matters worse, Kitiara managed to regain some semblance of calm. "Do you believe him, my lord, a shit-eating elf, or will you believe me? I had nothing to do with the death of Verminaard! He died through his own folly!"

Ariakas removed his sword and tossed it on the table.

"Highlords, you have heard the evidence. What is your verdict? Is Kitiara uth Matar guilty of the murder of Highlord Verminaard or do you find her innocent?"

"Guilty," said Lucien, with an orgish grin.

"Guilty," said Salah Kahn, his dark eyes glinting.

"Guilty, guilty!" cried Toede, then added nervously, "Therefore she should most definitely be in leg irons!"

"I am sorry, Kitiara," said Feal-Thas gravely. "I enjoyed our meeting at Icereach, but my duty is to my emperor. I must find you guilty."

Ariakas shifted the sword around. The point faced Kitiara. "Kitiara uth Matar, you have been found guilty of the death of a Dragon Highlord. The punishment for that crime is death. At dawn tomorrow, you will be taken to the Arena of Death where you will be hanged, drawn and quartered. The remains of your body will be placed upon pikes at the Temple gates to serve as a warning to others."

Kitiara stood still. She no longer struggled. Her ravings ceased.

"You are making a terrible mistake, my lord," she said calmly. "I have been loyal to you when all these others have been false. But no longer, my lord. No more. It is you who have betrayed me."

Ariakas made a gesture to the bent-wing bozak as if tossing out garbage. "Take her away."

"Where to, my lord?" the bozak asked. "Does she go to the Pen or to the dungeons in the Temple?"

Ariakas considered. The Pen was the local prison house and it was always overcrowded, verging on chaos half the time. Escapes were not common, but they did occur, and if anyone could manage to escape confinement, it would be Kitiara. She would be put into a cell with other prisoners—male prisoners. He could picture her seducing the jailer, her guards, her fellow inmates, rousing them all to revolt.

The dungeons in the Temple were more secure and less crowded. Most political prisoners were jailed there, yet Ariakas hesitated to send Kitiara to the Temple. The dark priests and the Nightlord had no love for Kitiara, who had stated openly she considered them lazy toadies who did nothing except eat and sleep while the military undertook the hard and thankless work of winning the war. Still, the Nightlord was jealous of Ariakas and Kit might find a way to win him to her side.

No matter where she was incarcerated, so long as she lived, Kitiara was a danger. Ariakas began to wish he'd scheduled her execution immediately, not waited for the public spectacle. Too late to change his mind. The other Highlords would scent weakness. He could think of only one place where she would be safe and completely inaccessible to anyone.

"Lock her up in the storeroom in my private chambers in the Temple," Ariakas said. "Post guards at the door. No one is to enter my chambers. No one is to speak to her. Any who fail me in this will suffer a fate identical to hers."

The bent-wing bozak saluted and started to lead Kitiara out the door. She had one last bold and desperate plan in mind. She had only to decide where and when to strike.

As if reading her mind, Ariakas remarked casually, "Oh, and by the way, Targ, be careful. She has a knife concealed in her dragon scale armor."

"The knife!" the draconian demanded, holding out his clawed hand.

Kitiara glared at him defiantly and made no move to comply.

"You can either show Targ where it is, Kitiara," said Ariakas dryly, "or he will strip you naked here and now."

Kitiara showed Targ where to find the knife. The bozak removed the weapon and then took off all her armor, leaving her in her gambeson. He searched her again from head to toe, just in case, and then placed her in the custody of two baaz draconians.

Kit endured these indignities with her head held high, her fists clenched. She'd be damned if she would give her enemies the satisfaction of seeing her sweat.

"Take her out," ordered Ariakas.

As the baaz were about to haul her away, Kitiara turned to Feal-Thas.

"You have the gift to look into hearts," she said. "Look into mine, now."

Feal-Thas was startled. He was about to refuse, but he saw Ariakas watching him and the thought came to him that this was some sort of test. Perhaps she meant to prove him a liar. Shrugging, he did as she requested. He cast the spell of the winternorn and gazed into her heart. He saw three Solamnic knights and a powerful cleric of Paladine leaving Tarsis, traveling the road to Icereach, intent upon stealing his dragon orb.

Feal-Thas shivered in rage, as though he'd been nipped by his own chill winds. He stood up from the table.

"I beg your pardon, my lord, but I must leave at once." The elf cast a pale, cold glance at Kitiara. "Events require my immediate return to Icereach."

The other Highlords stared at him. Kitiara's lip curled. Turning on her heel, she allowed her captors to lead her away.

The emperor looked out his window where he had once stood with Kit, watching traitors hang. Kit walked down the street in the midst of her guards, her head high, shoulders thrown back. She was laughing.

"What a woman," Ariakas muttered. "What a woman!"

On their way to the Temple, Kitiara attempted to bribe her baaz guards. The bent-wing bozak heard her talking to them and he ordered the two to leave, replacing them with two more.

Next Kit tried to bribe the bozak. Targ didn't even deign to reply to her generous offer. Kitiara sighed inwardly. She had guessed the attempt would fail, for the draconian guards were known to be extremely loyal to Ariakas. Still, it had been worth the attempt. The bozak would report back to Ariakas that she'd tried to bribe them, but what did that matter? What would he do to punish her? He couldn't kill her twice.

Ariakas's servant had run ahead of them to alert the Temple authorities. When informed that he was to house a Highlord on charges of treason, the Nightlord was confounded, did not know how to react. He was angered at first; he felt he should have been informed of Kitiara's treachery and consulted in the decision to execute her. He most certainly should have been told in advance that Ariakas planned to imprison her inside the Temple.

That being said, the Nightlord was not sorry to see the arrogant Blue Lady humbled and humiliated, nor would he fail to enjoy watching her execution.

The Nightlord sent a terse reply back to Ariakas, but that was the extent of his protest. He dispatched several acolytes to the Arena of Death to insure that his private box was supplied with food in case Kitiara's demise was prolonged. People had been known to survive an amazingly long time in screaming agony after having been disemboweled.

The Temple of Neraka was located in the center of the city, which had grown up around it. The Temple existed simultaneously on two planes—the material and the spiritual—and was a strange and eerie place. One felt as if one were walking in a building that existed in a dream, rather than reality. Organic in nature, having sprouted from the seed of the foundation stone, the Temple's walls were twisted and misshapen, its hallways twisting and tortured. As in a dream, corridors that appeared to be short and straight were actually long and winding. Those who attempted to walk through the Temple alone, without the guidance of the dark priests, would either end up lost or insane.

Kitiara, like the other Highlords, had her own furnished quarters in the Temple. Each Highlord had his own entrance, guarded by his own soldiers. The Highlords used these only on ceremonial occasions, all of them preferring the warm and homely comforts of an inn or even their own barracks to the unnerving atmosphere of the Temple.

Ariakas's imperial suite was the most luxurious in the Temple, second only to that of the Nightlord. Ariakas rarely spent much time there. He did not trust the Nightlord, nor did the Nightlord trust him.

The bozak, Targ, knew his way around the temple, but he was glad to have one of the dark priests serve as escort. They marched Kitiara through the distorted halls. But even those who worked in the Temple often found the hallways confusing. Their escort was forced to halt at one point to wait for another dark pilgrim to provide direction.

As Kitiara trudged along in between the two baaz, who wouldn't even look at her, much less speak to her, she tried to devise some plan of escape. Ariakas was smart. The Temple made an excellent prison. Even if she managed to free herself from her confinement, she might wander these halls forever and never find the way out. The dark priests would not help her. They would be just as happy to see her dead.

This was the end. She was finished. She cursed that idiot Verminaard for getting himself assassinated, cursed Tanis for killing him, cursed Feal-Thas for spying on her, cursed Toede for having been born, and cursed Ariakas for not letting her pursue the war in Solamnia. Fighting the knights would have kept her out of trouble.

The bent-wing bozak, Targ, led her to the imperial suite which was located far below ground level, hidden from public view. The chambers belonging to the Highlords were all at the top of the temple structure, above the Hall of Audience. Kit had often wondered why Ariakas had chosen subterranean rooms for his apartment. When she saw them, she understood. This was not a dwelling place. It was a bunker. Here, underground, accessible only by a steeply winding staircase, were quarters for his troops and an attached storehouse stocked with supplies. A small force could hold out here for a long time, perhaps indefinitely.

The priest lit a torch and went on ahead down the staircase to disable the traps. The air was fetid and damp. Murder holes lined the walls. Any force descending those stairs would have to move in single file, and the narrow stairs were deliberately rough and uneven. Even the draconians with their clawed feet had to watch their footing or risk a fall. At the bottom, a massive iron door, operated by a complex mechanism, stood open. The bozaks led Kit through this door and into the apartments that were spacious, luxurious, dark, and oppressive.

No wonder Ariakas refused to live here, Kitiara thought with a shiver. This was where, if all went badly, he would make his final stand, fight his last battle, and, if defeat were imminent, this was where he would die.

At least he would die fighting, Kitiara reflected bitterly.

Ariakas had said she was to be locked in the storeroom. Targ escorted her to the room, which turned out to be a large pantry, dark and windowless, off the kitchen. The dark pilgrim brought her a blanket to spread on the cold stone floor and a slop bucket for her needs, and asked if she wanted anything to eat. Kit declined with scorn. The truth was, her stomach was clenched in knots. She feared she would throw up if she ate a morsel.

The dark priest asked about manacles. Despite Toede's insistence on shackling Kit, the bozak had not thought to bring any along, and there were none to be found in the apartment. At length it was decided between Targ and the priest that for the moment manacles would be unnecessary. Kit obviously was not going anywhere until morning, when she would be led to her execution. The priest promised he would have manacles for her then. Targ shoved her inside the storeroom and started to shut the door.

"Targ, tell Ariakas I am innocent!" Kitiara pleaded with the draconian. "Tell him I can prove it! If he will only come to see me—"

Targ slammed the door shut and turned the key in the lock.

Alone in pitch darkness, Kitiara heard the clawed feet of the bozak scraping over the stone floor.

Then there was silence.

She could hear the beating of her own heart, each beat falling into the silence like grains of sand, counting out the seconds to her death. Kitiara listened to her heartbeat until the thudding grew so loud the walls of her prison seemed to expand and contract with this sound.

Kit was, for the first time in her life, almost sick with fear.

She had witnessed people being hanged, drawn, and quartered. The ordeal was terrible. She'd known veteran soldiers forced to turn away their heads, unable to stomach the gruesome sight. First, she would be hanged, but not until she died, only until she lost consciousness. Then she would be roused and staked down on the ground. The executioner would cut her organs from her still-living body. Screaming and writhing in unbearable agony, she would be forced to watch as her entrails were thrown into a fire and burned. She would be left to slowly bleed to death until, near the end, they would hack the limbs from her body and cut off her head. The various parts of her would be thrust onto pikes and left to rot at the Temple gates.

Kitiara imagined what the knife would feel like as it sliced into her gut. She imagined the cheers of the crowd as the blood spurted, cheers that, though loud, would not drown out her screams. The chill sweat rolled down her face and neck. Her stomach heaved; her hands began to shake. She could not swallow; she could not breathe. She gasped for air and jumped to her feet with some wild idea of flinging herself headlong into the wall, to end it by dashing out her brains against the stone.

Reason prevailed. Fearing she was on the verge of madness, she forced herself to think this through. She was down, but not out. It was only mid morning. She had the rest of the day and all the night to come up with a plan of escape.

What then? What if she did escape?

Kitiara sank down upon the chair. She would be alive, that was true, and that counted for something, but she would spend the rest of her life on the run. She, who had been a Dragon Highlord, a leader of armies, a conqueror of nations, would now skulk about the woods, forced to sleep in caves, reduced to thieving. The ignominy and shame of such a wretched existence would be harder for her to endure than the few terrible hours of agony she would suffer at her execution.

Kitiara let her head sink into her hands. A single tear burned her cheek; she angrily dashed it away. She had never known such despair, never been in such a hopeless position. She might try to make a bargain with Ariakas, but she had nothing to give.

A bargain.

Kitiara raised her head. She stared into the darkness. She could strike a bargain, but not with Ariakas—someone higher. She didn't know if it would work. Half of her thought it might, the other half scoffed. Still, it was worth a try.

Kitiara had never in her life asked a boon of anyone. She had never said a prayer, was not even certain how one went about praying. Priests and clerics went down on their knees, humiliated and abased themselves before the god. Kitiara did not think any god would be pleased with that, particularly a strong goddess, a warrior goddess, a goddess who had dared to wage war on earth and in heaven.

Kitiara stood up. She clenched her fists and shouted out, "Queen Takhisis. You want Lord Soth. I can bring him to you. I am the only one of your Highlords, my Queen, with the skill and the courage to confront the death knight in his keep and convince him of the worthiness of our cause. Help me escape this prison tonight, Dark Majesty, and I will do the rest."

Kitiara fell silent. She waited expectantly, though she was not sure for what. Some sort of sign, perhaps, that the goddess had heard her bargain, accepted her deal. She'd seen the priests receive such signs, or so they claimed. Flames flaring upon the altar, blood seeping from solid stone. She had always assumed these were nothing more than tricks. Her little brother, Raistlin, had taught her how such fakery could be accomplished.

Kitiara did not believe in miracles, yet she had asked for one.

Perhaps that was the reason no sign came. The darkness remained dark. She heard no voice, heard nothing except her beating heart. Kit sat back down. She felt foolish, but also calm—the calm of despair.

She had only now to wait for death.

7

The white bear. The Ice Folk.

he day that started out disastrously for Kitiara proved better for her rival. Laurana had asked the griffons to take them to Icereach and the griffons did so, though they refused to go near Ice Wall castle, telling her it was inhabited by a white dragon. The griffons made it clear they did not fear the dragon, but said they would have difficulty fighting a dragon while carrying riders.

The griffons told Laurana she and her companions would need help if they were going to remain in this region, stating they would not survive long without shelter, food, and heavier clothing. The land was inhabited by nomadic humans, known as the Ice Folk, who might be able to assist them, if they could convince the people they had no hostile intent.

Once they crossed the sea and were over the glacier, several griffons left the group to scout, keeping an eye out for the dragon and searching for the Ice Folk. The scouts soon returned to say they had found the nomad encampment. The griffons deposited their riders at some distance from the camp, for they feared if the Ice Folk saw the great winged beasts they would turn against the strangers immediately.

The Ice Folk have no love for Feal-Thas, the griffon told Laurana, as they made ready to depart, telling her the wizard and his thanoi had been waging war on the nomads for the past few months. The griffon left her with a final warning: make friends with the Ice Folk. They were fierce warriors who would be valuable allies, deadly foes.

After the griffons departed, the group sought shelter in the ruins of a large sailboat that appeared to have crashed and overturned on the ice. The boat was like nothing any of them had ever seen, for it was made to sail on ice, not water. Large runners carved of wood were attached to the hull. When the sail was hoisted, the boat would apparently skim over the surface of the ice.

The boat's hull offered some protection from the frigid wind, though not from the bone-chilling, flesh-numbing cold. The group discussed how best to approach the Ice Folk. According to the griffons, most of the nomads spoke Common, for during the summer months, when the fishing was good, they would sell their fish in the markets of Rigitt. Elistan proposed sending Laurana to speak to them, due to her diplomatic skills. Derek objected, saying that they had no way of knowing how the Ice Folk felt about elves or if they had ever even seen an elf.

They were huddled together in the wreckage of the boat, arguing or trying to argue—their mouths were stiff from cold and it was difficult to talk—when the argument was interrupted by a hoarse cry, a roaring and bellowing sound, as of some creature in pain. Ordering the rest to stay in the boat, Derek and his knights left to see what was wrong. Tasslehoff immediately chased after the knights. Sturm chased after Tas, and Flint went with him. Gilthanas said he did not trust Derek, and he followed, accompanied by Elistan, who thought he might be of some use. Laurana had no intention of remaining behind alone, and thus the entire group trailed after Derek, much to his ire.

They came upon an enormous white bear being attacked by two kapak draconians, who were jabbing at the bear with spears. The bear was on her hind legs, roaring and batting at the spears with enormous paws. Red blood marred the bear's white fur. Laurana wondered why the bear did not simply run off, and then she saw the reason. The bear was trying to protect two white cubs who crouched together behind her.

"So the foul lizards are here, too," Flint stated dourly.

He fumbled at his axe, trying to draw it from its harness on his back. His gloved hands were clumsy from the cold, and he dropped it. The axe fell to the ice with a clang.

At the sound, the draconians halted their attack and looked over their shoulders. Seeing themselves vastly outnumbered, they turned and started to run.

"They've seen us!" said Derek. "Don't let them get back to report. Aran, your bow!"

Aran removed his bow from his shoulder. Like Flint, the knight's hands were chilled to the bone, and he could not force his stiffened fingers to grasp the arrow. Derek drew his sword and started to run for the draconians, shouting for Brian to come with him. The knights slipped and slithered over the ice. The draconians, getting far better traction with their clawed feet, soon outdistanced them, disappearing into the white wilderness. Derek came back, cursing beneath his breath.

The white bear had collapsed and lay bleeding on the ice. Her cubs pawed her wounded body, trying to urge her to get up. Heedless of Derek's shouts that the wounded bear would attack him, Elistan walked over to kneel at the bear's side. The bear growled weakly at him, bared her teeth, and tried to raise her head, but she was too weak. Murmuring to her comfortingly, Elistan placed his hands on the bear, who seemed soothed by his touch. She gave a great, groaning sigh and relaxed.

"The draconians will be back," Derek stated impatiently. "The creature is dying. There is nothing we can do. We should leave before they return in greater numbers. I'm going to put a stop to this."

"Do not disturb Elistan at his prayers, sir," said Sturm and when it seemed Derek was going to ignore him, Sturm placed a restraining hand on Derek's arm.

Derek glared at him and Sturm removed his hand, but he remained standing between the knight and Elistan. Derek muttered something and walked off. Aran went with him, while Brian remained to watch.

As Elistan prayed, the gaping wounds and bloody gashes in the bear's chest and flanks closed over. Brian gasped and said softly to Sturm, "How did he do that?"

"Elistan would say that he did nothing; it is the god who brings about this miracle," Sturm replied with a smile.

"You believe in . . . this?" said Brian, gesturing toward Elistan.

"It is difficult not to," Sturm replied, "when the proof is before your eyes."

Brian wanted to ask more. He wanted to ask Sturm if he prayed to Paladine, but asking such a personal question would be ill-mannered, and therefore Brian kept silent. He had another reason. If Derek found out Sturm Brightblade believed in these gods and actually prayed to them, it would be yet another black mark against him.

The bear was starting to try to regain her feet. She was still a wild beast with young to protect, and Elistan prudently and hastily backed away, dragging Tasslehoff, who had been making friends with the bear cubs. The group returned to the boat. Glancing back, they saw the bear on all fours starting to lumber off, her cubs crowding near her.

Derek and Aran were talking over the fact that draconians were this far south.

"The draconians must be in the service of Feal-Thas," Derek was saying. "They will report back to him that three Solamnic knights are now in Icereach."

"I'm sure that this news will have the Highlord shaking in his fur-lined boots," said Aran dryly.

"He will guess we are here after the dragon orb," said Derek, "and he will send his troops to attack us."

"Why should he immediately jump to the conclusion that we're after the orb?" Aran demanded. "Just because you are obsessed with this artifact, Derek, doesn't mean everyone is—"

"Did you two see that?" Brian cried excitedly, joining them. "Look! The bear is walking around. Elistan healed her wounds—"

"You are such an innocent, Brian," said Derek caustically. "You never fail to fall for some charlatan's tricks. The bear's wounds were only superficial. Anyone could see that."

"No, Derek, you're wrong," Brian began, but he was interrupted by Aran, who took hold of each man's arm and gripped it tightly, warningly.

"Look around. Slowly."

The knights turned to see a group of warriors clad in skins and furs heading their way. The warriors were armed with spears and some of them held strange-looking axes that glistened in the chill sunshine as though they were made of crystal.

"Get everyone into the boat!" Derek ordered. "We can use that for cover."

Brian ran back, shouting at the others and yelling at them to run for the boat. He grabbed hold of Tasslehoff and hustled him off. Flint, Gilthanas and Laurana hurried after them. Sturm assisted Elistan, who was having difficulty keeping his footing.

The warriors continued to advance. Aran began blowing on his hands, trying to warm them so he could use his bow. Flint peered out over the hull, fingering his axe and staring curiously at the odd-looking axes of the enemy.

"These must be the Ice Folk the griffons mentioned," said Laurana, hastening up to Derek. "We should try to talk to them, not fight them."

"I will go," Elistan offered.

"It's too dangerous," said Derek.

Elistan looked at Tasslehoff, who was blue with the cold and shaking so badly that his pouches rattled. The others were not much better.

"I think the most urgent danger we face now is from freezing to death," Elistan said. "I do not think I will be in danger. These warriors have not rushed to the attack, as they would have if they thought we were with the armies of the Highlord."

Derek considered this. "Very well, but I will be the one to talk to them."

"If you will allow me to go, Sir Derek, it would be more prudent," said Elistan mildly. "If anything should happen to me, you will be needed here."

Derek gave an abrupt nod.

"We will cover you," he said, seeing that Aran had managed to warm his fingers enough to be able to use his bow. He had an arrow nocked and ready.

Laurana stood close to Tasslehoff, pressing the shivering kender against her body and wrapping her coat around him. They watched in tense silence as Elistan raised his arms to show he carried no weapons and walked out from the shelter of the boat. The warriors saw him; several pointed at him. The lead warrior—an enormous man with flaming red hair that seemed the only color in this white world—saw him too. The lead warrior kept going and urged his warriors forward.

"Look at that!" Aran exclaimed suddenly, pointing.

"Elistan!" Brian called a warning. "The white bear is following you!"

Elistan glanced around. The bear was trotting over the ice on all fours, her cubs running along behind her.

"Elistan, come back!" Laurana cried fearfully.

"Too late," said Derek grimly. "He would never make it. Aran, shoot the bear."

Aran raised his bow. He started to pull back the string, but his arm jerked and he lost his grip.

"Let go of me!" he cried angrily.

"No one has hold of you," said Brian.

Aran glanced around. Flint and Sturm were standing on the other side of the boat. Tasslehoff—the most likely suspect—was shivering in Laurana's grasp. Brian stood next to Derek, and Gilthanas was over beside Flint.

Aran looked foolish. "Sorry." He shook his head, muttered, "I could have sworn I felt someone."

He lifted the bow again.

The bear was on Elistan's heels. The warriors had seen the animal as well, and now their red-bearded leader called a halt.

Elistan must have heard the warning shouts. He must have heard the beast scrabbling over the ice close behind him, but if he did, he did not turn. He kept walking.

"Shoot!" Derek ordered, rounding on Aran furiously.

"I can't!" Aran gasped. He was sweating, despite the cold. His hand grasped the arrow, his arm shook with his great effort, but he didn't fire. "Someone has hold of my arm!"

"No, someone doesn't," said Tasslehoff between chatters. "Should one of us tell him?"

"Hush," said Laurana softly.

The bear reared up on her hind legs, towering over Elistan. She lifted up her great paws, held them over him, and gave a great, bellowing roar.

The leader of the warriors gazed long at the bear, then, turning around, he made a motion to his men. One by one, they threw their weapons onto the ice. The red-bearded warrior walked slowly toward Elistan. The bear relaxed down on all fours, though she still kept her gaze fixed upon the warriors.

The red-bearded man had bright blue eyes and a large nose. His face was seamed and weathered, and his voice rumbled like an avalanche. He spoke Common, though with a thick accent. He gestured at the bear.

"The bear has been hurt. She is covered with blood. Did you do this?" he asked Elistan.

"If I did, would she walk with me?" Elistan returned. "The bear was attacked by draconians. These valiant knights"—he pointed at Derek and the others, who had come out from the shelter of the boat—"chased them off. They saved the bear's life."

The warrior grunted. He eyed Elistan and he eyed the bear and then he lowered his spear. He bowed to the bear and spoke to her in his own language. Reaching into a leather pouch he had tied to his belt, he threw some bits of fish to the bear, who ate them with relish, then, rounding up her cubs, the bear lumbered away, heading at a rapid pace over the glacier.

"The white bear is the guardian of our tribe," the warrior stated. "You are fortunate she vouched for you, otherwise we would have killed you. We do not like strangers. As it is, you will be our honored guests."

"I swear to you, Derek," Aran was saying as the knights went to meet Elistan, "it was as if someone had hold of me in a grip of iron!"

"Good thing, too," remarked Brian. "If you'd killed that bear, we would all be dead now."

"Bah, he's missing his liquor, that's all," said Derek in disgust. "He's having a drunkard's dream."

"I am not!" said Aran, speaking with dangerous calm. "You know me better than that, Derek. Someone had hold of my arm."

Brian caught Elistan's eye.

The cleric smiled and winked.

◆━━━━━━━━◆

The Ice Folk made them welcome. They offered them smoked fish and water. One took off his own thick fur coat to wrap around the half-frozen kender. The red-bearded warrior was their chief, and he refused to talk or answer any of their questions, saying they were all in danger of frostbite. He hustled the group back to the camp, which consisted of small snug tents made out of animal hides stretched over portable frames. Trickles of smoke rose from the center holes in each tent. The heart of the camp was a long-house known as the chieftent. Long and narrow, the chieftent was made of furs and hides draped over the large rib cage of some dead sea beast whose carcass had been frozen in the ice. The small tents were used only for sleeping, being too cramped for much else. The Ice Folk spent most of their time either fishing the glacial pools or in the chieftent.

Those gathered in the chieftent sewed hides, braided and repaired nets, hammered fishhooks, fashioned spear and arrow heads, and performed countless other tasks. Men, women, and children worked together, and while they worked someone would tell a story or the group would sing, discuss the fishing prospects, or share the latest gossip. Little children played underfoot; older children had their tasks to perform. In this harsh clime, the tribe's survival depended on every person doing his part.

The Ice Folk gave their guests clothing designed for living on the glacier, and they snuggled thankfully into the warm fur coats, slipped their feet into thick fur-lined boots and thrust their chilled hands into heavy gloves. Laurana was given a tent of her own. The three knights shared another, and Sturm, Flint and Tas had a tent to themselves. Elistan was on his way to his tent when he found his way blocked by an elderly man with a long white beard, heavily bundled and wrapped in furs and a gray robe. All that could be seen of him was a hawk-like nose poking out of a gray cowl and two glittering eyes.

The old man planted himself squarely in Elistan's path. Elistan halted obligingly and stood smiling down at the old man whose bent body did not come to his shoulder.

The old man snatched off a fur glove, revealing a gnarled hand with enlarged joints, permanently crooked fingers, and spider webs of blue veins. He lifted his hand toward the medallion Elistan wore around his neck. He did not touch it. His hand, shaking with a mild palsy, paused near it.

Elistan took hold of the medallion, removed it, and pressed it into the old man's hand.

"You have waited long and patiently for this, haven't you, my friend?" Elistan said quietly.

"I have," said the old man and two tears trickled down his cheeks and were lost in his fur collar. "My father waited, and his father before him, and his father before him. Is it true? Have the gods returned?" He looked up anxiously at Elistan.

"They never left us," Elistan said.

"Ah," said the old man, after a moment. "I think I understand. You will come to my tent and tell me all that you know."

The two walked off together, deep in conversation, and disappeared into a tent slightly larger than the others that stood near the chieftent.

Laurana sat for a time alone in her tent. Her grief burned, her sorrow ached, but she no longer felt as though she was lost at the bottom of a dark well, with the light so far above her that she could not reach it. Looking back on the past several days, she could not remember much about them and she was ashamed. She saw clearly that she had been walking a terrible path, one that might have led to self-destruction. She remembered with horror how, for a brief moment, she had wished the stranger in Tarsis would kill her.

The griffons had saved her. This frozen, white, stark world had saved her. Paladine, in his mercy, had saved her. Like the white bear, she had come back to life. She would always love Tanis, always mourn him, always think of him, but she resolved now that she would work for him, work in his name to bring about the victory over darkness he had died fighting to achieve. Laurana said a silent prayer giving thanks to Paladine, then went to join the others in the chieftent.

Peat fires burned at intervals in the tent, the smoke rising through the holes in the ceiling. The Ice Folk sat cross-legged on the floor on furs and hides, going about their work. Their songs and tales were silenced, however, as they listened to the conversation their chief was holding with the strangers.

The chief's name was Harald Haakan. He spoke to Derek, who had taken it upon himself to announce he was the group's leader. Flint huffed at this, but was quieted by Sturm.

"You said 'draconians' attacked the bear," Harald said. "I have not heard of such creatures. What are they?"

"Monstrous beings never before seen on Ansalon," Derek replied. "They walk upright like men, yet they have scales, wings and the claws of dragons."

Harald nodded, scowling. "Ah, so that's who you meant. Dragon-men we call them. The foul wizard, Feal-Thas, brought these monsters to Ice Wall castle, along with a white dragon. None of us had ever seen a dragon before now, though we have heard tales that they lived here in ancient times. None of us knew what the great white beast was, until Raggart the Elder told us. Even he did not know these dragon-men, however."

"Who is Raggart?" Derek asked.

"Raggart Knug, our priest," Harald replied. "He is the eldest among us. He reads the signs and portents. He tells us when the weather is about to change, when to leave the pools before they are fished out and he shows us where to search for new ones. He warns us when our enemies are coming, so that we may prepare for battle."

"Is this man a priest of the white bear, then?"

Harald was clearly put out. He glared at Derek. "What do you take us for, Solamnic? Savages? We do not worship bears. The bear is our tribal guardian, honored and respected, but not a god."

Harald had a temper to match his fiery hair, it seemed. He muttered to himself in his own language, shaking his hairy head at Derek, who said many times he was sorry for the mistake. Eventually the chief calmed down.

"We worship no gods at the moment," Harald continued. "The true gods left us, and we wait for them to return. That could happen at any time, according to Raggart. The white dragon is a portent, he says."

"By the true gods, do you mean Paladine, Mishakal and Takhisis?" Sturm asked, interested.

"We know them by other names," Harald replied, "though I have heard them called such by the fisher folk in Rigitt. If those are the old gods, then, yes, it is for their return we wait."

Laurana looked about for Elistan, thinking he would be interested in this, but he had not come with them into the tent and she did not know where he had gone.

Derek steered the conversation to the Dragon Highlord, Feal-Thas.

Harald said that Feal-Thas had resided in Icereach for hundreds of years and up until now the wizard had kept mostly to himself. Harald had heard that Feal-Thas was calling himself a Dragon Highlord, but Harald knew nothing about that, nor did he know anything about dragonarmies or the war raging in other parts of Ansalon.

"I care nothing either," he said, waving it away with his large hand. "We are locked in a never-ending war waged on a daily basis—we fight every day just to stay alive. We fight foes far older than dragons and just as deadly—cold, disease, starvation. We fight the thanoi, who raid our villages for food, and so we care nothing about what is happening in the rest of the world." Harald fixed Derek with a shrewd stare. "Does the rest of the world care about us?"

Derek was discomfited, not knowing what to say.

Harald nodded and sat back. "I didn't think so," he grunted. "As for the wizard, he is stirring up trouble, bringing in these dragon-men to join with the thanoi to attack us. His armies have wiped out smaller tribes. They slaughter women and children. Feal-Thas has told us openly he means to destroy us all, so that no Ice Folk will be left alive in Icereach. Our tribe is large and my warriors are strong, and thus far he has not dared attack us, but I fear that may be about to change. We have caught his wolves prowling about, spying on us, and he has sent small forces against us to test us. I mistook your group for his soldiers."

"We are the foes of Highlord Feal-Thas," said Derek. "We are pledged to the wizard's destruction."

"We would welcome your swords in a fight, Sir Knight," Harald returned, "but you won't meet Feal-Thas in battle. He stays holed up in his ice palace or in the ruins of Ice Wall castle."

"Then we will go there to fight him," Derek stated. "Are there other tribes in the area? How large an army could we raise in a short time?"

Harald stared at him a moment, then the big man let out a laugh as hearty as himself. His large guffaws shook the ribs of the tent and caused all the people gathered within to join in.

"A rare jest," Harald said when he could speak. He clapped his hand on Derek's shoulder.

"I assure you, I was not jesting," said Derek stiffly. "It is our intent to go to Ice Wall castle to challenge the wizard to battle. We will go by ourselves if need be. We have been sent to Icereach on an important secret mission—"

"We're here to find a dragon orb!" Tasslehoff called out excitedly from the opposite end of the tent. "Have you seen one around anywhere?"

This brought Derek's conversation with the chief to an abrupt end. Rising angrily to his feet, the knight excused himself and stalked out of the chieftent. He motioned for Brian and Aran to accompany him. Derek cast a scathing look at Tas as he passed, which look went in one side of Tas's head and shot out the other without the kender ever noticing.

Shortly after the knights' departure, Gilthanas rose to his feet. "I beg you to also excuse me, Chieftain," the elf said politely, "but I find I cannot keep my eyes open. I am going to my tent to rest."

"Gil," Laurana said, trying to detain him, but he pretended not to hear her and walked out.

———————

The three knights were a tight fit inside the small tent. None of them could stand upright, for the ceiling was too low. They crouched on the floor, crowded together, shoulders jostling, practically bumping heads.

"All right, Derek, we're here," Aran said cheerfully. He was hunched nearly double, his knees up alongside his ears, but he was in a good mood again, the chief having provided him with a replacement for his brandywine. The drink was clear as water and was distilled from potatoes, which the Ice Folk received in trade for fish. Aran gasped a bit at the first gulp and his eyes grew moist, but he claimed that after one was used to it the liquor went down quite smoothly.

"What was so important you had to insult the chief and march us out of there in such a hurry?" Aran asked, tilting his flask to his lips.

"Brian," said Derek, "pull aside the tent flap—slowly. Don't draw attention to yourself. What do you see? Is he out there?"

"Is who out there?" Brian asked.

"The elf," said Derek.

Gilthanas was loitering nearby, watching some children drop lines through a hole in the ice to catch fish. Brian might have thought the elf was truly interested in the fishing, except he gave himself away by casting sharp glances at the knights' tent.

"Yes," said Brian reluctantly, "he's out there."

"What of it?" Aran asked, shrugging.

"He's spying on us." Derek motioned them closer. "Speak Solamnic and keep your voices down. I do not trust him. He and his sister mean to steal the dragon orb."

"So do we," said Aran, with a cavernous yawn.

"They mean to steal it from *us*," Derek said, "and if they get their hands on it, they will take it back to the elves."

"Whereas we're taking it for humans," said Aran.

"There's a difference," said Derek sternly.

"Oh, of course," said Aran, grinning. "We're humans and they're elves, which makes us good and them bad. I understand completely."

"I will not even dignify that with a comment," Derek returned. "We knights should be the ones to determine the best way to make use of the orb."

Brian sat up as straight as he could, given that his head brushed the tent ceiling. "Lord Gunthar has promised that the knights will take the orb to the Whitestone Council. The elves are part of that council and they will have a say in what happens to the orb."

"I have been giving that matter some thought," said Derek. "I am not certain that is the wisest decision, but we can determine all that later. For the moment, we must keep an eye on that elf and his friends. I believe they are all in this together, including Brightblade."

"So we're spying on them now? What does the Measure have to say about that?" Aran asked dryly.

" 'Know your enemy,' " Derek replied.

———————————

Laurana knew quite well Gilthanas was leaving to spy on Derek. She also knew she could do nothing to stop him. She squirmed uncomfortably. Only hours before she had thought she could never be warm again. Now she was growing uncomfortably hot and was feeling slightly nauseated from the smell of the smoke of the peat fires, the closeness of so many bodies, and the strong odor of fish. She started to leave, but Sturm detained her with a look, and Laurana sat back down.

Harald had been extremely astonished at Derek's statement about laying siege to Ice Wall Castle. Frowning, the chief turned his gaze on

Sturm. He sat patiently under the chief's scrutiny, waiting for him to speak.

"Crazy, is he?" Harald said.

"No, Chieftain," Sturm returned, startled by the comment. "Derek Crownguard is a high-ranking member of our knighthood. He has traveled a great distance on his quest for this dragon orb."

Harald grunted. "He talks of raising armies, of going to Ice Wall Castle to attack the wizard where he lairs. My warriors do not lay siege to castles. We will fight, if we are attacked. If we are outnumbered, we have our swift boats to carry us across the ice and away from danger."

Harald eyed Sturm curiously. "You're a knight, aren't you?" The chief pointed at Sturm's long mustaches. "You travel in the company of knights. Why aren't you with them, making plans or whatever it is they are doing?"

"I am not one of their party, sir," said Sturm, avoiding the question of whether he was or was not a knight. "My friends and I met up with Derek and his fellow knights in Tarsis. The city was attacked and destroyed by the dragonarmy, and we barely escaped with our lives. We thought it prudent to travel together."

Harald scratched his beard. "Tarsis destroyed, you say?"

Sturm nodded.

"I had not realized this war you spoke of was so close to Icereach. What about Rigitt?" Harald looked worried. "Our boats sail those waters. We take our fish to their markets."

"The city had not been attacked when last we saw it," Sturm replied. "I believe that for the moment Rigitt will be safe. The dragonarmies extended their reach too far when they attacked Tarsis and were forced to withdraw. But if Feal-Thas grows in strength here in Ice Wall, he can provide the protection the armies of darkness need to maintain their supply lines and Rigitt will fall, as will many other cities along the coastline. Then the darkness will cover all of Ansalon."

Harald was perplexed by this. "Feal-Thas is not alone in his evil ambitions? There are others?"

"Your priest is right," Laurana told him. "The white dragon was a portent. Takhisis, Queen of Darkness, has returned and brought with her evil dragons. She has raised armies of darkness. She seeks to conquer and enslave the world."

The other Ice Folk in the tent had stopped their work and were listening silently, their faces expressionless.

"A man sees the darkness coming and he fears only for himself," Harald remarked. "He never thinks of others."

"And if he does think of others, too often he says, 'Let them fend for themselves'," Laurana added sadly.

She was thinking of the dwarves of Thorbardin, who had decided to fight the dragonarmies but had refused to do so in the company of humans and elves. Gilthanas was here to obtain the dragon orb for the elves, to make certain the humans did not take it. If Derek and the knights were the ones to claim the dragon orb, they would take it for their own.

"I do not see your people coming to help the Ice Folk," said Harald, bristling. He had mistaken her meaning and was offended.

"We have come—" Sturm began.

Harald snorted. "You would have me believe you came all this distance to fight for the Ice Folk? The kender says you are here seeking some sort of dragon something."

"A dragon orb. It is a powerful magical artifact. Feal-Thas is rumored to have it in his possession. It is true the knights have come seeking the orb, but if Feal-Thas is killed, that would benefit your people as well."

"What of the wizard who will come after him?" Harald asked. "Or will you and this dragon orb stay here in Icereach to help us fight the next evil?"

Sturm seemed as if he was about to say something more. He let the words go in a sigh and lowered his gaze, stared down at his hands that were unconsciously smoothing and stroking the white fur sleeve of his coat.

Harald eyed Sturm and frowned. "You have the look of a man who has eaten bad eel."

"As to fighting Feal-Thas," said Sturm, "you may have no choice, sir. The draconians got a good look at us. They must have recognized us for Solamnic knights. They will report back to the wizard, who will wonder what Solamnics are doing so far from home. You say his wolf-scouts are watching your camp. They will tell him you have taken us in—"

"—and Feal-Thas will bring war down on us whether we want it or not," Harald finished. He glared at Sturm and growled, "This is a fine kettle of fish!"

"I am sorry, sir," Laurana said, guilt-stricken. "I did not realize we might be putting your people in danger! Sturm, isn't there something we can do? We could leave—" She stood up, as though prepared to depart on the instant.

"I'm sure Derek and the others are making plans for this now," said Sturm.

"I'm not," Flint muttered into his beard.

Harald drew in a breath, but his words were interrupted. The old man, the priest Raggart, came hobbling into the chieftent, accompanied by Elistan. Everyone in the tent rose in respect, including Harald. Raggart walked up to Harald. There were tears in the old man's eyes.

"I have joyful news," said Raggart, speaking Common out of deference to the strangers. "The gods are with us once more. This man is a cleric of Paladine. At his suggestion, I prayed to the Fisher God, and he answered my prayers." The old man touched a medallion similar to Elistan's, but graced with the symbol of the god known as Habakkuk to some, the Fisher God to the Ice Folk.

Harald clasped Raggart's hand and said something in low tones to the old man in their own language. The chief turned to Sturm.

"It seems you bring death in one hand and life in the other, sir. What are we to do?"

"I'm sure Derek will tell us," Sturm said dryly.

8

Midnight prayers in the Dark Abbey.

Kitiara spent some time searching the storeroom prison for something she could use as a weapon. This was a thankless task, considering she had been left in total darkness. The bozak had inspected the room before locking her in here, and she herself had looked around swiftly before he took the light, and she had not seen anything. Still, she had nothing else to do except think about her upcoming demise, and anything was better than that. She stumbled over crates and stubbed her toes on barrels, scraped her hand on a bent nail, and bumped her head walking into a wall, eventually coming up with a weapon—of sorts.

She kicked apart a packing crate and fashioned one of the broken slats for use as a club. To make it more lethal, she pried out some nails from the lid of a barrel, and, using another plank as a hammer, drove the nails into the end of her makeshift club, so that it was studded with points. Kit did not hope to be able to fight her way free. She hoped to put up such a vicious battle they would be forced to kill her.

This done, there was nothing else to do. She paced the storeroom until she was exhausted, then sat down on the chair. She lost all sense of time. The darkness swallowed the minutes, the hours. She was determined not to sleep, for she had no intention of wasting her few remaining hours of life in slumber, yet the silence and the boredom, the fear and the tension got the best of her. She closed her eyes. Her head sank down on her breast.

She woke suddenly from her fitful doze, thinking she'd heard sounds outside the door. She was right. Someone was putting a key in the lock.

It was time. Her executioner was here.

Kit's heart clogged her throat. She could not catch her breath, and she thought for one moment she might die of sheer terror. Then, with a gasp, she could breathe again. She grabbed hold of the club and crept across the room, groping her way in the darkness until she found the door. She put her back against the wall. When the door opened, those looking in would not see her. They would be surprised and she would have her chance. She crouched, club in hand, and waited.

The door creaked open slowly, an inch at a time, as though someone were pushing it stealthily, fearing to make too much noise. This was odd. An executioner would have just thrust it open. Light spilled inside, not the harsh light of day or the flaring light of torches, but a thin beam of light that went stabbing and poking about the storeroom, falling on the empty chair, then glancing off barrels and boxes. The air was scented with the fragrance of exotic flowers.

No executioner smelled that good.

"Kitiara?" whispered a voice—a woman's voice.

Kitiara lowered the plank. Keeping it hidden against her thigh, she stepped around the door. A woman swathed in a black velvet cape with a deep purple lining stood in the door. She pulled the hood back from her head. The light of her ring shone full on her face.

"Iolanthe?" Kit asked in profound astonishment, the name coming to her at the last moment.

"Thank the Queen!" Iolanthe breathed, seizing hold of Kitiara's arm and hanging onto it as though relieved to touch something solid and real. Light beamed from a ring on her finger, stabbed wildly about the room. "I didn't know if I would find you still alive!"

"For the time being," said Kitiara, not certain what to make of this unexpected visitor. She shook loose the woman's grip and looked out past Iolanthe, thinking she must have brought guards with her. There was no one there. She could not hear breathing or the jingle of armor or the shuffle of boots.

Suspicious, fearing some trap, though she could not possibly imagine what, Kitiara rounded on the witch.

"What are you doing here?" Kit demanded. "Did Ariakas send you? Is this some new torment?"

"Keep your voice down! I silenced the guards at the door, but others may come at any moment. As for why I am here, Ariakas did not send me." Iolanthe paused, then said quietly, "Takhisis did."

"Takhisis!" Kitiara repeated, her astonishment growing. "I don't understand."

"Our Queen heard your prayer and she bid me set you free. You must keep your vow to her, however," Iolanthe added. "You must spend the night in Dargaard Keep."

Kitiara was stunned. She had said that prayer out of desperation, never believing for a moment there were immortal ears to hear, or immortal hands to turn the key in the lock. The thought that Takhisis had not only heard but had answered and now expected her to keep her promise was almost as frightening as the cruel death she was facing.

Kit would have felt considerably better if she had known that while Takhisis may have been listening, it was Iolanthe's ears that had heard her prayer. The witch had splashed perfume on her hands to mask the scent of burnt hair.

"Did you bring me a weapon?" Kit demanded.

"You won't need one."

"I will if they try to capture me. I won't die with my guts hanging out," she added harshly.

Iolanthe hesitated, then she reached into her tight-fitting sleeve and drew out a long poignard, the type that wizards are permitted to carry in their own defense. She handed it to Kit, who grimaced at the light-weight, fragile-looking blade.

"I guess I should thank you," said Kit ungraciously. She didn't like to be beholden to anyone, much less this perfumed trollop. Nevertheless, a debt was a debt. "I owe you one . . ."

Thrusting the poignard in her belt, she started to walk out the door.

"Bless the woman!" Iolanthe exclaimed, aghast. "What are you doing?"

"Leaving," said Kit shortly.

"Will you walk about the Queen's temple dressed like that?" Iolanthe gestured at Kit, who had on what she usually wore beneath her armor—a blue gambeson embroidered in golden thread with the symbol of the Blue Dragonarmy.

Kit shrugged and kept walking.

"No strangers are allowed in the Temple after the close of evening worship," Iolanthe warned her. "The dark priests patrol the halls. You might as well not bother leaving your prison at all, for they will be returning you to it shortly. And what will you do about the magical dragon traps at each gate?"

Each of the gates was guarded by the armies of a different Highlord, each dedicated to one of the colors of chromatic dragons. Thus there was a red gate, a blue gate, a green gate, and so on. Each gate had traps that mimicked the breath weapon of the dragon it honored. The corridor leading to the red gate was lined with the stone heads of red dragons that would breathe fire on any hapless interloper, incinerating him before he was halfway down the corridor. The Gate of the Blue Dragon crackled with lightning, that of the green dragon spewed poisonous gas.

"I know the phrase to disarm the traps," Kit said over her shoulder. "Every Highlord does."

"Ariakas ordered the phrases changed after you were arrested," said Iolanthe.

Kitiara halted. Her hands clenched. She stood a moment, cursing beneath her breath, then turned to face the witch.

"Do you know the new password?"

Iolanthe smiled. "Who do you think worked the magic?"

Kitiara didn't trust this witch. She didn't understand what was going on. She found it difficult to believe Iolanthe's story that Queen Takhisis had sent her, yet how could the witch have known about Kit's prayer? Like it or not, Kit was going to have to put her life into this woman's hands, and Kit did *not* like it!

"So what is your plan?" she asked.

Iolanthe shoved a bundle of cloth at Kit. "First, put this on."

Kit shook out the folds of the black velvet robes worn by the dark priests. A sensible idea, she had to admit. She fumbled her way into the garb, trying to shove her head into the sleeve hole in her haste, and then putting the robes on backward. With Iolanthe's help, Kit managed to sort it out. The black, smothering folds enveloped her.

"Now what?"

"We will attend the midnight rites in the Dark Abbey," Iolanthe explained. "There we will mingle with the crowd and leave with them, for the dragon traps will be disabled to allow them to pass. We must hurry," she added. "The service has already started. Fortunately, the Abbey is not far from here."

They left the storeroom; the glow from Iolanthe's magical ring lit the way through Ariakas's chambers. The main door stood slightly ajar.

"What about the guards?" Kit asked in a whisper.

"Dead," Iolanthe replied dispassionately.

Kit peered cautiously around the door. By the light of the witch's ring, she saw two piles of stone dust—the remnants of two baaz draconians. Kitiara regarded the witch with new respect.

Iolanthe lifted the hem of her robes to keep them out of the dust and stepped gingerly over the remains, her mouth twisting in disgust. Kit walked right through the piles, kicking dust everywhere.

"We should get rid of that," she said, pointing back at the disturbed dust heaps. "Anyone who sees it will know that's a dead draco."

"No time," said Iolanthe. "We'll have to take our chances. Fortunately, this hall is rarely lit. And few people ever have reason to come to this part of the Temple. This way."

Kitiara recognized the staircase by which she had descended in the company of the guards. She and Iolanthe passed it and continued on, and soon she could hear voices chanting, praising the Dark Queen. Kitiara had never attended one of the services in the Dark Abbey. She had, in fact, gone out of her way to avoid them. She was not even sure where the Dark Abbey was located. She had the vague idea it was opposite the dungeons. The corridors were lit with a purplish-white light that had no apparent source, but seemed to shine eerily from the walls. The light had the effect of washing out all color, all distinguishing features, all differences, making every object ghastly white etched with darkness.

Everyone who walked these corridors, even those who walked

them daily, experienced the sense of unreality. Floors were not quite level, walls slanted oddly, corridors shifted position, chambers were not where they should be, doors were not where they had been the day before. Iolanthe, guided by the light of her ring, walked the strange halls with assurance. On her own, Kit would have been hopelessly lost.

She assumed the chanting emanated from the service. She had thought it would be easy to follow the voices, but sounds were distorted down here. Sometimes the chanting dinned in her ears and she was certain they must have arrived at the Abbey, only to find, with another turning, the chants fading away almost to silence. Then they would boom loudly again at the next turning. At one point in the service, a shrill scream reverberated through the corridors, causing the hair on the back of Kit's neck to prickle. The horrible scream ended abruptly.

"What was that?" Kit asked.

"The evening's sacrifice," said Iolanthe. "The Abbey is up ahead."

"Thank the Queen," Kit muttered. She had never before been on the dungeon level, and she could not wait to leave. Kit liked her life uncomplicated, not cluttered up with gods—which reminded her uneasily of her bargain with her Queen. Kit put that out of her mind. She had more urgent matters to consider and, besides, Takhisis hadn't saved her yet.

Rounding a curve, she and Iolanthe almost ran into one of the dark priests. Kitiara yanked her cowl down to hide her face, and she kept her head lowered. Her hand, folded in the capacious sleeve, grasped the poignard's hilt.

The dark priest eyed them. Kit held her breath, but the man's frowning gaze was fixed on Iolanthe. He pulled back his hood to glare at her. He was pale, gaunt, and cadaverous. A hideous red weal ran across his nose.

"You are here at a late hour, Black Robe," he said to Iolanthe in disapproving tones.

Kit's grip on the poignard tightened.

Iolanthe drew back the folds of her hood. The eerie light illuminated her face, shimmered in her violet eyes.

The dark priest looked startled, and fell back a step.

"I see you recognize me," Iolanthe said. "My escort and I are here for the service and I am late, so I ask that you do not detain us."

The dark priest had recovered from his shock. He glanced without interest at Kit, turned back to Iolanthe. "You are indeed late, Madame. The service is almost half over."

"Therefore I am certain you will excuse us."

Iolanthe swept past him, her black robes rustling around her, the scent of flowers lingering in the hallway. Kit followed humbly. She glanced over her shoulder, pushing aside her cowl to keep an eye on the dark priest. He stared after them and for a moment Kit thought he meant to come after them. Then, muttering something, he turned and stalked off.

"I'm not sure you're such a safe companion," said Kitiara. "You're not very popular around here."

"The dark priests do not trust me," said Iolanthe calmly. "They do not trust any magic-user. They do not understand how we can be loyal to Takhisis and at the same time serve Nuitari."

She smiled disdainfully. "And they are jealous of my power. The Nightlord is trying to convince Ariakas that wizards should be banned from the Temple. Some of his clerics want us thrown out of the city. Hardly feasible, considering the Emperor is himself a user of magic.

"Hush now," she cautioned. "The Abbey is ahead. Do you know any of the prayers?"

Kitiara, of course, did not.

"Then make this sign if someone asks you why you do not join in." Iolanthe moved her hand in a circle. "That means you have taken an oath of silence."

The Abbey was crowded. Kitiara and Iolanthe found places inside the entryway. A strong smell of bodies sweating beneath black robes, burning candle wax, incense, and fresh blood wafted from the chamber. The body of a young woman lay across the altar, blood streaming from a gash in her throat. A priest with blood smeared over his hands was chanting prayers, exhorting the crowd to praise Takhisis.

Kitiara stood, fidgeting, in the crowd, the smell of blood in her nostrils, the sound of off-key yammering in her ears, and suddenly she felt she had to leave. She couldn't bear to stand here and just wait for someone to discover that she was missing from her prison and raise the alarm.

"Let's just get the hell out of here," Kit whispered urgently.

"They would stop us at the gate and ask questions," said Iolanthe in a smothered whisper, grasping hold of a fold of Kit's sleeve. "If we go out with the crowd, no one will notice us."

Kitiara sighed, frustrated, but she had to admit this was sound planning. She steeled herself for the ordeal.

The Abbey was a circular room, with a high, domed ceiling beneath which stood a large statue of Queen Takhisis in her dragon form. The statue was a wonder. The body was carved out of black marble, with each of the five heads done in different colored marble. The ten eyes were gems that shone with magical light that illuminated the room. By some miraculous means, the heads of the statue seemed to move; the eyes looked this way and that, with the dread light of their watchful gaze constantly sweeping the crowd.

Kit stared at the statue of Queen Takhisis as the heads bobbed and weaved, and glanced at Iolanthe, standing beside her, barely visible in the ever-shifting colored lights. Kit could not see the witch's face for the cowl she had again drawn over her head. Kit was jittery, gripping the poignard in a sweaty palm, wishing the time to pass, wishing herself far away. Iolanthe was calm, not moving, not the least bit nervous, yet if Ariakas found out she had helped Kit escape, Iolanthe's life would not be worth living. Whatever punishment Kit would face, Iolanthe would find it trebled.

"Why are you doing this?" Kit whispered under the cover of the chanting. "Why are you helping me? And don't give me that crap about being the answer to my prayers."

Iolanthe glanced at Kit sidelong from under her hood. Her violet eyes glittered in the light of the Queen's multi-colored and multi-faceted eyes. Iolanthe shifted her gaze back to the statue, and Kit thought that she was going to refuse to answer.

At length, however, Iolanthe whispered, "I do not want you for my enemy, Blue Lady." The violet eyes, wide and intense, fixed on Kit. "If you do what you say you mean to do and you succeed, you will have one of the most powerful beings on Krynn on your side. Lord Soth will make you a force to be reckoned with. Don't you understand, Kitiara? Her Dark Majesty is starting to have doubts about Ariakas. She is looking for someone else to wear the Crown of Power. If you prove to be the one—and I think you will—I want you to think well of me."

And if I fail to return alive from Dargaard Keep, Ariakas retains the Crown and the witch has lost nothing in the attempt, Kitiara reflected. She is what I thought: cunning, self-serving, scheming, and conniving.

Kit was starting to like her.

The chanting had reached a fever pitch, and Kit was hoping fervently this meant that the service was about to end, when the statue's blue head shifted in Kit's direction. The light of the Queen's sapphire blue eyes illuminated the crowd around her. The lighted eyes paused for a moment on the worshipper standing to Kit's left and slightly in front of her—a bozak draconian with a bent wing. At that moment, the chanting abruptly ended, leaving ear-pounding silence behind. The Queen's heads ceased to move. The miracle had ended. The statue was once more marble, if it had ever been anything else; Kit had thought she'd heard the squeak and rumble of a machine. The Abbey glowed with white light. The service had ended.

The crowd blinked and rubbed their eyes. Those who knew from experience that the service was nearing its close had already started to edge their way out, hoping to beat the rush. People were heading for the exit. The bozak with the bent wing turned, walking straight toward her. Kit had her hood pulled over her head, but it did not cover her face and it had slipped somewhat during the service. She turned swiftly, but not before Targ had caught a glimpse of her. Kit was certain she saw a flicker of recognition in the reptilian eyes of Ariakas's pet bozak.

She could be mistaken, but she didn't dare take a chance. Kit slowed her pace, let the crowd flow around her. She gripped the knife and waited for the bozak to come near.

The crowd gave a surge that sent Targ stumbling into her. Perhaps Takhisis *was* on her side. Hoping desperately that the fragile-looking blade wouldn't break, Kit drove the poignard in between Tag's ribs, aiming for the lungs, hoping to nick the heart, not kill him outright.

The bozak gave a grunt indicative more of surprise than pain. Kit jerked the blade free and hid it in her sleeve. The bozak, an astonished look in his eyes, was just starting to crumple. Kitiara grabbed hold of Iolanthe's forearm and dragged her out of the doorway.

"Which way to the nearest gate?" Kit shoved aside several pilgrims, nearly knocking them down.

"Why? What's wrong?" Iolanthe asked, alarmed by the look on Kit's face.

"Which way?" Kit demanded savagely.

"The right," said Iolanthe, and Kit tugged her along in that direction.

They had not gone far when a blast shook the walls, sending dust and debris flying. As the noise of the explosion died away, shouts, screams, and moans began to echo down the corridors. Some pilgrims halted in shock, others cried out in panic. No one had any idea what had happened.

"Nuitari save us, what did you do?" Iolanthe gasped.

"The bozak in front of me was one of Ariakas's guards. He recognized me. I stabbed him. I didn't have any choice," said Kitiara, hurrying down the corridor. Seeing Iolanthe look bewildered, Kit added, "When bozaks die, their bones explode."

Guards and dark pilgrims pushed past them, some running to the site of the blast, others running from it.

"Nuitari save us," Iolanthe repeated. She pulled her cowl low over her face and, catching up the skirts of her robes, began to run. Kitiara joined her. She had no idea where they were and hoped that Iolanthe did. They rounded a corner and came face to face with draconian Temple guards pounding down the corridor. The guards were upon them before they could escape.

"What happened?" one demanded, blocking their path. "We heard an explosion."

Iolanthe burst into tears. "In the Abbey. A White Robe . . . disguised . . . cast a spell . . . dead draconians . . . a blast . . . it's horrible!" She used a little-girl voice, far different from her own throaty contralto.

"The White Robe got away," Kit added. "If you hurry, you might be able to catch him. He's dressed as a dark priest. You can't miss him. He has a long red scar across his nose."

The draconian commander wasted no more time in asking questions. He led his troops off in pursuit.

"Good thinking," Iolanthe said, hurrying on.

"You too," said Kit.

They climbed the winding stairs leading up out of the dungeon level. Their way was constantly impeded by troops shoving past them, racing to the scene of the disaster. Kit and Iolanthe reached the top of the stairs, ran down another corridor, and there stood the Gate of the White Dragon.

With the Temple under attack, all gates had been shut and sealed, the traps activated. The draconian guards, weapons drawn, were tense and on edge.

"Oops," said Kitiara. She hadn't foreseen this.

"Stay calm," Iolanthe said quietly. "Let me do the talking."

She lowered her cowl and tearfully repeated her tale about the dastardly White Robe. The draconians knew Ariakas's witch; Iolanthe had been there only that afternoon, working her magic on the white dragon trap that would hit anyone who set it off with a blast of frost, paralyzing them with cold. Iolanthe knew the password, of course, but the guards didn't even bother to ask her. They were interested in her companion, however.

"Who is this?" Reptile eyes stared suspiciously at Kit.

"My guide," Iolanthe stated. She sighed a helpless sigh and the violet eyes gave the commander a languishing look. "The corridors are so confusing. They all look alike. I get hopelessly lost."

"What's your name?" the draconian demanded, speaking to Kit. She remembered Iolanthe's advice and made the sign of the circle with her hand.

"She's taken a vow of silence," Iolanthe explained.

The draconian eyed Kit, who stood with her head humbly bowed, clutching the bloody poignard in her hand, keeping it hidden in the capacious sleeves. The commander waved them on through the gate.

They were almost out of the Temple when they heard clawed feet running after them. Kit halted, tensed, ready to strike.

"Madame Iolanthe," the draconian called, "the commander sent me to ask if you would like an escort home. The streets might not be safe."

Iolanthe gave a deep sigh. "No, thank you," she said. "I would not take you away from your post."

The two women walked through the gate, kept walking through the Temple environs, and into the street.

Kitiara was free. She breathed in the fresh air and gazed at the black sky sparkling with stars that she had never thought she would see again. She was almost giddy with joy and relief and barely heard what Iolanthe was saying.

"Listen to me!" Iolanthe pinched her arm to command her attention. "I must hasten to Ariakas. It would look strange if I didn't go straight to him with this news and I don't have much time! Where are you headed?"

"To my blue dragon," said Kit.

Iolanthe shook her head. "I thought as much. Don't waste your time. Ariakas ordered all the blue dragons in Neraka to return to Solamnia. He knows the blues are loyal to you and feared what would happen if your dragons found out you were going to be executed."

Kitiara swore softly.

Iolanthe pointed down a side street. "At the end of this street is a stable where Salah Kahn houses his horses. The horses of Khur are the fastest and the best in the world," she added with pride. "They are also the smartest. To protect them from being stolen, my people teach them a secret word. You must speak this word, or the horse will not permit you to mount. The horse will buck and lash out at you with its hooves and might kill you. Do you understand?"

Kit understood. Iolanthe told her the word. Kit repeated it and nodded.

"One more thing," said Iolanthe, detaining Kit as she was about to leave.

"What's that?"

Iolanthe looked at her searchingly. "Will you keep your vow? Will you ride now for Dargaard Keep?"

Kitiara hesitated. She thought about life on the run. Ariakas would offer a reward for her the moment he discovered she was missing. It would be a large reward. Every bounty hunter in Ansalon would be searching for her. She'd never be able to show her face in any city or town again. She'd be constantly looking over back, afraid to go to sleep.

"I will keep my vow," Kit said.

Iolanthe smiled. "I think you mean it. You will need this when you enter Dargaard Keep."

The witch took hold of Kitiara's hand and slid a large silver bracelet decorated with three jewels carved of onyx onto her wrist.

Kit grinned. "You want me to look my best for the death knight? Does it have earrings to match?"

"What do you know of Lord Soth?" Iolanthe asked.

"Not much," Kit admitted. "He's a death knight—"

"He can kill you with a single word," Iolanthe said. "He has an army of undead warriors who are bound to defend him, and if you fight your way past them, which is doubtful, you will encounter banshees. Their song is so horrific that if you hear but one wailing note, your heart will cease to beat and you will drop down dead. You will not survive five minutes in Dargaard Keep, much less an entire night."

Kit was subdued.

"So I take it this bracelet is magical." Kit eyed the piece of jewelry doubtfully. "Will it protect me in some way?"

"It will save you from dying of sheer terror. In addition, the onyx gems will absorb magical attacks made against you, though they will only take so much punishment. After that, they will crumble and the bracelet will be useless. Still, it should at least get you inside the front door. Its power is limited. Don't put it on until you intend to use it."

Kitiara clasped her hand over the bracelet.

"Good luck," Iolanthe added. She placed her hand over a ring she wore and began to mutter to herself.

"Wait, Iolanthe," said Kit, and the witch halted her incantation.

"Well, what now?"

Kit wasn't used to being grateful. The words stuck in her throat and came out gruff and awkward. "Thank you."

Iolanthe smiled. "Do not forget what you owe me," she said and disappeared, her black robes melting into the dark night.

Kitiara hurried down the alleyway. Behind her, she could hear more shouts as the tale spread among the outraged followers of Takhisis that a murderous White Robe had used his magic to infiltrate their Temple.

She found the stables and chose a black horse, liking the look of his powerful musculature, noble stance, the proud arch of his neck and the glint in his eye. She spoke the word Iolanthe had taught her. The horse permitted her to saddle him and within a few moments she was galloping out of the city.

Kitiara took the road north, toward Dargaard Keep.

Back in the Temple, the account of the White Robe caught the imagination of the worshipers and by the time the Nightlord arrived on the scene and was able to interrogate witnesses, several dark priests swore they had been standing right next to the daring wizard. The dark priest with the bald head and the scar across his nose was apprehended by a squad of draconians. Angered over the death of Targ, they gutted the man on the spot, only to discover after he was dead that he was not and never had been a user of magic. By dawn, the entire city of Neraka was being turned upside down as the draconians went house to house searching for the now-infamous White Robe wizard.

Such was the furor and outrage over the killings in the temple that everyone lost interest in the execution of Kitiara uth Matar. Guards were sent to bring her to the Arena of Death, only to find that she had managed to escape during the night's chaos. Ariakas was given this information by a quaking aide, who expected nothing less than death himself. Iolanthe was weeping and having hysterics in a corner. The Nightlord was raving about his ruined Abbey and demanding to know what the emperor was going to do to fix it. While he was talking, Salah Kahn came storming in, shouting in fury that his favorite horse had been stolen.

Ariakas received all this news with a calm equanimity that astonished everyone. He said nothing. He did not kill the messenger. He listened to the Nightlord's ravings and Salah Kahn's rants and Iolanthe's hysterics in silence, then ordered the Nightlord, the Highlord, the witch, and everyone else to leave.

Once he was alone, Ariakas paced the floor and considered the amazing coincidence that had brought a White Robe wizard to blow up the Dark Abbey on the very same night Kitiara happened to be locked up in the store room in the Temple awaiting execution.

The Emperor shook his head and said to himself in admiration, "What a woman. What a woman!"

9

Che spy. Che dream.
Fire and rainbows.

rian woke from the deep sleep of exhaustion with sudden alertness. He lay still, listening, until he was certain he'd heard the voices, not dreamed them. They spoke again and he flung off the fur blankets, and, moving silently and stealthily, he crept around the slumbering form of Aran to the tent opening.

"Whassamatter?" Aran mumbled.

"My turn at watch," Brian whispered, and Aran pulled the furs over his head and snuggled down deeper among the animal skins that formed his bed.

Brian, bundled in furs, opened the tent flap and peered into the darkness. No one was stirring. Derek was out there somewhere. He had insisted they set their own guard, though Harald had assured him the Ice Folk kept careful watch. A light shone from under a nearby tent—Sturm's tent. Brian crept closer.

Night in Icereach was black and silver, brittle with cold, spangled with stars. He could see well in the lambent light and if he could see he could be seen. He stayed in the shadows.

The voice that had awakened him had been Laurana's. She'd said something about Silvanesti. She was inside Sturm's tent, and as Brian watched from the shadows, he saw the dwarf join them.

Their voices were muffled. Brian circled around to the back of the tent to hear what they were saying. He despised himself for spying on those he had come to consider friends, but the moment he had heard Laurana's voice mention the ancient elven kingdom, his suspicions were aroused.

"We know," Laurana could be heard saying as Flint entered the tent. "You had a dream about Silvanesti."

"Apparently I'm not the only one?" Flint asked, making it a question. His voice was hoarse. He sounded nervous, uneasy. "I suppose you—you want me to tell you what I dreamed?"

"No!" Sturm spoke out harshly. "No, I do not want to talk about it—ever!"

Laurana murmured something Brian could not hear.

He was perplexed. They were talking about a dream, a dream of Silvanesti. It didn't make sense. He shuffled his feet to keep them warm and kept listening.

"I couldn't talk about mine either," Flint was saying. "I just wanted to see if it *was* a dream. It seemed so real I expected to find you both—"

Brian heard footsteps and shrank back into the shadows. The kender came dashing right past him, so excited he never noticed the knight. Tas flung open the tent flap and crawled inside.

"Did I hear you talking about a dream? I never dream, at least not that I remember. Kender don't, much. Oh, I suppose we do. Even animals dream, but—"

The dwarf made a growling sound and Tas returned to the subject. "I had the most fantastic dream! Trees crying blood. Horrible dead elves going around killing people! Raistlin wearing black robes! It was the most incredible thing! And you were there, Sturm. Laurana and Flint. And everyone died! Well, almost everyone. Raistlin didn't. And there was a green dragon—"

None of the others inside the tent said a word. Even the dwarf had gone silent, which was odd, since Flint rarely let Tas ramble on with such nonsense. Tas faltered in the silence. When he spoke again, he was apparently trying to nudge them into responding.

"Green dragon? Raistlin dressed in black? Did I mention that? Quite becoming, actually. Red always makes him look kind of jaundiced, if you know what I mean."

Apparently no one did, for the silence continued, grew deeper.

"Well," said Tas. "I guess I'll go back to bed if you don't want to hear anymore." He spoke hopefully, but no one took him up on it.

"Good night," Tas said, backing out of the tent.

Shaking his head in perplexity, he walked right past Brian—again without seeing him—muttering, "What's the matter with everybody? It was only a dream! Though I have to say," he added somberly, "it was the most *real* dream I've ever had in my whole entire life."

No one spoke inside the tent. Brian considered this all very strange, but he was relieved to know that they weren't plotting against them. He was about to slip back to his tent when he heard Flint say, "I don't mind having a nightmare, but I object to sharing it with a kender. How do you suppose we all came to have the same dream? What does it mean?"

"A strange land—Silvanesti," Laurana said in thoughtful tones. The light wavered beneath the tent. She opened the tent flap part way and Brian hunkered down in the shadows, hoping fervently she didn't see him.

"Do you think it was real?" Laurana's voice trembled. "Did they die—as we saw?"

"We're here," Sturm replied reassuringly. "*We* didn't die. We can only trust the others didn't either, and—this seems funny, but somehow I *know* they're all right."

Brian was startled. Sturm sounded very sure of himself, but after all it had been only a dream. Still, it was odd that they had all shared it.

Laurana slipped out into the night. She carried a thick candle and its flame illuminated her face. She was pale from the shock of the nightmare, and she seemed lost in wonderment. Gilthanas emerged from his tent, which was directly across from Brian's, so the knight was trapped. As long as the two stood there, he couldn't go back.

"Laurana," her brother said, coming up short at the sight of her. "I was so worried. I had a dream that you died!"

"I know," said Laurana. "I dreamed the same thing, so did

Sturm and Flint and Tas. We all had the same dream about Tanis, Raistlin, and the rest of our friends. The dream was horrible, yet it was comforting at the same time. I know Tanis is alive, Gil. I know it! The rest are alive, as well. None of us understand it—"

She and her brother went into his tent to finish their discussion. Brian was about to return to his, deeply ashamed of himself, when he heard movement. The dwarf and knight were walking out of the tent. Again Brian ducked back into the shadows, vowing he would never spy on anyone else so long as he lived. He was not cut out for this!

"Well, so much for sleep," Flint was saying. "I'll take my turn at watch now."

"I'll join you," Sturm offered.

"I suppose we'll never know why or how we all dreamed the same dream," said the dwarf.

"I suppose not," said Sturm.

The dwarf walked out of the tent. Sturm was about to follow when he appeared to find something on the ground just inside his tent flap. He stooped down to pick it up. The object glittered with a bright blue-white light, as though a star had dropped from the sky to rest in Sturm's hand. The knight stood staring at the shining object, turning it over in his hand. Brian could see it quite clearly—a pendant formed in the shape of a star. The pendant gleamed with its own sparkling radiance. It was incredibly beautiful.

"I suppose not," Sturm repeated, but as he stared at the jewel he now sounded thoughtful. He clasped it tightly, thankful to have recovered it.

Passing Gilthanas's tent, Sturm heard Laurana's voice inside, and ducked in there. Brian hurried thankfully to his own tent, slipped inside, stumbled over Aran's feet, and found his own bed. He could overhear the three talking in the tent opposite.

"Laurana," said Sturm, "can you tell me something about this?"

He heard her gasp. Gilthanas said something in Elvish.

"Sturm," Laurana said, awed, "that is a starjewel! How did you come by such a thing?"

"The Lady Alhana gave it to me before we parted," Sturm replied in a hushed and reverent tone. "I didn't want to take it, for I could see it was extremely valuable, but she insisted—"

"Sturm," said Laurana, and her voice was choked with emotion. "This is the answer—or at least part of it. Starjewels are gifts given by a lover to his beloved. The jewels connect them, keep each in the heart and mind and soul of the other, even if they are parted. The connection is spiritual, not physical, and is impossible to break. Some believe it lasts even beyond death."

Sturm's reply was muffled, and Brian could not hear it. His thoughts went to Lillith—they had not been far from her this entire trip—and he could only imagine what the knight must be feeling.

"I have never heard of a starjewel being given to any human," said Gilthanas, adding caustically, "Its value is incalculable. It is worth a small kingdom. You have done well for yourself."

"Do you truly believe I would ever *sell* this?" Sturm demanded. His voice trembled with his rage. "If so, you do not know me!"

Gilthanas was silent a moment, then he said quietly. "I do know you, Sturm Brightblade. I was wrong to imply such a thing. Please forgive me."

Sturm muttered that he accepted the apology and walked out of the tent. As he left, Gilthanas asked again for Sturm to forgive him. Sturm said nothing; he simply walked out.

Laurana spoke angrily to her brother in Elvish. Gilthanas replied in Elvish. Brian couldn't understand the words, but the elf lord sounded contrite, though sullen.

Laurana emerged from the tent and ran after Sturm.

"Gil didn't mean it—" she began.

"Yes, Laurana, he did," Sturm said. His voice was stern. "Perhaps he came to think better of his cruel remark, but when he first spoke those words, he knew exactly what he was saying."

Sturm paused then added, "He wants the dragon orb for your people, doesn't he? I've seen him hanging about the knights. I know he's been spying on Derek. What does your brother know about this orb?"

Laurana gave a little gasp. Sturm's blunt accusation had taken her by surprise. "I don't think he knows anything. He's just talking—"

Sturm cut her off in exasperation. "You keep trying to pour honey over everything. You placate Derek. You coddle your brother. Stand up for yourself and what you believe in for once."

"I'm sorry," she said, and Brian heard her boots crunch in the snow.

"Laurana," said Sturm, relenting, "I'm the one who is sorry. After what you've been through, I shouldn't have spoken to you like that. You've kept us together. You brought us here."

"For what?" she asked in hopeless tones. "So we could freeze to death?"

"I don't know," he returned. "Maybe the gods do."

The two were silent, friends comforting each other.

Laurana spoke. "Could I ask you one question before you go?"

"Of course," Sturm replied.

"You said you *knew* Tanis and the others were alive . . . "

"They did not die in Tarsis as we feared. He and our friends are with Lady Alhana in Silvanesti and though they have been in great peril and they feel great sorrow, for the moment they are safe. I don't know how I know that," he added simply, "but I know it."

"The magic of the starjewel," Laurana said. "Lady Alhana speaks through the jewel to your heart. The two of you will always be connected . . .

"Sturm," she said softly, so softly Brian could barely hear, "that human woman I saw in the dream, the one who was with Tanis. Was that . . . Kitiara?"

Sturm cleared his throat. He sounded embarrassed. "That was Kit," he said gruffly.

"Do you think . . . are they together?"

"I don't see how that's possible, Laurana. The last I saw of Kit, she was traveling to Solamnia, and anyway I doubt she would be in Silvanesti. Kit never had much use for elves."

Laurana gave a sigh that was audible even to Brian. "I wish I could believe that."

Sturm tried to reassure her. "We were all in the dream together and *we're* not in Silvanesti. Tanis and the others are alive and that is good to know. But remember, when all is said and done, Laurana, it was just a dream."

"I suppose you're right," Laurana replied, and she bid him a good night and returned to her tent, but as she walked past Brian's tent, he heard her murmur, "A *magical* dream . . ."

Brian lay awake for a long time, unable to sleep. He had lived his life, for the most part, having nothing to do with magic. Wizards were viewed with deep suspicion in Solamnia, and those wizards who chose to live in that realm—and there were few—kept to themselves. The only magic he had ever seen had been performed at fairs and even then his father had told him it was all sleight-of-hand and make believe. As for holy miracles, he had seen for himself when Elistan healed the wounds suffered by the white bear. He did not agree with Derek that it was trickery, though Brian could not quite bring himself to believe it was the gods either.

Yet now he was in the company of people who had been around mages since they were small; a wizard of the red robes had been a childhood companion. Though they did not understand its workings, they accepted magic as a part of their lives. They were convinced they had all shared a dream because of a shining bit of jewelry. Even the gruff and dour old dwarf believed it.

Perhaps, Brian thought, the magic is not so much in the jewel as it is in their souls. Their love and friendship for each other runs so deep that even apart they are still together, still in each other's hearts and minds. He saw daily the close bond that existed between these people and he remembered a time when there had been such a bond between three young men. Once, long ago, those three young men might have shared a dream. Not anymore. Brian realized he had been trying this entire journey to find their bond of friendship again, but that could never happen. War and ambition, fear and mistrust had changed them, driven them apart instead of bringing them together. He, Derek, and Aran were strangers to each other.

Because of Derek's suspicions, Brian had learned the innermost secrets of friends who trusted him, and though he was impressed and touched by what he'd heard, he knew quite well he should have never heard it. When Derek came off watch, muttering that he didn't trust the dwarf and Brightblade and the Ice Folk to keep a good look-out, Brian had to work hard to keep from leaping up and slugging him.

———————————————

The next morning, Derek and Aran set out to take a look at Ice Wall Castle to see it for themselves. They took along Raggart's grandson, who was also named Raggart, as a guide.

Raggart the Younger, as he was called, though he was close to thirty, had eagerly volunteered to accompany the two knights. Raggart was the tribe's historian, which meant that he was the tribal storyteller.

The Ice Folk kept no written history (few could read or write), and thus all important events were chronicled in song and story. Young Raggart had learned the history from the previous historian, now dead some fifteen years, and he related the stories on a daily basis, sometimes singing them, sometimes acting them out, with himself taking all the roles, sometimes making a tale of them. He could mimic any sound, from the swishing of the runners of the ice boats as they sped across the frozen landscape to the wailing howl of wolves and the quarreling cawings of sea birds, and he used the sounds to enliven his recitals.

Young Raggart foresaw adding a glorious episode to the tribal lore, one he would witness firsthand. He presented the knights with a crude drawing of the castle's interior, though exactly what good this was going to do them was open to question, since they had no intention of going inside. When Derek asked him how he knew what the castle's interior looked like, since he had admitted that he'd never been inside Ice Wall, Raggart had replied that he'd put it together from information found in a very old poem composed by a long-lost ancestor who had investigated the castle three hundred years ago. Though Derek had grave misgivings about the map, it was, as he said, better than nothing, and he accepted it and studied it with interest before they left. Their number included Tasslehoff, not because he was wanted, but because Derek could not find any way short of running a sword through the kender to get rid of him.

Brian had been supposed to accompany his fellows, but he had declined. Derek had not been pleased and he had been on the point of ordering Brian to come, but there was something oddly rebellious and defiant in Brian's manner. Not wanting to make an issue of it, Derek had swallowed his anger and instead told Brian to keep an eye on Brightblade and the others. Brian had stared at Derek in grim silence and then turned and walked off without a word.

"I think our friend has fallen in love with that elf woman," Derek said in disapproving tones to Aran as they departed. "I will have to have a talk with him."

Aran, who had seen the fond looks Brian and Lillith gave each other, knew Derek was completely and utterly wrong in this, but it amused the knight to let Derek remain under his misapprehension.

Trekking over the snow after their guide, Aran looked forward glee-fully to hearing one of Derek's sonorous lectures on the evils of loving anyone who wasn't "our own kind".

Brian had been going to eat a solitary breakfast in his tent. Laurana, hearing he remained behind, was concerned and came to ask after his health. She was kind and gracious and truly seemed to care about him. Remembering that he had spied on her last night, Brian felt worse than the meanest scoundrel that ever roamed the sewers of Palanthas. Brian could not refuse her invitation, and he joined her and her friends, along with the chief of the Ice Folk, in the chieftent.

The companions were much more cheerful this morning. They spoke of their absent comrades freely, without the sorrow of loss, wondering where they were and what they were doing. Brian acted surprised to hear their joyful news. His acting wasn't very good, but the others were so happy none of them noticed.

The conversation turned to the dragon orb. Harald listened to all they said, keeping his thoughts to himself. Gilthanas made no secret of the fact that he believed the orb should go to the elves.

"Lord Gunthar has pledged that the orb will be taken to the Whitestone Council. The elves are part of the Whitestone Council—" Brian began.

"We *were*," Gilthanas interrupted. His lip curled. "We are no longer."

"Gil, please don't start—" Laurana began.

Then, glancing at Sturm, perhaps thinking what he'd said about honey-coating everything, she fell silent.

"Here now!" Flint was saying. "What does this dragon orb do that is so blasted important?" His bushy brows came together in a frown. The dwarf looked first at Brian, then at Gilthanas.

"Well?" Flint demanded, and when neither answered, he grunted, "I thought so. All this fooferah to find something the kender said he read about in a book! *That* should tell you the answer right there—mainly that we should leave the fool orb where it sits and go home." Flint sat back, triumphant.

Sturm smoothed his mustaches preparatory to saying something. Gilthanas opened his mouth at the same time, but they were both interrupted by Tasslehoff who burst into the chieftent, agog with excitement, brimming with importance, and shivering with cold.

"We found Ice Wall Castle!" he announced. "Guess what? It's made of ice! Well, I guess it isn't really. Derek says underneath all the ice are stone walls and the ice has simply accumulated"—Tas brought out the big word proudly—"over the years."

He plopped himself down on the floor and gratefully accepted a warming drink of some steaming liquid. "That burns clear down to my toes," he said thankfully. "As for the castle, it's perched way, way, way up on top of a mountain made of ice. Derek has this great idea about how we're going to storm the castle, find the dragon orb, and kill the wizard. The castle is a wonderful place. Raggart sang us a song about it. The song tells about underground tunnels and a magical fountain of water that never freezes and then, of course, there's the dragon's lair with the dragon orb and the dragon inside. I can't wait to go!"

Tas took another gulp of his drink and let out a moist breath. "Whew, boy, that's good! Anyway, where was I?"

"—getting my people slaughtered," Harald stated angrily.

"Was I?" Tasslehoff looked surprised. "I didn't mean to."

"In order to reach Ice Wall Castle, my people will be forced to travel over the glacier, where we will be visible for miles along the way—easy pickings for the white dragon," Harald went on, growing angrier the more he talked. "Then those who by some miracle manage to survive the dragon's attack will be targets for the dragon-men who will shoot my warriors as full of arrows as a prickly pig!"

"What's a prickly pig?" Tas asked, but no one answered.

Derek had entered the tent.

Harald was on his feet, glaring at the knight. "So you would send my people to their deaths!"

"I had intended to explain my plan myself," Derek stated, with an exasperated glance at the kender.

Tasslehoff grinned and waved and said modestly, "That's all right, Sir Knight. No need for thanks."

Derek turned to Harald. "Your people can slip up to the castle under the cover of darkness—"

Harald shook his head and gave an explosive snort that seemed to expand the walls of the tent. The Ice Folk inside the chieftent put down their work to give him their full attention.

"What is wrong with that idea?" Derek demanded, disconcerted by the sight of so many dark and emotionless eyes fixed upon him.

Harald looked to Raggart the Elder. The old priest in his gray robes rose, tottering on shaking legs, leaning on the arm of his grandson for support.

"Wolves roam about the castle by night," Raggart stated. "They would see us and report back to Feal-Thas."

Derek thought at first he was joking, then realized the old man was serious. He appealed to the chief. "You are a man of reason. Do you believe such nonsense as this? Wolf guards—it is a child's tale!"

Harald once again swelled with rage and it seemed likely he would blast Derek out of the tent if he got started. Raggart rested a warding hand on Harald's arm, and the chief choked back his rage and was silent.

"According to you, the gods themselves are child's tales, aren't they, Sir Knight?" asked the old man.

Derek replied in measured tones, "I had a beloved brother who believed in these gods. He died a terrible death when our castle was attacked and overrun by the dragonarmies. He prayed to them to save us, and they did nothing. This proves to me there are no gods."

Elistan stirred at this and seemed about to speak.

Derek saw this and forestalled him. "Spare your breath, Cleric. If there *are* such gods of so-called 'good' who refused to heed my brother's prayers and let him die, then I want nothing to do with them."

He looked about the tent, at the eyes watching him. "Many of your people may die, Chieftain, that is true, but many people in other parts of Krynn have already laid down their lives for our noble cause—"

"—so that you can find this dragon orb and take it back to *your* homeland," said Harald dourly.

"And we will slay the wizard Feal-Thas—"

Harald gave another terrific snort.

Derek was flushed with anger, at a loss for words. He was accustomed to obedience and respect, and he was getting neither. He was obviously baffled by Harald's stubborn obtuseness, for that is what he considered it.

"You do not understand the importance—" Derek began impatiently.

"No, it is you who do not understand," Harald thundered. "My people fight only when we must fight. We do not go seeking battle. Why do you think our boats are swift? To carry us away from the conflict. We are not cowards. We fight if we must, but *only* if we must. Given a chance, we run. There is no shame in that, Sir Knight, because every day of our lives of we fight deadly foes: shifting ice, bitter wind, biting cold, sickness, starvation. We have fought these foes for centuries. When you leave, we will continue to fight them. Will this dragon orb of yours change anything for us?"

"It may or it may not," interjected Elistan. "A single pebble falling into a lake sends out ripples that expand and keep expanding until they reach the shore. The distance between Solamnia and Icereach is vast, yet the gods have seen fit to bring us together. Perhaps for the dragon orb," he said, looking at Derek, then shifting his gaze to Harald, "or perhaps to help us learn to honor and respect one another."

"And if Feal-Thas were destroyed, I think it unlikely Ariakas would send anyone to take his place," Sturm said. "To my way of thinking, the attack on Tarsis did not prove the Dark Queen's strength; it showed her weakness. If there was a way we could work together—"

"I have told you the way," Derek interrupted angrily. "By attacking Ice Wall castle—"

Laurana quit listening. She was sick of the quarreling, sick of the fighting. Derek would never understand Harald. The chief would never understand Derek. Her thoughts turned to Tanis. Now that she too believed he was alive, she wondered if he was with that human woman, Kitiara. Laurana had seen her with Tanis in the dream. Kit was lovely, with her black curly hair, crooked smile, flashing black eyes . . .

There had been something familiar about her. Laurana had the feeling she'd seen those eyes before.

Now you're being silly, she told herself. Letting your jealousy run away with you. Sturm's right. Kitiara's nowhere near Silvanesti. Why should she be? Strange that I feel this connection to her . . . as if we've met . . .

"We will carry on with our plans, Chieftain, no matter what you choose to do—" Derek was saying heatedly.

Laurana rose to her feet and walked off.

Tasslehoff had long since grown bored with the conversation. He was in the back of the chieftent having a grand rummage through his pouches to the delight of several children squatting on the floor around him. Among his treasures was a broken piece of crystal whose smooth planes and sharp edges formed a triangular shape.

He must have picked it up in Tarsis, Laurana realized. It looked as though it might have once graced an elegant lamp or maybe was part of the stem of a broken wine glass.

Tasslehoff was squatting directly beneath one of the ventilation holes in the roof. The midday sun streamed down, forming a bright halo around the kender.

"Watch this!" he said to the children. "I'm going to do a magic trick taught to me by a great and powerful wizard named Raistlin Majere."

Tas held the crystal to the sun. "I'm going to say the magic words now. *'Oooglety booglety'*." He twitched the crystal to make tiny rainbows go dancing about the tent. The children shouted in glee and Derek, in the front of the tent, cast them all a stern look and ordered Tasslehoff to stop fooling around.

"I'll show you fooling around," Tas muttered and he twitched the crystal again, causing one of the rainbows to crawl over Derek's face.

The knight blinked as the sunlight hit his eyes. The children clapped and laughed and Tas smothered a giggle. Derek rose angrily to his feet. Laurana gestured to him that she would deal with it, and Derek sat back down.

"Did Raistlin really teach you how to do that?" Laurana asked, sitting beside Tas, hoping to distract the kender from his torment of the knight.

"Yes, he did," said Tas proudly, adding eagerly, "I'll tell you the story. It's very interesting. Flint was designing a setting for a jeweled pendant for one of his customers, and the pendant went missing. I offered to help him find it, and so I left to go to Raistlin and Caramon's house to ask if they might have seen it. Caramon wasn't home and Raistlin had his nose in a book. He said I wasn't to bother him and I said I would just sit down and wait for Caramon to come back, and

Raistlin asked me if I meant to stay there all day, annoying him, and I said yes, I had to find this jeweled pendant, and then he put down the book and came over to me and turned all my pockets inside out and, would you believe it? There was the pendant!"

Tas had to stop for breath before continuing. "I was really happy to think I'd found it and I said I'd take it back to Flint, but Raistlin said, no, he would take it to Flint after supper and I was to go away and leave him alone. I said I thought I would wait for Caramon anyway, because I hadn't seen him since yesterday. Raistlin eyed me in that way of his that kind of sends crawly feelings through you and then he asked would I go if he taught me a magic trick? I said I would *have* to go, because I'd want to show the trick to Flint.

"Raistlin held the jewel up to light and he said the magic words and he made rainbows! Then he had me hold the jewel up the to the light and taught me the magic words and *I* made rainbows! He showed me another magic trick, too. Here, I'll do it for you."

He held the crystal to the sun so that the light passed through it and beamed brightly on the floor. Tas shoved aside one of the fur rugs, exposing the ice beneath. He held the crystal steady, focusing it on the ice. The light struck the ice and it began to melt. The children gasped in wonder.

"See?" said Tas proudly. "Magic! The time I did that for Flint, I set the tablecloth on fire."

Laurana hid a smile. It wasn't magic. Elves had been using prisms for as long as there had been elves and crystals, fire and rainbows.

Fire and rainbows.

Laurana stared at the melting ice and suddenly she knew how the Ice Folk could defeat their foes.

Laurana stood up. First she thought she would tell the others, and then she thought she wouldn't. What was she doing? Here she was, an elf maiden, telling battle-hardened Solamnic knights how to fight. They wouldn't listen to her. Worse, they might laugh at her. There was another problem. Her idea depended on faith in the gods. Was her faith strong enough? Would she bet her life and the lives of her friends and the lives of the Ice Folk on that faith?

Laurana walked slowly back. She imagined speaking out and felt suddenly queasy, as she had the very first time she'd played her harp for her parents' guests. She'd given a beautiful performance, or so her mother had told her. Laurana couldn't remember any of it, except throwing up afterward. Since her mother's death, Laurana had acted as her father's hostess. She had performed numerous times for their guests. She'd spoken before dignitaries and later, she'd talked to the assembled refugees, and she had not been nervous, perhaps because she had been in her father's shadow or in Elistan's. Now, if she spoke up, she would have to stand on her own in the glaring sunlight.

Keep quiet, you fool, Laurana scolded herself and she was determined to obey and then she thought of Sturm, telling her to stand up for what she believed in.

"I know how to assault Ice Wall Castle," she said and, as they stared at her in astonishment, she added breathlessly, surprised at her own courage, "With the help of the gods, we will make the castle attack itself."

10

Too much of a good horse.
The priest of Takhisis.

itiara rode all night. Salah Kahn's horse had been languishing in his stall for several days and was spoiling for a gallop. Kitiara had to occasionally rein him in, so as not to tire him out. They had a long journey ahead of them. Dargaard Keep was hundreds of miles distant, and danger crouched behind every bush, watched every crossroads.

She tried to calculate, as she rode, when her absence would be discovered. She hoped not until dawn, at the time of her scheduled execution, but with the chaos over the destruction of the Dark Abbey, she couldn't be certain. Dragons would carry the news of her escape far and wide. Word would spread fast.

The one advantage she had was that Ariakas would assume she would head for Solamnia, there to join up with her blue dragon command and lead them in rebellion against him. It was what he would have done in her place. He would concentrate his searchers on the roads leading to Solamnia. Those bounty hunters would be disappointed. Kit wasn't heading west. She was riding north, to the accursed realm known as Nightlund, a land no one visited unless he had a death wish or an exceptionally good reason for not being anywhere else.

Part of Solamnia, the realm had originally been known as Knightlund. The land was heavily wooded, rugged, and mountainous. Not suitable for farming, at the time of the Cataclysm it was only sparsely populated. A wealthy and influential Knight of the Rose, Sir Loren Soth, was ruler of the region. His family's keep was built in the northern part of Dargaard Mountains. Designed to resemble a rose, the castle was considered a marvel of architecture. Family legend had it that Soth's grandfather imported dwarven craftsman to build the castle and that its construction took one hundred years. A city called Dargaard grew up around the keep, but most of the other settlements in Knightlund were located along the river and did brisk business in milling, logging, and fishing.

The Cataclysm devastated Knightlund. Earthquakes split the mountains. The river overflowed its banks and, in some places, shifted course. Every settlement along the river was destroyed. Lives were lost, livelihoods ended.

The people in other regions of Solamnia were also hard-hit by the disaster. Concentrating on their own survival, they could not worry about what was happening in Knightlund. Most believed the lord of the region was dealing with the disaster.

Then survivors came stumbling out of that land, telling strange and terrible tales. The once-magnificent Dargaard Keep was destroyed, and that was not the worst of the story. Murder had been done in the keep; its mistress and her little child had died horribly in a fire that had swept through the wondrous castle, leaving it blackened and crumbling. With her dying breath, so it was said, she had called down a curse on the man who could have saved her and his child, but in his jealousy and rage, he had walked off and left them to perish in the flames.

Sir Loren Soth, once a proud and noble knight of Solamnia, was now a knight of death, doomed to live in the shadowy realm of the undead. The wailing voices of the elf women who shared his curse moaned night after night, repeating to him the tale of his tragic downfall. Warriors of fire, bone and blackened armor, stained with their own blood, were constrained by their master's curse to mount eternal patrol atop the crumbling walls and slay in fury any living person who challenged them.

The gods of Light had doomed Lord Soth to a tormented existence, forced to constantly reflect upon his own guilt. They hoped eventually he would ask forgiveness, redemption. Takhisis wanted to claim him for her own and she gifted him with powerful magicks, hoping to persuade him to turn his back on salvation and serve her. But Soth had apparently turned his back on all gods—good and evil, for he would not march forth to terrorize the world as Takhisis had hoped. He remained in his keep, brooding and terrible, dealing merciless death to those who dared disturb him.

These were the reports from Knightlund, and few believed them at first, but more stories came out of that dark land and all told the same tale. The city of Dargaard, which had escaped the Cataclysm relatively unscathed, was abandoned; its citizens fled in terror, vowing to never go back, but with the stories of dread banshees and undead warriors came tales of fabulous treasure, wealth unimaginable stashed away in the storerooms of the keep. Many were the greedy and venturesome who traveled to Dargaard in search of fame, wealth, and glory. The only ones who ever returned were those who had been so stricken by terror at the sight of the keep's blackened walls and broken towers that they never went closer. Such was the land's evil repute that some grim jokester suggested the name be changed from "Knightlund" to "Nightlund". Over time, that was how the realm became generally known, and now it was written thus on the maps.

No one had actually seen Lord Soth, or, if any person had, he had not lived to tell of it. Was the death knight a myth, a creation of mothers trying to scare children into good behavior? Perhaps it was a tale from the excited mind of some inventive kender? Or did he really exist?

Kitiara would have been the first to discount such fanciful stories but for Queen Takhisis, who had been so persistent in her urging, and for another reason. Kit's father had traveled to Nightlund. Drawn by rumor of wealth untold and scoffing at the "granny tales", Gregor uth Matar was one of the few to make it back alive. This happened because, as he freely admitted, his instinct for self-preservation had convinced him that no amount of money was worth the danger. He had always joked about his journey to Nightlund, but when, as a little girl, Kit had pressed him for details, Gregor had told her that some things were best forgotten. He had laughed when he said it, but there had been a shadowed look in his eye that she had never seen before, a look she had never forgotten.

And here she was, riding to this dread land, home to the living as well as the dead, a haunt for the desperate and dangerous, driven to hiding in Nightlund because they were hunted everywhere else.

As Kitiara rode that night, she thought of this, thought of her father, recalled the horror stories she had heard. Not far from Neraka, she came to a fork in the road. One highway led west. The other led north. Kit reined in her horse. She looked to the west, to Skie, who would be over his sulking fit by now and wondering what had happened to her. She was sorely tempted to take the western route, return to her troops, challenge Ariakas. Do just what he feared she would do.

She considered this option, forcing herself to examine it. Skie would side with her, she was sure of that. She would not be able to count upon the other blue dragons. Queen Takhisis, angry over Kit breaking her vow, would turn her back on her and the blue dragons would not go against their Queen. Kit's own troops would be divided. She might rally half of them to her cause. The others would desert. Handsome Bakaris would join her, but he was not all that trustworthy. He'd turn on her in an instant if the money was good enough.

Kitiara shifted in the saddle. There was one other reason, the most important, why she would not ride west. She might break her vow to her Queen, but Kitiara uth Matar could not break a vow to herself. She had vowed to return to Ariakas in triumph, strong and powerful, so strong he would not dare cross her. To accomplish that, she needed a strong and powerful ally—an ally such as Lord Soth. It was either victory or death.

Kitiara rode north.

Day dawned, bright and cold, and Kit realized the horse was going to be a problem. The magnificent stallion with his jet-black glossy coat, his long mane, sweeping tail, and powerfully muscled body was obviously a valuable animal. People stopped and stared at him in admiration. Their gaze shifted to his rider, to Kit, clad once more in her gambeson. She had used the poignard to slash the threads' embroidered design off the quilted fabric of her gambeson, already worn from much use. She had no cloak in this cold weather and that made her look even more down-at-the-heels. Everyone who saw that horse would instantly wonder how a shabby sellsword such as herself had managed to acquire the rare and noble beast. Everyone she met would be certain to remember the expensive horse and its beggarly rider.

Kit left the main road, seeking shelter in the woods. She searched until she found a shallow depression where she could tether the horse. Worn out from her exhausting ordeal, she needed sleep. Kit's mind was busy with the problem of the horse as she drifted off. She had named him Windracer and she needed his strength, power and stamina to carry her to Nightlund. She needed his speed in case Ariakas's forces closed in on her. She had to find some way they could ride openly on the road and not call attention to themselves.

Her mind worked as she slept, and Kit woke refreshed in the early evening, with what she hoped was a solution to her problem.

Leaving the horse concealed in the forest, Kit made herself even more disreputable-looking. She smeared dirt on her face, shook her hair over her eyes, then returned to the highway. She was still too close to Neraka for comfort, and her heart beat rapidly when a troop of goblin soldiers marched past on their way into the city. She crouched behind a tree and the goblin soldiers passed by her, never noticing she was there.

A merchant caravan approached, but it was guarded by several well-armed mercenaries and she allowed it to pass. After that, with night closing in, the number of travelers dwindled. Kit was starting to grow frustrated and impatient. She was wasting valuable time, and she had just about decided to risk riding as she was when the traveler she had been hoping to meet came along—a priest of Takhisis, obviously of high rank, probably a spiritor. A large medallion of faith dangled ostentatiously from a heavy golden chain around his neck. He wore black velvet robes and a lamb's wool cloak of fine quality. His fingers were adorned with rings of jet and onyx set in gold. His saddle and trappings were expensive hand-tooled leather.

He was a short man, of stout build with a ruddy complexion.

Unlike the dark priests of the Temple, he obviously enjoyed his dinner and his wine. He carried no weapon other than a riding crop. Kit waited for his armed escort to appear, but no one came. She heard no sound of hoofbeats. Though he was riding the roads near Neraka alone, the priest did not seem worried or nervous. Kit should have wondered about this odd circumstance but she was in haste and this victim was too perfect to pass up.

As the priest's horse drew near, Kit rose from her place by the tree. Keeping her head lowered to conceal her features, she limped up to the priest, her hand extended.

"Please, dark father," she said, her voice harsh, "spare a steel coin for a soldier wounded in the service of our Queen."

The priest cast her a baleful glance and raised his riding crop in a threatening manner.

"Wretched cur, I have nothing to give you," he said churlishly. "It is unseemly for one of our troops to be caught begging. Take your miserable carcass off the public road!"

"Please, father . . ." Kitiara whined.

The priest lashed out at her with the riding crop, striking for her head. The blow missed, but Kit gave a cry and fell back as though it had landed.

The priest rode on without a look. Kit waited a moment to be certain he was alone and no guards were following at a distance. Seeing no one else on the road, she ran lightly and silently after him. She leaped, vaulted onto the back of the horse, and wrapped her arm around the priest's neck. She put her knife to his throat.

The priest was taken completely by surprise. At the touch of cold steel, he gasped and went stiff in the saddle.

"I asked you nicely the first time, dark father," Kit said reproachfully. "You refused to give me anything, so now I'm insisting. It's only because you are a servant of the Dark Queen that I don't slit your throat, so you might want to thank her. Now get down off the horse."

She shifted the knife to the man's ribs and gave him a prod. She could feel his pudgy body quivering, and she assumed it was with fear. The dark priest sullenly dismounted. Kitiara slid deftly off the horse to land on the ground behind him. He started to turn. She kicked his knees out from under him, and he sagged to the ground with a groan.

"Hand over your money—" Kit began.

To her astonishment, the priest surged to his feet. Grasping his medallion, he held it out in front of him and cried out in fury, "May Queen Takhisis hear my prayer and shrivel your heart. May she flay your flesh from your bones, suck the breath from your body, and destroy you utterly!"

His flabby body shook with rage, his voice resounded with confidence. He had no doubt that the dark goddess would answer him, and for a terrifying moment, neither did Kitiara. The night air crackled with the power of his prayer and she cringed, waiting for the wrath of Takhisis to immolate her.

Nothing happened.

The crackling subsided and dwindled away. Kitiara's flesh remained intact. Her heart continued to beat. She kept right on breathing.

Kit raised her head. The priest was still holding the medallion, but he was starting to look uneasy. "Takhisis!" he cried, and now there was a note of panic in his voice, "shrivel this miscreant's heart and flay the flesh—"

Kitiara burst out laughing.

"You are calling on the wrong god if you want to stop *me*, dark father. Next time, try praying to Paladine. Now strip off those robes. I want your belt, your jewelry and that fat purse of yours. Quickly!"

She emphasized her words with her knife, prodding him in the midriff. The priest tore off his chain and his rings and flung them to the ground at her feet. Then he stood there, glowering, his arms crossed over his chest.

"Dark father, the only reason I don't gut you is that I don't want to ruin those warm robes," Kit told him.

She was nervous, fearing someone might come. She walked forward, the point of her blade darting at his neck.

"But if you force me—"

The priest tossed his purse at her head, then, cursing her to every dark god he could think of, he dragged his robes off over his head. Kit made a bundle, tying up the money and the jewels inside the robes and cloak. She slapped his horse's rump, so that the animal bounded off down the road, leaving the dark priest to stand shivering in his breeches, still calling down imprecations on her.

Chuckling, Kit entered the forest, wending her way through the thick underbrush to where she had Windracer concealed. The last she saw of the priest, he was running down the road, yelling loudly for his horse. Kit had seen the slash marks made by his riding crop on the animal's neck, and she guessed the horse was not going to be inclined to stop and wait for him.

Kitiara pulled on the sumptuous black velvet robes of a high rank-ing priest over her own clothes. She draped the golden chain with the Queen's medallion around her neck. The rings he'd worn were too big for her fingers. She put them in the purse that was filled with steel coins.

"How do I look?" she asked Windracer, modeling for the horse, who appeared to approve. Perhaps he, too, could foresee the best inns, the finest oats, the warmest stables.

Kitiara was transformed from a lowly sellsword into a wealthy priest of Takhisis. No one would think to question how she came to be in possession of such a valuable horse. She could ride the main roads by day. She could sleep in real beds, not spend her nights in ravines. Her pursuers would be searching for a renegade Highlord, a warrior woman. They would never think to look for a high-ranking spiritor. The wretched priest would tell his tale to the first sheriff he encoun-tered, but as far as he knew, he'd been attacked by a beggar or perhaps, since she'd mentioned Paladine, a servant of the God of Light.

Kitiara laughed heartily. She ate a good meal—the priest's own dinner—and then mounted her horse. She rode on, heading north. She had left one danger behind.

Unfortunately, that left her plenty of time to reflect upon the truly appalling danger that lay ahead.

II

The frostreaver.
The making of a squire.

aurana's idea for the attack on Ice Wall Castle caused an uproar. The knights were opposed, her friends were in favor, while Harald was dubious but interested. They spent that night and the next day arguing about it. Harald eventually agreed to go along with it, mainly because Raggart the Elder approved it, but partly because Derek was opposed to it. Derek said tersely that no military man of any sense would go into battle armed with only faith in gods who, if they existed at all, had proved themselves faithless. He would have no part of it.

Brian had to admit that on this issue he sided with Derek. Laurana's plan was ingenious, but it depended on the gods, and even Elistan said that he could not guarantee the gods would join the battle.

"Yet you are willing to risk your life because you believe the gods, on the off-chance, *might* come to your aid," Aran pointed out, politely offering his flask around before taking a drink himself.

"I did not say that. I said I have faith the gods will aid us," Elistan replied.

"But in the next breath, you say you can't promise they will do so," Aran argued good-naturedly.

"I would never presume to speak for the gods," Elistan said. "I will ask them humbly for their help, and if they deem it right, they will grant it. If for some reason they refuse to give their aid, then I will accept their decision, for they know what is best."

Aran laughed. "You're giving the gods a break. If they help you, they get the credit, but if they don't, you supply them with excuses."

"Let my try to explain," said Elistan, smiling. "You told me that you have a dearly loved nephew who is five years old. Let us say this child begs you to allow him to play with your sword. Would you give him what he wants?"

"Of course not," said Aran.

"You love your nephew very much. You want him to be happy, yet you would deny him this. Why?"

"Because he is a child. For him, a sword is a toy. He does not yet have the mental capacity to understand the danger he would pose to himself and others around him." Aran grinned. "I see what you are saying, sir. You claim this is the reason the gods do not give us everything we ask for. We might cut ourselves to ribbons."

"Granting us all our wishes and desires would be the same as allowing that little child to play with your sword. We cannot see the gods' eternal plan and how we fit into it. Thus, we ask in faith and hope we will be given what we want, but if not, we have faith that the gods know what is best for us. We accept the will of the gods and move forward."

Aran considered this, washing it down with a pull from the flask, but he still shook his head.

"Are you a believer in these gods?" he asked, turning to Sturm.

"I am," Sturm replied gravely.

"Do you believe that the gods truly know what is best for you?"

"I have proof," Sturm said. "When we were in Thorbardin, searching for the Hammer of Kharas, I prayed to the gods to give the hammer to me. I wanted the sacred hammer to forge the legendary dragonlances. At least, that is what I told myself. I was angry with the gods when they saw fit to give the hammer to the dwarves."

"You're still angry about that!" Flint said with a shake of his head.

Sturm gave a wry smile. "Perhaps I am. I do not to this day

understand why the gods saw fit to leave the hammer in the dwarven kingdom when we need it so sorely. But I do know why the gods did not give the hammer to me. I came to realize I did not want the hammer for the good of mankind but for my own good. I wanted the hammer because it would bring me glory and honor. To my shame, I even went so far as to agree to participate in a dishonorable scheme to keep the hammer and defraud the dwarves.

"When I realized what I had done, I asked the gods for forgiveness. I like to think I would have used the hammer for good, but I am not sure. If I was willing to sink so low to obtain it, perhaps I would have sunk even lower. The gods did not give me what I thought I wanted. They gave me a greater gift—knowledge of myself, my weakness, my frailties. I strive daily to overcome these faults, and with the help of the gods and my friends, I will be a better man."

Brian looked at Derek as Sturm was speaking, especially the part about wanting the hammer for his own glory. But Derek wasn't listening. He was still arguing with Harald, still trying to persuade the chief to go along with his scheme. Perhaps it was just as well Derek did not hear Sturm's admission. Derek's opinion of Sturm, already low, would have dropped below sea level.

Aran continued to question Elistan about the gods, asking their names and how Mishakal differed from Chislev, and why there were gods of neutrality, such as Lillith had talked about, and how the balance of the world was maintained. Aran listened to Elistan's responses attentively, though Brian guessed that Aran's interest in these new-found gods was purely academic. Brian couldn't imagine the cynical Aran embracing religion.

Derek's voice rose sharply, stopping the discussion.

"You expect me to entrust the success of my mission to the ravings of a couple of old men and the foolish notions of a girl? You are mad!"

Harald stood up and gazed down at Derek.

"Mad or not, if you want my people to attack the castle, Sir Knight, then we do it my way—or rather, the way of the elf woman. Tomorrow morning at dawn."

Harald walked out. Derek fumed, frustrated, but ultimately impotent. He had to either take this offer or forego his mission. Brian sighed inwardly.

An unwelcome thought suddenly crossed Brian's mind. No one knew anything about this dragon orb. What if it turned out to be an artifact of evil? Would Derek still take it back to Solamnia just to realize his own ambition? Brian had the unhappy feeling Derek would.

Brian looked at Sturm, a man who had freely admitted he'd been weak, who spoke openly of his flaws and faults. Compare that to Derek, a Knight of the Rose, tested and proven in battle, confident, sure of himself—a man who would scorn to admit he had faults, would refuse to acknowledge any weakness.

Are you sure he's a knight? the kender had asked.

In many ways, Sturm Brightblade was a truer knight than Derek Crownguard. Sturm, with all his weaknesses, flaws, and doubts, strove every day to live up to the high ideal of knighthood. Sturm had not come on this quest seeking the dragon orb. He had come because Derek had commandeered the kender, and Sturm would not abandon his friend. Whereas Brian knew quite well that Derek would sacrifice the kender, the Ice Folk, everyone, including his friends, to gain what he wanted. Derek would say (and perhaps he would believe) he was doing this for the good of all mankind, but Brian feared it was only for the good of Derek Crownguard.

Derek left the chieftent in a rage. Aran went after Derek to try to calm him down. Harald, Raggart, and Elistan, along with Gilthanas and Laurana, removed to a tent that Raggart had now dedicated to the gods to discuss their plans for assaulting the castle on the morrow. Tasslehoff had not been seen in hours, and Flint, certain the kender had fallen into a hole in the ice, said he was going to see if he could locate him.

Brian had an idea regarding Brightblade. Derek would be furious and likely turn against Brian forever, but he felt this could be the right thing to do. Brian had just one doubt about Sturm, one question to ask him before putting his plan in motion. Sturm was about to go with Flint to search for the kender, when Brian stopped him.

"Sturm," said Brian, "could I speak to you a moment in private?"

Flint said he could find the dratted kender on his own and left Sturm alone with Brian. Brian's tent being occupied, Brian asked Sturm if they could go to his.

"I have a question for you," Brian said, once they had settled themselves among the furs. "This is none of my business, and my question is impertinent. You have every right to be angry with me for asking. If you are, that's fine. I will understand. I will also understand if you refuse to answer."

Sturm looked grave, but indicated Brian could go ahead.

"Why did you lie to your friends about being a knight? Before you answer"—Brian admonished, raising a warning hand—"I have seen the regard and esteem in which your friends hold you. I know it wouldn't have made any difference to them whether you were a knight or not. You agree that this is true?"

"Yes, that is true," Sturm said in a low voice, so low Brian had to lean forward to hear him.

"And when they found out you had lied, that made no difference to them either. They still admire you, trust you, and look up to you."

Sturm lowered his head and passed his hand over his eyes. He could not speak for his emotions.

"Then why lie?" Brian asked gently.

Sturm lifted his head. His face was pale and drawn, but he smiled when he spoke. "I could tell you that I never lied to them. You see, I never told them in so many words that I was a knight. But I led them to believe I was. I wore my armor. I spoke about the knighthood. When someone referred to me as a knight, I did not deny it."

He paused, gazing thoughtfully into the past. "After my return, if Tanis had said to me, 'Sturm, are you now a Knight of Solamnia?' I think I would have found the strength to tell him that my candidacy had been turned down."

"Unjustly," Brian said firmly.

Sturm looked startled. He had not expected support from this quarter.

"Please go on with your explanation," Brian urged. "Don't think I'm asking out of smugness or idle curiosity. I'm trying to sort out some things for myself."

Sturm appeared slightly perplexed, but he proceeded. "Tanis did not ask me that question. He took it for granted I was a knight, and so did my other friends. Before I could put things right, all hell broke loose. There was the blue crystal staff and hobgoblins and a lady to protect. Our lives changed forever in an instant, and when the time came when I could have told my friends the truth, it was too late. The truth would have caused complications.

"Then there was my pride." Sturm's expression darkened. "I could not have endured Raistlin's smug triumph, his snide remarks."

Sturm sighed deeply. His voice softened and he seemed to be speaking to himself, as though Brian were not there, "And I wanted to be a knight so badly. I could not bear to relinquish it. I vowed to be worthy of it. You must believe that. I vowed I would never do anything to disgrace the knighthood. I believed that if I lived my life as a knight, I could somehow make the lie right. I know what I did was wrong, and I am deeply ashamed. I have ruined forever my hopes of becoming a knight. I accept this as my punishment. But if the gods will it, I hope someday to stand before the Council, confess my sins, and ask their forgiveness."

"I think you are a better knight than many of us who bear the title," said Brian quietly.

Sturm only shook his head and smiled. He started to say something, but was interrupted by Flint, who thrust his head into the tent to yell, "That blasted kender! You won't believe the fix he's got himself into *this* time! You better come."

Sturm excused himself and hurried off to rescue Tas from his latest predicament. Brian remained in the tent, thinking things over, and at last he made up his mind. He would do it, though he thought it likely Derek would never speak to him again.

That night, the Ice Folk held a celebration to honor the gods and ask their blessing for the attack on Ice Wall Castle. Derek grumbled that he supposed he would have to attend, since otherwise it would offend his host, but he added grimly that he wouldn't stay long. Aran stated that, for his part, he was looking forward to it; he enjoyed a good party. Brian was also looking forward to the celebration, but for a different reason.

The chieftent had been cleared of all work, leaving room for dancing. Several of the elders sat around an enormous drum, and they beat on it softly as Raggart the Elder related tales of the old gods he had heard from his father and his father before him. Sometimes chanting, sometimes singing, the old man even performed

a few dance steps. Raggart the Younger then took over, relating stories of heroes in past battles to embolden the hearts of the warriors.
When he was finished, Tasslehoff, sporting a black eye but otherwise fine, sang a bawdy song about his own true love being a
sailing ship, which completely mystified the Ice Folk, though they
applauded politely.

Gilthanas borrowed a whalebone flute and played a song that
seemed to bring with it the scent of spring wildflowers borne on
warm, gentle breezes. So evocative was the elf's playing that the
chieftent, hazy with the smoke of the peat fires and the strong odor of
fish, smelled of lilac and new grass.

When the singing and story-telling was done and they had all
eaten and drunk, Raggart the Elder raised his hands for silence. This
took some time, as the children (and the kender) were excited by the
festivities and could not settle down. Eventually, however, a hush
spread through the chieftent. The Ice Folk looked at Raggart expectantly; they knew what was going to happen. Derek muttered that
he supposed they could leave now, but since neither Aran nor Brian
moved, Derek was bound to stay.

Raggart the Elder reached down to an object wrapped in white
fur that had been lying at his feet. He raised it up reverently in both
hands and held it out in front of him. He said something softly and
his grandson, Raggart the Younger, gently released the leather thongs
that held the fur in place. The fur fell aside. The object glistened in the
light of the fire.

The Ice Folk gave a soft sigh and all rose to their feet, as did the
guests, once they understood this was expected of them.

"What is it?" Tasslehoff asked, standing on tiptoe and craning his
neck. "I can't see!"

"A battle axe made of ice," said Sturm, marveling.

"Truly? Ice? Flint, give me a boost!" cried the kender, putting his
hands on Flint's shoulders, prepared to jump up on him.

"I will do no such thing!" said the outraged dwarf, batting away
Tas's hands.

Raggart frowned at the disruption. Sturm grabbed hold of Tas and
dragged him around to stand in front, giving the kender a good view
and allowing Sturm to keep firm hold of him, for he could see Tas's
fingers twitching with longing.

Raggart began to speak. "Long, long ago, when the world was new-made, our people lived in a land far from here, a land parched and scorched by the fierce young sun. There was no food, no water. Our people withered in the heat, and many died. At last, the chief could stand it no more. He begged the gods for help, and one of the gods, the Fisher God, answered. He knew of a land where fish were plentiful and fur-bearing animals abounded. He would show our people the way to that land, for he feared evil beings were trying to take it over. There was one problem—the land knew summer only briefly. It was a land of winter, a land of snow and ice.

"The chief and his people were heartily sick of the burning sun, the sweltering heat and constant hunger. They agreed to move, and the Fisher God gave them clothes suitable to the cold and taught them how to survive in the long winter. Then he lifted them in his hand and brought them to Icereach. The last gift the god gave them was the knowledge of how to make weapons of ice.

"The frostreavers were blessed by the gods, and even when the gods turned from us in their righteous anger, those of us who waited patiently for the gods to return continued to make frostreavers, and though the gods were gone, their blessing lingered as did our faith in them.

"On the eve of battle, it is tradition for the cleric who makes the frostreavers to look into the heart of each person and select the one who has the skill and courage, wisdom and knowledge to be a great warrior. To that person, the gods give the gift of a frostreaver."

The warriors of the Ice Folk formed a line at the side of the chieftent and Harald, with a gesture, indicated their guests were to join them.

Flint frowned and shook his head. "Plain steel is good enough for Reorx and it's good enough for me," he said. "No offense to you or the Fish God," he added hastily.

Raggart smiled at the dwarf and nodded. Laurana did not join the line. She remained standing beside Flint, along with Elistan. Sturm and Gilthanas took their places in line, Sturm being there mainly to keep an eye on Tasslehoff. Brian, Derek and Aran stood at the end.

Raggart, bearing the weapon swathed in white fur, walked along the line. He walked past the Ice Folk warriors, past Gilthanas and Sturm, and, to the kender's vast disappointment, he carried the glistening weapon past Tasslehoff, who reached out to touch it.

"Ouch!" Tas snatched back his fingers. "I burned myself on ice!" he cried happily. "Look, Sturm, the ice burned me! How did that happen?"

Sturm shushed the kender.

Raggart continued on toward the three knights.

Derek muttered in disgust, "What am I going to do with a weapon made of ice? I suppose I'll have to take it. It would insult them, otherwise. I still hope to persuade their chief to go along with my plan."

Raggart walked past Aran, who eyed the weapon curiously and gave it a toast with his flask. The cleric walked past Brian and headed toward Derek, only to move past him.

Raggart halted, frowning. He glanced around, and his brow cleared. He turned from the line of warriors and walked over to Laurana. With a bow, he held out the frostreaver.

Laurana gasped. "There must be some mistake!"

"I see a tall tower, a blue dragon, and a bright silver lance whose light is dimmed by great sorrow," said Raggart. "I see an orb broken and another orb stained with the blood of evil. I see golden armor shining like a beacon-light in the forefront of the battle. The gods have chosen you, lady, to receive their gift."

Raggart extended the frostreaver. Laurana looked about in bewilderment, silently asking what to do. Sturm smiled encouragement and nodded. Gilthanas frowned and shook his head. Elf women train for battle, as do elf men, but the women do not fight unless the situation is desperate, and no elf woman would ever put herself forward as a leader of men!

"Take it, Laurana!" Tasslehoff called out eagerly. "But be careful. It burned me. See, look at my fingers!"

"The axe is well-crafted, I'll say that for it," said Flint, eying the weapon critically. "Heft it, lass. See what it feels like."

Laurana flushed. "I am sorry, Raggart. I am truly honored by this gift. But I have the strangest feeling. I fear that by taking it, I'm taking hold of destiny."

"Perhaps you are," said Raggart.

"But that isn't what I want," Laurana protested.

"We each seek our destiny, child, but in the end, it is destiny that finds us."

Laurana still hesitated.

Derek muttered to Brian, "If there was any evidence needed that the old man is a crackpot, we now have it."

He spoke in Solamnic and kept his voice low, but Laurana heard, and she understood. Her lips tightened. Her face set in resolute lines. She reached out her hand, and, flinching a little in anticipation of the flesh-burning, bone-chilling cold, she grasped the frostreaver and lifted it from its fur bed.

Laurana relaxed. She held the weapon with ease. Strangely, the ice was no colder than the hilt of a steel sword. She lifted it to the light, admiring the beauty. The frostreaver was made of crystal-clear ice, cut and polished so that it was smooth, its lines elegant and simple.

The weapon appeared quite large and heavy, and her friends winced a little, expecting to see her drop it or lift it clumsily. To their astonishment, when Laurana hefted it, the frostreaver was perfectly suited to her grip.

"It seems to have been made for me," she said, marveling.

Raggart nodded as if this was nothing out of the ordinary. He instructed her on the weapon's use and care, warning her to keep it out of direct sunlight and away from the heat of the fire.

"For," Raggart said, "although the ice from which we craft these is blessed by the gods and is unusually thick and dense, the frostreaver will melt, though not as fast as ordinary ice."

Laurana thanked him and the Ice Folk, and lastly she thanked the gods. She swathed the frostreaver in its fur blanket, and, her cheeks still flushed, she asked in a low voice that the celebration continue. The drumming started again, when Brian, his heart beating fast, raised his hand.

"I have something to say."

The drums fell silent. Aran and Derek stared at him in astonishment, for they knew how much their friend hated public speaking. Everyone else regarded him warmly, expectantly.

"I . . . um . . ." Brian had to stop a moment to clear his throat and then he continued, speaking rapidly to get this ordeal over. "There is one among us whom I have come to know well on this journey. I have been witness to his courage. I have come to admire his honesty. He is the embodiment of honor. Therefore"—Brian drew in a deep breath, knowing well the reaction he was going to get—"I hereby take Sturm Brightblade, son of Angriff Brightblade, as my squire."

Brian's cheeks burned. The blood pounded in his ears. He was dimly aware of polite applause from the Ice Folk, who had no idea what this meant. Finally, he dared to raise his head. Sturm had gone quite pale. Laurana, seated next to him, was applauding warmly. Gilthanas played a martial flourish on the flute. Elistan said something to Sturm and pressed his hand. The color returned to Sturm's face. His eyes shimmered in the firelight.

"Are you certain about this, my lord?" Sturm asked in a low undertone. He cast a sidelong, meaningful glance at Derek, whose face was dark, suffused with anger.

"I am," Brian said, and he reached out to clasp Sturm's hand. "You realize what this does for you?"

Sturm nodded and said brokenly, "I do, my lord. I cannot tell you how much this means . . ." He bowed deeply. "I am honored by your regard, my lord. I will not fail you."

Overcome with emotion, Sturm could say no more. Flint came over to congratulate him, as did Tasslehoff.

Laurana leaned over to ask Brian, "I heard you say this will do something for him. What will it do? Isn't Sturm too old to be a squire? I thought squires were young lads who acted as servants to a knight."

"Generally they are, though there are no age restrictions. Some men remain squires all their lives, content in that position. By making him my squire, Sturm may now apply to take his knightly trials, something he could not have done otherwise."

"Why is that?"

"Because I have named Sturm my squire, the transgressions he committed which would have barred him from the knighthood are now expunged."

A small frown line creased Laurana's smooth forehead. "What transgression could Sturm have possibly committed?"

Brian hesitated, unwilling to say.

"I know he lied about being a knight," Laurana said. "Sturm told me. Is that what you mean?"

Brian nodded, then looked up as a blast of frigid wind blew through the chieftent, causing the fires to waver. Derek had stalked out.

Laurana's troubled gaze followed him. "You mean Derek would have used that to block Sturm's application?"

"Oh, yes," said Brian, nodding emphatically. "By making Sturm my squire, I'm telling the Council that I have decided his error in judgment should be forgiven and forgotten. Derek won't even be able to bring up the fact that Sturm lied about being a knight."

Sturm was patiently answering Tasslehoff's questions, promising him that if he ever rode in a tourney, Tas could be the one to carry his shield, an honor that left the kender aglow with pleasure.

"I do not think Sturm lied," said Laurana softly.

"As it happens, neither do I," said Brian.

Aran walked over to shake Sturm's hand and extend his congratulations, then went to Brian.

"Derek wants to see you outside," he said in Brian's ear.

"Is he very angry?" Brian asked.

"I figure he's out there gnawing the edge off his sword blade," Aran said cheerfully. He clapped Brian on the shoulder. "Don't worry. You did right. I'll say as much over your grave."

"Thanks," Brian muttered.

The dancing started. The elders began beating out a lively rhythm on the drums and chanting. Young and old took the floor, forming a circle, joining arms, dipping and bobbing and weaving. They drew Laurana in, and even persuaded Flint, who kept falling over his own feet and tripping up the line, much to everyone's mirth. Brian, sighing, headed for the tent opening.

Sturm stopped him. "I fear this will cause trouble between you and Derek."

"I fear you're right," said Brian with a wry smile.

"Then don't go through with it," said Sturm earnestly. "It is not worth it—"

"I think it is. The knighthood needs men like you, Sturm," Brian said. "Maybe more than it needs men like us."

Sturm started again to protest. Brian unbuckled his sword belt and handed it to him. "Here, Squire. Have that weapon cleaned and polished by morning when we ride to battle."

Sturm hesitated, then he accepted the sword with a grateful smile. "I will, my lord," he said, bowing.

Brian walked into the icy wind blowing off the glacier. He saw pale shapes slinking outside the ring of tents—wolves, watching them. He wondered if Raggart was right, if the wolves were spies. They certainly seemed intent upon them. He shivered in the cold, and found more cold awaiting him—cold fury.

"You did that deliberately to discredit me!" Derek said accusingly. "You did it to destroy my credibility and make me look the fool!"

Brian was astonished. Whatever else he had expected, it wasn't this. "I don't believe it! You think I made Sturm my squire just to get back at you?"

"Of course," Derek returned. "Why else would you do it? Brightblade is a liar, quite possibly a bastard. Ye gods, you might as well have made the kender your squire! Or perhaps you're saving that for tomorrow night!" he snapped viciously.

Brian stared at Derek in amazement too great for words.

"I want both you and Aran in our tent before moon rise," Derek continued. "You will need your rest for the morrow. And tell Brightblade he is to report to me then as well. As a squire, he now falls under my jurisdiction. He will obey my orders. No more siding with the elves against me. Mark my words—the first time Brightblade disobeys me will be the last."

Derek turned and walked off toward the tent the knights shared, his boots crunching on the ice, his sword clanking at his side.

Brian, sighing deeply, went back to the warmth and merriment of the chieftent. He saw, out of the corner of his eye, the wolves slinking and sidling about the outskirts of the camp.

12

Feal-Thas sets a trap.
Derek dreams of dragons.

pon his return to Ice Wall Castle from Neraka, Feal-Thas
sent for the leader of the draconians to ask if any strangers
had been seen in the vicinity. The draconians reported that
a group of outsiders, including three Solamnic knights, had attacked
two draconian guards. The knights and the rest of their companions
were skulking about the camp of the Ice Folk. Feal-Thas had no doubt
these were the knights sent by Kitiara, part of Ariakas's scheme to
plant the dragon orb among the Solamnics.

Ariakas had explained his plan to Feal-Thas when he'd been
in Neraka. The emperor had used the analogy of besieging armies
throwing the carcasses of plague-ridden animals over the walls into
the enemy city so the disease could infect the defenders. Ariakas was
applying the same principle here, except that the dragon orb would
take the place of a plague-ridden cow. The knights would carry the
dragon orb into Solamnia and there fall under its sway, as had the
wretched King Lorac of Silvanesti.

Feal-Thas had agreed to go along with the scheme. He could do nothing else. Ariakas wore the Crown of Power. Takhisis loved him, while the Queen and Feal-Thas were barely on speaking terms. Feal-Thas took comfort in the fact that accidents happened, especially to glory-seeking knights. Ariakas could hardly fault Feal-Thas if this Solamnic ended up in the dragon's belly.

There was another problem that Ariakas had not considered, because Feal-Thas had not told him. The dragon orb had its own plots and schemes.

For hundreds of years, ever since the dragons had gone to sleep following the Dark Queen's defeat at the hands of Huma Dragonbane, the dragon orbs, made of the essence of dragons, had waited for their Queen's return. Finally they heard Takhisis's voice call out to them, as it had called out to her other dragons. Now this orb yearned to be free of its prison and back in the world. Feal-Thas heard its whispered temptations, but he was wise enough to shut his ears to them. Others—those who wanted to hear it, wanted to believe it—would listen.

Having heard the draconian report, Feal-Thas hastened to Sleet's lair to make certain the dragon orb was safe. The white dragon had been ordered to guard the orb, and she would obey that order to the best of her abilities. Unfortunately, Sleet's abilities did not fill the wizard with confidence. The white dragon was not particularly intelligent, nor was she clever, subtle, or cunning, whereas the dragon orb was all these and more.

Feal-Thas walked the frozen tunnels beneath the castle. He carried no light. At his coming, an icy enchantment caused the tunnels to shimmer with blue-white radiance. He passed the chamber that had once housed the orb and glanced inside. The traces left by the Guardian's victims was still visible—blood covered the floor, spattered the walls. He paused to regard the gruesome scene. Some of that blood was Kitiara's. Feal-Thas had been informed, just as he was leaving Neraka, that Kitiara had escaped her execution. Feal-Thas was disappointed, but hardly surprised. She was lucky, that one, lucky and fearless and smart—a dangerous combination. Ariakas should have never allowed her to live this long. Feal-Thas would be doing everyone a favor by getting rid of her.

He just had to find the way to get around that luck of hers.

Feal-Thas entered the white dragon's lair. A magical snow, created by the dragon, drifted down around her. The snow kept her cool, kept her food—two dead thanoi and a human—from spoiling until she was at leisure to eat it. Sleet was dozing, but she woke up fast enough when she smelled elf. Her nostrils twitched. One eye was a red glittering slit. Her claws dug into the ice floor and her white lips curled back over her yellow fangs. She did not like Feal-Thas, and the feeling was mutual.

The whites are the smallest of the Dark Queen's dragons and the least intelligent. They are good at killing and not much else. They obey instructions, but only if they are kept simple.

"What do you want?" Sleet muttered.

Her white scales glittered blue in the wizard-light. Her wings were folded over her back, her long tail curled around her massive, snow-covered body. Though small compared to a red dragon, she nearly filled the vast cavern she had inherited from some other white who had built it long, long ago, perhaps around Huma's time. Pallid sunlight gleamed through the lair's entrance at the far end, sparkling on walls coated with snow and hoar-frost from the dragon's breath.

"I am here to ascertain that you are comfortable and have all you require," said Feal-Thas smoothly.

The dragon snorted, blasting frost from her nose. "You came to check on your precious dragon orb because you don't trust me. It's safe. See for yourself. Then go bury your head in a glacier."

The white dragon rested her head in the snow. Her red eyes watched Feal-Thas.

The orb stood upon an icy pedestal. Its colors static, suspended, the orb looked dead. As Feal-Thas approached the orb and his thoughts focused on it, it came to life. The colors began to swirl around the globe's interior, making it look like a rainbow-glistening soap bubble—blue, green, black, red, white—changing and shifting, merging and separating.

Feal-Thas drew near. As always, his hands itched to touch it. He longed to try to exert his power over it, take command of it, become the orb's master. He knew he could. It would be easy. He was powerful, the most powerful elf archmage who had ever lived. Once he had the orb, he would wrest the crown from Ariakas, challenge Queen Takhisis herself . . .

"Ha, ha." Feal-Thas laughed gently. He came to stand before the dragon orb, his hands clasped tightly in his sleeves. "Nice try. You might as well give up," he advised the orb. "I will not relinquish you. I know the danger you pose. You must try your blandishments on someone else, such as this Solamnic knight who has come to free you."

The colors flashed briefly, swirled furiously, then settled back into a slow, drifting, seemingly-aimless motion.

"I thought that might interest you. I am certain if you apply yourself, you can snag him. You are the object of his desire. You should find it easy to seize hold of him, lure him to you, as your sister orb did Lorac." Feal-Thas paused, then said quietly, grimly, "As you did me."

The orb darkened, its colors blending, black with hatred.

"With me you failed," Feal-Thas continued, shrugging. "You might well succeed with the knight. You could summon him here, then send the dragon away on some trumped-up errand. But you don't need me to tell you that." Feal-Thas wagged a finger at the orb. "You are toying with me, hoping to ensnare me."

He again clasped his hands and said scornfully, "Spare yourself the trouble. Your tempting promises haven't worked in three hundred years; they won't work now."

The colors swirled again, and this time green was uppermost.

"You are suspicious of my motives, as you should be. Of course it's a trap. You bring the knight; I will slay him." Feal-Thas gave another shrug. "Still, you might succeed. I might fail. Take the gamble." He paused, then said quietly, "What choice do you have?"

Feal-Thas turned and walked away. He could see the light of the orb reflected on the ice walls flashing red, then purple, then going sullen, greenish black. He did not see, as he left, all the colors merging together in a riotous display of triumph.

Derek woke again from a dream of dragons. He gasped, breathing hard, not from fear, but with exultation. He lay awake, staring into the darkness, reliving the dream, which had been vividly real.

Usually his dreams were gray and black and nonsensical. He dismissed dreams, considering them wild forays of the slumbering, undisciplined mind. Derek never thought about his dreams or bothered to remember them, and he viewed with impatience those who yammered on about them.

But these dreams were different. These dreams were splashed with color: reds and blues, greens, blacks and shades of white. These dreams were filled with dragons, enemy dragons, clouding the skies. The sun shining on their scales made a hideous rainbow. People fled from them in open-mouthed, screaming terror. Blood, smoke, and fire spilled and billowed and crackled around him. He did not run. He stood firm, gazing up at the beating wings, the open mouths, the dripping fangs. He should have been holding his sword, but in its place he held a crystal orb. He raised up the orb to the heavens and he cried out a stern command and the dragons, shrieking in rage, fell from the skies, dying like shooting stars, trailing flame.

Derek was bathed in sweat and he threw off the fur blankets. The bitter cold felt good to him, slapped him out of the dream, brought him to conscious awareness.

"The orb," he said softly, exultantly.

13

The assault on Ice Wall Castle.

ake up, you two," Derek ordered sharply.

"Huh? What?" Aran sat up, still half-asleep, muddled and alarmed. "What's happened? What's wrong?"

Brian reached for his sword, feeling about for it, since he couldn't see in the darkness. Then he remembered—he'd given his weapon to Sturm. Brian groaned inwardly. A knight without his sword. Derek would view that as a most serious transgression.

"Be quiet," said Derek in a low voice. "I've been thinking things over. We're going to go along with this insane plan of the elf woman to attack the castle—"

"Derek, it's the middle of the night," Aran protested, "and cold as a goblin's backside! Tell me in the morning." He flung himself down and pulled the furs over his head.

"It is morning, or near enough," said Derek. "Now pay attention."

Brian sat up, shivering in the chill. Aran peered at him over the edge of the blanket.

"So we go along with the plan to attack the castle," Aran said, scratching his stubble-covered chin. "Why do we need to talk about it?"

"Because I know where to find the dragon orb," said Derek. "I know where it is."

"How do you know?" Brian asked astonished.

"Since you appear to be so enamored of these new-found gods, let us say *they* told me," Derek returned. "How I know is not important. This is my plan. When the attack starts, we will leave the main body, sneak into the castle, recover the orb, and—" He halted, half-turned to stare outside. "Did you hear that?"

"No," said Brian.

Derek, muttering something about spies, ducked out of the tent.

"The *gods* told him about the orb!" Aran shook his head in disbelief and reached for his flask.

"I think he was being sarcastic. This isn't like Derek," Brian added, troubled.

"You're right. Derek may be a stiff-necked, sword-up-the-butt, arrogant lunkhead, but at least he's been an *honorable*, stiff-necked, sword-up-the-butt, arrogant lunkhead. Now he's lost even that endearing quality."

Brian pulled on his thick boots, figuring he might as well get up. The gray light of dawn was seeping into the tent. "Maybe he's right. If we sneak into the castle—"

"That's my point," interrupted Aran, gesturing with the flask. "Since when does Derek *sneak* anywhere? This is the same Derek who had to turn the Measure upside down to find a way for us to enter Tarsis without proclaiming ourselves as knights to all and sundry. Now he's sneaking into castles and stealing dragon orbs."

"The castle of the enemy," Brian pointed out.

Aran shook his head, unconvinced. "The Derek we once knew would have walked up to the front of that castle, banged on the door, and challenged the wizard to come out to do battle. Not very sensible, admittedly, but *that* Derek would have never considered turning sneak thief."

Before Brian could respond, Derek crawled back inside the tent. "I'm certain the elf was eavesdropping, though I couldn't catch him. It doesn't matter now. The camp is starting to stir. Brian, go wake Brightblade. Tell him what we're doing, and order him to keep this to himself. He's not to tell the others, especially the elf. I'm going to talk to the chief."

Derek left again.

"Are you going to go along with this crazy scheme of his?" Aran asked.

"Derek gave us an order," Brian replied, "and . . . he's our friend."

"A friend who's going to get us all killed," Aran muttered. Buckling on his sword belt and taking a final pull on the flask, he stuffed it into his coat and stomped out of the tent.

Brian went to wake Sturm and found the knight already awake. A thin sliver of light spilled out from underneath the tent.

"Sturm?" he called softly, pushing open the flap.

The light came from a burning wick placed in a dish of oil. Sturm sat cross-legged on the floor, rubbing the blade of Brian's sword with soft, brushed hide.

"Almost finished, my lord," said Sturm, looking up. The light of the flame shone in his eyes.

Brian squatted down. "The order to clean my sword was meant to be a jest."

"I know," said Sturm, smiling. His hand with the cloth glided slowly, carefully, over the sword's blade. "What you did for me meant more to me than you can ever know, my lord. This is my poor way of showing my gratitude."

Brian was deeply touched. "I need to talk to you," he said. He explained Derek's plan to use the attack as a diversion, slip into the castle, and steal the orb.

"Derek says he knows where the orb is located," Brian added.

"How could he?" Sturm asked, frowning.

Brian didn't want to repeat Derek's sarcastic gibe about the gods, and so he evaded the question. "Derek has ordered you to accompany us."

Sturm regarded him in troubled silence. The frown line in his forehead deepened. "Far be it from me to question the orders of a Lord Knight of the Rose—"

"Oh, go ahead—question!" Brian said wearily. "Aran and I have been doing nothing else since we came on this mission." He lowered his voice. "I'm worried about Derek. He's become increasingly obsessed with this dragon orb. Almost consumed by it."

Sturm looked very grave. "I know something of magic, not by choice, mind you, but because I was around Raistlin so much—"

"Your friend the Red Robe wizard," Brian clarified.

"Not friend, exactly, but, yes, he's the one I meant. Raistlin always cautioned us that if ever we came upon any object that might be magical, we were to leave it alone, have nothing to do with it. 'Such artifacts are designed to be used by those who have studied magic and know and understand its deadly potential. They pose a danger to the ignorant'."

Sturm grimaced. "The one time I did not heed Raistlin's warning, I paid for it. I put on a magical helm I had found and it seized hold of me—" Sturm stopped, waved the story aside. "But that's another tale. I think if Raistlin were here, he would caution us against this orb, warn us against coming anywhere near it."

"You make it sound like the orb has something to do with changing Derek, but how is that possible?" Brian argued.

"How is it possible for a dwarven helm to steal a man's soul?" Sturm asked with a rueful smile. "I don't know the answer."

Tossing aside the cloth, he held the blade to the flame, watched the light flare off the gleaming metal. Sturm placed the sword on his bent arm, knelt on one knee, and offered it, hilt-first, to the knight.

"My lord," he said with profound respect.

Brian accepted the sword and buckled it on beneath his coat. The belt was not large enough to fit over the bulky fur.

Sturm picked up the ancient blade of the Brightblades, his most valued inheritance from his father. He gestured toward the tent's entrance. "After you, my lord."

"Please, call me Brian," said Brian. "I keep thinking you're talking to Derek."

❦

It seemed the gods were with Derek and the Ice Folk, at least at the start, for the day dawned clear, the sun shone bright, and a brisk wind sprang up, an unusually warm wind for this time of year, Harald told them. He consulted Raggart the Elder, who said the gods sent this good weather as a sign they favored the venture. And because the gods were with them, he was going to go on the raid.

Harald and Raggart the Younger were both shocked. The old

man could scarcely walk on his own. Both attempted to dissuade Raggart the Elder, but he would not listen. He tottered out to the ice boat unaided, carrying with him his frostreaver. When Raggart the Younger tried to assist him, the old man testily ordered his grandson to quit hovering around him like some damn mother bear.

Laurana brought her own frostreaver. She had planned to bring along her sword to use in battle. She was honored by the gift of the axe, but felt uncomfortable using it, since she was not trained in wielding such a weapon. But her sword was not in her tent. Laurana searched and searched and eventually realized it was probably inside Tasslehoff's tent, along with everything else that had gone missing from the camp during the past few days. She had no time to go rummaging through the kender's treasure hoard, so, fearing she would be late, she grabbed the frostreaver and hastened out into the morning.

She was gazing into the bright sunshine, thinking her plan might work after all, when Gilthanas caught up with her.

"Don't you think you should stay here in camp with the other women?"

"No," said Laurana indignantly and kept walking.

Gilthanas fell in beside her. "Laurana, I overheard Derek talking to his friends this morning—"

Laurana frowned and shook her head.

"It's a good thing I did," Gilthanas said defensively. "When the attack starts, the knights are going to use it as a diversion to enter the castle after the dragon orb. If Derek goes, I'm going with him. Just so you know."

Laurana turned to face her brother. "You want me to stay here because you plan to take the dragon orb for yourself and you think I'll try to stop you."

"Won't you?" he demanded, glowering.

"What will you do? Fight the knights? All of them?"

"I have my magic—" Gilthanas said.

Laurana shook her head and walked on. Gilthanas called angrily after her, but she ignored him. Elistan, walking toward the ice boat, heard Gilthanas's shout and saw Laurana's angry flush.

"I take it your brother does not want you to go," said Elistan.

"He wants me to stay with the women."

"Perhaps you should heed his concerns," Elistan said. "The gods have blessed us thus far and I have faith they will continue to aid us, but that doesn't mean we will not be in danger—"

"He's not concerned about my safety," Laurana said. "Derek and the other knights plan to use the battle as a diversion. They're going to sneak into Ice Wall Castle to steal the dragon orb. Gilthanas intends to go after them, because he wants the dragon orb. He's prepared to kill Derek over it or at least he thinks he is, so you see why I have to go."

Elistan's graying eyebrows came together; his blue eyes glinted. "Does Harald know of this?"

"No." Laurana's cheeks burned with shame. "I can't tell him. I don't know what to do. If we tell Harald, it will only cause trouble, and the gods are smiling on us this day—"

Elistan looked up at the bright sun, the cloudless sky. "It certainly seems they are." He regarded her thoughtfully. "I see you carry the frostreaver."

"Yes, I didn't want to. I don't know how to use it. But I couldn't find my sword. Tasslehoff must have run off with it, though he swears he didn't." Laurana sighed. "But then, that's what he always swears!"

Elistan gave her a keen look, then said, "I think you should go with your brother and the others." He smiled and added enigmatically, "This time, I think Tasslehoff is telling the truth."

He walked off to join up with Harald, leaving Laurana to stare after him, puzzled, wondering what he meant.

The Ice Folk kept their boats hidden in a cove created by a natural formation of the glacier. The warriors crowded on board, as many as the ice boats could carry. Those who doubled as sailors took hold of the ropes, ready for the order to raise the massive sails. They looked to Harald to give the command. The chief opened his mouth, but the word died on his lips. He stared uneasily up into the sky.

"What is it now?" Derek demanded, irritated.

"I feel it," Sturm said, and he crouched in the shadow of a mast and yanked Tasslehoff down beside him.

"The dragon. I think you should take cover, my lord."

Derek said nothing in reply, but he did duck down, squatting on the deck, muttering in Solamnic that this was yet another attempt by Harald to avoid making the assault.

The warriors sought shelter, either flattening themselves on the deck or climbing over the rails to hide on the ice beneath the boat. Everyone felt a sense of unease. They could hear the wind whistling through the rigging, but nothing more. Still, no one moved, the feeling of terror growing on everyone. Even Derek crouched back farther in the shadows.

The white dragon, Sleet, was suddenly above them, white wings spread, her scales glittering like snow crystals in the morning sun. The fear of the dragon squeezed hearts and stopped breathing. Men cowered on the decks. Weapons fell from limp hands. In the camp, children wailed and dogs howled in terror. The dragon's head dipped. Her red eyes looked toward the camp. Those warriors who had been able to overcome the terror gripped their weapons and prepared to defend their families.

Sleet gave a lazy flap of her wings. She snarled and snapped her teeth at them, but that was all. She flew on, skimming low over the ice boats.

Those crouching terrified on the boats watched the dragon's massive underbelly pass over the masts. No one dared move or even draw breath as she flew ponderously above them. Sleet had an odd habit of using her legs to fly, almost as though she were swimming through the air, so that when her wings swooped downward, her legs came together, then spread apart as her wings lifted. This tended to slow her flight and it was some time before she flapped and swam out of sight, flying straight into the sunrise.

No one moved until certain she was gone. Then, the fear lifting from their hearts, they rose and looked at each other in amazement, hardly daring to speak what they were now daring to hope.

"The dragon has left the castle!" cried Harald in disbelief. He stared into the bright sunshine until the tears blurred his vision, then turned to Raggart the Elder and grabbed the cleric in a bear hug that, fortunately, was fur-lined or he might have crushed the old man's frail bones. "The gods be praised! The dragon has left Icereach!"

Elistan rose to his feet, his hand still clasping his medallion. He looked a little dazed and overwhelmed by the gods' largess. He'd expected a miracle, but nothing quite this miraculous.

The warriors started to raise a cheer, but Harald feared the dragon might hear and return, and he shushed them and ordered them to get on with their business. They raised the sails. The wind caught hold of the canvas and propelled the ice boats forward, sending them sliding on their sharp blades across the ice.

Flint had, of course, raised objections to riding in the boat, claiming that he always fell overboard. The dwarf had been persuaded by Sturm that the ice boats were not like boats that sailed upon water; there would be no bobbing and tossing on the waves. If Flint did fall overboard, which was highly unlikely, there was no chance he could drown.

"No, I'll just break my head on the glacier," Flint grumbled, but since it was either go on the boat or be left behind, he agreed to go with them.

Sadly, Flint soon discovered ice boats were far worse than any other type of transportation he'd ever encountered, including griffons. Ice boats could travel over ice far faster than a boat could sail the water, and they careened across the glacier, sometimes going so fast the wind lifted them up onto one runner and they tilted sideways. The Ice Folk grinned and opened their mouths wide when this happened, swallowing the wind.

Poor Flint huddled in a recessed corner, his arms wrapped tightly around a rope, his eyes squinched shut in order not to see the horrendous smash-up he was convinced was coming. Once he opened one eye, only to see Tasslehoff clinging to the neck of the figurehead carved in the shape of a beaked sea monster. The kender shrieked in delight as tears from the stinging wind whipped off his cheeks. His topknot flapped behind him like a flag. Shuddering, Flint swore that this was the end. He meant it. No more boats of any kind. Ever.

Derek paced the deck, or tried to. He kept stumbling sideways and eventually, realizing this ineptness was impairing his dignity (the Ice Folk had no difficulty standing on the canting deck), he took his place at the rail alongside Harald. Raggart the Elder and Elistan sat on barrels, appearing to enjoy the wild ride. Gilthanas kept near Derek. Sturm stood beside Tasslehoff, ready to grab the kender should he lose his grip and go flying. Laurana kept away from the others, especially Derek, who had not been at all pleased at her decision to accompany them and had tried his best to send her back to camp. He had appealed to Harald, but received no support from the chief. Laurana had been given a frostreaver. She was an acknowledged warrior and welcome to come. Harald might have changed his mind had he known her true intent.

Sitting on the deck, the wind blowing in her face, Laurana considered what she was planning to do and she was appalled at herself. She trembled at the thought and was not certain she had the courage to go through with it. Several times, her heart would fail her and she would decide that when they reached their destination, she would stay in the boat. No one would fault her. Everyone would be relieved. Despite the fact that she'd been given the frostreaver, the warriors were uncomfortable having a woman in their midst. Derek was angry, and even Sturm cast her worried glances.

Laurana had fought draconians in Pax Tharkas and she had acquitted herself well. Tanis and the others had praised her skill and her courage in battle. Though elf women are all trained to fight—a tradition that dates back to the First Dragon War, when the elves fought for their very survival—Laurana was not a warrior. But she could not let Gilthanas end up in a fight with the knights, and she had the terrible foreboding that this was what it would come to if no one was there to stop him. She might have once relied upon Sturm to side with Gilthanas, keep him out of trouble, but Sturm had other loyalties now. He was bound to obey his lord, and Laurana would not force him to make a choice between duty and friendship.

The ice boats sped across the glacier, racing toward the castle. The warriors crowded the sides, enjoying the wild ride. The plan of attack was simple. If the gods came to their aid, the warriors would fight. If not, they would use the swift-sailing boats to carry them away. The only enemy who could catch them was the dragon, and she was gone. But they all had faith that the gods, who had already done so much, would do more.

Victory was assured.

The single tower of Ice Wall Castle, rising high in the air, appeared to be the only part of the fortress made of stone. The castle walls were covered in centuries of accumulated ice. The guards atop the ramparts walked on ice. Stone stairs had long since disappeared, covered by ice. So many layers of ice coated the walls that the tops of the watchtowers were now practically on a level with the ramparts.

As the boats drew nearer, they saw soldiers massing on the icy battlements. The soldiers were enormous, large and hulking.

"Those are not draconians," said Derek.

"Thanoi," said Harald, glowering. "Our ancient enemy. They are also called walrus-men, for they have the tusks and massive girth of a walrus and they walk upright, like men. They have no love for Feal-Thas. They have come just for a chance to kill us. So much for a surprise assault. The wizard was warned of our coming."

"The wolves," said Raggart the Elder knowingly. "They were prowling about the camp last night. They heard our war-feast and they told him we were coming."

Derek rolled his eyes at this, but he kept quiet.

"Yet Feal-Thas sent away the dragon," Sturm said in puzzled tones. "That makes no sense."

"Perhaps it was a ruse," suggested Raggart the Younger. "Perhaps the dragon is lurking nearby, ready to attack us."

"No," Raggart the Elder returned. He pressed his hand over his heart. "I do not feel her presence. The dragon is gone."

"There could be many reasons," said Derek briskly. "The war rages on in other parts of Ansalon. Perhaps the dragon was needed elsewhere. Perhaps this Feal-Thas is overconfident. He thinks he does not need her help against us. What it means," he added in a low voice to his friends, "is that the dragon orb has been left unprotected."

"Except by a thousand walrus-men and a few hundred draconians, not to mention a dark elf wizard," Aran grumbled.

"Don't worry." Derek stomped his feet on the deck to warm them. He was in a good humor. "Brightblade's gods will assist us."

Sturm did not hear Derek's sarcastic remark. He was watching the thanoi crowding the ramparts, brandishing their weapons and leaning over the walls to shout insults at their foes. The warriors shouted back, but they seemed daunted. The thanoi clustered thick on the walls, forming a dark, unbroken line of steel that encircled the top of the fortress.

"Feal-Thas brings in thousands of troops to guard the castle, yet he sends away the dragon," Sturm remarked, shaking his head.

"There are white bears up there," cried Tasslehoff. "Like the bear we saved!" He turned to the chief. "I thought bears were friends of your people."

"The thanoi make slaves of the white bears." Harald told him. "They goad them and torment them until the bears come to hate anything that walks on two legs. They will attack on sight."

"First draconians, then walrus-men, now mad bears. What next?" grumbled Flint.

"Have faith," said Elistan, resting his hand on the dwarf's shoulder.

"I do," said Flint stoutly. He patted his axe. "In this. *And* in Reorx," he added quickly in dwarven, fearing that the god, who was known to be touchy, might take offense.

The ice boats were sailing within arrow range. At first the warriors were not worried. The thanoi, with their thick hands and claws, were not archers. But then arrows began thunking into the ice ahead of them, and they realized draconian archers were on the walls. Two arrows struck the side of the boat, their shafts quivering in the wood, and Harald ordered the boats to a halt. They lowered the sails. The boats slowed and slid to a stop.

The warriors stared up at the walls in grim silence. No cheers, no elation, as there had been when they started. The Ice Folk numbered about three hundred, and they faced an army of over a thousand. They were exposed, out in the open. Their enemy was safely ensconced in a fortress of ice. Derek had not yet admitted defeat, but even he was daunted.

A large boulder, thrown from the wall, crashed on the ice near the lead boat. If the boulder had found its mark, it would have smashed through the bottom of the boat, perhaps snapped the mast, killing any number of warriors. Other boulders began to rain down on them, hurled by the strong arms of the thanoi.

Harald turned to Elistan. "We cannot stay here waiting for them to make a lucky hit. The gods must either aid us, or we must retreat."

"I understand," said Elistan. He looked at Raggart the Elder, who nodded his head.

"Lower the ladder," Raggart ordered.

Harald was astonished. "You mean to leave the boat?"

"We do," said Elistan calmly.

Harald shook his head. "Impossible. I won't allow it."

"We must move closer to the castle," Elistan explained.

"That will take you into arrow range. They would use you for target practice." The chief shook his head. "No. Absolutely not."

"The gods will keep us safe," declared Raggart. He gave Harald a shrewd look and added cannily, "You either believe or you don't believe, Chieftain. You can't have it both ways."

"It is easy to have faith when you are safe and snug in the chieftent," Elistan added.

Harald frowned, rubbed his beard and looked from one to the other. The warriors clustered around them, watching their chief, waiting to see what he would do. Laurana was assailed by sudden doubt. This had been her idea, but she never meant for Elistan to place his life at risk. As he said, it was easy to have faith when you were snug and safe. She longed to try to dissuade him. As if reading her thoughts, he glanced over at her and smiled reassuringly. Laurana smiled back, hoping her smile radiated confidence, hoping it didn't look as shaky as it felt.

"Lower the ladder," Harald said at last, reluctantly, grudgingly.

"I will go with them," Sturm offered.

"No you will not," said Derek. "You will remain with us, Brightblade," he added in Solamnic. "If this crazy scheme of theirs works, which I doubt, I plan to enter the castle and you will be close by to attend us."

Sturm didn't like it, but there was nothing he could do. He was a squire, pledged to serve the knights.

"You could do nothing to protect us anyway, Sir Knight," Raggart the Elder told him, "but I thank you for the thought."

The cleric of Habakkuk clasped hold of his medallion in one hand and raised his other hand, calling for silence. The warriors hushed. Many bowed their heads.

"Gods of Light, we come to you as children who ran away from home in anger and now, after years of wandering, lost and alone, we have at last found our way back to your loving care. Be with us now as we go forth in your name, Fisher God, and in your name, Father God, to fight the evil trying to claim the world. Be with our warriors, strengthen their hands, and banish fear from their hearts. Be with us. Grant us your divine blessing."

His prayer finished, Raggart walked off. He walked strongly, no longer tottering, and he shoved away the hand of his grandson. The old man walked over to a rope ladder hanging from the rail, and, grasping it with firm hands, climbed down it as nimbly as he had when he was a lad more than seventy years ago. Elistan followed more slowly, being unaccustomed to boats and ladders, but at last both stood safely on the ice.

The enemy crowded the walls, curious to see what was happening. At the sight of two elders, one clad in long white robes and the other in blue-gray, walking fearlessly toward them, the thanoi began to hoot and snort in derision.

"Do you send your old women to fight?" one shouted, and raucous laughter went up along the walls, followed immediately by a flurry of arrows.

Laurana watched in terror, her heart in her throat. The arrows landed all around the clerics. One arrow pierced Elistan's sleeve. Another stuck in the ice in between Raggart's feet. The two kept walking, unafraid, their hands clasping their medallions.

"The archers will find their aim the next time," said Derek grimly. "I knew this was folly. Come, Brightblade, we must go fetch the two old fools back."

"No!" Harald stood barring the way. "They went with my sanction."

"Then you must answer for the consequences," said Derek.

Another flight off arrows sped from the walls. These missed their targets as well. More arrows fell around Elistan and Raggart, none hit them.

A warrior started to cheer, but his comrades shushed him. They watched in silence, reverent, awe-struck. The jeering on the walls had ceased, replaced by a rumble of anger and cries of "shoot again!"

Elistan and Raggart paid no attention to the jeers or the arrows. They came to a halt within the shadow of the castle walls. Lifting their medallions in their hands, they held them high to meet the rays of the morning sun.

The wind strengthened and shifted, blowing with unusual warmth, bringing with it a hint of spring. Everyone waited tensely, not one sure what was going to happen.

"They didn't say the magic words," Tas whispered, worried.

Sturm hushed him.

The bright sun struck first one medallion and then the other. Both blazed with light. The clerics held the medallions steady and the light grew in intensity until those watching had to avert their eyes. Then a single beam of radiant, blazing white light shot from Elistan's medallion. The beam, strong and powerful, struck the wall of Ice Wall Castle. A moment later, another beam of light, this one blue in color, lanced out from Raggart's medallion, hitting a different section of wall.

No one moved or spoke. Many gasped in awe. Everyone stared transfixed, except Derek, who was engrossed in fixing a loose buckle on his sword belt. Sturm started to say something to call his attention to what was happening.

"Don't waste your breath," said Brian quietly. "He won't look, and even if he did, he wouldn't see."

Elistan's beam of light burned into the ice on the castle wall, and the ice shuddered. A sound like thunder splintered the air. The ice cracked and sheered off the wall, sliding down to the ground with a dull roaring sound. Where Raggart aimed his beam of holy light, huge chunks of ice broke apart and slid down the wall.

The two beams shone more brilliantly by the moment as the gods grabbed hold of the sun and hurled it against the walls of ice. The thanoi crowding the battlements had ceased their jeering and were staring down in astonishment. At first they did not recognize their danger. But then one, less thick-headed than the others, saw what was bound to happen if the assault on the icy castle walls continued.

The archers redoubled their efforts. But the arrows continued to miss their marks, while those that passed inside the beam of holy light vanished in puffs of smoke. The ice cracked and sloughed off, and those watching began to see the stone beneath.

Elistan shifted his beam of light to strike the ice-covered battlements. Some of the thanoi standing near that blazing light panicked and tried to flee, only to run into those packed in around them. The trapped thanoi shoved the others out the way. Their fellows shoved back. Roars of fear and rage rose into the air and were drowned by another thunderous crack. The ice on the battlements shifted and shook, and with no more ice to support it, the icy battlements cracked and fell with a sound like an avalanche.

The thanoi, hundreds of them, came down with the ice, their shrieks and bellows terrible to hear. The thanoi standing on the wall Raggart had under assault tried frantically to escape, but their battlement gave a shake and a shiver and collapsed. Ice and thanoi cascaded to the ground.

The cracks in the ice continued to spread outward, like the web of a demented spider, running around the side of one wall, racing up over the next. Then it seemed as if the entire castle was collapsing, its ice walls sliding and slipping, rumbling and falling. Only the stone tower stood immovable, seeming invulnerable.

Harald gave an exultant roar, and, waving a gigantic frostreaver over his head, ran toward the side of the boat, bellowing for his men to follow. He did not bother with the ladder, but vaulted over the rail. His warriors poured after him. The warriors on the other ice boats did the same, and soon the entire force was running across the ice, eager to attack any of the enemy who had managed to survive the collapse.

Derek ordered the knights to wait until the boat was cleared. He leaned over the rail, staring at the castle wall intently, then seemed to find what he was searching for. He ran for the ladder, ordering Sturm, Brian and Aran to follow. Tas did not hear his name included in the order, but he assumed this was simply an oversight. The kender gleefully vaulted over the railing and was soon running happily alongside Derek.

The knight, without missing a stride, gave the kender a shove that sent him flying. Tasslehoff landed on his belly on the ice, arms and legs akimbo. He did a couple of spins before he slid to a halt and lay there, gasping for breath.

Sturm turned to go back to see if Tas was all right. Derek snapped an order at him. Sturm seemed about to disobey.

"I'll take care of him!" Laurana shouted, hurrying to Tas's side.

Sturm looked grim, but he turned to run after the knights.

Gilthanas had been right. Derek was not going to join the fight. He was angling away from the battle.

Laurana helped Tas to his feet. The kender was unharmed but extremely indignant.

"Derek said he didn't need me! After all the help I've been to him! He wouldn't have known anything about that stupid old orb if it wasn't for me. Well, we'll see about that!"

Before Laurana could catch him, Tas had dashed off.

"I told you so," said Gilthanas. He took hold of her, detaining her as she would have gone after Tas.

"I'm not staying behind," she said defiantly.

"I know you're not," he said curtly. "I just want to let them get a head start, so they don't know we're following."

She sighed. Part of her was glad he hadn't tried to force her to remain behind and another part desperately wished he had. She felt the same dread she had felt when the dragon flew overhead, though she did not know why, for there was no dragon around. She and Gilthanas caught up with Tasslehoff, whose short strides were no match for the long legs of the knights.

"I'm coming with you," Tas announced, his breath puffing in the cold air.

"Good," said Gilthanas. "You might be useful."

"I might?" Tas was pleased, but dubious. "I don't think I've ever been useful before."

"Where is Derek going?" Laurana wondered, mystified.

Derek had been heading for the castle wall, but now he slanted off, leading his small force around a corner to the back of the castle, on the very edge of the glacier.

Gilthanas squinted his eyes against the bright light to see, then pointed to an area close to the ground. "There! He's found a way in."

The ice had broken away from beneath the wall and, like slicing through the side of honey-comb, the removal of the ice wall laid bare scores of tunnels beneath the castle.

Derek chose the nearest tunnel and ordered his small force inside.

Gilthanas and Laurana and Tas held back, waiting for the knights to get far enough ahead so they could safely pursue them. The three were about to enter when they heard heavy footfalls and a gruff voice calling out loudly, "Wait up!"

Laurana turned to see Flint, slipping and sliding, come running clumsily over the snow.

"Make haste! We're going to lose them!" Gilthanas said irritably. Walking soft-footed, he crept inside the tunnel. "Keep behind me," he ordered his sister, "and take care you don't hurt yourself with that thing." He glared at the frostreaver.

"What are *you* doing here, doorknob?" Flint demanded, glaring at Tas.

"Gilthanas says I might be *useful*," Tas said importantly.

"In a pig's eye!" Flint snorted.

Doubting herself, feeling she was in the way, Laurana followed. She had to go. Gilthanas was acting strangely. Derek was acting strangely. Neither was himself, and it was all because of this dragon orb.

She began to hope fervently they never found it.

14

The wolf pack. The trap. Laurana's destiny.

nside Sleet's lair, now empty, the white wolf stood near his master. Though the dragon was gone, her magical snow continued to fall, drifting down around them in large flakes that landed on the wolf's fur, forming a woolly white blanket. The wolf blinked his eyes free of the snow. The other members of the wolf pack stood or paced around him, ears twitching, pricking, listening. The lead female, mate to the wolf, lifted her nose and sniffed the air. She stiffened.

The other wolves stopped their pacing, lifted their heads, alert, their attention caught and held. The she-wolf looked over her shoulder at her mate. The male wolf looked at Feal-Thas.

The winternorn stood unmoving. The snow matted his fur robes, forming a second cloak. He stared down the tunnels, lit with the enchanted light, for he did not want his foes bumbling about in the dark, and he, too, sniffed the air. His ears pricked.

The ground shook as though with an earthquake. The tunnels creaked and groaned. He could hear above him the screams of the injured and dying—the sounds of battle. The castle was under assault. Feal-Thas didn't give a damn. Let the gods of Light throw their temper tantrums. Let them melt this place to the ground. It only needed to hold together long enough for him to destroy the thieves who were after his dragon orb.

The snow stopped falling as Feal-Thas spoke words of magic, chanting a powerful spell. He sang words at the beginning of the chant, but it ended in a howl. The white fur of his robes adhered to his flesh. His nails grew long and curled under, transforming into claws. His jaw jutted forward, his nose lengthened to become a snout. His ears shifted, elongated. His teeth were fangs, sharp and yellow and hungry for blood. He stood on all fours, feeling muscles ripple across his back, feeling the strength in his legs. He reveled in his strength.

He was a massive wolf, lord of the wolves. He stood head and shoulders over the other wolves of the pack, who slunk around him, staring at him with their red eyes, uncertain, wary, yet prepared to follow where he would lead.

His senses heightened, Feal-Thas could smell what the other wolves smelled—the scent of humans borne on the frost-crusted air. He could hear the rasping of their breath and their firm footfalls, the clank of a sword, the occasional scrap of conversation, though not much, for they were saving their breath for breathing.

His trap had worked. They were coming.

Feal-Thas leaped forward on all fours, muscles bunching, expanding, bunching, expanding. His legs gathered up the ground, pushing off from it, reached out for more. The wind whistled past his ears. The snow stung his eyes. He opened his mouth and sucked in the biting air, and saliva spewed from his lolling tongue. He grinned in ecstasy, reveling in the run, the hunt, and the prospect of the kill.

Inside the icy tunnel, Derek stopped to consult the map given to him by Raggart the Younger. The tunnels in which they stood had not been here three hundred years ago. The dragon's lair was on the map, though it had not been named by the ancestor, since dragons had not been seen on Krynn for many centuries. The lair was denoted as a "cave of death" on the map, for the ancestor had seen a great many bones lying about, including several human skulls.

An abandoned dragon's lair would be the logical place for Sleet to use as her lair, or so Derek concluded. He knew the general location of the lair from the map and he chose a tunnel that led in that direction. Sunlight lit their way, shining through the ice, turning the tunnel a shimmering blue-green. They had walked only a short distance when they came to a place where their tunnel intersected with two others. Derek gazed, frowning, at his map, not making much sense of it. Aran suddenly jabbed a finger at the icy wall.

"Look at this!" he exclaimed.

Arrows had been carved into the ice. One pointed straight up. Another pointed at what appeared to be a crude drawing of a dragon—a stick figure with wings and a tail. The knights investigated the other tunnels and found that each had similar arrows.

"The arrow pointing straight up must indicate that this tunnel leads up to the castle proper," guessed Brian.

"And this tunnel leads to the dragon's lair," said Derek in satisfaction.

"I wonder what that X means," Aran asked, taking a pull from his flask.

"And who put these here," said Sturm.

Derek shrugged. "None of that matters," he said, and led the way down the tunnel adorned with the figure of the dragon.

❦

Gilthanas and Laurana, accompanied by Flint and Tas, shadowed the knights, creeping silently down the icy corridors. They halted when they heard the knights halt and listened to the discussion about the marked tunnels. When the knights continued on, they continued after them.

The small group moved silently, keeping their distance, and the knights did not hear them. Due to the cold, Flint had been forced to leave his chain mail and plate behind. Though he wore a sturdy leather vest and was wrapped to his eyeballs in layers of leather and fur, he maintained he was naked without his armor. The crunching of his thick boots was the only sound he made, aside from his grumbling.

Tasslehoff was so charmed by the idea of being useful that he was determined to obey Gilthanas's orders to be quiet, even though that meant keeping all his interesting observations and questions bottled up inside him until he began to feel like a keg of ginger beer that had been sitting in the sun for too long—he was fizzing and about to explode.

The knights would sometimes pause to listen, to try to determine if any enemy was either in front of them or behind. When the knights stopped, Laurana and her group stopped.

Flint found this puzzling. "Why don't we just catch up with them now?"

"Not until Derek leads me to the dragon orb." The elf's voice was grim. "Then he'll find out I'm here—with a vengeance."

Flint regarded Gilthanas in astonishment and shifted his worried gaze to Laurana. She gave Flint a pleading look, asking for understanding. Flint walked on, but he no longer grumbled, a certain sign he was upset.

The four continued to pursue the knights through the maze of tunnels. They passed the chamber where Feal-Thas had kept the dragon orb and its magical monstrous guardian. The knights noticed the chamber, but went on by, although they could hear Aran stating he'd found an X on the wall. At this, Gilthanas, who had also noticed the Xs on the walls, took a moment to investigate. Laurana went with him, leaving Flint and Tasslehoff to stand guard outside.

Laurana stared in shuddering horror at the bones, severed limbs and blood frozen in the snow.

"Look at that pedestal," said Gilthanas triumphantly, pointing. "It was made to hold the dragon orb. Look at these runes. They speak of the orb and how it was created. That explains the carnage," he added, looking about at the blood and gore. "We're not the first to come in search of it."

"You're saying the orb was here and something or someone was guarding it, but it's not here now. Perhaps we're too late." Laurana sounded hopeful.

Gilthanas cast her an angry look and was about to say something when they heard Flint bellow.

"The blasted kender," the dwarf stated. "He ran off that way." He pointed at a dragon-marked tunnel.

Almost immediately, Tasslehoff came dashing back. "I think I found it!" he said in a loud whisper. "The dragon's lair!"

Gilthanas hastened off, with Tas leading the way, and Flint and Laurana hurrying behind him. Rounding a corner, the elf jumped quickly back into the tunnel. He motioned the others to come forward slowly.

"They're here," he mouthed, pointing.

Laurana peered cautiously around the corner into a large empty chamber. Icicles hung from the ceiling like white stalactites. The knights stood in the middle of the chamber, looking around.

"Where are the guards?" Brian was asking tensely. "We've come this whole way and not a sign of anyone."

"If there were soldiers guarding this area, they have probably run off to join the battle," said Derek. "Aran, you and Brightblade remain here, keep watch. Brian, you will come with me—"

"It's a trap, my lord," said Sturm, speaking with such calm and conviction that the knights were shocked into silence.

Derek quickly recovered. "Nonsense," he said testily.

"I think he may be right, Derek," said Aran. "I've had the feeling all along that someone was following us."

Gilthanas sidled farther down the tunnel and pulled Laurana with him.

"That explains why Feal-Thas sent away all those guarding the orb, including the dragon," Brian added tensely. "He wanted to lure us into doing exactly what we are doing—walking into a trap."

As if someone was listening, an eerie howl wailed in the darkness, bestial, mocking laughter that throbbed with enmity and a terrible threat of blood and pain and dying. The single voice was joined by countless more voices, their howls and cries reverberating through the tunnels.

Laurana clutched at her brother, who grabbed hold of her. Flint whipped out his axe, looking about wildly.

"What was that?" Laurana gasped. Her lips were numb with cold and fear. "What is that dreadful sound?"

"Wolves!" Gilthanas breathed, not daring to speak aloud. "The wolf packs of Feal-Thas!"

At a sharp command from Derek, the knights took up positions back to back, facing outward, their swords drawn. Steel glinted in the magical light.

The wolves surrounded the knights. White fur against white snow, red eyes glowing, the wolves circled the knights, padding quietly, closing in on them. Now the wolves had gone silent, intent on the kill, on avoiding the sharp steel, on leaping and dragging down and tearing apart, on gulping the hot blood.

One wolf, larger than the rest, held apart from the others, remaining outside the circle. This wolf did not join in the attack. He was watching, a spectator. It seemed to Laurana the wolf had a cruel smile in his dark eyes.

Elves have long studied the habits and nature of the animals who share their forest homes. They do not kill their animal neighbors, not even the predatory beasts, unless forced to do so.

Laurana knew the ways and habits of wolves, and no wolf would behave like this—sitting on his haunches, watching his fellows.

"Something's not right. Wait, Flint!" she cried desperately, as the dwarf would have dashed off to join the battle. "Tas! Do you have those magical glasses of yours? The ones that see things for what they are!"

"I might," said Tas. "I'm never sure what I have, you know, but I try to keep those with me."

Laurana watched in agony as the kender, hampered by his fur gloves, began peering into and rummaging through his numerous pouches. From their hiding place in the tunnel, Laurana could see, out of the corner of her eye, the wolves closing the circle. There must be fifty of them or more. And still the one wolf watched the doomed knights and waited.

Tasslehoff continued rummaging. Frantic, Laurana grabbed one of the pouches, upended it, dumping stuff on the ground. She was about to do the same with the others, when Gilthanas pointed. The glasses sparkled and glittered in the magical light. The elf made a grab for them, but Tasslehoff was quicker. He snatched them up and, giving Gilthanas a reproachful glance, settled them on his nose.

"What am I looking at?" he asked.

"That big wolf." Laurana knelt beside the kender, bringing herself to his eye level, and pointed. "The one there, standing apart from the others."

"It's not a wolf. It's an elf," said Tasslehoff, then he added excitedly, "No wait! It's an elf *and* a wolf . . ."

"Feal-Thas . . ." Laurana whispered. "You know something of this wizard, Gil. How do we stop him?"

"An archmage!" Gilthanas gave a bitter laugh. "One of the most powerful wizards on Krynn—"

He halted. His expression grew thoughtful. "There might be a way, but you would have to do it, Laurana."

"Me!" She gasped, appalled.

"You're the only one who has a chance." Gilthanas pointed. "You have the frostreaver."

She had thrown the weapon to the ground to help Tasslehoff search through the pouches. It lay, gleaming crystalline clear, at her feet. She made no move to pick it up.

Gilthanas gripped her arm, speaking very fast. "Your weapon is magical. The wizard is a winternorn and the weapon is made of the same elements that fuel his magic. It is the one weapon that might kill him."

"But . . . he's a wizard." Laurana quailed.

"He is not! Not now. Now he's a wolf. He's trapped in the wolf's body, and he'll be hampered in his spell casting! He won't be able to speak the words of magic or make the gestures or use his spell components. You must attack now, before he shifts back!"

Laurana stood shivering, staring at the enormous white wolf. The other wolves continued to circle the knights, wary of the sharp steel, yet hungry for blood.

"You can do this, Laurana," said Gilthanas earnestly. "You have to. Otherwise, there's no hope for any of us."

If Tanis were only here . . . Laurana stopped herself from thinking that. Tanis wasn't here. She couldn't depend on him or anyone else. This was up to her. The gods had given her the frostreaver. She didn't know why. She hadn't asked for it. She didn't want it. She seemed a very poor choice. She wasn't a knight. She wasn't a warrior. Yet even as she thought this and railed against her fate, ideas on how she could attack the wizard began crystallizing in her mind. She spoke her thoughts as they came to her, almost without realizing what she was saying.

"He mustn't see me coming. If he does, he might start to shift back to his true form. Gil, find somewhere you can use your bow. Keep his attention fixed on the battle, and if you can, drive him away from the rest of the pack."

Gilthanas looked at her, startled, then gave an abrupt nod. "I'm sorry I dragged you into this. It's my fault."

"No, Gil," she said. "I made my own choices."

She thought back to the day she had run away from home to follow after Tanis. That choice had led her to the knowledge of the gods, to knowledge of herself. She was a far different person from the spoiled little girl she had once been. A far better person, or so she hoped. She wasn't sorry, no matter what happened.

The circle of wolves began closing, moving in on their prey. Flint stood by her silently, stoutly.

"You can do it, lass," he said in gruff assurance, then he added wistfully, "I wish I had time to teach you the proper way to wield that axe!"

She grinned at him. "I don't think it's going to make much difference."

Gilthanas slipped to the tunnel opening, seeking a good location from which to use his bow. Laurana and Flint hurried down the tunnel's slight incline and ventured out into the open. Feal-Thas did not hear them or see them, nor did the wolves. They were focused on the prey at hand, focused on the kill.

Tasslehoff had been having fun flipping his glasses up and down, seeing an elf one moment and a wolf the next. When this grew boring, he took off the glasses, looked about, and saw that he was alone.

Gilthanas had taken up a position at the end of the tunnel. He had drawn his bow and was nocking an arrow. Laurana, her frost-reaver in her hands, was slipping up behind the pack of wolves. Flint was behind her, keeping one eye on the wolves and the other on Laurana.

"Try to hit his back, lass," Flint told her. "Aim for the biggest part of him, and put your own back into it!"

Tas hurriedly thrust the glasses into a pocket and reached into his belt. There was Rabbitslayer, just where it always was, whether he had thought to bring it or not.

"Maybe after this I'll rename you Wolf-Killer," he promised the knife.

Tas started after his friends. He hadn't been paying attention to Laurana's orders to keep quiet, and he was about to raise his voice in a gleeful taunt when the words stuck in his throat.

<hr />

The knights closed ranks, facing, as best they could, the coming onslaught. The wolves padded toward them, their eyes glittering red in the eerie light. Then snow began to fall, magical snow, drifting down out of the air. The light dimmed, hampering their ability to see.

"You damn fool!" Aran swore savagely at Derek, his voice rising in fury with each word. "You bloody, stupid, arrogant fool! What do you say now? What bloody words of wisdom are you going to spout at us before we all die?"

"Aran," said Brian softly, his mouth so dry he could barely speak, "you're not helping . . ."

Sturm was to Brian's left. Sturm stood tall and steadfast, his sword point unwavering, his gaze fixed on the wolves. He was talking, but only to himself, the words low and barely audible. Brian realized Sturm was praying, asking for Paladine to aid them, commending their souls to the god.

Brian wished in sudden agony that he believed in a god—any god! That he was not staring into a hideous, eternally silent, eternally empty void. That the pain and the terror held some meaning, that his life held some meaning. That his death would have some value. That he had not found love at last only to lose it in an icy cave on some pointless venture. A bitter taste flooded his mouth. The gods might have returned, but too late for him.

"Brightblade, be silent," said Derek, his voice rasping. "All of you, silence."

He was the cool, calm commander, the leader in charge of the situation, a courageous example, an inspiration to his men as described in the Measure. If he had doubts, he wasn't giving in to them. He believed in something, Brian thought. Derek believed in Derek, and he couldn't understand why they didn't believe in him as well. He expects us to die believing in him, Brian suddenly realized. That struck him as funny, and he gave a crackle of bitter laughter that brought another sharp rebuke from Derek.

"Pay attention!"

"To what?" Aran raved. "To the fact that we're going to die horribly, torn apart by wild beasts, our bones hauled off to be gnawed in some den—"

"Shut up!" Derek shouted furiously. "All of you, shut up!'

According to the Measure, the leader never shouted, never lost his calm demeanor, never wavered or doubted, never showed fear . . .

Snowflakes fell into Brian's eyelashes. He blinked them away rapidly, keeping his gaze fixed on the wolves. As if acting on some unheard signal, the wolves suddenly came at them in a rush.

Sturm gave a great roar of defiance and swung his sword in a slashing arc. A huge white wolf fell at his feet, blood welling from a wound in its neck.

Another wolf came bounding at Brian, snarling, fangs glistening. It suddenly sailed sideways, its body skidding on the ice. Brian saw, as it slid past him, an arrow sticking out of its ribs. A second arrow took another wolf in mid-air, felling it. Brian had no time to wonder or to look around. An enormous wolf galloped over the snow, charging at him. Brian tried to hit it with the blade of his sword, but the wolf, launching itself into the air, leaped on top of him. Huge paws thudded into his chest. The wolf's weight bore Brian to the ground. His sword flew out of his gloved hands and went spinning away over the ice.

The wolf's breath was hot on his face, smelling of rotting meat. Yellow teeth slashed his flesh. Saliva, now red with blood—his blood—splashed over him. The wolf had him pinned. He pummeled it with his hands, to no avail. The wolf sank its fangs into Brian's neck, and he screamed. He knew he screamed, but, horribly, there was no sound except gurgling. The wolf savaged his neck, ready to rip out his throat. Then it gave a hideous yelp and tumbled or was kicked off him. Brian looked up to see Sturm yank his sword out of the wolf's flank.

Sturm bent over him. Brian could barely see him in the falling snow.

Sturm gripped Brian's hand, held it fast, even as he stabbed and slashed with his sword, fending off more wolves.

"I'll get up in a minute," Brian meant to tell him. "I'll help you fight. I just have to . . . catch my breath . . ."

Brian held onto Sturm's hand and tried to breathe, but no breath would come.

He held Sturm's hand and the snow fell and the flakes were cold upon his lips and . . . he let go . . .

Laurana saw Brian fall. She saw Sturm bending over him, still fighting, trying to keep the wolves from attacking him. A wolf leaped on Sturm's shoulders. With an enormous effort, he rose up, heaving the beast off him. The wolf landed on its back. Sturm drove his sword into its belly, and the beast yelped and snapped in pain, feet flailing in the air.

Aran fought expertly. His sword was slippery-wet with blood, and bodies lay about his feet. The wolves fell back, eyeing him, then several ganged up to bring him down. One dashed in behind him, digging its sharp fangs through his leather boot, sinking deep into his ankle, severing the tendon. Aran stumbled and the wolves leapt on him, snarling and growling, ripping and tearing. Aran cried out, shouting for help. Sturm could do nothing, could not come to his aid. A wolf had hold of the sleeve of his sword arm and was trying to drag him off-balance. Sturm beat at it with his fist, trying to force the jaws loose.

Laurana heard Aran's cries and turned to look. "Flint, go help him!" she shouted.

Flint looked at her, frowning, doubtful, not wanting to leave her.

"Go!" she said urgently.

Flint cast her an agonized glance, then ran to Aran's aid. The dwarf descended on the attacking wolves, coming at them from behind. Flint roared and hacked, and his axe was soon red with gore. The wolves, maddened with the smell of fresh blood, paid him little heed. They continued their assault on Aran, who had ceased to struggle. One wolf died with its teeth still clamped in Aran's flesh.

Flint dragged the carcass off Aran, then stood over the knight's body, fending off the wolves.

"Reorx aid me!" Flint cried, swinging his axe and the steel, covered with blood, flared red in the tunnel light. The wolves did not like the light and kept clear, but they continued to eye him.

"Aran?" Derek cried, half-turning. But he was fighting his own battle and could not see what had happened.

Flint glanced down at Aran, buried beneath wolf carcasses, but he dared not take his attention from the wolves. "Tas," Flint yelled. "I need you! Over here! See to Aran," he ordered as Tas came dashing up.

Tasslehoff frantically shoved and kicked aside the bloody bodies until he found Aran. The knight's eyes were wide open and unblinking as the snowflakes fell into them. Half his face had been torn off. Blood pooled and froze on the ice beneath him.

"Oh, Flint!" Tas cried, choking in dismay.

Flint glanced over his shoulder.

"Reorx walk with him," he said gruffly.

Tas yelled a warning, and Flint turned, swinging his axe as more wolves descended on them.

Sturm put his back to Derek's, to keep the wolves from taking them down from behind as they had Aran. The two men stood in a circle of bodies. Some of the wolves, wounded, whimpered and tried futilely to stand. Others lay still. The ice was red with gore. The knights' swords were slippery with blood that ran down the blade and gummed up the hilt. They were sweating beneath the fur coats. Their breath came fast and frosted their mustaches and eyebrows. The wolves watched, waiting for an opening. Every so often, an arrow would fly through the darkness and take down another, but by now Gilthanas was running low on arrows, and he had to make every shot tell.

"Aran?" Derek asked harshly, gasping for breath.

"Dead," said Sturm, breathing hard.

That was all. Derek did not ask about Brian. Derek knew the answer. At one point, he had almost fallen over his friend's body. The wolves closed in again.

Flint was on the defensive, battling for his life. He no longer roared; he had to save his breath. A wolf leaped at him. He swung his axe and missed, and the beast was on him, bowling him over. Tasslehoff jumped on the wolf's back. Tas had gone into a sort of kender fury, screaming taunts that had no effect, for the wolves couldn't possibly understand or care. Riding the beast, Tas stabbed the wolf in the neck, stabbed it again and again and again with all the strength in his small arm until it toppled over and lay dead.

Tasslehoff stood over the wolf, watching it grimly, ready to kill it all over if it should somehow spring back to life. When it moved, he gave a savage cry and started to strike again and nearly stabbed Flint, who was trying to crawl out from underneath the twitching body.

Laurana could see the chaos out of the corner of her eye. Using the wizard's own magical snow as cover, Laurana circled around Feal-Thas to come at him from behind. Gilthanas fired at Feal-Thas, and the large wolf that was no wolf was driven away from the rest of the pack by Gilthanas's arrows. Forced to remain on the fringes of the assault, Feal-Thas paced back and forth, watching the attack, his tongue lolling, fangs dripping as though he tasted the blood. He did not see Laurana until she was almost upon him, coming at him from behind. He did not hear her over the wolves' howling and snarling.

Laurana saw Brian's crumpled body lying on the bloody ice. She had been afraid, but now anger subsumed her fear. She lifted the frostreaver, and remembering Flint's hastily imparted instructions, she started to swing, to strike the wolf-elf in the back, sever the spine . . .

Feal-Thas sensed her. He turned his wolf's head and gazed at her, gazed deep into her heart. His eyes pinned her as the wolf had pinned Brian. She halted in mid-stride. The frostreaver hung in the air, poised, ready to strike a killing blow. But Laurana's will seeped out of her. Feal-Thas stared at her, yellow eyes probing deep inside her, his thieving hand rifling her heart's secrets, sifting and sorting, keeping what was valuable, tossing out the rest.

Laurana realized, horror-stricken, that Gilthanas had been wrong. The archmage could still work his magic from inside a wolf's body. She was in the grip of enchantment, and she could do nothing except flutter helplessly like a butterfly on a pin.

The wolf growled, and she heard words in that bestial snarl.

"I have seen you before!"

"No!" Laurana whispered, quaking.

"Oh, yes. I saw you in Kitiara's heart. I see her in your heart, and I see the half-elf in both. What fun is this?"

Laurana wanted to flee. She wanted to kill him. She wanted to sink to her knees and bury her face in her hands. But she couldn't do anything. The wolf trotted closer and she was paralyzed, unable to break free of the fell gaze.

"Kitiara wants Tanis," said Feal-Thas, "and she means to have him. If she succeeds, Lauralanthalasa, he will be lost to you forever. I am the only person powerful enough to stop her. Kill me, and you give Tanis to your rival."

Laurana heard the din of shouts mingled with the howling of the wolves. She glanced over her shoulder, saw Brian with his throat torn, Aran dead, Flint crawling out from under the bodies and Tasslehoff fighting as tears ran down his cheeks, forming trails in the blood.

Feal-Thas knew in that moment he'd lost her. He saw his danger. First Kitiara had made a fool of him. She'd brought disaster on him, and now this elf woman was here to finish him off. He saw the two of them, Kitiara and Laurana standing together, laughing at him.

Rage boiled inside Feal-Thas. If he had been in his body, he would have destroyed this feeble woman with a word and a gesture. He would have to settle for tearing her apart, feasting on her flesh, drinking her blood. And someday, he would do the same to Kitiara.

Laurana felt the wizard's grip release her. She saw the fury in the yellow eyes. She saw the attack coming. She gripped the frostreaver tightly, putting all her strength into it. Laurana forgot about Tanis, forgot about Kitiara. She gave herself and her past and her future into the hands of the gods. She took hold of her own destiny.

Fangs snapping, the wolf leaped at her.

"So be it," Laurana said calmly, and she swung the frostreaver at the wolf's throat.

The magical blade blessed by Habakkuk sliced the winternorn's magic and cut deep into his neck. Blood spurted. Feal-Thas howled. The white wolf slumped to the ice, jaws open, tongue lolling, blood and saliva dribbling from its mouth. The yellow hate-filled eyes stared at her. The wolf's flanks heaved, feet scrabbled and clawed the ice that was red with blood pouring from the fatal wound.

Faint words, dark and piercing as fangs, sank into her.

"Love was *my* curse! Love will be your curse *and* hers!"

The hatred and the life faded out of the wolf's yellow eyes, and in the moment of his death the enchantment that had transformed Feal-Thas into the wolf snapped. One moment Laurana was staring at the corpse of a wolf. She brushed her eyes to clear them of snow, and when she looked again, the body of the elf lay on his back in a vast pool of blood. His head was nearly severed from his neck.

Laurana gasped and shuddered and turned away. She was sick with shock and horror. She started shaking, and she couldn't stop. She had some dim realization that she was still in danger—the wolf pack might turn on her, attack her. She looked up to see one wolf running toward her, and she struggled to lift the frostreaver, but it seemed suddenly immensely heavy. Gasping for breath that wouldn't seem to come, she braced herself.

The wolf paid no heed to her. It padded up gently to the body of the elf, sniffed at the blood, then it threw back its head and gave a wailing howl of grief. The other wolves, hearing the howl, broke off the attack and began to wail. The wolf nuzzled Feal-Thas. The beast looked at Laurana, its gaze going to the glittering, blood-stained frostreaver. The wolf snarled at her, turned, and slunk away. The rest of the pack trailed after, disappearing down the tunnels.

Laurana sagged to her knees. She still held the frostreaver clutched in her hands. She did not think she could ever let go.

Gilthanas knelt beside her, putting his arm around her.

"Are you all right?" he asked fearfully, when he could speak.

"I'm fine," she said through stiff lips. "The wizard didn't hurt me."

She realized, suddenly, this was true. Feal-Thas had tried to hurt her with his terrible curse, but he had not touched her. If love had been the elf's curse, it was because he had let something beautiful grow into something dark and twisted. She didn't know about Kitiara. None of that made sense. For Laurana, love was her blessing and would continue to be, whether Tanis returned her love or not.

She was not perfect. She was well aware there would be times when she would know despair, jealousy, and sorrow, but with the help of the gods, love would bring her closer to perfection, not hinder her in the pursuit.

"I'm all right," she repeated firmly and, rising to her feet, she threw the frostreaver down on top of the body of the dead wizard. "How are the others?"

Gilthanas shook his head. Sturm stood protectively over the bodies of Aran and Brian. Sturm was covered in blood, pale and exhausted, but he did not appear to be hurt. Flint had firm hold of Tasslehoff, who was wildly waving the blood-smeared Rabbitslayer and screaming that he was going to kill every wolf in the world.

Laurana hurried to the kender and put her arms around him. Tas burst into tears and collapsed into a sodden and blood-covered heap on the ice.

Derek had a gash on his face and claw marks on his hands and arms. One of the sleeves of his fur coat hung in tatters. Blood oozed from a bite on his thigh. He gazed down at the bodies of Aran and Brian with a slight frown, as if trying to recollect where he'd seen them before.

"I'm going into the dragon's lair to find the orb," he said at last. "Brightblade, stand guard. Don't let anyone come after me, especially the elves."

"Gilthanas and Laurana probably saved your life, Derek," said Sturm hoarsely, his throat raw.

"Just do as you're ordered, Brightblade," Derek said coldly.

He limped out of the chamber, heading for the dragon's lair.

"The gods go with him," Laurana murmured.

"Hah! Good riddance to bad rubbish is what I say," said Flint, patting the hiccupping kender on the back.

15

The Dragon Orb. The Knight.

he dragon orb was pleased. All was going better than hoped. The powerful archmage who had kept the orb prisoner—kept it safe, too, though the orb now gave no thought to that—was dead. Over the centuries, the orb had come to hate Feal-Thas. The orb had repeatedly tried to lure the wizard into using it, hoping to bring the wizard under its control. Feal-Thas had been too smart for that and the orb had seethed and schemed, seeking a way out of this godforsaken place.

Then the place was no longer godforsaken. Takhisis returned and spoke sweet words of blood, fire, and victory, and the orb heard her blandishments and longed to be a part of her new world. But Feal-Thas would not let the orb go. He was so powerful, with his own powerful advocate among the gods, that the wizard could turn a deaf ear to Takhisis.

Then Ariakas came up with a scheme to use the orb to bring about the downfall of the Solamnics. Kitiara came to set his plan in motion. She killed the guardian, and Feal-Thas was forced to hand over the orb to the care of an obtuse and thick-skulled dragon. More, in his arrogance, the wizard was foolish enough to use the orb to lure his enemies into an ambush. The orb had not taken an active role in the destruction of Feal-Thas, but it was pleased to think that it had, in some small way, been of use.

Now the victorious knight was coming to claim his prize. The essences of the five dragons trapped inside the orb roiled and writhed in anticipation. The orb glowed with a hideous light that sank to nothing the moment the knight set foot in the chamber. The orb went clear as a crystal lake on a fine midsummer's day. Not a ripple disturbed its placid surface. Pure and innocent-seeming, benign, harmless, it sat upon its pedestal and waited.

The knight entered the lair in naïve glory and total ignorance. He limped in, moving slowly and cautiously. Sword drawn, he looked about for the dragon or any other guardians. He would find none. The lair was empty, except for Sleet's victims—dead bodies encased in ice to be thawed and eaten when she, the lazy beast, did not feel like hunting.

The knight found the orb immediately. The dragon minds inside could both see and feel his yearning. He proceeded warily, however, advancing at a crawl, constantly looking over his shoulder, fearful of something sneaking up behind him. The orb waited patiently.

At last, certain he was alone in this chamber, the knight sheathed his sword and limped toward the orb. He took from his belt a sack made of deer hide. He looked at the orb, looked at the sack, and frowned slightly. The orb was too large. It would not fit inside.

A sound came from behind him and the knight dropped the sack, drew his sword, and turned around. Instantly, the orb shrank itself down, becoming just the right size. The sound was not repeated and the knight turned back. He was startled to see the orb appeared to be smaller. His eyes narrowed in suspicion. He fell back a step.

The orb sat on its pedestal, blandly innocent.

The knight shook his head. He was wounded, bleeding, exhausted. He'd been mistaken. He again sheathed his sword, picked up the sack and spread it on the icy floor, ready to receive the orb. He reached out his hands and placed them on the crystal orb, prepared to lift it off its stand and put it in the sack.

Oh, the things about magic the knight did not know, but which he would soon find out!

To his everlasting sorrow.

There are magical words that must be spoken by the person who touches the orb. These words would not assure the orb would come under the person's control, but they would weaken the will of the dragons caught within. The person placing his hands upon the orb should have a strong and powerful will and should be ready to seize hold and dominate the essence of the trapped dragons. He must be ready to meet the hands that will reach out, grab hold, and try to drag him down.

The knight thought he had only to pick up a globe of clear crystal. He was suddenly and terrifyingly disabused of this notion. Light flared from the globe and struck him directly in the eyes. He closed his eyes against the blinding glare and did not see the colors start to swirl and dance. He did not see the hands that reached out and grabbed hold of his.

The knight gasped. He tried to free himself, but he was not strong enough. His will wavered. He was ignorant, confused, and horribly afraid. He did not understand what was happening and the orb had an easy time of it. It dragged him down and dragged him under, held him fast until he ceased to struggle.

The dragons began to whisper to him, words of despair, meant to destroy hope.

When they were finished with the knight, they let him go.

Pleased with himself, never realizing that forever and always he would hear the voices whispering doom to him in the night, Derek Crownguard bore the dragon orb out of Ice Wall Castle.

16

Cʜe ᴅᴇᴀᴅ ᴀɴᴅ ᴛʜᴇ ʟɪᴠɪɴɢ.

he wolves had fled, but the danger had not. Derek had gone off to the dragon's lair to find the orb. Laurana and the others remained in the tunnels beneath a castle under siege. Sounds of fighting echoed faintly down the tunnels. The Ice Folk had managed to fight their way inside the castle and were battling the enemy within its walls. Their day was not finished. The wizard was dead, but those who served him were not.

Sturm sheathed his sword and knelt down to compose the bodies of his comrades. He shut the staring eyes and covered Aran's ghastly face with his own cloak. He washed the blood from Brian's face with handfuls of snow.

Laurana had feared Gilthanas would rush off after Derek, perhaps even fight him for the dragon orb. Gilthanas did not leave. He stared at the bodies of the two knights, remembering that only last night they had been alive, laughing, talking, smiling, and singing. He bowed his head, his eyes filled with tears. Laurana stood at his side. He put his arm around her, and together they knelt in the snow to pay their respects to the dead. Flint made a swipe at his eyes and cleared his throat. Tasslehoff smeared blood over his face as he blew his nose on Caramon's handkerchief.

The dead lay in some semblance of peace, their arms crossed over their breasts, their swords clasped in their still hands.

Sturm raised his eyes skyward and prayed quietly, " 'Return this man to Huma's breast, beyond the wild, impartial skies; grant to him a warrior's rest, and set the last spark—' "

"Time for that later," Derek interrupted.

He came from the dragon's lair and he held a leather sack in his hand tied with a drawstring. "I have the dragon orb. We must get out of here before we are discovered."

He glanced down at Aran and Brian, lying on the blood-stained ice, and a spasm passed over his face. His eyes dimmed; his lips trembled. He pressed his lips tightly together. His eyes cleared.

"We will return for the bodies after we have made certain the dragon orb is safe," he said, cold, impassive.

"You go on, my lord," said Sturm quietly. "I will remain with the fallen."

"What for? They are not going anywhere!" Derek rasped angrily.

Flint scowled and growled deep in his throat. Laurana stared at Derek in shock.

Sturm stood quiet, unmoving.

Derek flashed them all an irate glance. "You think me callous, but I am thinking of them. Listen to that!" He gestured down a tunnel. They could all hear the unmistakable sounds of battle—clashing metal, shouts and oaths and screams—and those sounds were growing louder.

"These knights gave their lives to secure the dragon orb. Would you have their sacrifice go to waste, Brightblade? Perhaps you think we should all stay here and die with them? Or do we finish our quest and live to sing of their bravery?"

No one said a word.

Derek turned and walked off, heading back the way they had come. He did not look behind to see if the others were following.

"Derek is right," said Sturm at last. "We should not let their sacrifice be in vain. Paladine will watch over them. Harm will not come to them until we can return to claim them and take them home."

Sturm gave a knight's salute to each of the fallen, then he walked after Derek.

Gilthanas retrieved what arrows he could find and went after Sturm. Flint harumphed and rubbed his nose and, grabbing hold of Tasslehoff, gave the kender a shove and told him to get a move on and quit standing there sniveling like a big baby.

Laurana lingered in the chamber with the dead. Friend. Foe. Picking up the frostreaver, stained with the wizard's blood, she walked to her destiny.

The Fall of Ice-Reach Castle

AN ICE FOLK SONG

By Lester Smith

Attend now, Ice Folk, to my tale,
Of the day that Ice Wall Castle fell,
And heed the lessons it reveals.

The tower had stood for ages long,
With walls of ice on walls of stone;
And wizard Feal-Thas called it home.

This dark elf magus held in thrall
A thousand thanoi to man its walls—
Fierce walrus-men. Nor was this all:

For ice-bears these fiends had enslaved,
Taunted, and tortured, till they raved
For blood and flesh to sate their rage.

Draconians, too, in their hundreds
Upon the Ice Tower's walls abounded,
To do whate'er Feal-Thas commanded.

And more than this, a great white dragon
Served the wizard's will! Its might again
Affirming Feal-Thas' right to reign.

For the dark elf had resolved to rule
With iron fist, and intent cruel,
Where long our people had endured.

The Ice Folk seemed to face their doom.
Against this threat, we had no boon.
Our hope upon the wind was strewn.

Listen, Ice Folk, to my tale!

Then Habakkuk, our old god, came
To Agéd Raggart, in a dream,
And promised victory in his name.

And strangers, too, were come to join
The Ice Folk's cause, for which they gained—
Knights, elves, and dwarves—welcome as kin.

Chief Harald, frostreaver in hand,
Called all true souls to take a stand
And cleanse the ice of Feal-Thas' stain!

The day that Ice Wall Castle Fell!

Our ice boats launched as day dawned fair.
And though our hearts had long held fear,
A breath of hope was in the air.

Then we a miracle beheld!
Even as Habakkuk had vowed:
When we set forth, the dragon fled!

Heed the lessons here revealed!

Cheered by this sign, our sailors sailed
With joyful hearts; while alongside
The ice boats, camp dogs raced and bayed!

But tower's shadow dimmed our mood,
For high and mighty still it stood,
With thanoi taunting—the ugly brood.

Then Agéd Raggart, with Elistan—
A priest of foreign Paladine—
Debarked their boats with this command:

"Watch now, and learn how gods of light,
Prepare a path for those who wait
And trust, so men may do what's right!"

Hearken, Ice Folk, to my tale!

Then these two graybeards walked alone
Toward the evil wizard's home
Through hail of arrows, and boulders thrown.

Untouched, they stopped below the tower,
And, catching sunbeams from the air,
Brought them upon the walls to bear.

Beneath those beams, the ice walls steamed,
Then cracked in giant rifts and seams,
And fell—while thanoi plunged and screamed.

And now from every ice boat's deck
Our warriors rushed into the wreck,
To Feal-Thas' fiends delivering death!

And as for Feal-Thas and his magics:
The dark elf fell to an elf maid's axe
And bled his life out on the ice.

The day his mighty castle fell!

Where once a mighty fortress stood,
Now Ice Folk warriors freely strode,
The threat of Feal-Thas done for good.

Think on this tale, when hope seems far,
And let its lessons guide your heart,
For we, my brethren, Ice Folk are.

We, O brethren, Ice Folk are!

BOOK IV

I

The Oracle of Takhisis.
Kit Gives an Ultimatum.

The winter deepened on Ansalon. Yule came and went. The hunt for Kitiara continued, though it was half-hearted. Ariakas did not send his troops out after her. He did send assassins and bounty hunters, but they were ordered to conduct their search circumspectly. After a time, it seemed they forgot about her. No longer were bounty hunters handing steel coins about, asking if anyone had seen a warrior woman with black curly hair and a crooked smile.

Kitiara did not know it, but Ariakas had called off the hounds. He was starting to regret the entire incident. He realized he'd made a mistake with regard to Kit. He began to believe in her claimed innocence. He tried to place the blame for his belief that Kit had betrayed him on Iolanthe. She cleverly shifted it to the elf wizard, Feal-Thas. The elf had proven to be a vast disappointment to Ariakas, who had never expected much from Feal-Thas in the first place, for word came that the blasted elf had gotten himself killed and Ice Wall Castle had fallen.

At least the knight, Derek Crownguard, had fallen victim to Ariakas's scheming. He had taken the dragon orb back to Solamnia, and Ariakas's spies reported that contention over the orb had caused a rift between elves and humans and was further demoralizing the knighthood.

Ariakas wanted Kit back. He was finally ready to launch the war in Solamnia and he needed her expertise, her leadership skills, her courage. But she was nowhere to be found.

Queen Takhisis could have informed Ariakas of Kit's whereabouts, for Her Dark Majesty was keeping a close watch on the Blue Lady. But Takhisis chose to keep Ariakas in ignorance. Ariakas might have welcomed Lord Soth's entry into the war, but he would not be pleased to see a Soth/Kitiara alliance. Kit already had an army behind her, an army loyal to her. She commanded a wing of blue dragons, also extremely loyal to her. Add to this a powerful death knight and his forces, and Ariakas would start to feel the Crown of Power resting uneasily on his head. He might try to stop Kitiara from going to Dargaard Keep, and Takhisis could not allow this.

The bounty hunters were a nuisance to Kit, though never a danger. None recognized her in her guise as a high-ranking spiritor, and no one bothered her. She even had an enjoyable conversation with a bounty hunter, giving him a description of herself and sending him on a long and fruitless search. When she took the road leading to Nightlund, pursuit ended. None would follow her into that accursed land.

Her journey was long and wearisome, giving Kitiara plenty of time to think about her confrontation with Lord Soth. She required a plan of attack. Kit never went into any battle unprepared. She needed information about exactly what sort of enemy she faced—solid information, not legend, myth, granny stories, kender tales, or bard's songs. Unfortunately, such information was difficult to come by. Of those who had encountered Lord Soth, none had come back to tell of it.

All she had was the information Iolanthe had provided following their brief and eventful encounter in the Temple in Neraka. Kit wished she'd taken more time to listen to the witch, asked her more questions. But then, she'd been fleeing for her life. Not the right moment for chitchat. Kit went over everything Iolanthe had said, mulled over it all, hoping to devise a strategy. All the stories agreed on certain points: an army of undead warriors, three heart-stopping banshees, and a death knight who could kill her with a single word. So far as Kit could see, developing a strategy for this encounter was rather like developing a strategy for committing suicide. The only question was how to die as quickly and painlessly as possible.

Kit had the bracelet Iolanthe had given her. Iolanthe had instructed her in its use, but Kit wanted to know all there was to know about this bracelet. Not that she didn't trust Iolanthe. The witch had saved her life.

It was just that Kit did *not* trust Iolanthe. She took the bracelet to a mageware shop.

The owner—a Red Robe wizard, as most tended to be, since they had to deal in black, red, and white magic—latched onto the bracelet and was loathe to let it go. His eyes lit up at the sight of it; his mouth watered. He stroked and caressed it. His voice grew husky as he spoke of it. The bracelet was very rare, he told her, and very valuable. He knew of such bracelets only by reputation. He'd never seen one before. He mumbled magic over it, and the bracelet did prove to be magical. Though he wouldn't swear by his god the bracelet would do what Iolanthe had promised—protect Kit from magic-induced fear and magical attacks—he thought it likely the bracelet would perform as required. Finally, holding the bracelet lovingly in his hand, he offered her the pick of any object in his shop in exchange. When she refused, he offered her his shop.

Kit eventually pried her bracelet from the man's hands and left. The Red Robe followed her down the street, begging and pleading. She had to spur her horse into a gallop to get away from him. Kit had been rather careless with the bracelet, stuffing it into a sack and not thinking much about it. From then on, she treated it with more care, checking frequently to make certain she still had it in her possession. The bracelet did not make Kit feel easier in her mind about her upcoming encounter with the death knight, however. Quite the opposite. Iolanthe would not have given Kit a gift this precious unless certain Kit would need it.

That was very disheartening.

Kitiara decided she would do something she'd never done in her life—seek the help of a god. Queen Takhisis was the one responsible for sending her on this mission. Hearing of an oracle not far from the border of Nightlund, Kitiara made a detour to visit the old crone to request Her Dark Majesty's aid.

The oracle lived in a cave, and if the stench counted for anything, she was extremely powerful. The smell of body waste, incense, and boiled cabbage was enough to gag a troll. Kit walked into the cave entrance and was ready to turn around and walk right back out when a beggarly youngster, so filthy it was impossible to say if it was a he or a she, seized hold of her and dragged her inside.

The crone had lank, ragged, yellow-white hair that straggled about her face. Her flesh hung flaccid off her bones. Her breasts beneath her worn garments sagged to her knees. Her eyes were blurred and unfocused. She sat cross-legged in front of a fire and appeared to be in some sort of stupor, for she mumbled, drooled, and rolled her head. The youngster held out a hand, demanding a donation of a steel piece if Kitiara wanted to ask a question of the Dark Queen's oracle.

Kit was dubious, but also desperate. She handed over the steel piece. The youngster inspected it to make certain it was not counterfeit, then muttered, "It's good, Marm," and remained to watch the spectacle.

The crone roused herself long enough to toss a handful of powder onto the fire. The powder crackled and hissed; the flames changed color, burning green, blue, red, and white. Tendrils of black smoke coiled around the crone, who began to moan, rocking back and forth.

The smoke was noxious and made Kit's eyes water. She could not catch her breath and she tried again to leave, but the youngster grabbed hold of her hand and ordered her to wait; the oracle was about to speak.

The crone sat up straight. She opened her eyes and they were suddenly focused and lucid. The mumbling voice was clear and strong, deep and cold and empty as death.

" 'I will pledge my loyalty and my army only to the Highlord who has the courage to spend the night with me alone in Dargaard Keep'."

The crone collapsed back into herself, mumbling and mewling. Kitiara was annoyed. She'd spent good steel for this?

"I know about the death knight's promise," said Kit. "That's why I'm going. What I need is for Her Dark Majesty to look out for me. I won't be of any use to her if Soth slays me before I even have a chance to open my mouth. If Her Majesty would just promise me—"

The crone raised her head. She looked directly at Kitiara and said snappishly, in a querulous tone, "Don't you know a test when you see one, you stupid chit?"

The crone sank back into her stupor, and Kitiara left as fast as she could.

A test, the oracle said. Lord Soth would be testing Kit. This might be comforting. It could mean the death knight would refrain from killing her the moment she set her foot in the door. On the other hand, it could also mean he would keep her alive just for her entertainment value. Perhaps he only killed people when he grew bored of watching them suffer.

Kit continued her journey north.

━━━━━━━━━━━━━◆━━━━━━━━━⋗⋲━━

She knew she had crossed the border into Nightlund when she started seeing abandoned villages and the road on which she traveled could scarcely be termed a road anymore. Solamnia had always been known for its system of highways. Armies marched faster on roads that were in good condition. Merchants traveled farther and reached more cities. Good roads meant a strong economy. Even after the Cataclysm, when there was so much turmoil and upheaval, those in charge of the cities made highway upkeep a priority—everywhere but in Nightlund.

Many of the roads had been destroyed during the Cataclysm, sunk under water when the river flooded or shaken apart in the earthquakes. Those roads that had survived fell into disrepair, and in some parts they disappeared altogether as nature reclaimed the land. The roads Kit traveled now were overgrown with weeds, dusted with snow, and devoid of travelers. Kit went for days without seeing another living soul.

She had made good time up to this point. Now her progress was slowed. She had to ride miles out of her way to find a place to ford a river because the bridge had washed out. She had to fight her way through tall grass that came up to her horse's flanks and was as tough as wire. Once, the road dumped her in a ravine, and another time led her straight into the side of a cliff. She would sometimes cover only a few miles in a single day, leaving herself and her horse exhausted. She also had to spend time hunting for food, for the only inns and farm houses she came across were long-since abandoned.

Kit had not used a bow and arrow since she was young, and she was a clumsy shot at best. Hunger sharpened her skills, however, and she managed to bring down the occasional deer. But then she had to butcher it and dress it, and that took more valuable time.

At this rate, she would be as old as the crone by the time she reached Dargaard Keep—if she reached it at all.

Not only did she have to deal with broken roads and impassable forests and near starvation, she had to keep constant vigilance against the outlaws who now made this part of Ansalon home. She had discarded the garb of a wealthy cleric, foreseeing that would make her a valuable target. She replaced it with the clothes she had been wearing when she escaped Neraka: her gambeson and some leather armor she had picked up along the way. She resembled a down-on-her-luck sellsword again, but even that wouldn't save her. There were those in Nightlund who would kill her for her boots.

During the day, she rode with her hand constantly on the hilt of her sword. Once, an arrow struck her in the back. The arrow hit the armor and bounced off. She was ready to fight, but the coward who fired the arrow did not have nerve enough to confront her.

By night, she slept with one eye open, or tried to, though sometimes she would be so weary she'd sink into a deep slumber. Fortunately for Kit, the horse of Salah Kahn had been trained to keep its master safe from the assassination attempts that were a way of life in Khur. Kit was constantly jolted out of sleep by the horse's whinny of alarm. Leaping to her feet, she had to grapple with a knife-wielding thug, or, drawing her sword, watch a shadowy shape slither off into the darkness.

Thus far, she had been lucky. She had been attacked by assailants acting alone. But the night or the day would come when a roving gang of thieves would fall upon her, and that would be the end.

"I can't do it, Your Majesty," Kit said one day as she was trudging through the snow, leading the horse by the reins, for the road was too rough for the beast to traverse without risking injury. "I am sorry to break my vow, but it will be broken anyway, for I will never live long enough to even see Dargaard Keep."

Kit stumbled to a halt. She did not like to admit defeat, but she was too hungry, too tired, too cold and dispirited to keep going. She started to turn around, to head back down the road along which they had just come when Windracer gave a terrified shriek and reared up on its hind legs, hooves flailing. Kit had been holding tight to the reins, and the horse's sudden, unexpected move nearly dragged her arm out of the socket.

Kitiara dropped the reins and grabbed her sword. The horse landed on its feet again and stood in the road, shivering and sweating, foam dripping from its mouth, its eyes rolling wildly. Kit looked and saw nothing, but she felt the horse's terror. Then she heard hoofbeats behind her.

Kit whipped around, steel blade flashing in the sun.

An enormous jet-black horse with fiery red eyes stood blocking the road. A woman was mounted on the horse. She rode side-saddle, as did the noble gentry. She was clad in a dress of fine black velvet. The skirt fell in graceful, sweeping folds down the horse's flank to the road. Her face was concealed by a long black diaphanous veil. She sat straight and tall, her black-gloved hands loosely holding the reins.

Kitiara dropped her sword. Quaking inside, more terrified than she had been at the thought of facing her executioner, she fell to her knees.

"Your Majesty!" she gasped fearfully. "I didn't mean—"

"Yes, you did," said Takhisis, and her voice was soft as the black velvet of her dress and as hard as the frozen ground on which Kit knelt. "I heard your ultimatum."

Kit shivered. "Your Majesty, it wasn't—"

"Of course it was. What you are saying is that if I want you to go to Dargaard Keep, I should find some means of getting you there in a timely manner."

And *alive*, Kitiara thought, but she did not dare say that.

She risked sneaking a look from beneath her long lashes, but she could see nothing of the woman's features hidden beneath the veil.

"If you command me, Your Majesty," Kit said humbly, "I will keep going . . . as far as I can . . ."

Takhisis tapped her gloved hands in irritation. She sat straight in the saddle, turned this way and that, taking in the forest and the wretched excuse for a road.

"I give you credit," Takhisis said. "You have done well to come this far. I knew this place was a mess, but I didn't know how bad it was."

She turned her veiled face to Kit. "I will help you one more time, Blue Lady, but that will be the last."

The Dark Queen lifted a gloved hand to point skyward.

Kitiara looked up and gave a glad cry. Skie came into view, flying slowly overhead, his head down, searching this way and that. Kitiara shouted his name and leapt to her feet, waving her arms. Either the dragon heard her or he heard his Queen's command, for he shifted his gaze, spotted her, and began spiraling downward.

Kitiara looked back to Takhisis. "Thank you, Your Majesty. I will not fail you."

"If you do, it will not matter, will it? You will be dead," Takhisis replied. "I suppose I will have to return Salah Kahn's horse. I'll never hear the end of it otherwise."

She took graceful hold of Windracer's reins and rode off down the road, leading the terrified steed behind her. When the goddess had disappeared into the darkness of the woods, Kitiara had a joyous reunion with Skie.

She was so glad to see the dragon, she felt strongly inclined to fling her arms around his neck and hug him, but she knew Skie would be deeply offended and likely never forgive her. She began by apologizing to the dragon, admitting that Skie had been right, her foolish search for the half-elf had landed her in trouble, nearly gotten her killed. Skie did not say "I told you so," but instead he magnanimously apologized in turn, saying he was wrong to have deserted her.

After that, he informed her that she was back in Ariakas's good graces. Ariakas had asked Skie—almost begged him—to go searching for her. This bit of news caused Kit to smile wryly, particularly when she learned that Feal-Thas was dead and the Solamnic knights were stirring up trouble.

Ariakas had an important assignment for Kitiara in Flotsam. The emperor also wanted her to begin planning for an attack on the High Clerist's Tower.

"Now he decides that!" Kit fumed. "Now, after the knights are talking of sending troops to reinforce the tower. And if Solamnia is suddenly so important, why does he talk of sending me to Flotsam, to the other side of the continent on some secret mission? Bah! The man is losing his grip!"

Skie flicked his tail in agreement and dropped down on his belly so that Kitiara could climb up on his back. Skie had brought with him the blue armor and helm of a Dragon Highlord, given to him by Ariakas on the off-chance that Skie should find her. Kitiara put on her armor with relish. She felt herself vindicated. She placed the helm on her head and vowed that Ariakas would one day come to regret his treatment of her. She was not yet strong enough to challenge him. That day would come, however, maybe sooner than later if she succeeded at Dargaard Keep. Clad once more in her armor, Kitiara felt strong enough for anything, even a death knight.

His Blue Lady restored to him, the dragon was also in excellent humor. His blue scales rippled and he dug his claws into the ground, ready to take off.

"Where do we go?" he asked. "Solamnia or Flotsam?"

Kitiara sucked in a deep breath. This was going to be difficult.

"Her Majesty didn't tell you?" she hedged.

"Who? Tell me what?" Skie swiveled his head around, suddenly suspicious.

"We fly north," Kit said. "To Dargaard Keep."

Skie stared at her, then said flatly, "You're joking."

"No," said Kitiara calmly. "I'm not."

"Then you're crazy!" the dragon snarled. "If you think I'm going to fly you to your death—"

"I promised Queen Takhisis I would undertake this," Kitiara said. "What did you think I was doing here in Nightlund anyway?"

"Traipsing after the half-elf maybe. How in the Abyss should I know?" Skie flared.

"Trust me, I have forgotten all about Tanis Half-elven," Kitiara assured the dragon. "I've had more important things on my mind, such as trying to figure out some way to live through this encounter."

She explained the vow she had made to Queen Takhisis.

"You know our Queen," Kit added. "I can't back out now. It would be as much as my life was worth."

Skie did know Takhisis, and he had to admit facing Takhisis in her wrath was something the mightiest dragon would go out of his way to avoid. Still he didn't like Kit's plan and he let her know it.

"I cannot believe you were going to go without me!" Skie boomed. "As it is, with me along, you have at least a chance of surviving. I will blast the keep into rubble, bring it down on top of him. The death knight can't be killed, but I can at least weaken him, give him something to think about, like crawling out from several tons of rock."

Kitiara wrapped her arms around the dragon's neck, gripped him tightly, and ordered him to take off.

His idea was good. She didn't want to tell him it wasn't going to work.

2

A Night at Dargaard Keep.

kie flew over the forests and swamps, rivers and hills, ruined dwellings, broken roads, predators and outlaws of Nightlund, accomplishing safely in hours what would have cost Kitiara days of hard work and danger. They came within sight of Dargaard Keep late on the afternoon of the second day.

The keep was built high upon a cliff, most of it carved from the cliff's peak. The only way to reach the keep was by climbing up a road that wound around and around the cliff face. Kit might have considered this path, but one look at the road made her thankful she had Skie. The road was split and cracked and in some places huge chunks had fallen off, gone sliding down the mountainside. What remained was strewn with rock and boulders and rubble from the ruined keep.

The beauty of Dargaard Keep itself had once been legendary. It had been built to resemble a rose half-open, blooming, full of promise. Now the rose was shattered, the petals blackened and ugly. The gardens, once green and flourishing, were home to malignant weeds.

The only rose growing inside the crumbling garden walls bore a flower of hideous black hue, its thorns deadly to the touch.

Skie slowed his flight. The dragon feared little on Ansalon, yet he did not like the look or the feel of this place. "Should I go on?"

"Yes," said Kitiara, and she had to repeat herself, for, the first time, the word stuck in her throat.

No sun shone on Dargaard Keep, which languished always in the shadow of the gods' anger. The moment Kit and Skie flew above the outer wall, the sunlight vanished. The sun still shone, but it was a fiery orb burning in a black sky, and it shed no light on Dargaard Keep. The undead standing on the walls would see, far off in the distance, the sunlit world, a green and growing world, a world of life and warmth, a world lost forever to those trapped within the curse of Dargaard Keep.

The sudden, terrible thought occurred to Kit that she might herself become one of those lost souls. Her undead spirit might be forced to join those warriors held in thrall to Lord Soth. Kitiara shuddered and shoved that thought hurriedly out of her mind.

She looked down over the dragon's wings. Below, the keep was dark and deserted. No light shone from the broken windows, yet Kitiara had a sudden vision of flames blazing, bursting through the roof, ascending heavenward in a spiraling whirlwind of ash and cinders. She smelled smoke and the stench of burning flesh, and she heard a baby screaming in agony on a single, high-pitched note, screaming on and on until the scream died, horribly, away. Kitiara's throat tightened, her stomach clenched, a muscle in her thigh spasmed. She felt a tremor shake the dragon's body.

"An accursed house," said Skie, his voice harsh and strained. "The living have no place here."

Kitiara agreed whole-heartedly. She had never known fear like this; she was literally sick with terror and she had yet to put her foot inside the gate! Her stomach roiled. A horrid taste, like blood, caused her to gag. She could not take enough air into her lungs. She clung to Skie and was ready to order him to turn back, fly away as fast as he could. Facing the Dark Queen's fury would be better than this horror. The command rattled in Kit's throat, coming out in a croak tinged with hot and bitter bile.

"What did you say?" Skie shouted. "Should we leave?"

Kitiara drew in a shivering breath.

"Land," she ordered, the word squeezed out of her.

Skie shook his head and spiraled down, searching for a place to settle. The only area large enough was the courtyard located directly in front of the keep's main gates. He had to make tight turns in a steeply banking descent. He was forced to pull in his wings at the last moment, so as not to strike them on a tower; he came down hard, skidding on the cobblestones and nearly smashing into a wall.

Kit sat motionless for long moments after the bone-jarring landing. She felt as though she were being smothered, and she took off her helm. Her dark eyes narrowed. Her jaw set. She licked her lips and tried to speak, but no words would come out. Skie understood her.

"A good idea. You dismount, my lord, and find cover. I will do the world a favor and destroy this vile place!" Skie hissed his words, lightning crackling between his teeth.

Kit slid down off the dragon's back. She did not leave, but kept her hand on his neck, loathe to let him go.

"Be careful," she said at last, and stood back to give him room.

Skie gave a convulsive leap off his hind legs, pushing himself upward. He had to gain altitude enough with his jump to be able to spread his wings and not clip any of the stonework around him.

He cleared the keep. Spreading his wings, he prepared to circle around and blast the towers and battlements with his lightning breath. But a blast of wind, hot and seething, came roaring down from the sky and struck the dragon in the chest. He fought against it, wings flapping wildly, feet scrabbling at the air. The wind blew hard and he could make no headway against it. Then the wind picked up the dragon and began to tumble him about, pushing him away from the courtyard, carrying him away from the keep, away from the cliff, back into the sunlit world. There the wind suddenly died, dumping the disoriented dragon in a field.

Furious, Skie raised his head, his wings flapping defiantly. He knew quite well who had sent that wind, but he wasn't going to give up. Kitiara needed him. Seeing him start to take off again, the wind came roaring out of the sky and slammed into him. The dragon groaned and dropped to the ground, stunned, insensible.

Kit watched in calm despair. She'd known Takhisis would not allow the dragon to interfere. Kit was on her own.

Flinging down her helm, Kit stood, shivering in the deserted courtyard, and looked around. She could see no one here, but eyes watched her. The keep was silent, and voices screamed, shrieked and moaned. No fire burned, and she could feel the heat of the flames.

All around her, the threat, the menace of the tormented dead throbbed and pulsed with horrid life. They wanted her, wanted to make her one of them. They meant to keep her here for all eternity. Corpses of the brave and the foolish who had come before her lay strewn about the courtyard. All had died of sheer terror, judging by the contortions of the limbs, the mouths gaping wide in screaming panic. None had made it as far as the front gate.

The fear grew inside her, relentless, grinding, wringing her and twisting her. Her legs wobbled and trembled. Her heart thudded painfully, erratically. She couldn't catch her breath. Chill sweat trickled down her breast.

Fear . . . terror . . . A voice saying something . . . Iolanthe's voice . . .

It will save you from dying from sheer terror. . . .

The magical bracelet. Kit had tried to put it on before she entered the courtyard, but the bracelet would not fit over her riding gloves. She had taken it off and thrust it beneath her breastplate, intending to put it on when she arrived at the keep. She had been so unnerved, however, that all thought of the bracelet had fled her mind. Now Kit fumbled for the bracelet with shaking hands, found it, seized hold of it, and clutched it tightly.

Warmth potent as dwarf spirits surged through her, easing her fears. Her racing heart slowed, her stomach stopped twisting, her bowels quit cramping. She could breathe again. She started to clamp the marvelous bracelet over her wrist.

A woman's song sounded from within the keep. The woman sang a single note, beautiful and awful, piercing, wailing, keening. The note struck Kitiara like a steel bolt. She gasped and flinched. Her hand jerked. She dropped the bracelet and it fell, clattering, to the cobblestones.

The fear surged back, crashing over her, crushing her. Panic-stricken and desperate, she dropped to her hands and knees. She couldn't find the bracelet in the darkness, and that was maddening because she could see clearly because of the roaring fire. She groped about for it with her bare hands. The cobblestones were covered with black, greasy soot and ash. Water ran in rivulets among the cracks and crevices. Kit drew back her wet hand and saw in horror that it wasn't water. Her palm was smeared with blood.

The light of the fire grew brighter, and she saw her bracelet lying just out of reach. Kitiara made a frantic lunge for it. She was just about to grab the bracelet when two polished black boots stepped over it, standing on either side of it. A long, ragged-edged cape fell around the boots. A gloved hand reached down and picked up the bracelet.

Kit raised terror-stricken eyes.

A knight stood over her. Eyes of fire glowed behind the eye-slits of a bucket helm. The blaze of the burning keep reflected off steel armor. A rose emblazoned on the breastplate was cracked, charred black, and smeared with blood.

Lord Soth held the bracelet in his gloved hand. The fire in the eye-slits seemed to flicker in amusement. He lifted the bracelet up for her to see, then, as she watched, he slowly closed his hand over it. There was a snapping sound, rending metal. Soth opened his fist. Silver and onyx dust trickled from between his fingers, sparkled briefly in the firelight, and dissolved into mud on the blood-wet cobblestones.

"That's cheating," said Lord Soth.

He turned on his booted heel. His cape flowed around him like a ripple in the fabric of darkness. He flung wide his hands.

"You are my guest this night," Soth added.

The gates to Dargaard Keep opened.

3

Kitiara's fight. Lord Soth's vow.

itiara crouched on her knees in the blood and stared into the open gates. Before her was a grand entry hall, dark, empty, and bright with candlelight flaring from a wrought-iron chandelier that hung from the ceiling and lay, broken and twisted, on the floor. If Kit did not stand up and walk into that hall, she would be just one more corpse lying in the courtyard. Skie would fly over Dargaard Keep tomorrow morning and see on the cobblestones her bones and her rotting flesh encased in the blue armor and horned helm of a Dragon Highlord. Skie would mourn her—he would be the only one to mourn her, yet he would find another rider. Ariakas would laugh when he heard and term her a fool who deserved her fate. Takhisis would despise her. Lord Soth would pick up her horned helm and add it to his trophies and that would be the end. Kitiara uth Matar would be forever a nobody. She would fade into obscurity and be forgotten.

"A little fear is healthy," Gregor uth Matar had once told his daughter. "Too much fear makes you worthless in a fight. When you start to feel the terror beat in your throat, you're hanging on to life too tight, daughter. Let go of what may come and live for what is—because that may be all you have . . ."

A soldier walked forth from the entry hall. He was clad in armor adorned with the rose, one of Soth's men-at-arms. Flames consumed him as he walked, blackening his armor, blistering his skin. The flesh melted from his face, leaving a bloody skull. He held a sword in his smoldering hand. His eyes saw nothing but death . . . and her. He meant to slay her, if she did not kill him first, except that he himself was already dead.

Let go of what may come and live for what is . . .

Kitiara let go of her ambition, her hopes and dreams and plans. She let go of love and hate, and, when she had nothing left inside her, she realized that fear had let go of her.

Rising to her feet, Kit drew her sword and walked forth boldly to meet the undead warrior. Her dragon armor protected her against the heat of the flames. She yelled in defiance and struck the corpse's blade a testing blow, judging his strength, his skill. The corpse's strength was daunting; his counter strike almost shattered her arm. She broke off, fell back, and waited for him to attack her.

But death seemed to have robbed the dead man of his brains as well as his skill. He raised his sword over his head and brought it down on her as though he were chopping wood. Kitiara dodged, then leaped and spun, slamming her foot into his chest, knocking him over backward.

He lay floundering on his back. Kit put her foot on his chest and drove her blade into his throat between his armor and his helm. The flames disappeared. The warrior lay still. He wasn't finished, though. She couldn't kill what was already dead.

Hearing clanging and rattling behind her, she turned around, but not fast enough. A sword struck her on the left shoulder. Her armor saved her from a broken collarbone, but the blow was powerful enough to dent the armor the Dark Queen herself had blessed. While the undead warrior recovered from his swing, Kitiara swept her blade into his neck, severing his head. That second corpse was still falling when another came lunging at her, and she heard, behind her, the first attacker clambering to his feet.

Kitiara glanced behind her and saw the first attacker aim a thrust at her back. The one in front was surging forward. She dropped to the ground. The warrior behind her stabbed the warrior in front and both fell. Kitiara crawled out from beneath the bodies to find another warrior waiting for her, jabbing at her with a spear.

Kit rolled frantically from to one side to the other. He hit a glancing blow, and Kit gasped in pain as the spearhead sliced open a gash in her thigh. Seeing an opening, she smashed both feet into his legs, kicked them out from under him. She hacked the point off the spear, but she didn't waste her energy "killing" him. It wouldn't make any difference. He couldn't die.

More undead troops came at her, so many she couldn't begin to count them. They were jumping off the battlements, running down the stairs, trailing fire that glowed in the blades of their swords and blazed in their eyes that were empty of life but not of hatred.

Kit was wounded and exhausted. Her fear had been costly, draining her of strength, and she had to keep fighting. She risked another glance behind. The gates to Dargaard Keep stood wide open. The great hall, lit by candlelight, was empty. No warriors were inside the keep, not since the one had come forth to do battle. The undead soldiers were massing in front of her. If she could win her way inside the keep, make it through the gates alive . . .

Drawing her boot knife, she stabbed one warrior in the midriff, below his breastplate, and took a step backward. She drove her sword through the eyeslits of another's helm and kept moving backward.

She had to keep the warriors from flanking her, crowding around behind her, coming between her and the open gate. She thrust her sword between the legs of a warrior and brought it upward, tearing into his crotch. He toppled forward, and Kitiara moved another step closer to the gate.

A blow knocked off one of her bracers. Blood oozed from a deep wound in her left forearm and more blood trailed down her thigh. Another blow struck her on the head and the flames wavered and swam in her vision. But she fought against the bursting pain and blinked her eyes until they focused and kept fighting. And she kept moving backward.

Her breath came in gasps. Her arms ached. Her sword was unbelievably heavy. The hand holding the dagger grew slippery with her own blood. When she lashed out with the dagger at a foe, the knife flew from her hand. She made a desperate grab for it, but booted feet trampled it and she had to let it go.

A sword thrust into her side. Her armor saved her from death, but the blow damaged her ribs and made every movement, every breath, splintered pain. She kept moving backward, kept swinging her sword, kept ducking and dodging. In front of her, the warriors jammed together, fighting without reason or skill, hitting each other as often as they hit her. What did it matter? They died, fell, and rose to fight again.

Candlelight streamed out from behind her. She had reached the gate. Wooden doors banded with iron stood open. Above her gleamed the wicked teeth of a portcullis.

Kit drew in a breath and gave a strangled shout of fury and defiance and launched a last, frenzied attack. Slashing and hacking at them with her sword, she drove back the warriors, sent them tumbling and falling over one another, then she turned tail and ran with her last remaining strength through the gate.

A thick rope attached to a mechanism held the portcullis in place. Hoping time and fire had weakened the stout rope, Kit swung her sword, tried to sever it. The rope parted, but did not break. She gritted her teeth. The sweat rolled down her face, half blinding her. She drew in a breath. Pain lacerated her. The warriors were coming after her. She could feel the heat of the flesh-consuming flames wash over her. She took another swing. The rope snapped. The portcullis came thundering down, smashing some of the warriors beneath its sharp points.

The warriors vanished. Disappeared. The fight was over for them. They returned to their bitter darkness to keep endless watch, mount eternal guard.

The clamor of battle ceased and all was, for the moment, silent; blessedly silent.

Kitiara groaned. The pain was like a red-hot knife inside her. She doubled over, pressing her hand against her side. Tears wrung from agony stung her eyes. She whimpered, then clamped her teeth on her cries. Biting her lips until the blood ran, she waited for the pain to wash over her and ease.

Someone started to sing. The voice was a whisper at first, but it raised the hair on her head and sent a shudder through her. Kitiara opened her eyes and looked wildly about.

Three elf women came floating toward her, moving as if on hot air currents rising from unseen flames. Their mouths were open, their hands outstretched, and Kitiara realized in despair that she had escaped one enemy only to be trapped by another. She had already experienced the debilitating effects of a single note of their lethal song.

That song would strengthen, grow more powerful. The hideous notes would swell around her in shattering anguish, lamentation, and grief so poignant and piercing it could literally stop the heart.

The elf women came nearer, their long hair floating around them in tendrils, their white robes burned and blackened, their bodies trembling with the wailing song.

Blonde hair, blue eyes, pale complexion, slanted eyes, pointed ears . . . elves . . . elf maidens . . .

Laurana . . .

"Elf bitch!" Kitiara cried savagely. "If it's the last thing I do, I'll kill you!"

Heedless of the pain, screaming curses, she swung her sword at the elf maid in great, huge, furious, slashing arcs, back and forth, slicing and stabbing.

Laurana disappeared. Kit sliced at nothing but air.

She lowered her sword and stood panting and sweating, hurting and bleeding in the entry hall. Raising her blood-dimmed gaze, she saw at her feet an enormous, wrought-iron chandelier. Though it had fallen down centuries ago, the candles in it still burned. A pool of blood, still fresh—always horribly fresh, fresh as memory—lay beneath the twisted metal.

Beyond the chandelier was a throne. The death knight, Lord Soth, sat there watching her. He had been watching her the entire time. The eyes in the slits of the helm burned steadily, reflecting the flames that had died three hundred years ago. He did not move. He waited to see what she would do next.

Kitiara's left arm was drenched in blood that still oozed from the wound. The fingers of that hand had gone numb. Her breath came in wrenching, painful gasps. The slightest movement sent pain lancing through her. She had wrenched her knee; she only noticed that now. Her head ached and throbbed. Her vision was blurred. She felt sick to her stomach.

Kitiara drew herself up as best she could, considering that she limped on her left leg and could not put her full weight on her right. She blinked back her tears and shook back her black curls.

Her arms shaking with fatigue, she managed through sheer effort of will to raise her sword and move awkwardly into a fighting stance. She tried to talk, but no voice came out. She coughed, tasting blood, and tried again.

"Lord Soth," said Kitiara, "I challenge you to battle."

The fire in the eyes flared in astonishment, then flickered. Soth shifted upon his throne, the black cape, its hem drenched in the blood of his wife and child, stirring about him.

"I could kill you without ever leaving my seat," he said.

"You could," Kitiara agreed, her words coming in whispering gasps, "but you won't. For that would be cowardly. Not worthy of a Solamnic knight."

The eyes of fire regarded her intently; then Lord Soth rose from his throne.

"You are right," he said. "Therefore, I accept your challenge."

Sweeping aside his cape, he drew from a blackened scabbard an immense, two-handed great sword, and circling around the fallen chandelier, he strode forward to meet her. Limping painfully, Kitiara pivoted to keep him in clear sight, holding her sword at the ready.

He was taller than she was, stronger than she was, to say nothing of the fact that he was deader than she was—though not by much. He felt no physical pain, though the gods alone knew the spiritual torment he suffered. He would never grow tried. He could fight for a hundred years, and she had maybe a couple of moments left in her. His reach was longer. She would never even get close to him, but this was what Kitiara had vowed to do, and by the Dark Queen, she was going to do it, though it would be the last thing she ever did.

Soth feinted left. Kit did not fall for it, for she saw the real attack coming. She blocked the blow, her sword clashing against his.

The chill of death and worse than death, the bitter cold of unending life, struck through her flesh to the bone. She shuddered in agony and gagged and sobbed for breath and held her ground, unmoving, blocking his blade with hers, holding him at bay with the last vestiges of her courage, for her strength had long since drained away.

Her sword shattered. The blade burst into slivers of steel. Splinters and shards of metal flared in the firelight. Kitiara staggered, almost falling.

Menacingly, Soth advanced on her. Kit reached into the dragon armor, snatched out the hidden dagger, and, shivering, trembling, she flung herself at him.

Soth caught hold of the hand holding the dagger and gave it a wrench. Kitiara's flesh froze at his touch. She gave a soft, involuntary moan, then her teeth clamped down on her lips. She would not give him the satisfaction of hearing her scream. She waited, in silence, to die.

Lord Soth released her hand.

Kitiara clasped the wrist and gazed at him dully, so far gone she didn't much care what happened, only that it should happen quickly.

He raised his sword, and Kitiara braced herself.

Lord Soth shifted the blade in his gloved hands. He held it out to her, hilt-first, and knelt down on one knee before her.

"My lady," he said. "Accept my service."

Kitiara stared at the sword. She stared at him. She smiled her crooked smile, then she collapsed in a heap on the floor, one hand crumpled under her, the other outstretched, fingertips touching the pool of blood beneath the chandelier.

Soth drew off the black cape and laid it over Kitiara, covering her to keep off the chill of night. In the morning, he would summon her dragon and see her safely on her way to her destiny. In the meantime, he would guard her sleep.

That night, for the first night since his downfall, Lord Soth forbade the elf women to sing to him the song of his crimes, lest they wake Kitiara.

4

FINIS

"That ends our tale for today," said Lillith Hallmark.

She had held her audience spellbound as she related the story of the momentous events that had taken place during the winter of 351 AC. She had spoken very calmly and quietly of the death of the two knights, Brian Donner and Aran Tallbow, and she had reminded her listeners that they could see the monument erected in their memories in the Hall of the Knights on Sancrist Isle. The Aesthetics who had gathered to listen to her had exchanged sorrowful glances. Lillith had never married, and all knew that her heart was buried in the tomb with Brian Donner.

The people were reluctant to leave, however, and many wanted to know what happened next.

"I'll tell just a little more," said Lillith, smiling.

"After leaving the chamber where the two knights had died, the Heroes of the Lance—Laurana, Sturm, Flint, Tasslehoff, Gilthanas, Elistan—joined with Sir Derek Crownguard and fought alongside the warriors of the Ice Folk to defeat the armies of Feal-Thas and drive them from Ice Wall Castle," Lillith told them. "Their mission accomplished, they left Icereach, taking with them the dragon orb and another artifact they found in the castle, one that turned out to be of far greater value. They also took with them the bodies of Aran Tallbow and Brian Donner to be buried as heroes in their homeland. What happened to the Heroes there is chronicled in the book *Dragons of Winter Night*.

"Many years have passed since that fateful day, and the song of their adventures in Icereach is still sung on a long winter's night by Raggart the Younger. One of the tribe's most honored possessions is Laurana's frostreaver, which she gave to Harald before she left, fearing it would melt if she took it with her. The frostreaver stands always in a place of honor in the chieftent.

"Following the departure of the Companions, Harald pursued the war against the dragonarmies. He brought together the other tribes of the Ice Folk, and they attacked Sleet with such ferocity they drove her from her lair. The Ice Folk occupied Ice Wall Castle and held it. Harald's task was made somewhat easier by the fact that Ariakas could not find anyone willing to take the place of Feal-Thas. Ariakas decided he did not care much about this unprofitable region of Ansalon anyway, so after a half-hearted attempt to retake Ice Wall Castle that ended in disaster, Ariakas pulled his forces out of Icereach, leaving it to the white bears and the nomads and the wolves.

"As for Kitiara, her continuing adventures can also be found in *Dragons of Winter Night*. Suffice it to say here, she and Tanis would meet again. Their liaison would have unforeseen consequences for both of them, for their companions, and for final victory in the War of the Lance."

Her story for the day finished, Lillith rose to her feet. "Thank you, friends, for coming today and learning a portion of the history of Ansalon. In our next session, we will pick up the story of Kitiara's half-brother, Raistlin Majere, who made a momentous decision right here in the Great Library. His tale is called *Dragons of the Hourglass Mage*. We, the Aesthetics of Gilean, hope you will return to share this with us."

Author's Notes

Feal-Thas

The full story of the wizard Feal-Thas can be found in the Dragonlance game accessory *Dragons of Winter*, published by Margaret Weis Productions, Ltd. It is interesting to note that Feal-Thas was in fact innocent of the crime of which he was accused. He was, in his youth, a brilliant and promising mage. But for this terrible tragedy and subsequent injustice, Feal-Thas might well have used his magical powers in the battle to save his homeland of Silvanesti, instead of betraying Lorac and trying to destroy it.

The Siege of Castle Crownguard

Details of the attack on Castle Crownguard and the death of Derek's brother, Edwin, can be found in the short story, "Glory Descending" by Chris Pierson, in the Dragonlance anthology, *Dragons at War*.

Rabbitslayer

Many readers noticed in *Dragons of the Dwarven Depths* the odd fact that Tasslehoff gives his beloved knife, Rabbitslayer, to Tika only to have Rabbitslayer once more in hand when he needs it in the dwarven kingdom. This was not a mistake, as many of you thoughtfully pointed out, or rather, it was a mistake in that we meant to insert a little explanatory note in the back of that book, but that never happened.

Some have speculated that Tasslehoff called any old knife that came to hand by the name Rabbitslayer—a good theory and a logical one, considering a kender's short attention span. However, as those of you who have read other Dragonlance books know, Rabbitslayer is a magical blade that always returns to an owner it likes. Tasslehoff proudly carries the one and only Rabbitslayer throughout his long and illustrious career as a Hero of the Lance.

Dragons of the Hourglass Mage

The next and final book in the Lost Chronicles series, *Dragons of the Hourglass Mage*, will complete the tales we have left to tell. We will follow Raistlin Majere from the library of Palanthas, where he takes the black robes, to the Dark Queen's city of Neraka. His journey is fraught with peril, for Raistlin decides to play a dangerous game, one in which he is prepared to gamble his very life for a chance at even greater power.